SWEET BLACK WAVES

KRISTINA PÉREZ

[Imprint]
MAKE YOUR MARK

NEW YORK

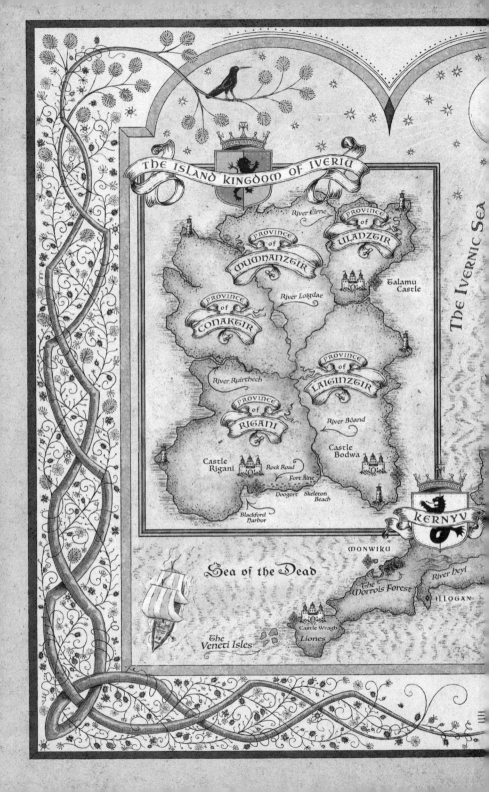

THE WINTER SEA

THE OLD NORTH

RHEGED

LUGUWALOS

The Wild Mountains

River Carr

River Ardu

DYFED

River Temeskos

CLOTEN

EBRAUC

USA

ALBION

ORDOWIK

DEVA

ECENI

VENTA

River Kamulos

THE SAOZONE SEA

CAERLEON

River Abona

River Dubras

ISCA

LOGRES

MEONWARA

THE SOUTHERN CHANNEL

[Imprint]
MAKE YOUR MARK

A part of Macmillan Publishing Group, LLC
175 Fifth Avenue, New York, NY 10010

Library of Congress Control Number: 2017958062

ISBN 978-1-250-13285-7 (hardcover) / ISBN 978-1-250-13286-4 (ebook)

Our books may be purchased in bulk for promotional, educational, or business use. Please
contact your local bookseller or the Macmillan Corporate and Premium Sales Department at
(800) 221-7945 ext. 5442 or by e-mail at MacmillanSpecialMarkets@macmillan.com.

Book design by Ellen Duda

Map by Virginia Allyn

Imprint logo designed by Amanda Spielman

First edition, 2018

1 3 5 7 9 10 8 6 4 2

fiercereads.com

An té a dhéanfadh cóip den leabhar seo, gan chead, gan chomhairle,
dhíbreodh é go Teach Dhuinn.

For Jack

Ne vus sanz mei, ne mei sanz vus
—Marie de France, "Chevrefoil"

DRAMATIS PERSONÆ

IVERNIC ROYAL FAMILY

HIGH KING ÓENGUS OF IVERIU—father of Princess Eseult, uncle of Lady Branwen; he holds his court at Castle Rigani, in the province of Rigani

QUEEN ESEULT OF IVERIU—mother of Princess Eseult, wife of King Óengus, aunt of Lady Branwen, sister of Lady Alana and Lord Morholt; she's originally from the province of Laiginztir

PRINCESS ESEULT OF IVERIU—daughter of King Óengus and Queen Eseult, cousin of Lady Branwen, niece of Lord Morholt and Lady Alana

IVERNIC NOBILITY

LADY BRANWEN CUALAND OF LAIGINZTIR—heir to Castle Bodwa, daughter of Lady Alana and Lord Caedmon, cousin and lady's maid of Princess Eseult, niece of Queen Eseult and King Óengus

LORD MORHOLT LABRADA OF LAIGINZTIR—the King's Champion, uncle of Branwen, brother of Queen Eseult and Lady Alana

LADY ALANA CUALAND OF LAIGINZTIR (*deceased*)—Lady of Castle Bodwa, mother of Branwen, sister of Queen Eseult and Lord Morholt

LORD CAEDMON CUALAND OF LAIGINZTIR (*deceased*)—Lord of Castle Bodwa, father of Branwen

LORD DIARMUID PARTHALÁN OF ULADZTIR—heir to Talamu Castle, son of Lord Rónán, northern clan leader, and Lady Fionnula; he's a descendant of High King Eógan Mugmedón

LORD RÓNÁN PARTHALÁN OF ULADZTIR—Lord of Talamu Castle, father of Diarmuid; he's a descendant of High King Eógan Mugmedón

LADY FIONNULA PARTHALÁN OF ULADZTIR—Lady of Talamu Castle, mother of Diarmuid

LORD CONLA OF MUMHANZTIR—nobleman from the province of Mumhanztir, former love interest of Princess Eseult

MEMBERS OF THE ROYAL GUARD AND HOUSEHOLD

SIR KEANE OF CASTLE RIGANI—member of the Royal Guard and bodyguard to Princess Eseult; he's from a coastal village along the Rock Road

SIR FINTAN OF CASTLE RIGANI—member of the Royal Guard and bodyguard to Queen Eseult

TREVA OF CASTLE RIGANI—head royal cook

DUBTHACH OF CASTLE RIGANI—servant at the castle, son of Noirín

NOIRÍN OF CASTLE RIGANI—castle seamstress, mother of Dubthach

MASTER BÉCC OF CASTLE RIGANI—the royal tutor to Princess Eseult and Lady Branwen

SAOIRSE—becomes an assistant to Queen Eseult in the infirmary at Castle Rigani; she's from the coastal village of Doogort

SIR COMGAN OF CASTLE RIGANI—member of the Royal Guard

GRÁINNE—an orphan girl from the Rock Road befriended by Princess Eseult

KERNYVAK ROYAL FAMILY

KING MARC OF KERNYV—uncle of Tristan, brother of Princess Gwynedd, son of King Merchion and Queen Verica of Kernyv

PRINCE TRISTAN OF KERNYV—heir to the protectorate of Liones, nephew of King Marc and the King's Champion, son of Princess Gwynedd and Prince Hanno

PRINCE HANNO OF LIONES (*deceased*)—navigator with the Royal Kernyvak Fleet who became a prince through marriage to Princess Gwynedd of Kernyv; he's the father of Tristan, and his ancestors came to Kernyv with the Aquilan legions from Kartago

PRINCESS GWYNEDD OF KERNYV (*deceased*)—mother of Tristan, older sister of King Marc, daughter of King Merchion and Queen Verica

CREW OF THE *DRAGON RISING*

MORGAWR—Captain of the *Dragon Rising*, member of the Royal Kernyvak Fleet

CADAN—cabin boy on the *Dragon Rising*, member of the Royal Kernyvak Fleet

PART I

THE
OLD WAYS

KISS OF LIFE

SMOKE AND SCREAMS AND LOVE.

Fractured images swirled in the back of Branwen's mind, transporting her a thousand leagues away from Castle Rigani. She dug her fingernails into the armrests of her chair as her heartbeat accelerated. The dreams always grew worse this time of year. Snatches of color like stained glass that collided together and burst apart.

"Really, Branny," said Essy, interrupting her thoughts. "You're such a mopey drunk."

Branwen inhaled. Her cousin had forgotten what day it was. She spared an extra second's glance at the sea, preparing herself to meet Essy's gaze. The waves were rough through the small, circular windows of the princess's drawing room: indigo capped with white. She never liked to lose sight of them for long. A wildness stirred inside her as they broke against the shore. She did her best to smother it.

"Elderberries loosen your tongue altogether too much," Branwen said as she turned to her cousin.

The princess giggled and touched another thimbleful of elderberry wine to her lips.

Branwen kept her voice light. "What would dashing Lord Diarmuid say if he could see your cheeks so flushed?" Diarmuid was the son of Lord and Lady Parthalán from the province of Uladztir, whom King Óengus had invited to the castle for a feast this evening. Essy couldn't stop talking about him.

The princess responded by brandishing her bright pink tongue. "Diarmuid does make my cheeks flush all on his own." Another giggle and a hiccup. "But if we're going to be subjected to Lord Rónán recounting all of his youthful victories against the Kernyveu—again—then I think you'd do well to have another thimbleful yourself, Branny."

An anchor dropped in Branwen's chest simply thinking about the people who terrorized her kingdom. Thieves and pirates all of them. Their assaults on the coast of Iveriu were relentless. She didn't need any further reminders. Especially not today. Faceless raiders already lay in wait for Branwen whenever she closed her eyes.

Perhaps a hazy glow was just what she needed to make the anniversary pass more quickly. Although no drink would ever be strong enough to completely dull the memories.

Had it really been thirteen years?

Essy measured another pour of the sweet and tart wine into her thimble, declaring, "Delicious," while sighing in satisfaction. The princess had pilfered the wine from the personal supply of Treva, the head cook, which inspired a flicker of guilt in Branwen, but, then, there were certainly worse things Essy could do.

"Delicious," Branwen agreed as she swiped the wine-filled waterskin from her cousin, forgoing the thimble, and savored the taste of elderberries on her tongue. Essy clapped excitedly, giving her a con-spiratorial wink.

The princess adored making mischief and pulling pranks around the castle. One time she convinced Dubthach, the spinner's son, that a bowl of hard-boiled eggs was blind men's milky eyeballs and, as his future queen, commanded him to eat one. Poor Dubthach still couldn't stand the sight of eggs. Or chickens, for that matter.

Getting tipsy in Essy's chambers when they were supposed to be studying one of the great Ivernic love stories for their lessons with the royal tutor seemed a small crime by comparison.

Branwen pulled the waterskin away from her mouth, and her eyes flicked once more to the tumultuous waves below.

They called to her. Strange how much she could love the dark depths that carried destruction to her kingdom. In ancient times, so the bards sang, the island of Iveriu was invaded five times, and now the kingdom of Kernyv threatened to do it again.

Fire and sea and fighting men.

Branwen suspected peace was a dream as broken and elusive as her own, a puzzle from which key pieces had been stolen. She gave her head a small shake, the wine burning her throat nicely.

At the center of her fragmented dreams was love. Always love. A pair of lovers intertwined until they shared the same heart; their faces blackened, ashen. The tide pulled them out into the Ivernic Sea. They loved while they burned and they burned while they loved. And always, always their arms reached for Branwen.

It was her parents, she was sure of it.

"Share and share alike," said Essy, reaching for the waterskin. Branwen's gaze flitted back to her baby cousin, whose seventeenth birthday had just gone. With no male heirs, the peace and prosperity of Iveriu rested squarely on Essy's marriage. Ivernic law prohibited a woman from ruling in her own right—she needed a husband—and Branwen had heard rumblings that a foreign ally was crucial to protecting the waters that surrounded their small island. The difference in their stations had never been important, but Branwen sensed that one day it would be. Maybe one day soon.

Essy would, after all, become her queen.

A firm knock came at the heavy wooden door, and Branwen immediately stiffened in her seat.

Queen Eseult entered, her gait graceful, her spine straight. Surreptitiously, Branwen hid the waterskin beneath her thick brocade skirts. She spied Keane, the princess's bodyguard, make a face from the archway, but he said nothing. Keane was starkly attractive and he'd asked Branwen to dance twice at the last Imbolgos festival. Too bad he didn't cause her cheeks to flush. That was entirely due to the wine.

Scanning their rosy complexions, Queen Eseult lowered an eyebrow. "I see." She cleared her throat. "It must be a highly amusing lesson that Master Bécc assigned you both today. I could hear your laughter from halfway across the castle."

Branwen's eyes snagged on the queen's and she ducked her head. Technically, as a lady's maid, she was charged with keeping the princess safe—even from herself. Her aunt had never made her feel like a servant, however. She'd always treated her more like another daughter.

Queen Eseult dropped a comforting hand on Branwen's shoulder. She had an uncanny knack for reading other people's emotions. Whispers abounded that the Old Ones had gifted her with the ability to see into the Otherworld, but Branwen was undecided regarding things she couldn't hold in her hand and examine.

If the Old Ones truly existed and were protecting the kingdom of Iveriu, then why did they permit the Kernyveu to continue their slaughter?

Why hadn't they saved Branwen's parents?

Essy remained happily ignorant of the silent exchange between Branwen and her mother. "We're reading the most *marvelous* story, Mother," she slurred.

"And what is this marvelous story?" the queen asked.

"'The Wooing of Étaín.' It's terribly romantic."

Branwen snorted. "Terrible is right. She gets turned into a purple fly!"

Essy twitched her nose and stuck her tongue out at her cousin, no longer pretending to hide her intoxicated state.

"I don't fancy being turned into an insect, but Étaín *did* live for thousands of years. Everyone in Iveriu still knows her name. And to be fought over by two supernatural men..." The princess clutched melodramatically at her heart.

Branwen and the queen couldn't stop themselves from laughing. Essy's charm was nothing if not infectious, and she always drew Branwen back from the dark places in her head. Although Branwen didn't understand why Essy loved the story of Étaín so much. It never ended well. In one version she was cursed by her lover's jealous wife to be an insect. In another she was spirited away to the Otherworld forever. Maybe Branwen just wasn't a romantic.

Her aunt caught her eye, almost as if she knew precisely what Branwen was thinking. The corner of the queen's mouth arced upward and she winked.

Branwen would always be indebted to her aunt not only for raising her but also for taking her on as an apprentice healer. Queen Eseult was renowned throughout the kingdom for her skills with herbs. Branwen may not have believed in the Old Ones, but medicine was something she understood.

She often worked by candlelight long after Essy had fallen asleep, grinding and mixing new remedies to test or practicing her stitches on cushions. Branwen wanted to be able to save somebody else's parents, somebody else's children.

If her parents had reached a healer in time, could they have been saved? The queen made sure Branwen never learned the precise details of their deaths, but the question haunted her. Something had broken inside Branwen the day her parents died and never fully mended; something had ignited, too—a fiery hatred that she knew would consume her if she didn't keep it carefully controlled.

With a sly sideways glance at her daughter, Queen Eseult said to Branwen, "Once the princess has recovered her . . . wits, could I impose upon you to gather some mermaid's hair?"

Branwen nodded. Mermaid's hair was luminous turquoise seaweed that made the surface of the water glow like a lantern on moonless nights. Fresh air and a walk would do her good.

"Thank you, dear heart," the queen continued. "I'm making a balm for the king. Óengus is suffering from gout again. The weather has been so temperamental lately."

"Gout? *Gross*, Mother." The princess curled her top lip in disgust. "Gentlewomen do *not* discuss gout."

"Wait until you've been married a few years."

"I'd rather be transformed into a fly like Étaín than be married

8

to a man with gout!" With that, Essy liberated the elderberry wine from beneath Branwen's skirts and took an indelicate gulp.

The queen sighed. "Keep this up and *I'll* be the one who needs a drink," she said, wresting away the waterskin.

"Good. Maybe that would loosen you up, Mother."

Branwen held her breath. Any other queen would have struck her daughter for being so insolent and behaving with such impropriety. A lady's maid could also expect to be punished if her charge made such a remark.

Queen Eseult simply recorked the elderberry wine. Then she stooped down, kissing the princess on the forehead. Essy made a noise of complaint.

Branwen's aunt turned toward her and kissed her temple, too. As warmth from the kiss radiated outward, she was choked by shame for failing in her duties.

"Today is hard for me as well, my darling Branny," the queen murmured before sweeping out silently.

She remembered. A solitary tear slid down Branwen's cheek, frozen in the afternoon light.

"Come on." Essy pushed to her feet, catching hold of Branwen's hand. "The Queen of Iveriu commands us to catch a mermaid by the hair, and so it shall be." She glowered in the direction her mother had vanished.

"It wasn't a command, Essy. It was a request."

"A queen's request is always a command."

Branwen shrugged, letting her cousin tug her from the chair. Request or command, she would do anything to repay the queen's love. Gladly.

Essy stumbled along beside her as they wended their way from the castle to the beach below. When they were children, Branwen had resented her younger cousin's following her everywhere, constantly pestering her, but the gap in their ages eventually meant less and less, and Branwen could no longer imagine her own portrait without Essy painted by her side.

Keane kept a respectful but watchful distance from the princess and her lady's maid. Branwen was glad she didn't have a bodyguard of her own. It would get tiresome.

She usually spent her spare time on the rocks below the ramparts. They seemed fierce and protective to her, like Queen Eseult; in the fading sunlight, the stone of the four rounded towers shone like emeralds. Branwen always knew she was safe within the castle walls. Its bastions jutting out toward the sea were lined with archers to fend off any invaders, like the Kernyvak pirates who killed her parents. And yet she couldn't resist the urge to be free of them.

Most people would avoid the spot where they'd learned their parents had been murdered. But, for Branwen, this was also the last place she had known they were alive.

She felt closest to them here.

Sometimes she could almost make herself believe they were merely at Fort Áine, the destination of their final journey. That they would be coming back for her soon. Her pulse spiked as the breakers crashed in her ears.

"Did you even hear what I *said*, Branny?" Essy nudged her gently with her shoulder.

"What was that?"

Essy had the same eyes as Branwen's mother, Lady Alana—green like Rigani stones. It made her love her cousin that much more.

She, on the other hand, had inherited coppery brown eyes from her father, Lord Caedmon.

The princess twisted a straw-colored lock around her finger and pulled, scowling at her cousin. "I said, do you think any man will ever love me as much as Étaín? Do you think Lord Diarmuid could?"

Real sadness underscored her words and Branwen's heart ached. Her cousin spent too much time losing herself in old, romantic ballads. It wouldn't help prepare her for a political marriage. "I thought you didn't want a husband?" she said breezily.

"I don't want a husband. I want a *lover*. I want a man who loves me—not my kingdom or my titles."

"Don't let your mother catch you talking like that, Essy," Branwen said, chastising her with a swing of the small wicker basket that she'd brought to collect the mermaid's hair.

"Why not? I don't care who knows. I don't care if *everyone* knows!" the princess said, raising her voice. Sidelong, Branwen glimpsed Keane furrowing his brow. "Why shouldn't I choose whom I love?" Essy demanded.

They both knew why.

Essy *was* the kingdom. One day she'd be queen and her first duty would be to the Land. To Iveriu. When the time came, Essy would do the right thing for her people. Branwen only wished it wouldn't make her so miserable.

The princess blew out a shaky breath. "No one ever asked me what I wanted."

Branwen's gaze skated over the waves, darkening as the sun set, and thought of her parents. There was an Otherworld that supposedly lay beyond the waves. Were they there? Were they happy? The only thing Branwen knew for certain lay beyond the waves was the island of Albion and their enemy, the kingdom of Kernyv, on its western peninsula.

"We seldom get what we want, dear cousin," she said.

Essy followed her gaze to the beach. "I didn't forget what today is . . ." She nodded toward the water. "Are you all right, Branny?"

There was a pinch in Branwen's chest. She shouldn't have doubted her cousin. Essy knew her better than anyone. Branwen sighed. "This day happens every year."

"That's not an answer." A line appeared on the bridge of Essy's nose. "Just because we seldom get what we want doesn't mean we shouldn't try," said the princess, raising her chin.

Nothing would ever bring Branwen's parents back, and nothing would ever change the fact that Essy was born to royalty. Her blood dictated her future. Branwen squeezed her cousin's elbow. She'd try to be more understanding.

"If you don't feel like entertaining tonight," said Essy, "I'll make your excuses at the feast. You don't always have to be so stoic."

A small smile parted Branwen's lips. The princess might be self-centered at times, but she loved deeply in her own way. For months after Branwen's parents died, Essy would crawl into her bed so Branwen wouldn't have to face the dark alone. Branwen had been so angry—at the world, at Essy for still having a mother—that she wouldn't share her covers. But Essy still came, night after night, and slept in the cold.

"Thank you," said Branwen. The last thing she wanted to do was play hostess for pleased-with-himself Lord Diarmuid, but she was part of the royal household and she would perform her duty. Stoic was the only way she knew how to be. "I'll be fine, Essy. Truly."

"If you're certain."

"I'm certain."

"In that case . . . Will you fix my hair?"

Branwen laughed. "Never fear," she assured her. Essy always pushed her luck.

"You're the best, Branny!" the princess sing-songed as if she hadn't been on the verge of tears moments ago. Her cousin's moods came as fast and feverish as a tempest but broke just as quickly.

Branwen shoved Essy toward the castle. "Off with you!" She flicked a glance in Keane's direction. He inclined his head.

"Promise you won't stay too long by the waves," said Essy. "The coast isn't safe at night." She was right. The Kernyvak raids on Iveriu had begun when the Aquilan Empire retreated from the island of Albion to the southern continent, and they had intensified with each passing year.

Nevertheless, Branwen waved her hands, unperturbed.

"Perhaps I should leave Keane with you," said Essy.

"Nice try." The princess was forever trying to evade the vigilant eyes of her bodyguard.

Stubbornly, Essy complained, "I'd give all my jewels for a tenth of your freedom, Branny."

"Ah, yes, the freedom to collect seaweed and fungus from the forest floor. You would just *love* that." Her cousin's study of herbal remedies had ended precipitously after she forced Dubthach to drink one of her concoctions and he lay in bed with a stomachache for two weeks. Branwen stroked Essy's brow in a tender motion. "Jewels for mushrooms!" she teased. "Bards will sing my ballad far and wide: *Branwen of the Briars!*"

"Fine." With the speed of a falcon, Essy's pout dissolved into a mischievous grin. "Don't let the mermaids get you!"

Branwen watched Essy walk in the direction of the main gate, still a bit unsteady from the wine. Keane filed closely behind her. Just before the princess disappeared from view, she called back, "Love you, Branny!"

A laugh followed, which was echoed by the surf.

"Love you, too," Branwen whispered, but the sea beckoned to her.

Dying sunlight swirled around her. Some of her countrymen believed it was filled with invisible sprites. They believed you could cross the Veil into the realm of the Old Ones through hills like Whitethorn Mound, a short distance from the castle.

Branwen believed in what she could see. She believed the existence of sprites or Old Ones was about as likely as having one true love. The only true love she felt was for her aunt and her cousin. And for Iveriu.

Mermaid's hair was strewn across the wet sand. Branwen liked the feel of the slick granules as she picked up the seaweed and placed it in the basket. She had been on the beach the day her parents died, building them a sandcastle.

She remembered how she'd hollowed out the sand into a circular moat with the earnest concentration of a master builder. The first line of defense. Her people had been at war with the kingdom of Kernyv since before Branwen was born. At six years old, she'd already understood the importance of protecting what you loved.

The sandcastle was to have been a gift, an apology to her parents. She'd been very cross with them for leaving her behind, and she had refused to say good-bye. While they were away, she had longed for her mother's embrace, to bury her face in dark mahogany curls—Lady Alana always smelled of rosemary. She longed for it still.

Right as Branwen was packing the final sand wall of the intricate terraced structure, a tiny blond projectile had catapulted herself into Branwen's arms. She had lost her balance and they both collapsed on top of the castle.

You've ruined everything! Branwen had shrieked. Essy took no notice, rolling in the glistening grains merrily—completely oblivious to the destruction she had wrought. To her, it was just a game.

A rustle in the undergrowth surrounding the beach jolted Branwen back to the present. She gasped as her gaze caught a familiar shape.

The basket of mermaid's hair fell to the sand.

It was a fox, poised and curious. The same fox she'd seen the day her parents died. Thirteen years ago today. *Impossible.*

The fox barked as if it sensed her skepticism. Branwen had never told anyone how the creature appeared on the beach, its eyes intent, a story behind them, moments before Queen Eseult came bearing tidings of her parents' deaths. At the time, she'd wondered if it was a messenger sent by the Old Ones, like in the legends of her people. When she was older, she'd dismissed the memory as childish whimsy—a foolish hope that anyone in the Otherworld cared about her.

Regardless, Branwen would recognize the fox's gleaming redcurrant coat anywhere. And its white ears. So beautiful, so unnatural. Dusk shimmered around the creature, making it seem more illusion than flesh and bone.

The fox stared out to sea, indicating something with its nose and barking again. What was it doing here? What was it looking at?

She sucked in another sharp breath as she spotted it: a raft. She could just make out the form of a man sprawled across it.

Turning toward her, the creature regarded Branwen with Otherworldly grace. *Save the man*, it implored with ebony eyes. She shook her head. That was a *ridiculous* notion.

The fox swished its bushy tail in annoyance.

Her chest tightened with the urge to obey. *Move*, the beast seemed to say. Exhaling, Branwen ran toward the water, still apprehensive, and waded into the chilly depths.

When she was submerged halfway up to her chest, Branwen managed to seize one corner of the makeshift raft. She couldn't see the man's face but he wasn't moving.

She kicked as hard as she could, guiding the large plank of driftwood toward the shore. It took all of Branwen's strength to haul the raft onto the beach. As she felt the sand once more beneath her feet, she dropped down beside the stranger, shivering from exertion and the freezing waters. Scanning his body, she looked for injuries the way that Queen Eseult had trained her to do.

Hurriedly, she turned the man over. His tunic was in shreds, stained with blood. A gash started at his shoulder and sliced diagonally across his heart to his abdomen. It didn't seem too deep, but, unfortunately, his chest wasn't heaving. He wasn't taking in any air.

Branwen didn't know how long the stranger had been unconscious. There was a chance she could still save him if it hadn't been long enough for his soul to depart. The kiss of life, her father had called it.

She'd been on the beach with her father one afternoon when the villagers brought a drowned fisherman to him for help. Branwen watched in awe as her father revived the man. All of the peasants had loved Lord Caedmon. As a little girl, Branwen had understood that although he ruled over them, he never placed himself above them.

Trying to remember that distant day, Branwen began pounding on the stranger's chest. His wounds wept blood all over her hands. Nothing was happening. Fighting her panic, she raised her face above the man's.

She had not yet allowed herself to take in his features. But when she did, her own breath buckled in her throat. He was the most handsome man she'd ever seen, even with his cuts and bruises. A foreigner, certainly. Dark curls, wet and bloody, framed elegant cheekbones and a mouth that was almost too perfectly formed.

Collect yourself. Branwen's training was intended for a moment like this.

Without further delay, she felt the stranger's neck for a pulse. His brown skin was flaky like a snakeskin from the sun. Could he have been aboard a trading vessel from the southern continent?

Summoning all of her courage, she pressed her lips to his. They were salt-stained and irresistibly sweet. She pinched his nose with her fingertips and breathed life into him.

More than Branwen had wanted anything since her parents died, she wanted to save this stranger. She beat his chest again, shuddering as he took in her breath. Instantaneously, he coughed hard and sprayed her with seawater. Despite the cold seeping into her body, her cheeks burned hot. The stranger wheezed and spat so much water out onto the sand that it seemed as if he'd swallowed the entire Ivernic Sea.

After an eternity, the stranger opened his eyes. Hazel flecked a darker brown, matching the last glimmer of evening light on the waves. He regarded his savior as he rasped for air and gurgled salt water.

Branwen stepped back because for the first time in her life, she felt a pull she couldn't control. A pull stronger than the sea.

And then he smiled. "That was *some* kiss."

She touched her flaming lips as the words reverberated in her mind. The stranger's voice had an odd lilt to it. He spoke her language but he wasn't Ivernic.

Her eyes widened in disbelief. The beautiful stranger was a Kernyvman.

Branwen had just saved the life of her enemy.

ODAI ETI AMA

"**W**HY ARE YOU STARING AT me like that?" the Kernyvman asked, still struggling for air. She turned on her heel, heart pounding, and prepared to make a break for the castle. "Wait. Wait, lady—*wait*," he pleaded.

Branwen hesitated and she hated herself a little for it. She wouldn't be ensnared by the wiles of some striking Kernyvak pirate. She would *not*. She owed her parents' memory more honor than that.

"Please, dear lady," he said, voice low and grainy. "By my troth, no harm will come to you."

She whipped around to face him. "What good are the promises of Kernyvmen?" she demanded, and he flinched as if she'd slapped him.

"On the graves of my parents, I swear it."

His declaration gave Branwen pause. The day Lord Caedmon had restored the fisherman to life, her father explained he was now responsible for the man until he returned the favor. If her father failed to protect him, he would lose his own honor. It was the way of the Old Ones.

Branwen could help her enemy or leave him bleeding on the beach. Either would mean dishonor. Curling her hands into fists, she hissed, "If anything untoward should befall me—it will be the last thing you do."

The half-drowned man chuckled. "I'd rather lose a limb than let anything happen to you."

"That could be arranged."

"If you were injured on my account, I would deserve it." He wasn't laughing now.

"Very well," she said shortly. Branwen knew which choice her father would make in her position. "It seems a shame to have saved you from the waves only to let you die on the shore." She thrust out a hand.

"A shame, indeed," he said, accepting her hand, the callused pads of his palms startlingly soft. She began to lift him up when the Kernyvman flashed her a half smile. "One day, I hope to be able to repay you for saving me. If not with a life, then with another kiss."

Of all the nerve! Branwen relinquished her grasp and he tumbled back into the sand.

"Death is preferable to kissing a Kernyvman," she told him.

He arched an eyebrow. "Are you saying that if you'd known who I was that you would have let me drown?"

Branwen didn't answer. She honestly didn't know. When she saw him on the raft, she'd wanted to save him the way no one had been able to save her parents. But if an Iverman washed up on the coast of Kernyv, would anyone help him?

At the back of her mind, Branwen could practically hear her father's reproach that it didn't matter what the Kernyveu would do—only she was responsible for her own honor.

Curse them all!

Getting to his feet with great difficulty, the bedraggled stranger said, "What is your name, my lady? I should like to know to whom I owe my life."

She bit her lip, afraid to trust him with her name. If he knew she was the niece of King Óengus, he might kidnap her to gain concessions for the kingdom of Kernyv.

"Emer," Branwen said at last. That was her favorite heroine, the wife of the most famous Ivernic hero. "Just plain Emer. I'm not a *lady*."

The Kernyvman studied her face intently. Could he see through her lies? She turned quickly, feeling exposed.

"Follow me," she called over her shoulder.

If Branwen left him on the beach and he was discovered by the Royal Guard, it would mean a hasty end for the Kernyvman. She might as well toss him back into the murky depths. Against her better judgment, she led him to a cave concealed within the cliff face.

At high tide, it became inaccessible from the beach. She'd discovered the cave when she was a little girl. She used to come here to hide herself. Especially after her parents died. Essy could never find her here when they played hide-and-seek, and it used to drive the princess mad.

Branwen didn't look back at the stranger as they walked, but she listened to his labored breaths. Each of his footfalls seemed weightier, less assured than the last. From the corner of her eye, she glimpsed the fox monitoring their progress toward the cave.

She blinked. The creature was really there. And he was no

common fox. What interest did he—or the Old Ones—have in this shipwrecked stranger?

The Kernyvman suddenly staggered beside her, knocking into Branwen's shoulder. On instinct, she reached out to steady him. The stranger wore a brave face but his pupils were dilated. He was becoming woozy from so much blood loss. Queen Eseult had taught her the signs when she let her assist in tending to the Royal Guard. The Kernyvman might pose a danger to her—but not in his current condition.

Tentatively, hoping she wouldn't live to regret it, Branwen looped an arm around his shoulders and took his weight.

"Come along, Sir—?"

"No *sir*." His tone was teasing as he wheezed. "Just plain Tantris. I'm a minstrel."

She gave her head a little shake. "Right. Keep up, *just plain* Tantris." Branwen gripped him harder as they walked, and he winced. She'd never been wedged so closely against a man before. He shivered with cold and she shivered with . . . because he shivered.

"Tell me," she said, an edge to her voice. "How does a minstrel come to be floating half dead in the middle of the Ivernic Sea?"

"Pirates." His jaw clenched. "I'd caught passage on a merchant ship. We were attacked." A few strained breaths whistled through his teeth.

His story was plausible. Kernyvak pirates menaced all of the northern seas, including their own kingdom's ships.

"Your countrymen do you proud," she said.

Tantris stopped short. Branwen lurched forward, then rocked back against him. "Not all Kernyvmen love bloodshed, Emer," he said.

Icy-hot prickles of mortification spread across Branwen's chest before she remembered she shouldn't care if she'd offended her mortal enemy.

"What do they love, then, Kernyvmen?" she wanted to know.

"Poetry." He gave her a shameless wink.

Ugh. Tantris could barely stand, yet his attempts at charm didn't flag. "Poetry?" Branwen repeated.

"I suppose I can't speak for *all* Kernyvmen, but I, myself, have a weakness for verses."

She cast him a withering look. "Is that so? Recite me one of your favorite poems."

"You ask a lot of a man with a sword wound who's just returned from the dead."

"If you can't even recite a single verse, how am I to know you aren't a pirate rather than a poet?"

They neared the entrance to the cave and fresh fear gnawed at her gut. Was Branwen foolhardy enough to trap herself alone with him? Surely the fox wouldn't have wanted her to save a pirate. But then, why was she following the advice of a fox? A fox!

Breathing raggedly, Tantris said, "I suppose it's the least I can do for the selfless maiden who rescued me from the sea."

"Indeed." Although, to be fair, he was slurring slightly and looked increasingly poorly.

"*Odai eti ama,*" he began, his voice rich and rolling like the waves, and Branwen became inordinately grateful for her lessons in the language of the Aquilan Empire.

"I hate and I love," she whispered, almost to herself.

Tantris glanced at her, taken aback. "You speak Aquilan?"

Branwen froze. Aquilan was spoken by the nobility across the southern continent, the Western Isles of Albion and Iveriu, and as far north as the Skáney Lands. If Tantris entertained at royal courts, he would have a reason to study it. A commoner, such as she claimed herself to be, would not.

"Only a little," Branwen said, preparing to bolt. What a useless spy she would make!

He nodded. "*I hate and I love*," Tantris began again in Ivernic, appearing to believe her deception. She loosed a breath. "*Dark as dawn, light as midnight*," he continued, first in Aquilan—which Branwen pretended not to understand—then in her language.

"*Fire that numbs, rain that burns*." The poet glanced at her for an unbroken moment. "*This love that I hate and hate that I love*."

Tantris leaned his forehead against hers, his lips dangerously close. Her chest swelled, panic and excitement infusing her. She should push him away—she really, really should. The poet tottered beside her.

"Emer . . ." Instead of brushing her mouth with his, Tantris collapsed on top of her.

Branwen let out a sigh and, with enormous effort, lugged the Kernyvman into her hiding spot. Her secret place. The place she'd never shared with anyone.

Crimson light splayed across the walls of the cave. The dwindling rays made the unconscious poet even more alluring, warming his bronze skin. Most of the Kernyvak raiders who pillaged Ivernic shores were pale like Branwen. Tantris's family must have immigrated to Kernyv from elsewhere in the now diminished Aquilan Empire, which had ruled Albion until a few generations ago. Perhaps that was how he'd learned their poetry?

She noticed he had a tiny scar across his right eyebrow, and she found it disconcertingly endearing.

My enemy, she told herself. It didn't matter what color his skin was. *He's my enemy.*

He might be a poet not a pirate, but his people had still murdered her parents. Even if his ancestors came from beyond the Aquilan Sea, the poet was a Kernyvman. His charm alone proved it. As Branwen debated with herself, Tantris's thick eyelashes fluttered. He focused on her face and gave her a smile.

Refusing to reciprocate, she told him, "You should count yourself lucky, Tantris—lucky that I didn't know you were Kernyvak."

Queen Eseult always said that healers couldn't choose their patients. The Old Ones expected them to heal whoever crossed their paths, whether they were thieves or princes. Would the queen extend that mandate to Kernyvmen?

"It was more than luck, Emer, that brought me to you." His voice brimmed with a confidence Branwen wished she shared.

The fox, she wanted to say. *It was the fox that brought* me *to* you.

Until today, she'd convinced herself that the fox was simply the figment of a grief-stricken child's imagination. Until today, Branwen had thought the Otherworld was a bedtime story and the Old Ones nothing but false promises. After today . . .

Flattening her lips together, she tore a strip of cloth from one of the underskirts of her gown. This wasn't a subject she wanted to discuss—and definitely not with Tantris.

"What are you doing, my lady?" he asked.

She laughed at the hint of scandal in his tone. "I'm going to bandage your wound," she replied matter-of-factly. The ripping sound filled the space between them. It was good to have something practical to concentrate on rather than his eyes. Honor compelled Branwen to help him, but she would not *like* a Kernyvman.

"I'm sorry it's wet," she told him. "It's only temporary. I'll be back later with my salves." High tide wouldn't come till midnight, and she'd return before then.

He touched her hand, sending tingles all through her body. She fought the sensation. "You're a healer?" Wonder filled his voice.

"More like an apprentice." Queen Eseult was the true medicine woman; Branwen had much yet to learn.

Tantris tried to support himself with his elbows but he was too weak.

"Emer, my Otherworld savior."

Branwen rolled her eyes. "I'm not from the Otherworld." But it begged the question: Why did the Otherworld care about this Kernyvman and not her parents?

He reached toward Branwen and twined a stray lock of her hair around his forefinger. She pulled back, although part of her wanted to be pulled closer.

"You're Otherworld-sent," Tantris pronounced, "and I won't hear otherwise." His smile transformed into a grimace as he laughed.

A few seconds later, he heard nothing at all. Branwen sighed as Tantris succumbed to exhaustion. She finished bandaging his chest and lit a small fire to keep him warm. Before she set off toward Castle Rigani, Branwen skimmed her finger along the scar on his brow.

He didn't stir.

Somehow she knew the fox was still watching without being seen.

"*Odai eti ama*," she breathed.

HE LOVES ME, HE LOVES ME NOT

"WHERE HAVE YOU BEEN, BRANNY?" the princess complained, seated at her vanity. "Look at the state of my hair!" A crown of lopsided plaits adorned Essy's head.

Where had she been? Saving a sworn enemy of Iveriu, that was where. Branwen's breaths still came in pants from retrieving the basket of mermaid's hair on her dash back to the castle, dropping it off for the queen, and running up the stairs to Essy's chambers.

"I'm here now," she said, trying to steady her nerves. As usual, the princess was too preoccupied to notice that Branwen's dress was damp and sea-stained. She was thankful that Keane wasn't on duty. He would have noticed.

Essy caught her eye in the vanity mirror.

"Lord Diarmuid should be here any minute." She beamed an excited smile. Branwen hardly thought the northern lord deserved it.

Striding toward the princess, she wiped her grimy hands on her already dirty dress. "Then I'd better get to work," she said, and pulled the horsehair brush from Essy's grip.

As she began detangling the bird's nest her cousin had made of her hair, she noticed a few tufts missing from the base of Essy's skull. A few years ago, the princess began pulling at it whenever she was anxious. She'd begged Branwen not to tell the queen. Branwen gnashed her teeth but decided not to bring it up tonight. They both had enough on their minds.

Essy hissed as Branwen pulled loose the golden and ruby balls the princess had inexpertly attached to the ends of her flaxen braids. "*Ouch*, cousin," she cried.

Ignoring her protests, Branwen unraveled the knots with agile fingers. The princess closed her eyes. Branwen stroked the brush through her cousin's tresses in a soothing, rhythmic motion, like she'd been doing since they were children. It reminded Branwen of the ebb and flow of the tide. She found it comforting, too—she liked consistency. She did *not* like strangely pleasing Kernyvmen turning up on her beach.

Eyes still closed, the princess said, "Branny, there's something I've been meaning to tell you."

"Oh?" she replied as she selected vibrant red ribbons from a pile the princess had haphazardly discarded on the tabletop. Whenever her cousin began a conversation in this vein, it most often meant she'd borrowed something of Branwen's without permission and lost it. She didn't know how Essy would survive without a castle full of servants to look after her and, fortunately, the princess would never have to find out.

Branwen swept her cousin's hair into two loops on either side of her face. She threaded the winter cherry–colored ribbons through the braids, securing them with an intricate pattern called a sweetheart plait. The princess was blessed with a high forehead, which the plaits accentuated. Branwen's wasn't quite as high, but her heart-shaped face was pleasant enough. At least, she hoped it was.

She found herself wondering whether a certain Kernyvak poet would think so, too. *My enemy*, she repeated in her mind. *My enemy*.

"What did you want to tell me, Essy?" Branwen asked to distract herself.

Her cousin tapped her lower lip, drawing her eyebrows together the way she always did before confessing she'd eaten the last of the lavender candies or let the inkwells dry out.

"It's about Lord Diarmuid," she said, unable to meet Branwen's eyes.

Branwen tensed. "What about him?"

"He . . . he writes me letters." Scarlet splotches appeared on her cheeks. This was more serious than candies or inkwells.

"What kind of letters?" When the princess didn't answer, Branwen bent down to her eye level. "What *kind* of letters, Essy?" she said again.

"Love letters," her cousin admitted as she exhaled. "Wonderful love letters." A shy smile slipped across her face. "It's so romantic."

"It's not romantic, Essy! Your father could have his head." Quite literally. "It's reckless. What if someone finds them?"

"Who would find them? You?" She stabbed a finger in the air. "See—this is why I didn't tell you sooner," she said, a whine creeping into her voice. "I knew you'd react like this. But you really don't have to worry, Branny. Diarmuid is a descendant of High King Eógan Mugmedón. And, as eldest son, he'll inherit Talamu Castle. It's a fine match. Father will approve."

The princess fixed her with a glare, daring her to disagree.

Branwen opened and closed her mouth.

"Besides," Essy said, eyes bright. "I think tonight's the night that Diarmuid proposes!" She laughed and it held a trace of both exuberance and desperation. "His parents have accompanied him all the way from Uladztir. That must be why. Don't you think?"

"Maybe," said Branwen.

In order to combat the increasing Kernyvak raids, Iveriu might be forced to seek military help from abroad and the most expedient way to secure that help would be to marry the princess to a foreign ruler. No matter his lineage, Diarmuid couldn't supply an army.

Branwen regarded her cousin seriously. Weaving a string of freshwater pearls through the white-blond wisps of her hairline, she entreated, "But Essy, you hardly even know Lord Diarmuid."

"And how well am I likely to know any of the men my father chooses for me?"

She couldn't disagree. Still, she challenged, "What about Lord Conla? He was your favorite at the Imbolgos festival. You wouldn't stop babbling about him for months."

"Who?"

"Lord Conla of Mumhanztir," she said, tying off either end of the pearl strand.

"Oh *him*. He's such a boy. Diarmuid is a man. He's gorgeous and he said that the first time he laid eyes on me was like seeing the sun after years of night . . . he has the best turns of phrase. Practically a poet."

Branwen's heart tripped over itself. "Men will sugar you with sweet words until they get what they want." *Especially poets*, she reminded herself.

"How would you know, Branny?" Essy gave her a hawkish glance. "You've never been courted."

She swallowed. Opening her heart didn't come naturally to Branwen. She envied Essy's ability to throw her entire being into everything in her life—not that she would tell her so. Branwen dropped her eyes to the floor.

"Oh, Branny, I didn't mean it like that. I—"

"It's fine. You're right. I've never been courted." Flirtatious, half-dead Kernyvmen in caves definitely didn't count. *I hate and I love.*

Essy clasped her hand, tracing her forefinger in a familiar pattern against Branwen's palm. Her cousin's nail scratched into her skin. Branwen bit her tongue.

When Master Bécc taught the royal cousins the alphabet of the ancient language of trees—the first Ivernic writing, he'd pointed to an enormous hazel tree in the castle gardens and the honeysuckle vine wrapped around it. Neither could survive being separated from the other, he'd explained.

The girls had coupled the letter for hazel, which resembled a four-pronged comb, with the spiral that represented honeysuckle. It became their code, their secret language. To them, and only them, it meant *I love you, I understand, you're not alone*—and everything in between.

"Not you without me," said the princess as she finished tracing the symbol.

Branwen lifted her gaze. "Not me without you." She quieted Essy's finger, taking her cousin's hand in her own, and traced their emblem in return.

The sting of Essy's remark was gone. She kissed her cousin on the temple. Forgiving the princess her thoughtlessness had become second nature, and it was a small price to pay for her love.

One side of Essy's mouth tilted upward. "We'll find you a kind and swoon-worthy nobleman of your own, Branny," she insisted. "Don't be sad."

"I'm not."

Finding a swoon-worthy nobleman was the furthest thing from her mind.

"Here." Essy plucked a wilted blossom from her vanity. "I picked this for you on the way back from the beach."

Branwen smiled. As she closed her hand around the honeysuckle, she felt the pollen dissolve, staining her palm. They were the honeysuckle and the hazel tree, and they always would be.

"Thank you, cousin," she said.

Essy stole a glance at herself in the weathered looking glass. "Oh, Branny!" Her lips curved slightly, satisfied. "You have magic hands." She touched the pearls beaded along her brow. "Thank *you*!"

"I'm glad you like it."

Suddenly, the piercing blare of horns at the gatehouse rent the night. The glass in the narrow windows of Essy's bedchamber practically shook.

"They're here!" the princess exclaimed. "Tonight I'll find out if he loves me, or he loves me not!"

Branwen saw in her cousin's glinting eyes how much she wanted to rush to Lord Diarmuid's side. She wanted her to be happy, but she also wanted to protect her cousin's too-eager heart. Admiring her plaits once more, Essy said, "You really *are* a lifesaver, Branny!"

Her stomach cramped. There was someone whose life actually was depending on her this very moment. Branwen resolved to slip away from the feast as soon as she wouldn't be missed. She didn't want Tantris to catch a chill or go hungry or get a blood infection. Even if he *was* a Kernyvman.

Her honor required it. That was all.

"Go," she whispered in Essy's ear. "Go see Lord Diarmuid. I'll be along shortly. Just be careful with your heart."

"You're careful enough for the both of us, Branny." Essy giggled, regarded herself in the mirror one last time, and headed for the door. "Don't dally, cousin," she said, vanishing down the corridor in a ball of energy.

Branwen brushed off the petals of the broken flower as she took in her own appearance. Her gown was etched with sea salt, ruined, and her hair was a mess of black tendrils. It was a good thing the princess was so obsessed with Lord Diarmuid that she didn't ask too many questions.

She touched her lips, which tingled with the memory of the Kernyvman.

Spying the waterskin of elderberry wine that lurked beneath the bed skirts, she grabbed it and swigged a healthy gulp. A little buzz took hold.

It was nothing compared to the kiss of life.

✠ ✠ ✠

Branwen heard Essy's shriek of delight before she could see her.

She squinted. The princess and Lord Diarmuid lingered at the back of the feasting hall, illuminated by guttering candles. In the dim light, she glimpsed her cousin coquettishly tap him on the nose.

Branwen mustered all of her patience and walked toward them.

As the northern lord turned around to greet her, his smile seemed forced.

"Good evening, Lady Branwen." He dipped his head, raising her hand formally to his lips. Branwen knew the Parthalán clan was an important ally of King Óengus, controlling much of the northern Uladztir province and, for that reason alone, she gave him a curtsy in return.

"Lord Diarmuid. I hope I'm not disturbing you." Essy noticed the curtness of Branwen's tone—although Diarmuid did not—and lanced her with a sidelong glare.

"Not at all," he assured her. Again there was something about his civility that seemed contrived. "I was just informing our Lady Princess how we rousted some Kernyvak raiders on our way here."

Panic stabbed Branwen. Were those the same pirates who had attacked the vessel carrying Tantris?

"Oh really?" she said, feigning disinterest.

"We sent them back to their ships with their tails between their legs. Although, if you ask me, we should have pursued them all the way to Kernyv."

During her shifts in the castle infirmary, Branwen had eaves-dropped on guardsmen grumbling in a similar vein. Some of the provincial lords wanted to take matters more into their own hands. Anxiety was growing that King Óengus couldn't protect Iveriu against Kernyvak attacks.

There hadn't been a civil war in Iveriu for generations. How real was the threat? Branwen wondered. Could the king actually be plan-ning on marrying Essy into the Parthalán clan to quell dissent among the lesser lords?

That outcome would undoubtedly please Essy in her current frame of mind. The princess laid a possessive hand on the young lord's arm. She was besotted—for now. But Branwen didn't believe

Lord Diarmuid was the lover her cousin dreamed of. No, she suspected he was a crown-chaser, like most other noblemen.

Branwen was saved from further small talk by the trumpet heralding the arrival of the King and Queen of Iveriu.

Under the cover of the horn blowing, Essy whispered in Branwen's ear, "What do you think?"

She glanced at Lord Diarmuid, who she presumed could hear them. "He has a pleasing face," Branwen whispered back, which wasn't a lie. The northern lord was possessed of silver-gray eyes and a square jaw. Although comparing him with the Kernyvak poet was like making a bit of sea glass compete with a star. She blushed at the thought, twisting the right sleeve of her gown.

"I know!" Essy said happily, giving Branwen a wink. The trumpeting stopped and the princess returned her attention to Diarmuid.

The queen sought out Branwen with her gaze. She was always utterly elegant and exuded a regal authority. Tonight, however, Queen Eseult resembled her sister, Lady Alana, so closely that it nearly broke Branwen's heart. It was as if her mother were standing before her.

Queen Eseult processed toward Branwen and Essy while King Óengus was waylaid near the entrance speaking with other guests, including Diarmuid's parents, Lord Rónán and Lady Fionnula. She also spotted Lord Morholt, the King's Champion. Morholt was Branwen's uncle, but his manner was so unlike that of the queen or of her mother that it was hard for her to see any relation.

The sea of courtiers parted for the queen, bowing their heads. The esteem in their eyes wasn't affected. Queen Eseult was beloved by the Iverni.

One day, Branwen fully expected Essy to inspire the same devotion.

"Good evening, Lady Queen." She greeted her aunt with a deep curtsy.

"Good evening, Lady Branwen. I collected the mermaid's hair from the infirmary. Thank you." The queen squeezed her hand.

"My pleasure." Branwen swallowed the reply. Mention of the infirmary sent a dart of fear straight through her. A wound like Tantris's could take a turn for the worse at any moment. She needed to get back to the cave.

Essy gave her mother a much more perfunctory curtsy. Lord Diarmuid, on the other hand, practically scraped the stone floor with his chin as he bowed.

"Lady Queen, my family is honored that you have invited us to feast at Castle Rigani."

"The honor is mine," said the queen mildly as she appraised the nobleman standing so close to her daughter.

Unable to resist needling him, Branwen told her aunt, "Lord Diarmuid informs me that we have him to thank for fighting off some Kernyvak raiders."

"Ah, yes?"

Lord Diarmuid licked his lips, cheeks growing ruddy. "I— I'm always proud to draw my sword for Iveriu," he stammered. "But my family is, of course, obliged to the Royal Guard for their assistance."

"As it is our duty and pleasure to provide it," said Queen Eseult. "A united kingdom is a strong kingdom. Wouldn't you agree?"

Essy linked her arm with Diarmuid's. "I would, Mother." She showed a briary smile. "Completely." Unlike the ballads the princess adored singing, in real life, Branwen knew, a noblewoman rarely got to write the ending to her own story.

Lord Diarmuid coughed as if he'd swallowed his tongue. "One Iveriu forever," he mumbled as mother and daughter dueled with their eyes.

Branwen stifled a laugh at his discomfort as Lord and Lady Parthalán joined them. Further pleasantries were exchanged until the feast began, when polite conversation dwindled in favor of boar slathered with ambergris and sides of venison.

When the acrobats cartwheeled into the hall, Branwen made her escape. Essy was so absorbed with Lord Diarmuid that she wouldn't have noticed if boulders were being catapulted at the castle. Branwen skulked down to the kitchens, careful to avoid head cook Treva. Hands trembling, she filled a basket with freshly baked bread, tranches of cured rabbit, smoked haddock, and wild blueberries.

From the laundry, she filched a clean tunic and trousers. She'd already pocketed blood-stanching herbs from the queen's stores when she delivered the mermaid's hair. Her aunt wouldn't mind. She always encouraged Branwen to work on her healing arts; she didn't need to know her patient was a Kernyvman. Still, Branwen's heart raced faster than any stallion.

Now she had everything she needed. All that remained was to gather the nerve to sneak out of the castle. At night. When raiders had been spotted marauding along the coast.

She cast one last look toward the safety of the feasting hall. Inside lay her family, her countrymen, everyone she loved, everyone who trusted her. Outside lay danger. The unknown.

Branwen pictured Tantris bleeding and suffering. Essy and the queen weren't the only ones who trusted her anymore. The Kernyvman had put his faith in Branwen, too.

He was trusting her to return.

Just outside the east gate of the castle, in the shadow of the archway, a pair of vulpine eyes flashed in the darkness. Bright yellow like a hungry moon. The fox.

Branwen sensed that he would protect her, although she didn't understand why. She drew in a bracing breath. Was she really taking orders from a fox? He barked, hurrying her along. A quavery warmth spread from her heart throughout her body.

She followed the creature into the night.

A WOMAN OF HONOR

BRANWEN HAD WALKED THE TRAIL from the castle to the shore thousands of times, but never alone in the dark. Shoulders tensed, she listened carefully for the snapping of branches or the low rumble of hooves on dirt. But she heard nothing. She moved as swiftly and quietly as she could. The fox followed her from a distance the whole time.

As she neared the cave, Branwen gazed back at the crenellated façade of Castle Rigani, radiant in the light of the watch fires. This was her home. It was beautiful. She would do anything to protect it.

So why was she sneaking out in the middle of the night to heal a wounded Kernyvman? Several times she almost stopped and turned on her heel, but the fox urged her onward. Branwen's thoughts returned to her father's rescue of the fisherman.

She'd asked him later why he would risk himself for one of his subjects. "Branny," Lord Caedmon had told her, "if you want your people to fight and die for you, then you must be prepared to do the same. And if you want to rule in peace, it is better to turn enemies into friends."

Branwen had felt the truth of his words in her bones, but the more time that elapsed without hearing her father's hearty laughter, the more she doubted she could ever be so generous. Her heart wasn't honorable enough to uphold her father's legacy. Hers was brittle and more fragile than she liked to acknowledge.

Farther up the path, the fox made a plaintive noise, somewhere between a whine and a bark. It gave her the distinct impression it didn't want Branwen to tarry any longer.

At the entrance to the cave, the fox barked again. There was no light coming from inside. The fire must have burned itself out. With apprehension, she tiptoed inside.

Quicker than an arrow, a hand was around her waist, and another clamped over her mouth. All the supplies she'd brought tumbled to the ground. Branwen struggled but her attacker held her firm. Fighting the panic that numbed her mind, she recalled Keane's lessons on self-defense.

Physically, she was outmatched. Her only advantage was surprise.

She bit her attacker's hand.

He snatched it back. Triumph swelled in Branwen for an instant before a foot hooked her ankle and she fell onto the rocky floor with a thud. The Kernyvman sprawled on top of her.

"Are all the Kernyveu this mad?" she rebuked him.

A startled intake of breath. "Emer?" The voice was full of alarm, and shame. Tantris's voice.

"Who else would it be?" Branwen's chest heaved with an odd mixture of fear and relief. Their lips were once again close enough for the kiss of life. A riot of anger—and something else—pulled taut every muscle in Branwen's body. "Get off me!" She elbowed him in the ribs.

He yelped from the pain as he rolled to the side.

"You could have signaled your arrival," he said, tilting his head so that a thin sliver of moonlight bathed his face. He was both appealing and exasperating.

"What a wonderful suggestion," said Branwen. "I'll run and signal your location to the Royal Guard as well!"

"The Royal Guard? We're near Castle Rigani?"

Curse the Kernyvman! She'd said too much. Who knew what his true purpose was in Iveriu?

Tantris looked at her thoughtfully. "Are you a servant at the castle?"

Lady's maid wasn't quite the same but Branwen nodded. Let him believe it.

"The king won't pay a ransom for me," she lied. "If that's what you're thinking." How could she have played so easily into her enemy's hands?

Outrage followed by anguish gripped Tantris's features. "You think me a kidnapper, Emer?" he said, a roughness to his accusation. "If anyone's done the kidnapping, it's you."

"*Me?*"

"Yes, *you*. Dragging a half-drowned man to your cave. Utterly helpless."

"Helpless?" *What gall!* She gave Tantris another shove. "You should learn not to bite the hand that feeds you," she spat. He groaned and a wave of guilt crashed over her. Fear for his life had given him the strength to attack her, but he was still gravely injured.

"I believe *you* did the biting, Emer."

Branwen made an indignant noise. Just when she was feeling sympathy for him! "Fine then. You can suture yourself." She scrambled to her feet.

Tantris caught the hem of her skirt. "No, wait. Emer, don't go." He gazed up at her. "Forgive my rash words."

"Why should I?" she said, but she didn't run. She stood very still as Tantris pushed to his feet.

"Because what I should have said is how brave you are to leave the shelter of the castle to help a stranger." There was something so musical and enticing about his voice that he must have been a talented bard, indeed. "And to pull me from the sea."

"I know how to swim," Branwen told him, dismissive. Her father had taught her to swim as soon as she could walk. He didn't care that noblewomen were never supposed to reveal enough of themselves to swim. Lord Caedmon used to say that they lived by the sea and he wouldn't lose his daughter to the tide.

Tantris searched her face. "Regardless, I'm truly ashamed for attacking you. You caught me unawares."

She felt a strange thrumming in her chest. "I said I'd return, and I keep my word." Branwen was rattled by the authority in her own voice—she sounded like Queen Eseult herself.

Tantris dropped to one knee, the way a knight would before his lady. "You are truly a woman of honor, Emer. I will never doubt your word again. I'm in your service."

Her cheeks blazed, and she hoped the moonlight wasn't strong enough in the cave for him to notice. "Get up, Tantris. Only a knight can pledge his service—and you're just a minstrel."

"Of course," he answered with a tight-lipped smile, rising with some pains back to standing.

"Your clothes are in tatters. Here, I brought you these." Branwen held out fresh linens as a peace offering.

Tantris's hands brushed hers as he accepted the clothing, and she felt heat right down to her toes.

"Thank you," he said. His dark eyes seared her. She swallowed several times.

"You're welcome." A cough. "Now make yourself useful and kindle a fire," Branwen commanded as imperiously as Essy would have.

She expected a smart remark but he simply inclined his head in deference. This Kernyvman was quite the enigma. He set about making the fire as Branwen scoured the cave floor for the supplies she'd dropped.

With a cluck of the tongue, she said, "Your supper is spoiled, and you have only yourself to blame."

Stone struck stone and a spark glittered against the night. The twigs began to crackle. Firelight washed over them. For several suspended moments, it seemed like neither of them was breathing. Her eyes darted to the floor as she pointed at the strips of meat she'd recovered. "Come, you must be hungry. Eat."

"Again, I thank you," Tantris said from beside the fire. "Won't you join me?" There was uncertainty in his question, and Branwen found it infinitely more enticing than his compliments.

From within her skirts, she pulled a salve of birch bark, to prevent infection, and arnica petals, to relieve pain. Tantris eyed the jar quizzically.

"It's a balm for your wound. It might sting," she cautioned.

Queen Eseult had taught her how to make the remedy. "I will tend to it, and then I must return home before I'm missed."

"I'll escort you."

Branwen's pulse quickened. "To Castle Rigani? Do you have a death wish?" With Lord Diarmuid's talk of Kernyvak raiding parties, Tantris would meet an unceremonious end within the castle walls.

"You've already risked yourself for me by coming here alone, Emer. I can't let you do it again."

"I didn't ask for your permission."

His eyes were trained on hers, unyielding. "It's not safe," he said.

"You can blame your countrymen for that."

"King Marc is a good king," said Tantris, defensive. He obviously believed it.

Branwen's nostrils flared. "As is King Óengus."

He rubbed the back of his neck. "Let's not quarrel, Emer."

"No, let's not. You could barely make it to the cave without my help, Tantris. You won't be much protection tonight."

Shadows clung to his face as he admitted, "I suppose I wouldn't." He balled his hands into loose fists. She could tell his muscles ached.

Branwen crouched down beside him and tugged at the end of his blood-soaked tunic. "Here, let's see to your wounds." She began pulling it over his head, but Tantris stopped her.

"Won't your father mind you undressing a strange man?" He paused. "Or your husband?"

His reticence made her laugh. "If I did have a husband, would you prefer that I let your wound get infected?"

"I would rather die than dishonor a woman who has shown me such kindness," Tantris replied. His tone left Branwen in no doubt that he would.

She crinkled her nose. "Tantris, I am an apprentice healer and this is what my honor impels me to do." Speaking the words, Branwen realized they were true. "You will only dishonor me if you don't let me help you." Lucky for him, *she* wasn't a princess. The honor of Iveriu itself would be in jeopardy if Essy were ever discovered alone with a man who was neither a relative nor her husband.

Exhaling, Tantris nodded. Branwen began to remove his tunic and his body went completely still. He smelled of the sea. It was even more intoxicating than the elderberry wine. Worryingly, the make-shift bandage she'd torn from her underskirts this afternoon was bloody and, more critically, tinged with green and yellow pus. His ability to push through the pain was truly impressive, but it could also belie the danger.

Although his cuts might not be deep, they could still poison his blood. A blood infection could cause a fever and a fever could be lethal.

She ripped off the bandage. Tantris teetered forward, seizing her shoulders for balance. His forehead pressed to hers, his curls tickled.

"Sorry," Branwen said in a hush.

"You didn't answer my question about a husband," he said. The hazel flecks in his eyes sparkled like gold in the firelight.

"No husband." For a moment, she spared a thought for her cousin, wondering if Lord Diarmuid had, in fact, proposed at the feast. "No father, either," she told him.

Concern filled his gaze. "I'm sorry, Emer."

She replied by pushing him gently away from her so she could slather the balm into his wound. Tantris sealed his lips together as she worked the ointment around the puffy flesh. The only sound was the spluttering of the fire. When she was done, Branwen wrapped the wound in muslin and sighed deeply.

"I shouldn't like to ever make you sigh again." Raising an eyebrow, Tantris asked, "What has the patient done to displease his healer?"

"I hope the salve will be enough to stave off a fever," Branwen said, drumming her fingers across her chin. "I'll be back tomorrow—when the water is low."

Tantris put his palm to the fresh bandage over his heart. "Don't fear, Emer," he said, boldly sweeping his hand along her cheek to calm her agitated fingers, and then he took her hand with his own. "I will live to see you again."

He locked his eyes on hers as he kissed her hand with reverence. Branwen had received many formal kisses in her life, but none of them felt like this. The softness of his sunburned lips made her want to laugh or scream—or maybe both.

Deep inside, Branwen quivered. With her whole heart, she wanted him to live.

She stood abruptly. "Good night, Tantris."

A BLEEDING HEART

BRANWEN ROSE AT DAWN, BARELY able to contain her unease. She'd spent the night tossing and turning, feeling as if she were still among the waves. Every time she closed her eyes, she pictured Tantris's lips on her hand.

All this trouble for a Kernyvman, she scolded herself.

Her arms sagged from the weight of Queen Eseult's breakfast tray as she crossed the cobblestoned courtyard of the inner ward. Delivering it wasn't part of Branwen's regular duties, but she needed to speak with the queen and she wanted an excuse. If Treva found Branwen's request odd, the castle kitchens were too busy for the head cook to mind as she happily handed over the tray piled high with pots of butter and wild fruit preserves, scrambled eggs, bacon, and freshly baked sweet buns.

Queen Eseult's apartments occupied the entire west tower, while King Óengus had the north to himself. Branwen and Essy lived together in the south tower, which overlooked the feasting hall. When Branwen had returned from the cave, she found Essy still adhered to Lord Diarmuid. He didn't ask for her hand at the feast, but the princess had convinced herself that it was solely because he was waiting for Belotnia, the Festival of Lovers, in two moons' time.

Her cousin was not an early riser, especially after the wine and excitement of the previous evening, so Branwen knew she should have plenty of time with the queen—if she could work up the nerve to ask her what she wanted to know.

She flicked a glance toward the east tower, where the Crown Prince of Iveriu would have resided if the queen had given Óengus a son. When the princess was younger, Essy insisted she preferred being an only child but a brother would have made her life easier. Instead, Branwen's uncle Morholt called the east tower home— although there was nothing genial or homey about him.

Branwen glided under the pointed, green marble arch at the base of the west tower and began ascending the spiral staircase. The keystones at the center of all the arches in the queen's tower were engraved with the image of a harp, its body painted gold and its strings silver: the symbol of Laiginztir. Queen Eseult was a proud Laiginztir woman. Just as Branwen's mother had been.

She touched the harp with two fingers as she ducked her head in the low clearance of the hallway leading to the queen's bedchamber. It was both a tribute and a prayer.

Fintan, the head of the queen's bodyguards, threw his shoulders back when he saw Branwen. He was a bear of a man with a large nose and thinning hair. He'd survived many battles against the Kernyveu and he had the scars to prove it.

"Good morning, Lady Branwen," he said gruffly, tipping his head as he opened the door for her. The warrior's deepest scars, however, came from losing his wife in childbirth a decade ago. He had no interest in remarrying, he said, and Branwen occasionally wondered if his dedication to her aunt went beyond duty.

Queen Eseult stood beside her court cupboard, mixing herbs with a mortar and pestle, as Fintan announced Branwen's arrival. It looked like she'd been awake for some time. The queen dismissed Fintan with a nod and turned her attention to her niece.

"What a nice surprise," she said.

Performing a swift curtsy, Branwen asked, "Where would you like the tray?"

"Oh anywhere." She waved a hand toward the sideboard.

Branwen set down the tray and her gaze traveled to her aunt's furrowed brow. "Would you like some tea?"

A beat passed before Queen Eseult said, "Tea?" She ground the herbs with some force. "Oh yes." She lifted her eyes to Branwen. "Forgive me, I'm a little out of sorts today. Tea would be lovely."

"Not at all." Anticipation bubbled in Branwen's chest as she busied herself pouring the tea into a cup that was also branded with a golden harp.

"It's not an easy thing to be the mother of daughters," said the queen, mostly to herself, as she reduced the herbs to a fine powder. "You'll see yourself one day."

Branwen had never really considered having children. She simply assumed she would stay in the service of the princess when she became queen. At nineteen Branwen was more than eligible, but her own marriage didn't seem particularly important.

She brought over the tea as her aunt ensconced herself in a tapestry-covered armchair by the window. Down below, the waves broke against the cliffside. In the morning light, they glinted aqua. Branwen's stomach churned.

"Thank you." The queen looked at her shrewdly and motioned for her niece to be seated. "Branny—is Essy happy?"

Branwen chewed the inside of her cheek, uncertain what to say. She thought of the newly torn clump of hair, but she wouldn't betray her cousin's confidence. "Essy seemed to be happy in the company of Lord Diarmuid," she answered, reluctant to share her qualms about his motives.

Queen Eseult put the cup to her lips and took a small sip. "Yes." Another sip. "And he in hers." There was an undercurrent to the queen's words.

"Lord Diarmuid would be a suitable match," her aunt continued. "But there are many things to consider." Branwen understood Queen Eseult's veiled message—don't let Essy set her heart on him.

"Of course," she said. "Will Lord and Lady Parthalán be staying at Castle Rigani long?"

"A fortnight, perhaps. Morholt has gone out with Lord Rónán this morning to gather reports from the villages about the sightings of Kernyvak raiders." The queen always spoke fondly of her brother.

Branwen didn't understand why. She found her uncle Morholt a hard-nosed and somewhat volatile man—cold, distant. Maybe it was just his warrior's heart. She swallowed, thinking of Tantris, and felt guilt stir within her.

The queen noticed her niece had gone quiet and touched a palm lovingly to Branwen's face. "I'm sorry we had news of Kernyvak raiders yesterday of all days."

"It's nothing."

"Come now, Branny. It's always hard for me to hear such news as well. That is why the matter of Essy's marriage is of such importance."

"I know."

She scrutinized her niece. "Tell me, dear heart, to what do I owe the pleasure of your company so early in the morning?"

Branwen's shoulders rose as she took a breath, and said, "I wanted to ask you about the Old Ways."

The queen's eyes narrowed. All of her subjects knew Queen Eseult was a master of the Old Ways, but Branwen had never shown interest in them. She had rejected any part they might play in healing her aunt's patients.

"What is it you wish to know?" she asked.

Branwen sucked in air through the tiny gap between her two front teeth. After a moment, she dared, "Do you believe in the Otherworld? That you could cross over at Whitethorn Mound?"

"Do you?" she countered.

"I've never believed in things I can't see."

"Yet you believe in love."

She nodded and fidgeted uncomfortably with her plaits as the queen held her gaze. "The Otherworld is like love, Branny. You can't see it, but you can feel it. It's all around us, all of the time."

"But . . . but . . . ," she began with trepidation. Branwen had never believed it was a real place any more than you could reach out and grab fate with your hands. Maybe she had been wrong. "Can it truly send us messages?"

Her aunt rested her elbows on her knees, leaning toward Branwen.

"What have you seen?"

"I—I'm not sure."

"*Branny*," the queen said in a low voice.

"A fox," Branwen confessed, praying she wouldn't question her sanity. Was she really troubling the queen over a wild animal?

The queen's expression didn't change. "And what did the fox tell you?" she asked.

What had the fox told Branwen? To save Tantris. But she couldn't admit that to the Queen of Iveriu, even though she'd hate herself for lying. Lying to the queen was treason, no less. She worked her jaw.

Finally, Branwen told her aunt, "To make a friend of an enemy." That's what Lord Caedmon would say, wasn't it?

Queen Eseult's lips formed a crescent. "Sound advice."

"You really think the fox was sent from the Otherworld?" she said. "From the Old Ones?" Part of her wanted it to be true, and the other part of her was afraid of what that might mean. Everything she had believed until yesterday suddenly seemed so uncertain, everything she had believed until she met Tantris.

"It may very well be," the queen acknowledged, that august clarity in her voice. "What I am certain of is that you're a natural-born healer, just like Alana was. The Goddess Bríga has favored you both with her healing fire." Bríga was the goddess of the hearth and the sunrise, healing and keening—the poetry of loss.

Branwen's fingers tensed around the folds of her skirt, a deep sadness welling in her breast. She used to think healing fire was a metaphor. If the fox was real, however, maybe it was something more. Something she shared with her mother.

"A natural healer is not just a healer of men, Branny," said the queen. "But a healer of kingdoms." Her aunt stroked Branwen's chin. "The Old Ways will reveal themselves as they're required. As sure as I breathe, I know you will be instrumental in protecting Iveriu one day."

"I will protect it with my whole heart."

"I know you will, my niece. Iveriu is your first love—as it is mine. That is why the Otherworld has chosen to speak to you. Heed its messages."

"Thank you, Lady Queen," she said, feeling a knot grow in her stomach.

"Thank *you*, Lady Branwen. Now go see to Essy."

Branwen curtsied and exited the queen's chambers, lost in thoughts of the fox and of Tantris. The Otherworld had led her to the Kernyvak poet. It wanted her to save him, shelter him.

She would have to trust that the Old Ones wanted to protect her kingdom as much as she did. Even if Branwen remained skeptical as to their motives, Queen Eseult believed in them, and Branwen believed in her queen above all else. She would do whatever was necessary to preserve the Land.

She would defend Iveriu until her dying breath.

The breeze was fresh, and the sunlight on the sand made it gleam as brightly as snow. Before making her escape from the castle, Branwen had unknotted Essy's sweetheart plaits and steeped her willow bark tea—to counter the effects of too much wine—in record time while half listening to her cousin's praise of Diarmuid's dancing abilities.

What if Tantris had developed a fever in the night?

Moving quickly, Branwen checked over her shoulder to ensure she wasn't being followed. Strictly speaking, since she was a noblewoman, Branwen shouldn't leave the castle unescorted, but the Royal Guard had long ago stopped tracking her movements. The guardsmen were accustomed to her foraging in the wood along the coast for herbs and berries to fill her small leather satchel. Some even came to Branwen for simple remedies.

She supposed she could see why it seemed to Essy as if she had all the freedom in the world, but Branwen didn't feel free in this moment. Not at all. Forces beyond her control coerced her, held her hostage.

Glancing nervously along the beach, Branwen slipped through a network of lianas into the mouth of the cave. The tide had retreated and late morning light showered the rock, casting it with an emerald glow. The walls were made from the same veiny green marble that had been quarried to build Castle Rigani. Carrying a chip of Rigani stone in your pocket was meant to be good luck and keep away Otherworld-dwellers with more nefarious intentions.

"Emer," said a melodious, if tired, voice. "You are even more dazzling silhouetted by sunlight."

Branwen wrinkled her nose to mask her ratcheting pulse. "Did you sleep well, Tantris?"

Groaning, he propped himself onto his elbow. "Off and on," he answered.

She could see the pain and stiffness pervading his muscles. She tried to assess him clinically, not allowing her gaze to linger on the broad shoulders beneath his tunic or the way the light played on his sweat-laced curls.

Branwen approached him with caution; she was afraid of herself when she was around him. She was committing treason—and yet that seemed to be what the Old Ones dictated.

Tantris puckered his forehead. "Are you well?"

"Quite well," she snapped.

His gaze swept over her. "The blue suits you."

The bodice of her gown was a deep cerulean blue stitched with fine silver thread. Normally, Branwen would have considered it too extravagant for everyday use, but she'd worn it for him, and she'd woven a matching ribbon through her fishtail braids.

Flustered by the compliment, she looked away as she seated herself beside him, next to the ashes of the fire from the night before. "Here," Branwen said, handing Tantris a bacon biscuit she'd pilfered from the kitchens while Treva's back was turned.

He held it up to his mouth and as the scent of the fried meat filled his nostrils, he looked like he was going to be sick. Fear slithered across Branwen's chest. Lack of appetite was an early sign of fever.

"What about these?" she said, more anxious, and dropped a few hazelnuts from her pocket into the center of his palm.

"Hazelnuts?" Tantris cocked his head. "Did you pick these especially for your poet-patient?" he said, although his smile was less self-assured this morning.

Tamping down on her nerves, she said, "What?"

"In Kernyv, we believe hazelnuts are full of poetic inspiration."

"Oh. So do we." She twiddled one between her fingers. "I hadn't even thought of that."

Tantris caught her eye, pushing into a sitting position. "Perhaps we're not so different, the Kernyveu and the Iverni." He tossed a hazelnut into his mouth and began to chew.

"I wouldn't go that far," Branwen said.

Tantris paled as he finished chewing. "I'm not really that hungry."

She was afraid of that. Despite all logic, her concern for him exceeded what Branwen had ever felt for a patient. Knitting her brow, she surveyed him again. Tantris lowered his gaze to his chest when she gasped. Now that he was upright, a fresh crimson stain revealed itself on his new tunic.

"It would seem I have a bleeding heart." He shrugged then scowled from the effort.

"That's not funny."

"It's a little funny."

"It's *not*," she said harshly. Would the Otherworld punish Branwen—or her kingdom—if she failed to save the life of a man under its protection? She leaned in closer, perilously close. She pressed two fingers against his tunic. Tantris moaned. More blood leaked from the wound.

"The salve isn't working." She kept her voice impassive; she had learned from Queen Eseult not to upset a man in pain. "Lie back," Branwen instructed.

"I don't think any man could deny you that request." The way his eyes danced completely unsettled her. Tantris scanned her up and down. "You seem nervous," he said as he lay back against stone the color of summer leaves.

"I'm not nervous," Branwen lied.

"Concerned, then?"

"Yes, concerned." She smiled resolutely and, with great care, stripped Tantris of his tunic. Streamlets of blood zigzagged across his chest.

Branwen was overwhelmed with misgivings. She should have sewn up the wound last night, but she'd been worried about being missed at the castle. Her patient might die because of her haste.

"It'll be all right, Emer. I've survived worse."

"You've seen many battles as a *poet*?" She scoffed, trying to shutter her fear.

A deep ravine formed between his eyes. "I can hold my own. I'm descended from the great Kartagon warriors," said Tantris.

The corner of his mouth lifted at the wonder on Branwen's face. The siege of Kartago by the Aquilan Empire was legendary. The port city controlled the Strait of Alissar, and the Kartagons held out for more than a year before the city fell.

"Your family is from the southern continent, then—originally?" she asked, both because she was curious and because she wanted to keep him distracted while she determined how to help him.

"My father's ancestors came to Kernyv with the Aquilan legions."

Despite their defeat, the Kartagon warriors were celebrated for their bravery and they were recruited as soldiers by the Aquilan army. In Branwen's history lessons, Master Bécc said the Aquilan Empire was so successful because its military rewarded the worthy rather than the highborn.

As Tantris spoke, blacker blood began to flow from his heart. Branwen gulped.

"My mother's people are from the Kernyvak peninsula, though," he went on, hissing a breath. "I am a Kernyvman, through and through." He sounded almost defensive. Branwen wanted to know why but she didn't want to ask, and she disliked being reminded he was her enemy.

Tantris blinked rapidly. She touched a finger to the dark blood, raised it to her nose, and sniffed. Brackish. She couldn't delay any longer.

Pulling a vial from her healing kit, Branwen told him, "Drink this."

"What is it?" he asked.

"A tincture." Tantris's fingers grazed hers as he took the vial; tingles spread outward from the spot. "Clíodhna's dust and a few other things," Branwen said as she struck a small stone against the floor to rekindle the fire.

Clíodhna's dust was a pink flower found at the base of trees in the forest surrounding the castle. Named for the Otherworld queen whose song could heal the sick, the right quantity relieved a man quickly of his senses.

Tantris rolled the vial back and forth, still corked.

"Don't you trust me, Tantris?" Branwen asked. It came out as a reproach.

He rocked closer in response and skimmed his knuckles against her cheek in a fleeting, intimate gesture. The touch felt so right, so natural.

"With my life."

Looking Branwen in the eye, Tantris downed the vinegary concoction in one swallow. His pupils dilated almost immediately. "Who taught you the Old Ways?" he asked, somewhat dreamily.

She froze. She couldn't tell Tantris that the queen had taught her, or that Branwen wasn't really Emer, castle servant.

"The women in my family have always been healers." That was the truth, at least. "Now close your eyes and stop talking."

"Those are sweet words for any man to hear." A troublesome grin spread over his face even as the Clíodhna's dust took hold.

Ignoring his remark, Branwen withdrew an embroidery needle from her satchel and dipped the tip into the embers.

"You don't want to see this," she told him.

Branwen pulled a few threads from her skirt, braided them carefully together, then threaded the eye of the needle. She'd waited until its tip was white-hot before removing it from the embers. Queen Eseult had taught her there was less chance of infection if she heated the needle first.

She lifted one of Tantris's eyelids and saw that he was swimming in the dreamtime. He would soon be out cold. But she couldn't wait. She took a steadying breath.

The needle pierced his chest and the flesh made a whimpering noise. Tantris cried out before sucking down his anguish. Branwen felt her own heart stop and start several times. She had always preferred her Aquilan language lessons to embroidery, but for once she was glad that she'd applied herself to the pursuits of noblewomen.

Hurriedly, she spun an intricate web of stitches over Tantris's heart. With each stroke, she prayed to the Otherworld that her handiwork would be enough to save the poet's life. The stitch was called a love-knot, which seemed a strange thing to give her enemy.

As her fingers sewed together his flesh, however, Branwen no longer saw Tantris as a Kernyvman—just as a man. A man who needed her help. And his heart was literally in her hands.

He came in and out of consciousness. Branwen hoped the Clíodhna's dust would be strong enough for him to float through the worst of the pain in a sea of dreams. Before he dropped off entirely, Tantris opened his eyes. They were raven-dark and intensely alive.

"Emer, I do believe you've tied my heart up in knots."

Branwen couldn't resist a small, hopeful smile. He gave her a lopsided grin and she watched as the tide pulled him under.

SHADOW-STUNG

BRANWEN STAYED WITH TANTRIS UNTIL the worst had passed. Then she returned to Castle Rigani, shoulders slumped and weary. Early evening light warmed her cheeks as she headed directly to the castle kitchens, desperate for a reinvigorating cup of tea.

"Lady Branwen?" Treva looked up from stuffing a pig to roast. "The queen came by here looking for you. She's gone to the infirmary."

"When?"

"Maybe half an hour ago?"

Guilt erased Branwen's exhaustion as she dashed for the windy stairwell that led down to the castle cellars, where the infirmary was located. Treva didn't get a chance to ask her what she'd wanted before she was gone. Candlelight glinted on the marble of the subterranean corridor just like in the cave. She hoped Tantris's dreams were serene.

A woman's cry echoed off the walls as Branwen approached the queen's clinic. Fury simmered in her veins at the sound, pushing the poet from her mind.

"Branwen." Queen Eseult exhaled her name with relief as she leapt through the doorway. "Thank you for coming." Her aunt stroked the fever-damp brow of the woman whose scream she'd heard, and the gratitude on the queen's face clawed at Branwen's heart.

The woman who writhed on a narrow cot was no older than twenty.

"I'm sorry I was delayed, my queen. I came as soon as I heard."

Standing beside her mother, Essy winged her eyebrows as if to say, *Where were you?* Branwen ignored her. She couldn't explain.

"You've arrived at the perfect time," said Queen Eseult. "The sedative I've administered should be taking effect."

"What do you need?" Branwen asked.

"Another pair of hands."

"More expert hands, she means," muttered the princess as she dabbed at the patient's brow with ice chips.

"They're yours," Branwen told the queen, who showed her a quarter smile in return. Branwen felt it like a dagger to the breast. She should have been here. She should have been here serving her queen and her countrywoman. Not one of the Kernyveu.

The patient let out another howl and Branwen rushed to her bedside.

"This is Saoirse," said the queen. The red-haired woman moaned, delirious. Perhaps she recognized her name through the fog of pain. Perhaps not.

Queen Eseult murmured soothing words into her ear and pointed to where the woman's skirt had been ripped to expose her thigh. Branwen examined the wound. A gash made by a sword, indubitably. The thigh was swollen, seeping with black blood and sun-colored pus. It carried the distinctive smell of infection. This was exactly what she'd been trying to prevent with her ministrations of Tantris.

Branwen glanced in her cousin's direction. Essy's jaw was gritted tighter than a statue's. She was doing her best to make herself useful, Branwen could tell, but the princess hated the sight of blood. Her face grew whiter by the second.

When Essy was seven years old and Branwen nine, Essy had discovered a rabbit caught in a trap. She insisted on freeing the animal, not knowing that releasing the metal snare would cause the creature to bleed out. By the time the girls brought the rabbit to Queen Eseult in the infirmary, the creature was dead and Essy's dress was stained scarlet. To this day she refused to eat Treva's rabbit stew, and she avoided the infirmary at all costs.

The queen must have really been desperate for help.

Saoirse wailed again. Branwen returned her attention to the serrated flesh.

"Shadow-stung," she said quietly. The flesh around the cut was discolored, graying—dying. She'd seen a wound like this one on a guardsman once.

"Yes." The queen confirmed Branwen's diagnosis.

"What happened?"

"Kernyvmen." The word was a growl. Branwen jumped at Keane's voice. She arrowed her gaze at where he stood guard in the corner of the room. She hadn't noticed him. His muscles were tensed, poised to launch an attack. Their eyes met and his stance relaxed a fraction.

"The villagers from Doogort brought Saoirse in earlier this

63

afternoon," explained the queen. "They were attacked last week. I fear they waited too long."

How long had Tantris drifted on the raft before Branwen found him?

"Will she lose the leg?" she asked her aunt. The guardsman who'd been similarly afflicted had his arm amputated to save his life.

The queen touched a hand to Branwen's shoulder. "We will try to burn the infection out," she said. "It will be easier with two of us. After that, it is up to the Old Ones."

Branwen swallowed. She didn't like leaving things in the hands of the Old Ones.

Wriggling her nose, Essy said, "I'm glad you got here, Branny. I think I might be ill." Her tone was airy, but Branwen detected a trace of regret in her cousin's eyes.

"We all have our talents, dear heart," said the queen. She stroked the back of Essy's head and the princess cringed. Frowning, she said, "Fetch a bucket of hot coals from Treva, won't you?"

Essy stepped back from the patient's bed. "Of course, Lady Queen. I'm very talented at fetching and carrying."

The queen made a small *tsk*ing noise, which was as close to exasperation as she ever came. "Thank you," Branwen told her cousin, meeting her eye. Essy gave her a wink. "Anything for you, Branny," she said, and threw a haughty look at her mother before exiting the infirmary.

Saoirse jerked as the door banged closed; Queen Eseult heaved a sigh. "Keane," she said, "turn Saoirse on her side, then hold her firm. Branny, you will help me drain the fluid before we burn the flesh." The patient's engorged leg needed to be tilted at an angle so the pus would flow into the pail on the floor.

Keane and Branwen ducked their heads in assent, his gaze seeking hers for another brief moment. Branwen's nerves skittered, but she would not fail her queen. She would not fail her patient.

Saoirse groaned as Keane repositioned her on the cot, and Branwen spied his shoulders go taut. His countrywoman's pain affected him more deeply than Branwen would have suspected. When Queen Eseult handed her a thin metal pipe used for draining wounds, Branwen balked.

"I won't always be here," her aunt said, voice firm. "You're my apprentice; you know what to do."

Willing her fingers not to tremble, Branwen accepted the hammered tin instrument. She held the pipe steady as the queen kneaded the area around the wound in a circular pattern. Saoirse let out a doleful cry.

Why did the Old Ones send Branwen to Tantris today instead of here—where her family needed her?

Concentrate, she upbraided herself.

Gradually, bit by bit, Branwen and the queen drained the pus from the woman's thigh. Perspiration pebbled Keane's forehead as he held Saoirse down, but he never flinched. He didn't utter a sound. Branwen's own arms began to quake and she was only dimly aware when Essy reappeared, having retrieved a bucket of coals.

The princess dropped the bucket with a *thud*, its weight straining her shoulders. "Can I help?" she asked Branwen.

"Hold Saoirse's ankles," answered the queen.

Essy nodded and squeezed the patient's ankles against the flimsy straw pallet without further comment.

"You've drained the wound as best we can hope for," Queen Eseult said to Branwen, and her chest warmed. The queen's faith meant everything. "Now, take this." She plucked the pipe from Branwen's grasp and exchanged it for a fire-poker, like those a blacksmith wielded, only shorter and more delicate. "Dip the end in the coals, then insert it into the wound."

Branwen's stomach roiled. Not from squeamishness but from fear that she wasn't talented enough to save this woman's leg.

The queen indicated the soft flesh of Saoirse's upper thigh, right beside the wound. "Be careful not to touch the poker here. Beneath is the blood supply for the whole body. If it's severed, we won't be able to stop the blood loss."

Branwen looked up from the spot to meet her aunt's gaze, then her cousin's. Both she and Essy were thinking of the rabbit. Branwen released a shallow breath.

"You can do this, Branny," Essy assured her. "You have magic hands, remember?" Branwen stifled a nervous laugh as courage surged through her. The princess wasn't as different from her mother as she would like to believe.

Cautiously, methodically, Branwen lowered the iron instrument into the coals. When she'd dipped the needle she used on Tantris into the fire, only one end had grown hot; the coals heated the entire length of the poker. Grinding her teeth, she touched the glowing iron to the open wound.

Saoirse's scream pierced Branwen to her very core. Its echo would stay with her forever. But she didn't stop. She couldn't stop. She plunged it deeper. She couldn't stop until the blood ceased to flow.

Finally, she felt a hand on her elbow and the queen's placid voice in her ear.

"You did well. I believe we purged the infection." A kiss on the cheek. "I'll bandage the wound, Branny. You get some rest."

Branwen could only nod, relief robbing the last of her strength. At the same moment, Essy threaded her arm around Branwen's waist, pulling her closer, away from her mother. The queen sighed.

Just before the cousins exited the clinic, Keane stepped toward Branwen. Admiration filled his deep-blue gaze. "Lady Branwen—" She canted her head, and he swallowed audibly. "Rest— Rest well," he told her. It seemed like he was on the verge of saying more, but Essy pulled Branwen across the threshold.

She walked toward the south tower in a daze, the princess holding her tight, quiet for once.

Essy helped Branwen out of her dress; otherwise, Branwen would have crawled under the down-filled covers precisely as she was: disheveled and covered with other people's blood. The princess promptly clambered in after her. She blew out the candle on the night table, darkness eddying above them and below them.

"Shall I sing you a song?" suggested Essy. "*Once on the island of Iveriu, there was a girl called Branwen of the Briars,*" she began in her dulcet soprano.

Branwen laughed into her pillow, emboldening her cousin.

"*She did not care for balls or swoon-worthy lords, but of injured men and salves she never did tire!*"

"Oh, Essy!" She batted an exhausted hand at the princess's nose but missed her mark. Her cousin's tongue was too clever by half. A trait she shared with Tantris. Branwen shivered.

Could the Princess of Iveriu ever understand why she had felt obliged to protect the Kernyvman?

As Essy carried on with her lullaby, Branwen drifted along the boundary of sleep. She had nearly crossed over when her cousin said, "I have no talent for healing, Branny. I have no talent. I'm useless."

"You're not useless," Branwen mumbled, fatigued beyond reason.

"My only use is producing heirs. And I'm not even allowed to choose with whom I produce them!"

Branwen rolled toward her baby cousin, pulling her onto her breast, and stroked her hair. "You have a talent for loving people, Essy. For making people feel loved." Branwen kissed the princess between the eyes. "And that is the greatest talent a queen can have."

Essy began to protest and Branwen shushed her. "Not you without me."

"Not me without you."

THE LORD OF WILD THINGS

THE SUN HUNG LOW IN the sky when Branwen meandered her way toward the cave. It wasn't merely the fear of being followed that had encouraged her to take a circuitous route back to Tantris. She nearly hadn't come at all.

Despite her honor demanding it. Despite her father's belief in making friends of enemies. And, yes, in spite of the Old Ones, Branwen almost didn't come.

She'd spent the hours since she'd woken at Saoirse's bedside, mopping the woman's brow and changing the poultice on her thigh.

Someone needed to answer for what had happened to Saoirse. The Kernyveu had to answer. Tantris was on Ivernic soil, so why shouldn't it be him? Saoirse deserved justice from her attackers. Wasn't Branwen denying it to her by hiding the Kernyvman right under the noses of the Royal Guard?

Yes. Yes, she was. And yet she'd declined Keane's offer of company for her walk, claiming she needed to be alone. The look of understanding on his face had caused shame to creep down her spine—and rightly so.

The wind whipped Branwen's hair across her face, and she licked the salty tang of the sea from her lips. If only she hadn't come down to the beach that day, her loyalties wouldn't be divided. *If only.* The two most pointless words she knew.

Branwen folded her arms, spoiling for a fight, when she spied a man backlit against the waves.

Tantris!

What was he doing outside the cave? She was risking everything for him, and he exposed himself so heedlessly? She huffed a few of the swears she'd picked up from the guardsmen under her breath and broke into a sprint. Anger fizzing inside her, Branwen left furious footprints in the sand, kicking the grains up around her knees. The closer she got to the water, the denser the sand was packed, and the fleeter her stride.

When she was within striking distance of Tantris, she could barely contain the urge to tackle him to the ground and pummel him for his sheer stupidity. She raised her hand to grab his tunic or slap him or something—

"Emer!" he hollered, spinning on his heel. "Emer, look out!"

She stopped short, mouth agape. The leather satchel dangling from her shoulder whacked her hip.

Wriggling between Tantris's arms was the fox.

What? But . . . Branwen had thought the creature was an apparition. She'd been so certain. It growled. Apparently solid, the fox fidgeted its hind leg, nails scratching Tantris's forearm. Branwen pressed a hand to her chest, air whooshing out of her.

"He was caught in there," Tantris explained, and pointed a couple paces in front of them.

It was a pit. A trap. It had been covered with sand and dune grass. Not too deep but lined with sharpened sticks like ferocious jowls.

"You rescued it?" Branwen couldn't keep the incredulity from her tone.

He raised his eyebrows. "I heard the fellow crying. What else would I do?"

Just like Essy and the rabbit. "I didn't think a Kernyvman would care for a wounded animal," she snapped even as her anger extinguished.

"And you're the expert on Kernyvmen?"

The gaze Tantris turned on her was heated. Also hurt. Branwen's mouth went dry. She wouldn't have thought she had the power to hurt him.

Nevertheless, she declared, "I know everything I need to know." She wouldn't give Tantris the satisfaction of learning he was the first Kernyvman with whom she'd had a proper conversation.

"If that's what you believe." The heat in his eyes faded to sadness. The fox yipped and Tantris chided, "Try not to bite." Glancing at Branwen, he said, "Same goes for you."

Branwen snorted. "Are you sure you're not a court jester rather than a minstrel?"

He released a half-hearted laugh in response.

It sounded wrong. She wanted to hear him laugh, free and easy. Only the Old Ones knew why. Her gaze dropped from his face to his heart. Once again, the cloth above it was spotted a dark ruby. "You've torn a stitch," she said.

Tantris shrugged. Lowering himself into a squat, he murmured to the fox in low, calming tones like you might to a disconsolate child. He spoke in Kernyvak. The creature's snow-white ears twitched. Branwen had only gleaned a few simple phrases over the years, but she didn't need to know the words to understand their meaning. For the first time, she wished she'd studied the language of her enemies.

Tantris loosened his grip and the fox leapt into the sand, scrambling at the grains with its paws. Branwen assessed the creature as if it were one of her patients—it seemed no worse for wear. What did the beast want? She couldn't believe this was a coincidence.

"You've made a friend," she said to Tantris.

Capturing her gaze, he said, "I hope so."

Branwen rubbed her lips together. If the Kernyvman were an Iverman, she might want that, too. "We should get back to the cave," she said. "It's not safe here. For you."

Tantris nodded, pushing to his feet. At his full height, he stood more than a head taller than Branwen. "The fox's red coat is quite unusual," he remarked as the creature scurried toward the surf.

"Quite," she said. "Some of the Iverni believe the Old Ones send animals as messengers from the Otherworld."

"Do you?"

Excellent question. "I didn't used to . . ." She let her voice drift off. If Branwen had needed any further proof that the Old Ones had granted Tantris their protection, this was it. After a beat, he took a deep breath and Branwen's eyes darted back in his direction.

Staring down at her, "Emer," he began. "I know what you're risking by helping me. I don't take it—any of it—for granted." His eyes shimmered, and Branwen felt the same pull she had the day they met. Her lips ached, not unpleasantly.

"I—" She broke the stare, inclining her chin at the blossom of blood on his chest. "We should hurry." Readjusting her satchel, Branwen started for the cave.

"As my healer commands," Tantris acceded and followed half a step behind. She shouldn't want to be anything more than his healer. She really, really shouldn't.

After walking a few moments in silence, Tantris said, "We tell similar stories in Kernyv." He glanced in the direction the fox had vanished. "About the Old Ones."

Branwen cast him an inquisitive look over her shoulder. "What about the New Religion?" She'd heard that the Kernyveu were giving up the Old Ways in favor of a god from the Aquilan Empire. There were those who believed this new god was the reason Kernyvak raiders assaulted Ivernic shores.

Tantris caught up with her in one stride. "The Horned One, you mean?" Branwen tilted her head, urging him to continue. "He was called Carnonos. Before he became a god."

"How does one *become* a god?"

"His followers say that Carnonos and his father were hunting a great stag when they were set upon by thieves in the forest. As they fought off the bandits, the stag charged. Carnonos jumped in front of his father and was gored to death on the stag's antlers."

Branwen shivered. *What a grisly story.* Tantris pulled back the vines covering the cave's entrance to let her enter.

"For his sacrifice and selflessness," he carried on, "the other gods resurrected Carnonos and entrusted him with judging the souls of the dead. He decides who is worthy of resurrection."

Branwen made a noncommittal noise. Surveying the cave, nothing seemed disturbed. They were safe. She exhaled.

"This is what you believe?" she said, shoulders relaxing, as she started a small fire. She handed Tantris dried sausage from her satchel, which he dutifully began to eat, seating himself on a boulder. The fire crackled between them.

"The Horned One is growing more popular all across the island of Albion," said Tantris as he chewed, "but I don't see a reason to choose."

Branwen peeked up from the sparking twigs. "Why is he named the Horned One?"

Taking another bite, Tantris replied, "The animals of the forest were also moved by Carnonos's sacrifice. When he was reborn, they granted him a crown of antlers."

"A man with antlers?" she said, unconvinced, and Tantris nodded. "*Hmph.*" That seemed a strange god indeed. Satisfied that her patient had managed to eat, Branwen looked over her healing supplies, grateful she'd left them at the cave.

"Undress," she told him.

"With pleasure."

"Just the tunic," she clarified.

Smirking, Tantris whipped it quickly over his head but was unable to stifle a groan. Branwen scooted closer to examine the damage. Three popped stitches. "You must be more vigilant," she said crossly. "No more heroics."

"I don't regret it."

She traced her forefinger along the newly torn flesh and he hissed. Who was this mysterious Kernyvman who would risk his life to help an animal?

"Carnonos is also called the Lord of Wild Things," said Tantris.

"And are you a wild thing?" The question just slipped out of Branwen. She'd never sounded so brazen in her life.

A crafty grin. "Sometimes."

Coughing like she had a wasting sickness, Branwen pulled loose another couple threads from her hem. Wetting them, she threaded a needle.

"Do you have any more of that dust?" Tantris asked.

"I'm afraid not." She lowered the tip of the needle into the fire.

"Then tell me something about you, Emer. I'm sure it will be equally intoxicating." He winked. Branwen couldn't help laughing.

"What do you want to know?" she said. She should have been more disconcerted that his Kernyvak charm was wearing down her defenses.

"Anything. How about your family? I've told you about mine."

She stiffened. She couldn't tell Tantris the truth, and for some reason, she didn't want to lie. Well, she could tell him a version of the truth.

"I live with my cousin," she said, hesitant. The end of the needle began to glow. "She drives me mad, especially at the moment. We're opposites in many ways, too. Yet nobody knows me better." She thought about the lullaby Essy made up last night. "I drive her mad as well, I'm sure, but she—" Branwen lifted the needle from the embers. "She loves me as I am."

"I can understand why," Tantris said. Branwen's heart hiccupped.

"I'm sorry if I hurt you," she told him, shifting her attention to his wound. He inhaled a shallow breath.

"I'm sorry, too."

Before he could say anything else, Branwen punctured his flesh with her needle, fingers moving nimbly. Tantris gripped either side of the boulder with white knuckles. To distract him, she admitted,

"You're the first Kernyvman I've met—who wasn't a prisoner, that is." Another stitch. "I was wrong earlier. When I said I know everything I need to. There's obviously a lot I don't know about . . . you."

"Emer." He said her name with rough sweetness. "Ask me anything you want to know about the Kernyveu. Or me."

So she did. She asked as she stitched and he answered, and hours melted away. She always had more questions. Maybe that made her a traitor. Maybe . . . she couldn't help it.

Branwen wanted to know, needed to know—everything.

THE ONLY JEALOUSY OF EMER

O VER THE NEXT FEW WEEKS, she returned to the cave every afternoon as the light began to thin. With spring blossoming, Essy was so preoccupied with Lord Diarmuid—whose family was *still* at Castle Rigani—that, thankfully, she barely noticed Branwen's prolonged absences. Distance grew between the cousins with every excuse Branwen made, and it pained her, but the Old Ones had put Tantris's life in her hands.

Although, if she were being entirely honest, she also enjoyed hearing the Kernyvman recount the folktales of his people, tell her of their festivals. Gradually, the Kernyveu were becoming less of a faceless monster. More real.

As Branwen ducked to enter the cave this particular dusk, some of the flowering thorns caught in her hair, jerking her head backward. She felt foolish, graceless. Tantris hurried to her side.

"Watch your head." His grin was boyish. Now that the cuts had faded and the swelling had abated, his angular cheekbones were all the more eye-catching.

Tantris began pulling the thorns from Branwen's hair.

"I think I may well have just caught a wolf by the tail," he said. She felt his eyes rove her face and she averted her gaze. So many years of disappearing into the background at court served Branwen well when she needed to disguise her emotions. The touch of his fingers on her scalp, however, threading between her plaits, was undeniably thrilling. When she sensed Tantris lingering longer than was strictly necessary, she stepped away.

After she gained a little breathing room, she trailed her gaze over his tunic. For once, it wasn't soiled with fresh blood.

"You look well," she said. Better than well. Tantris's golden-brown complexion was no longer wan in the least. He seemed healthy, strong—strong enough to make the journey home, perhaps. An unwanted hollowness spread through Branwen at the thought.

Taking a step toward her, Tantris declared, "Only because my healer has worked her magic" with an open smile.

Branwen did wonder if it *had* been magic. Bríga's healing fire. "I don't think I can take all the credit," she told him, thinking of the fox. Saoirse still languished in the twilight of fever. If even Queen Eseult's expertise hadn't been enough for the woman to make a full recovery, Branwen doubted she could have healed Tantris on her own.

His expression grew inscrutable. She followed his eyeline to the harp peeking out from beneath her burgundy capelet and, when their gazes collided, Tantris grimaced.

"This is a test," he said.

It *was* a test, but Branwen hadn't intended for it to seem that way. A recalcitrant part of her needed to know that Tantris was who he said he was, needed to understand why the Old Ones had shown him their favor. Even if she couldn't reveal herself to him.

"I thought you trusted me, Emer."

The disappointment in his voice made Branwen feel as if the thorns caught in her hair were piercing her heart instead. She hated how much his rebuke affected her. And she hated that she had offended him.

Her swirling emotions coalesced into something more familiar—indignation—and she prickled. "I thought you were a bard?" Taking in his stricken expression, she tried to play it off. "I'd like to hear a song from your homeland, Tantris."

"I'm a fine bard, indeed." Fire flickered in his voice. He closed the space between them with unsettling speed. Grabbing the harp from her hands, he rasped in Branwen's ear, "*Odai eti ama.*"

Nervous energy flooded her entire body. Then Tantris retreated a few paces, seating himself on a large rock. Plucking the harp, he tested the strings, tuning them in turn. "Do you have any particular requests?" The edge to his voice had dulled somewhat.

"It's a *krotto*—you know how to play it?"

"An Ivernic harp is not so very different from a Kernyvak one. Nor is an Iverman so very different from a Kernyvman."

She wouldn't have believed that before she met Tantris. Now, on the other hand . . . Branwen didn't know what expression she displayed, but his softened. Suddenly it was *he* who was apologetic. "Please sit, Emer. You're making me anxious," he said jokily. "Like you're about to run off and leave me."

A blush bit into her cheeks but she did as she was told. She sat on another medium-sized Rigani stone, wrestling her hands in her lap.

"Do you play?" Tantris asked.

"Only a little. And not well. It was my mother's harp, she—" Branwen broke off her own words. Why had she divulged that? These past few weeks, she'd managed to keep references to her family extremely vague.

His eyes grew infinitely tender. Tantris stroked the curve of the golden wood like she imagined he might caress a lover. Just for a moment, Branwen envied the harp with her entire being.

"Laiginztir," he murmured.

"*What?*" Terror shot through her.

"A golden harp with silver strings is the symbol of Laiginztir." Tantris roamed her face with his eyes. "That's where you're from, isn't it, Emer? Before you came to work at Castle Rigani?"

The poet was frustratingly perceptive. Branwen ground the toe of her lambskin boot into the rocky floor of the cave. "How would you know that?" she demanded, a petulance in her voice that reminded her of the princess.

"I've traveled to all the provinces of your kingdom with a song in my heart: Conaktir, Mumhanztir, Uladztir, Rigani, *and* Laiginztir."

"Singing for your supper?"

"After a fashion," said Tantris, strumming his fingers across the strings in a running scale; the notes tinkled, reverberating in the confined space of the cave.

The music stirred something deep inside Branwen. A snatch of a long-forgotten memory. She used to sit at her mother's knee, listening to her play as her honeyed contralto told of battles fought and love lost. How had such a beautiful image faded from Branwen's mind?

She hid her face in her hands, unable to keep the tears at bay. She heard Tantris set down the harp, and then his warm body pressed against hers. She didn't dare look up.

"Oh, Emer," he said. "Please tell me what I've done to upset you."

Branwen turned her face from side to side, still masking her eyes with her hands.

"Never mind."

"No." Tantris circled her wrists and tugged them away from her face with a gentle but deliberate motion. "Is your mother still in Laiginztir?" There was something so guttural about how he asked his question that it was almost a growl. Branwen suspected he already knew the answer.

Tantris wiped away a tear from the corner of her eye as she told him, "She and my father are both in the Otherworld."

"How did it happen?" he asked, his voice almost a whisper.

Branwen's bottom lip quivered. "Kernyvak raiders." The five syllables were coated with rage—but not nearly as much venom as there used to be.

"I'm sorry, Emer. Now I know why you see me as your enemy." Tantris heaved a deep, exhausted breath. It was like the gasp of resignation at the end of a long argument. "And yet you risked yourself to save your enemy—repeatedly," he said, marveling.

"I don't—" she started, surprising herself. "I don't see you as my enemy anymore."

Branwen heard with increasing distress the rumors flying around the castle that King Óengus's war council was considering an invasion of Kernyv. A full-scale attack had always been deemed impossible because Kernyv possessed superior ships and superior numbers. Her uncle Morholt, however, agreed with the lesser lords that the Iverni should bring the fight to the raiders' homeland. They might be right: Branwen didn't know the strategies of war—but she could think only of the families that would be butchered.

She lifted her gaze back to Tantris, half afraid he could read her thoughts. She remained a loyal Iverwoman; she wouldn't dream of betraying her kingdom by warning Kernyv. Yet she didn't want to send Tantris home to slaughter, either. He held her gaze but he didn't appear to detect her warring impulses. No, his face was brightening, slowly, like the sun rising above the Ivernic Sea.

"Emer, if that's true, it's the best news I've had in a long, long time." He took her hand in his and dashed a too-brief kiss along her knuckles.

Exhaling a shaky breath, Branwen changed the subject. "You must miss your parents, back in Kernyv," she said. Then she was struck by a troubling thought. "Or, your wife?"

The night they'd met, Tantris had asked if Branwen had a husband; he'd failed to volunteer the same information about himself. Of course! He looked a year or two older than her, and someone as captivating as Tantris must have a wife. Why should she have hoped otherwise? She was as bad as Essy.

"No wife," he said with a soft laugh, not releasing her hand. "No parents, either," he added. She tasted the loneliness of that statement. "It's just me and my uncle."

Branwen shifted toward Tantris, angling one shoulder against his. "How?"

Grief shaded his features. "Ivernic raiders." His voice went cold as death. "My mother died having me the night my father was killed. Lord Morholt—the brother of Queen Eseult—was gathering villagers as tribute. *Children.* My father defended them, like the proud Kartagon warrior he was."

Branwen wanted to run away. Shame coursed through her. Her family had been destroyed, but so had his. And countless others. Tantris had never even known his parents. Her own uncle had been the instrument of that destruction.

"You're not usually at a loss for words, Emer."

In that moment, Branwen very nearly told him her true name. But then Tantris would know that her aunt was the queen and that her family was responsible for watering the fields of Kernyv with blood.

And Tantris would hate her. She couldn't stomach the idea of him hating her.

"I don't know what to say," she muttered, not knowing where to look, either.

His shoulders hunched in a sigh. "Our countrymen have dealt as much death as each other. They have wrought equal destruction." Gingerly, Tantris tipped her head back. Flames licked the rich brown of his eyes and she was enthralled.

"I hope I have made a friend of an enemy," she said hoarsely.

"You've made more than that, but I could never be your enemy."

Her pulse galloped in her ears. She believed him. She believed him yet she should pull away—she knew she should.

"*Emer.*" Tantris spoke her name so close to her lips that it took form, and cut her.

She didn't want him to utter a false name before he kissed her. She didn't want him to kiss Emer. She wanted Tantris to kiss *her*—Branwen—and she recoiled.

"Forgive me," he said, jumping to his feet. "I forgot myself for a moment." He raked a hand through his dark curls, tearing at them a little, furious with himself.

"There's nothing to forgive," Branwen assured him, because there wasn't. If anything, *she* was the one lying to him. She was the one who needed forgiving. With a slightly awkward smile, she said, "How about that song?"

All of his features slackened with relief. "Truly," Tantris said, "you have the noblest of hearts."

Or the most selfish, she thought.

He clapped his hands together as an idea came to him. "I know just the ballad. One for your namesake," he said, retaking his seat. A bit of the rogue returned to his voice. "*'The Only Jealousy of Emer'*!"

Branwen laughed as he began to tease the strings. She had chosen Emer as her identity that day on the beach because she was the most forthright of Ivernic heroines. "How is it you speak my language so well, Tantris? And know our stories?"

"I told you—I love poetry. And Ivernic poetry is beautiful." He caught her eye. "Like Iverwomen." Branwen dropped her gaze to her boots. He began to sing.

The Hound of Uladztir bites and hisses,
Longing for Lady Emer's sweet kisses.

The wooing of Emer by the Hound of Uladztir, the fiercest of Ivernic warriors, was celebrated across the kingdom. The Hound was returning from training with the warrior woman Skathak when he came across Emer and was instantly thunderstruck.

Hair like a raven's wing,
Only for her does he sing.

Branwen dashed Tantris a questioning look. In the stories, Emer was always blond. He answered with an artful smile. He had changed the words just for her. Essy would appreciate his talent, thought Branwen, but, of course, they could never meet. Tantris could never truly be part of Branwen's world.

Singing of how the Hound won Emer away from the man to whom she'd been promised, the poet's dexterous fingers danced over the strings. Branwen couldn't help but notice how elegantly tapered they were. His strumming grew to a crescendo as he reached her favorite part of the story: The goddess Fand seduces the Hound, luring him into the Otherworld—and Emer fights back, threatening the goddess with a silver blade.

At the same moment in the song that Emer rescued the Hound from the Otherworld, a shiver of foreboding shot down Branwen's spine.

Something was wrong. She launched to her feet, putting her finger to her lips. Hastily, Tantris ceased his playing.

She couldn't explain it, but she knew they were in danger. The shiver had been a warning. She motioned for Tantris to get back. He shook his head. Fear scorched each one of Branwen's nerves. She jabbed her forefinger toward the darkest, farthest reaches of the cave.

Please, Branwen mouthed. After their eyes battled for several more moments, Tantris's chest deflated and he slipped into the darkness.

Steeling herself, Branwen strode toward the cave opening, stooping to avoid the shroud of thorns.

"Keane!" Her voice was pitched too high. *Try not to be suspicious, Branwen.* Drawing in a breath, she said, "What are you doing here?"

"I could ask you the same thing." He held a torch in one hand, illuminating his stern expression. Then he smiled, almost shyly. She forced herself to return it.

"I asked you first."

"Princess Eseult was trying to find you."

"Oh," Branwen began, tone breezy. "You do realize she most likely sent you after me just so she could get Diarmuid alone?"

Keane's smile grew chagrined. "I'm aware, my lady. Although I would have accepted the mission to spend time alone with you."

Her eyebrows lifted skyward. Keane had never said anything so bold to her before. Was it being outside the castle that allowed him to speak more freely?

He coughed into his fist, seeming to realize his error.

"But on this occasion, I bring welcome news. Saoirse is awake. And she's asking for you."

Fear for Tantris momentarily abated and a true smile split Branwen's face. "That is most welcome news, Keane!"

"Then I'm glad to be the one to deliver it."

"Thank you. Thank you so much." They shared a moment of elation before Branwen wondered, "How did you know where to find me?"

Keane shifted his weight. "The princess isn't the only one I keep an eye on."

Oh no. Of course she wasn't. How often had Tantris nearly been exposed because of Branwen. So arrogant. She thought she'd been so careful, so clever, but she'd brought the Royal Guard right to his door.

Suddenly, the fox darted through the dangling lianas and barked up at them. Keane laughed in surprise. The guardsman wasn't half as surprised as Branwen. Her heart stopped and started again. The fox had materialized from nowhere—unless the cave was an entrance to the Otherworld?

"Whom do we have here?" said Keane.

Smoothing the shock from her features, Branwen said, "This is one of my patients. I found it trapped in one of the sand pits. I've been caring for the fellow here at the cave." The lie rolled altogether too easily from her tongue.

Keane creased his forehead. "I set those traps to catch Kernyvmen, not foxes. Although they can be one and the same." He reached a hand toward the fox in a conciliatory gesture. The animal nipped his fingers.

Hissing, he drew back his hand. "I'm glad you weren't hurt, my lady."

"You don't have to worry about me."

"Maybe not." A pause. "But I do." A swell of surf broke against the shore. "Come," said Keane. "I'll escort you to the infirmary."

"I can make my own way."

"It's grown dark. I insist."

Branwen didn't want to leave without saying good-bye to Tantris, but she couldn't give Keane any further reason to wonder about the cave. As if speaking to the fox, she raised her voice and said, "Stay here. I'll be back tomorrow."

The creature yapped once, its eyes glowing like candles in the dark, and dashed inside. *Keep Tantris safe*, she pleaded.

"The beast seems quite devoted to you," Keane remarked as they walked back toward the castle gates.

"Maybe so."

"Just don't forget it's wild."

In the torchlight, Branwen nicked him with a glance. "Meaning?"

"Meaning it's when you think you've tamed a wild thing that it can cause you the most harm."

She didn't reply. She knew Keane was right.

Her heart was the wildest thing of all.

SEA OF FLAMES

SMOKE SWIRLED IN HER LUNGS. Panic licked her gut. At her feet, briars were stinging, scrambling, clutching at her—keeping her in place.

Branwen saw a brilliant light far out at sea, crystalline and hypnotizing. It winked at her, signaling her. But she couldn't move. She couldn't breathe.

And then, fire danced upon the waves.

No! She tried to call out, but she had no voice.

Something feather-soft brushed her ankles. Ebony eyes became amber. The fox.

The creature growled and barked, angling its head toward the water. She knew it wanted her to follow, but Branwen was trapped. Thorny roots held her prisoner.

The fox barked again. *What's a little blood?* it seemed to say.

Time warped around her. The stars touched the horizon and the sea boiled.

Branwen yanked her feet from the sharp-toothed vines, jagged claw marks crisscrossing her calves. She bit down on the pain and broke into a sprint. The fox nipped at her heels as she ran.

As she neared the shoreline, she made out the silhouette of a man against the starlight and the flames. He moved with casual grace.

Her heart overflowed.

In the next moment, the glint of something silvery and deadly caught her eye. A broadsword. Raised high, drops of blood oozed toward its hilt.

Branwen knew the hand wielding that sword. Morholt. Her uncle.

He whirled it above his head. Once. Twice. Three times. The sound sliced the night.

As the death-bringing edge bore down on its victim, Branwen regained her voice.

Tantris!

But it was too late.

✢ ✢ ✢

"Tantris." She tasted his name on her lips in the sunlight. He had to go. Last night was too close. The dream was another warning. He would be discovered and Branwen would be branded a traitor.

You'll miss him. It didn't matter. She had to send the Kernyvman away.

Branwen was sure she must have woken the entire castle with her cries but, as she stretched and stumbled toward the window, she saw Castle Rigani was already bustling. Below, she spied the Royal Guard assembled in the inner ward. They were dressed in the saffron-colored tunics of war. Uncle Morholt, Lord Diarmuid, and Lord Rónán were among them. Fresh fear like the first snowfall settled over her body.

Was she too late? Had Keane returned to the cave and discovered Tantris? Did her family know how she'd betrayed them?

Branwen finished dressing in double time, then carefully opened her door and peered down the corridor toward Essy's apartment. She hated to abandon her cousin with trouble obviously afoot, but she needed to warn Tantris. Not seeing anyone, Branwen sprinted past Essy's door and, as if she summoned him with her thoughts, slammed straight into Keane at the top of the stairs. He caught her in a tight grip, startled, his posture battle-ready.

"Are you quite well, my lady?" Keane asked. His eyes gleamed with worry.

"Yes." At least he wasn't here to arrest her. She swallowed, wriggling under his grasp. "Thank you." Realizing their chests were still pressed together, Keane immediately relinquished his hold on her, reddening, and took a step backward.

"Keane," said Branwen, breaking the tense silence. "Why is the Royal Guard trooping?"

Please don't let it be Tantris. Please.

Wrath burned in his eyes as he answered. "Kernyvak raiders. Twenty leagues. We're going after them." He was itching to get in on the action.

Branwen gasped, raising a hand to her mouth.

"Don't be afraid, Lady Branwen. You'll be safe within the castle walls. No man has ever breached Rigani."

"I'm not afraid."

"That doesn't surprise me, my lady, but—" Daring to take her hand, Keane pulled Branwen closer, speaking low and urgently. "Promise me you won't visit your patient in the cave today."

"Patient?" she choked out.

"The fox," said Keane, his brow creasing. "The critter can live without you for one day. I want *you*—I don't want anything to happen to you." The admission was nearly a command. He stroked the back of Branwen's hand with his thumb, insistent. Although she'd made no promises, guilt flared as she thought of Tantris, of his serenade.

"I promise." The lie strangled her voice. "Be safe, Keane."

The Iverman squeezed her hand, then took a step down the stairs. "One Iveriu," he said. His eyes flashed as he disappeared and Branwen recognized the battle lust. She waited until she saw him exit the south tower through the turret window before she made her own escape.

Branwen had to get to the cave. She had to find Tantris.

What's a little blood?

If she didn't, the sea would turn to flames.

✦ ✦ ✦

The waves crashed, coming in fast and furious. She remembered her dream: Tantris had been swimming. Queen Eseult told Branwen to listen carefully to the messages from the Otherworld. She rushed toward the beach, where she had first laid eyes on him.

Her skirts caught on a piece of driftwood as she sloshed through key-cold sea-foam. Thick nettles scratched her legs. There was blood in the water. In the foam she spied a shard of Rigani stone and pocketed it quickly.

She prayed it would bring luck. Not to her, but to Tantris.

The sun rising like a fireball above the horizon was nothing compared with the sea of orange bodies dotting the cliffs along the coastline. The Royal Guard was under attack, trying to beat their enemies back to the beach. In no time, the cave would be surrounded.

Branwen realized that the only way to save Tantris would be to return him to her enemies. Her own countrymen would kill the Kernyvman, and she knew he would choose death before dishonor. He was far too brave for a poet.

There was a glimmer among the whitecaps. A wink. A signal.

The Otherworld bled into the sea as well. From the depths below, a dolphin leapt up over the booming waves. Coastal villagers believed these creatures protected the waters of Iveriu, but it seemed to be protecting the Kernyvman, too.

"Tantris!" Branwen called out, running as hard as she could against the tide, dragging the *kladiwos* that she'd stolen from the armory behind her. "Tantris!"

A new shape in the swell went utterly still. "Emer?"

All of the air rushed from her lungs. He was still alive. Tantris was still alive—for now.

His eyes landed on Branwen as he emerged from the waves. The howling of swordplay carried on the breeze, and he dashed toward her with equal speed.

Branwen's hair was loose and wind-tossed, shadowy tendrils down her back. She'd pulled a simple shift over her nightgown, fawn-colored—the better not to be seen in the wood. Brandishing the *kladiwos*, she looked less like a noblewoman and more like a warrior.

"Emer," he called out, pointing at the blade. "Have you come here to kill me?" Tantris cracked his usual sly grin, but there was doubt in his eyes.

She held out the weapon solemnly. It trembled between her sweaty palms. "My countrymen have," she told him. "I thought I told you not to leave the cave."

"I'm sorry, Emer. The fox wouldn't let me rest until we'd taken a dip in the sea."

She darted a glance to where the creature scampered in the foamy surf. The Otherworld wanted him away from the cave. How close *was* the Royal Guard?

When at last Tantris stood only a handswidth before her in the sand, Branwen felt her cheeks turn a wild shade of scarlet.

Salt water dripped down the firm ridges of Tantris's naked chest. His britches were soaked, clinging to his muscular thighs. Branwen could well believe he belonged to the races of Old Ones said to dwell beneath the sea, disarming and dangerous. A yearning for the unknown coursed through Branwen and she fought the urge to touch him.

She had seen him shirtless most days as she tended his wound, of course, but she was no longer looking at Tantris the way a healer regarded a patient.

Branwen sucked in a breath as he stepped in closer. Her eyes snagged on the tiny love-knots stitched over his heart. The scar was her mark. Tantris would always carry part of her with him, back across the Ivernic Sea.

"What is it, Emer?" he said. "What's happened?"

She held out the sword to him once more. "Tantris, listen to me." Branwen forced her eyes to his face. "The Royal Guard is trooping." She gestured at the cliffs. "Kernyvak raiders are within reach of Castle Rigani. They've never dared to come so close before."

He muttered something incomprehensible under his breath. Grimness set over his features. And something else: guilt. As if Tantris thought he was somehow responsible for the attack.

"Take the blade," she said sternly. "Go. Find your countrymen. The Iverni will be taking no prisoners today."

He put his hand over hers and they held the sword together. His touch was rough and kind at the same time, and Branwen didn't want him to ever let her go.

"Are you telling me to fight your own people?"

"No, Tantris. I don't want you to fight them. But you're my friend, and I want you to live." Her voice nearly broke as she spoke the words.

His fingers threaded through hers, and his back straightened as he took hold of the *kladiwos*. Tantris looked comfortable with a sword in his hand. Strong. His pose graceful.

He should run. Tantris needed to run. Why did he seem rooted to the spot? Why did she?

"There isn't much time," Branwen told him, trying to catch her breath. "Around the next bend in the shore, beneath the cliffs, you'll find fishing boats moored. Take one. *Please.*"

"You're not safe here, either. I won't leave you defenseless."

"I'm not defenseless." She pulled down the collar of her dress to reveal a protective curiet of boiled leather that she'd also pinched from the armory.

He flipped the sword over, glowering. "Kernyvak or Ivernic, men at war aren't to be trusted." Air hissed through his teeth. "I won't thank you for your kindness by abandoning you."

Damn stubborn poet. "Thank me by *living*, Tantris," Branwen told him, that unfamiliar authority bolstering her voice once more.

At the edge of her vision, Branwen glimpsed horses pounding the craggy cliffs with their hooves, drawing closer, closer. "Leave me, Tantris." She was almost yelling now. "You need to *go*!"

Such tenderness washed over his face that Branwen nearly choked on her next words. "Please, Tantris. Go back to your homeland knowing you made a friend in Iveriu."

"I would have peace between our peoples," he said with a conviction that was indisputable. Branwen wished ardently in that moment that Tantris were a king rather than a minstrel. Neither he nor she would ever have the power to truly bring peace.

"The peace between us is a start," Branwen said with a feeble smile. "But there will be no peace if you're dead."

"There is much more than peace between us, Emer. Let me fight for you."

With a shake of the head, she said, "This is me fighting for you." She withdrew the Rigani stone from her pocket and pressed it into his palm. "To remember me by."

"It would be easier to forget my own name than it would you." Tantris closed his fingers in a fist around the stone and held it to his chest. "But just in case—" He broke off and his lips were suddenly on hers.

Time stood still. There was no blood or fire, no Iveriu or Kernyv. There was only this—only this kiss. It was enough to make Branwen believe in things she couldn't see, to exist by feeling rather than thinking.

She allowed her hand to explore the finely packed muscles of his stomach, damp with seawater. Tantris tunneled his fingers through her loose black locks, pulling her closer, sharing the same sweet breaths. She wanted nothing more than to pull him down on top of her, let the tide rush over them.

If Branwen didn't break away now, she would never be able to let go. Maybe in the Otherworld, beyond the sea, lay a place where they could be together, but it wasn't in this world.

She pushed Tantris away and he stumbled backward in the wet sand.

"Emer—"

"You promised me you'd live."

Determination sparked in his eyes. "I *will* live and I *will* see you again."

She didn't know what she would have done then—maybe follow Tantris back to Kernyv—if she hadn't spied her uncle Morholt on the cliffs directly overhead.

"*Go,*" she commanded.

And then she ran away, and she didn't look back. She couldn't. Regret suffused her with each step she took away from him. Tantris would never know her true name.

Branwen was the sea of flames.

SERPENT AMONG THE WAVES

WHOOPING AND HOLLERING RESOUNDED FROM the inner ward as Branwen snuck back into the castle, making her way toward Essy's apartment, in the south tower. Her body buzzed from the fresh memory of the poet's mouth on hers.

She was terrified about what would happen to Tantris if he found his countrymen—they were pirates, after all.

She was even more terrified about what would happen to him if he didn't. And then there was her fear for the lives of the Royal Guard and the villagers along the coast.

An unholy howl slashed the air. It was animal. And another. Branwen needed to go hide herself with Essy before Keane realized she was missing. Yet there was something about the tormented cry that paralyzed her.

Dubthach burst from beneath the archway, nearly knocking her over. His eyes shone and there was a frenzy upon him.

"Lady Branwen," he said. "Beg your pardon." Then, excitedly he told her, "They caught some. They caught some of those bloody Kernyvak bastards down on the beach."

Ice spread though her veins, freezing her heart. "Where?"

"They're bringing them to the keep. Come on, Lady Branwen—let's go see them behead some Kernyvmen!"

Dubthach tugged on her shoulder. She followed him, but she felt as if she were watching the scene from somewhere else, floating. Far above Castle Rigani. Far above the waves battering the shore.

The throne room was on the ground floor of the keep. The Royal Guard dragged men across the courtyard, black hoods covering their faces. Her stomach flipped several times as she pictured Tantris's chiseled features beneath one of those hoods. Several of the prisoners had *kladiwos* blades dangling impotently from their belts.

That doesn't mean it's Tantris, she told herself. Plenty of Kernyvmen carried a *kladiwos*. The argument was almost convincing.

Dubthach pulled Branwen through the crowd that was forming to glimpse the prisoners. Not to mention the inevitable executions. "We beat them back," he recounted enthusiastically. "Now they'll know Ivernic justice."

She nodded faintly. As Branwen and Dubthach pushed their way toward the front of the throne room, her ears filled with the sounds of disdain and condemnation, jeering and whistling. She couldn't remember the last time prisoners had been brought to Castle Rigani. King Óengus obviously wanted to find something out. Somehow, this raid must have been different.

Branwen scanned the ten hooded men on their knees before the king. Their heads were all bowed, pressed to the floor, their hands bound behind their backs with coarse rope. They looked so weak, so helpless, crouched there like that. Which, she realized, was precisely the point.

King Óengus was making the Kernyvmen feel his dominion, the panic that came from knowing your enemy held your life in his hands. Branwen didn't want to feel a lick of sympathy for the captives—not an hour ago they were undoubtedly raping and murdering her countrypeople—but picturing Tantris beneath a hood, pity stirred inside her.

If one of them was Tantris, could she beg for mercy on his behalf? Would the king grant clemency if she asked him for it? But how could Branwen possibly explain? How could Essy or the queen see her as anything but a traitor if they knew the truth. Would it matter that he was a poet and not a pirate? Before she had met Tantris, she wouldn't have seen the distinction.

She sagged against Dubthach, trying to keep her wits about her.

"Don't worry, Lady Branwen," he whispered in her ear. "These Kernyvak bastards can't hurt you now. They won't hurt any Ivermen ever again." Dubthach lobbed a globule of spit at the prisoners and pumped a fist in the air. The zeal with which he spoke was petrifying.

Branwen's countrymen were crying out for Kernyvak blood. What would happen if King Óengus appeased his lesser lords with an invasion of Kernyv?

Essy caught her eye from where she stood behind Keane. Queen Eseult was seated at the right hand of the king, Fintan poised half a step between her and the prisoners, stance wary. The queen was right: Essy's impending nuptials might be the only way to prevent further innocence from being lost. Somehow, Branwen had to make her cousin understand what was at stake.

Morholt bowed before King Óengus, and he presented the captured raiders with a wave. Everything about her uncle smacked of arrogance, which Branwen supposed was only natural as the King's Champion. Even so, she'd never seen him show any grief over the death of Lady Alana, his youngest sister, and part of her had always hated him for it. He never marked the anniversary of his sister's death in any way.

The princess beckoned Branwen forward. Her stomach rioted but she obeyed. She had no choice. Her place was next to Essy.

The Kernyvmen were positioned in an uneven semicircle before the throne. Branwen skirted its edge as she hurried to her cousin's side, her pulse accelerating. She scoured the forms of the prisoners but they were all bloody and sand-stained, seawater clinging to their tunics. Some were larger than others, but it was impossible to tell them apart—to know if one of them was Tantris.

Keane frowned as Branwen sidled up next to Essy, the concern in his eyes genuine. His fingers hovered on the hilt of his sword like he was restraining himself from reaching for her. The queen spared her niece a questioning glance.

Branwen couldn't quite force an apologetic smile.

"I looked for you everywhere," Essy said in a harsh whisper. "You scared me out of my senses!"

The princess folded Branwen's hand into her own and held it tight.

Branwen traced her apology on Essy's palm.

Had she betrayed her family by trying to save Tantris? Her heart was torn between Kernyv and Iveriu—something she never could have imagined. But then, she never could have imagined Tantris.

"It's all right, Branny. Just don't frighten me like that again," the princess said, fierceness behind her beseeching. "Not you without me, remember?"

"You know I do."

"So, where *were* you? You've made a habit of disappearing lately."

Branwen was terror-struck once more. Did Essy *know*? Did she suspect?

Not daring to lift her eyes, she told the princess, "Off having my mad affair with Dubthach, of course! Where else?"

Her cousin let out a giggle, then covered her mouth. Essy trusted her. Why wouldn't she? Before Tantris washed up on her beach, Branwen had never had anything to lie about.

Cool relief tingled on her brow. "I went to fetch herbs for the queen and when I heard the fighting, I hid," said Branwen, despising how effortlessly she could deceive those who trusted her.

Essy screwed up her lips. "Mother shouldn't have sent you. You're *my* lady's maid," she said, and Branwen felt a pinch in her gut. The princess rarely called her that, true as it was.

"I didn't mean to upset you."

Her cousin nodded, her expression still troubled. "The raiders have never been within reach of Castle Rigani before."

Branwen squeezed her hand. "I know," she said. Managing Essy's moods required more energy than she possessed in this moment.

Morholt raised his broadsword in the air, rattling it a few times to silence the crowd. A tense hush fell over the throne room. When he was satisfied, Morholt turned toward the king and said, "My Lord King, we have slain more than forty men on the cliffs today. The Kernyveu grow even more confident."

He thrust his sword at one of the prisoners, jabbing the tip into his neck. Branwen saw a new trickle of blood leak from beneath his hood. "We have taken these ones alive so that you might question them. Still more escaped across the sea, serpents among the waves."

Lord Rónán stepped forward from the clump of Royal Guards watching over the captives with Diarmuid at his heels. "My Lord King," he began, "I believe these raiders had a more particular purpose than usual."

The king's face was expressionless. He raised one interested eyebrow. "Is that so?"

"Yes, my Lord King," Morholt answered before Lord Rónán had the chance. They were both trying to curry favor with King Óengus.

"Tell me what you know."

Now it was Lord Diarmuid who jumped in. "Let the captives tell us." He received death-promising glares from both his father and the King's Champion.

Essy leaned into Branwen. "Isn't he bold?"

"Who?" she asked under her breath.

"Diarmuid."

Too bold to be wise, she thought. "*Mmm*," was her response. During his stay at the castle, the nobleman had grown on Branwen like a fungus.

Unconsciously, the princess twirled her fingers through her plaits, pulling at the roots.

Diarmuid ripped the hood shrouding the face of the first prisoner. Branwen's entire body went as taut as a harp string. The crowd hissed and booed as his face was unmasked. She released into a sigh when she saw the captive wasn't Tantris.

This Kernyvman had several newly healed scars on his cheeks, the same golden-brown skin as the poet, and he jutted his chin out defiantly. Still, Branwen spied dread behind his eyes.

Morholt raised his sword again and the din quickly dissipated.

"Tell us why you attacked Castle Rigani this day?" he demanded of the prisoner. Her uncle's eyes blazed, and she thought she would surely confess to anything if he looked at her like that.

Diarmuid gave the captive a vicious kick to the back. He groaned as his face hit the stone. Branwen winced. The young northern lord smiled triumphantly and sought the princess's eyes to bask in his own reflected glory.

Branwen didn't think there was anything laudable about kicking a man already on the ground whose hands were tied. She angled her head toward Keane whose gaze drilled into the back of her neck. Breaking protocol, he leaned forward, whispering, "No need to feel compassion for the man, Lady Branwen. He isn't like us." Keane meant to reassure her, but he only frightened Branwen more.

The sickening crunch of bone being crushed and the clank of metal on stone tore through the throne room. Lord Diarmuid's broadsword smashed into the ground at the same moment the Kernyvman's head began to roll.

He hadn't said a word.

Branwen swayed on her feet. She imagined that the head belonged to Tantris, and she couldn't fight the sharp sting of tears.

The crowd cheered and Lord Rónán unveiled the next prisoner. He clapped his son on the back for a job well done. The spectators roared in approval.

It wasn't Tantris. Thank the Old Ones it wasn't Tantris.

The eyes of the second Kernyvman went wide as he took in the severed head of his comrade. The first prisoner's body was still twitching.

Branwen felt sick as she realized her uncle intended to play this beheading game with all ten captives. Her nerves were shredded; she didn't think she could watch.

Essy kissed her cheek, where a tear was streaming down. "You really are so tenderhearted, Branny."

She didn't know if that was so, but she evidently wasn't as hard-hearted as she would have liked to believe. Not even concerning her enemies. Branwen tried to tell herself these men were the kinsmen of her family's murderers and that she shouldn't care. But a little voice in her head insisted they were Tantris's kinsmen, too. If Morholt could play with their lives in this way, how were the Iverni any nobler than the Kernyveu?

The second captive appeared less defiant, more haunted. His face was paler than a killing frost.

"I'll repeat the question, in case you didn't understand," Morholt said cavalierly. "Tell us why you dared attack Castle Rigani. For your own sake, I hope you speak better Ivernic than your fellow pirate."

Her uncle took a jaunty step toward the disarticulated head and gave it a kick. It spun toward one of the pillars, resounding with a dull thump as it collided. The Ivermen throughout the throne room brayed, including Keane.

The captive wet his lips. He looked from Morholt to King Óengus. "Y-you've p-poached something of ours," he started in Ivernic, his teeth chattering.

"Shut your trap!" hollered one of the still-hooded prisoners.

The man spoke in Kernyvak but Branwen understood enough. As did the other Ivermen.

Diarmuid rushed toward the raucous, surly voice and exposed the speaker's visage. This Kernyvman was older than the other two. His orange hair burned like a firestorm. Again, Branwen's heart had leapt into her throat in the moment before the captive's face was revealed.

Three of the Kernyvmen weren't Tantris. Only seven left. She thought she would burst apart at the seams.

The older Kernyvman spat a gob of blood onto the floor. Diarmuid bashed the top of his head with the hilt of his broadsword.

Morholt returned his attention to the pirate who had spoken and whose entire body now quaked. "You were saying," he said coldly.

The king waited silently for the answer, his fingers drumming lightly on his thigh.

"Don't keep the High King of Iveriu waiting," Morholt roared in a sudden burst of anger.

"I . . . I . . ." His teeth clacked together so violently that Branwen could hear it from where she was standing.

"Don't you dare open your bone-box!" the older Kernyvman shouted.

Morholt and Diarmuid exchanged a glance. Then the edge of Diarmuid's blade bit into the defiant Kernyvman's neck. But the northern lord had been standing too close to the prisoner. He didn't get enough momentum for a clean strike. It took three more agonizing blows to hack off the captive's head.

Blood sprayed Diarmuid's tunic. This time Essy made no comment about his boldness. The gore was a revolting red.

Branwen's uncle turned to the young prisoner at his feet.

"So sorry for the interruption." Morholt wore a teasing smile. "What was it you wanted to add?" he asked, no mercy in his eyes.

The quaking Kernyvman looked sideways at the heads to his left and to his right. Staring at the floor, he said, "Iveriu will know no peace from King Marc so long as you hold his nephew captive."

King Óengus's eyebrows shot up. He glanced at Morholt, who gave his head one firm shake. The king folded his arms across his chest.

"You are misinformed," he said neutrally. "We have no princes of Kernyv here."

Morholt grabbed the prisoner by the hair and yanked his head up. "Show our king his due respect."

Maybe the Kernyvman sensed his end was near, because he met the king's gaze and told him, "King Marc is the only king I bow before. We will keep coming for his Champion until he is found. Ivermen are honorless liars."

Those were the last words he spoke. King Óengus had learned what he needed to know. Morholt slit the Kernyvman's throat and cut out his tongue before lopping off his head.

Branwen turned to her cousin, who was now even whiter than she was. *What of the other captives?* she wanted to ask. Then she got her answer.

The king signaled the Royal Guardsmen flanking the prisoners. Morholt, Diarmuid, and Lord Rónán took a prisoner apiece. As did Keane, and Fintan, and two other saffron-sashed men. Keane looked like he relished the order.

Branwen had to force herself not to close her eyes. She didn't want to see this. She didn't want to see her friend Keane as a murderer. She didn't want to see Tantris murdered.

"Let the justice of the Land, of Goddess Ériu, be done," declared King Óengus. Queen Eseult echoed him. She had sat stoically at his side throughout the entire spectacle. That was what it meant to be queen.

With terrifying synchronicity, the seven Ivermen raised their steel to the sky, and the heads of the seven Kernyvmen tumbled to the floor. Branwen couldn't breathe. They hadn't unsheathed the faces. Did one belong to her beautiful stranger?

Cheers and yowls erupted in the hall.

"Get the pikes," Queen Eseult instructed Fintan.

Unable to contain her nerves any further, Branwen rushed out a side exit and vomited in a darkened crevice of the hallway. She would have to search for Tantris's head among the pikes mounted on the ramparts. Air scorched her lungs as she dry heaved; vitriol ate at her throat. Her heart was cut to ribbons.

Rallying all the strength she had left, Branwen straightened up. She wouldn't curl in on herself. She wouldn't crumble. If Tantris was dead, she needed to know and she needed to honor him.

She needed to honor him because even though it went against everything Branwen had always believed—Tantris brought something alive inside her. Something that couldn't be contained.

True love was more powerful than death or dishonor.

Slowly, excruciatingly slowly, Branwen walked toward the main gate, where the Royal Guard was raising the pikes. Each footfall, each heartbeat, was a prayer that she would not see the poet's face. That she would never see his face again—except in her dreams. She was certain she would always see him there.

Branwen reached the main gate. The Royal Guard stood aloft,

Keane and Fintan among them. They removed the shrouds. Her breath hitched.

Seven heads. Seven moments of death. She felt each one.

But Tantris wasn't there. Tantris wasn't there.

Branwen fell to her knees, and she wept.

PART II

ACROSS THE VEIL

THE ROCK ROAD

BRANWEN SAT UNEASILY ON HER MOUNT. She longed to gather her horse's mane between her hands, letting the wind weave its fingers through her own loosened plaits, and gallop toward the horizon. But this was a solemn occasion. She was accompanying the princess as she visited the villages destroyed by the Kernyveu, bringing food and clothing. Although she was there in body, Branwen's mind was back at the cave.

As soon as she could after the raiders were executed, she'd returned to retrieve her mother's harp. Tantris was gone. The only sign he'd ever existed were a few scratches in green rock: ODAI ETI AMA. Branwen slinked away whenever possible to trace her finger in the grooves, although the cold stone could never compare to the poet's warmth, his smile . . . his kiss.

"Lady Branwen?" Keane said, disturbing her thoughts. "How do you fare?"

Startled, Branwen jerked back too fast on the reins and her

palfrey faltered. The mare blew out an annoyed breath through her nostrils, pinning her ears back, and shot the interloper an accusatory glare. Branwen leaned forward, patting the horse's neck while planting a soft kiss behind her ear.

"Lucky horse," Keane commented. His eyes fastened on Branwen's face, lingering on her lips. He sidled his mount closer to hers and his calf brushed briefly against her skirts.

Keane was an imposing man, taller than Tantris, with a broader frame that guardsmen training kept weighted with muscle. Branwen swallowed. Guilt seeped under her skin that she enjoyed the other man's flirtation. Just a little.

Essy's laughter rang out across the cliffs. Bright, like a bell.

Keane whipped his head toward the sound, breaking the charged moment. *Thank you, Essy*, thought Branwen. When the princess felt the bodyguard's gaze land on her, she shot him a challenging look and kicked her mount into a canter. Lord Diarmuid followed suit, pursuing Essy on his stallion. Essy winked at Branwen over her shoulder. The Festival of Lovers was drawing near, and her cousin was counting the days until Diarmuid proposed, as she was sure he would.

Keane heaved a small sigh. "If you stop chasing, she'll stop running," Branwen informed him with a laugh. "My cousin doesn't like to lose." Essy didn't realize Branwen had been letting her win their races for years.

"It's nice to hear you laughing, Lady Branwen. I—" Keane paused, his eyes combing her face; they gleamed midnight blue. "I wish you hadn't witnessed me dispatching the Kernyvmen."

Alarm prickled along her spine. It seemed a horribly sanitizing euphemism for what he had done. She gripped the reins, and her palfrey snorted in complaint.

"You carried out your duty to protect our kingdom."

Tentatively, he touched her elbow. "I did." He inhaled a heavy breath. "But you haven't looked at me the same way since."

There was no use claiming otherwise. Every time Branwen looked at Keane, she saw the headless captives. Even if there were no Tantris, she had been privy to a side of her friend that she would rather not have glimpsed. Her gaze skipped along the ancient Rock Road, strewn with the withering petals of spring and newly fallen rain, which traversed the coast. Keane allowed his forefinger to venture the distance from Branwen's elbow to her shoulder.

His touch wasn't unpleasant but he wasn't Tantris. By the Old Ones, what she wouldn't give to feel the poet's fingers tangle in her hair—just once more.

Branwen tipped her chin upward so that their eyes met. "I beg your pardon, if I haven't been myself," she said. "The attack has brought into the present, memories better left in the past." The only comfort she took lately was giving solace to the wounded—and the infirmary was filled with them.

Keane's face creased, disappointment replaced immediately by anger, like a storm changing course. His fist pounded his thigh. "Forgive me. It was on the Rock Road that your parents were felled."

Nodding, Branwen said, "I should have been there that day, you know. I was furious that they refused to let me travel with them."

Branwen's countrymen believed that when the spirit departed from the body, it would live on in the Otherworld, waiting to be reborn. Right after her parents were killed, Branwen had wished she'd died with them so they could all be reborn together. Later, she grew incensed that her parents hadn't found their way back to her. By her twelfth birthday, Branwen had stopped believing in the Otherworld altogether. Now, she supposed the Old Ones must have their reasons for keeping her parents beyond the Veil.

"Never wish that," Keane nearly barked, snapping Branwen out of her memory. "If anyone had hurt you . . . I would have killed as many Kernyvmen as it took to turn the Ivernic Sea red." The hatred that laced his words made them terrifying rather than flattering.

Keane scanned the retinue again, checking on the princess before allowing his gaze to settle once more on Branwen. His shoulders were tensed, nearly raised to his ears.

"We have more in common than you think," he said, softer now. The breeze toyed with his short chestnut-colored bangs. "I was only a little older than you were when I lost my own parents to the Kernyveu. I grew up not far from here."

Branwen fiddled with the reins. She realized she knew nothing of Keane's life before he came to Castle Rigani. Why had she never inquired?

"The day my parents died was the day I decided to join the Royal Guard." Keane set his jaw. "It was also the day I killed my first Kernyvman. And I lived up to my name."

His name could mean either "a battle" or "a lament," the song of Bríga.

"What happened?" Branwen asked, half afraid of the answer.

"I was playing on Skeleton Beach when I saw the ships approach." He shivered as if he were back in that distant moment. Branwen shivered, too. The Skeleton Beach massacre was infamous throughout

Iveriu. It was rumored that the dead washed ashore for months afterward, unburied souls who now belonged to the Sea of the Dead, claimed by Dhusnos—the Dark One.

"I ran," he said. "The pirates ran faster."

Need radiated from Keane as he spoke, and there was violence beneath it. On instinct, Branwen took his hand. He squeezed hers back. The surf climbed the side of the cliff before crashing back into the sea.

"By the time I reached my home, the thatched roof was on fire," he continued, visibly pained, the cords of his neck taut. "I didn't have a weapon, so I grabbed a rock. The raider didn't notice me enter. I flung myself on his back. He smelled of rotted fish." Keane screwed up his nose. "I bashed him over the head, again and again."

Branwen's throat went dry as she pictured the scene.

"It was for nothing. My parents were already dead. Sprawled by the hearth, throats slit." He swallowed. "Their hands were touching . . . like they'd been trying to say good-bye."

Branwen pulled back gently on the reins of Keane's mount, which he'd allowed to go slack. As they came to a halt, Branwen brushed her hand against his cheek in sympathy. "I am so sorry for your loss." She also comprehended more fully why Saoirse's suffering had unsettled him so much.

The sharpness in his eyes dulled. "I didn't mean to distress you, my lady. Only to say that I think we understand each other." Keane traced her cheekbone in return. His wasn't a sympathetic gesture, however; it was an intimate one. "Great things are built on understanding," he told her.

Branwen gulped because she knew it was true. Her love for Tantris had grown once she let herself see who he was inside—even if it was a love neither of their peoples would ever be able to understand.

"One Iveriu," she breathed.

"A woman after my own heart," said Keane, and she offered him a fleeting smile. Branwen could never be a woman after Keane's heart, however, because she was already fashioned after another.

And if an Ivernic heart could be made from the same stuff as a Kernyvak one, perhaps all was not yet lost.

✛ ✛ ✛

As Branwen accompanied Essy into the scene of desolation, it was hard to maintain any lofty hopes. The hardest of hearts had brought this village low and rent it asunder. The princess walked among the ruins while a dozen Royal Guardsmen distributed supplies to the remaining able-bodied adults.

Branwen spied only a few men amidst the survivors; raiders always killed the men first. The rational part of her brain understood their strategy: Women were less likely to resist. But the pirates had underestimated her countrywomen—to their peril. Several overconfident invaders dangled from the trees by their toes, heads severed.

Any satisfaction at the sight dissolved as she surveyed the haunted faces of the village children. Branwen had been inconsolable even without seeing her parents murdered before her very eyes. She could only imagine what Keane was feeling as he directed his men with curt orders; he must have seen himself in each face.

Branwen noticed one small girl, graced with sunset-colored ringlets, who hung back from the other children greedily gobbling up

Treva's famed apple cake. She stood and watched, clinging to the charred husk of a doll.

Essy made the rounds among the villagers, offering embraces and words of comfort. Tempestuous as she could be, the princess loved ardently and that love extended to her people—especially the children. All of the servants' children at Castle Rigani loved to listen to Essy's stories, and she loved telling them. They demanded nothing more of her than her imagination.

Another one of the princess's joyful squeals carried on the breeze as she called the youngest villagers closer for a story.

The children raced toward her, scrambling around her skirts. All except for the red-haired girl. They grabbed saltwater caramels from her palms like overexcited squirrels. And they laughed.

Essy smiled, laughing with them. Then her gaze drifted toward the quiet girl.

"Aren't you hungry?" she asked, approaching the child.

The girl's eyes went moon-round. She clasped the burned doll to her chest, wrapping her arms fiercely and protectively around it. The flinty look in her eye told Branwen she wouldn't let anything part her from her possession. Branwen's heart ached; a child shouldn't be that leather-tough.

Essy crouched down so that she was at eye level with the girl, who couldn't be more than five years old. Again, she held out a candy. No reaction.

Pointing toward the doll, she asked gently, "Who's your friend?"

The girl shrank back, holding Essy's gaze. Looking from the princess to the doll, she listed her head, considering. "Eseult," she answered finally, in a rasp. Branwen recognized a voice hoarse from too much screaming. "I named her for the princess." The redhead squinted. "Is that really you?"

Essy nodded once, closing her eyes for the briefest instant. "And what about you—what's your name?"

The girl glanced self-consciously around her at the other children, who had stopped feasting to gawk at her. "Gráinne," she said. Her chin wobbled.

"Gráinne is a lovely name," Essy told her. "Where is your mother?"

No answer.

"Your father?"

No answer.

"I see." The princess took a nibble of the caramel. "It's delicious. Are you absolutely certain you don't want to try it, Gráinne?"

The little girl's cheeks blazed a rosy pink. "A princess shouldn't see my hands."

Essy's brow pinched in concern. "Let me be the judge of that." Still, Gráinne hesitated. "I'm your princess, aren't I?" she persisted with a wink, resembling Queen Eseult completely.

Gráinne relented. Keeping one hand clutched around her doll, she showed Essy the other palm. It was peppered with tiny cuts, probably from brambles, that had become infected.

The princess worked her jaw. She really couldn't stand the sight of wounded flesh. Her eyes imploring Branwen for aid, Essy asked Gráinne, "Would you let me help you?"

The girl bit her lip uncertainly as Branwen joined them, squatting down beside Essy. She'd had the foresight to bring a wound-cleansing salve with her, just in case her cousin suffered from a similar injury on the road. Fishing the jar from the pocket of her heavy traveling skirt, Branwen warned, "It might hurt."

"Gráinne is brave," Essy declared. Then to the girl, she said, "But it's all right to cry."

Gráinne shook her head, fiery curls bouncing. "Mama told me not to cry. She made me promise."

The cousins shared a meaningful look. Essy turned her eyes downward, kissing the top of the child's head so she didn't see her princess blinking back tears.

"You kept your promise, Gráinne. Your mother wouldn't be cross. I'm your princess, and I would know. You're safe now."

But Branwen knew Gráinne wouldn't be truly safe until Essy was married. Perhaps the royal family—herself included—had been wrong to shelter the princess. If Essy was to rise to the occasion, she had to be given the chance.

"Ready?" asked the princess. Gráinne bobbed her head. Essy opened the jar and applied the salve liberally to the girl's right palm. Air escaped through her missing baby teeth and her lips trembled, but she did not cry.

When Essy reached for Gráinne's other hand, she yanked away. Inferring the problem, the princess said, "Eseult is your good-luck charm, isn't she?" The girl nodded. "Branwen is mine. Can she hold Eseult for you?" Essy stroked the singed dress of her effigy. "Only for a minute."

Reluctantly, Gráinne consented. Branwen accepted the doll, casting her cousin a sidelong glance, infinitely touched.

Essy finished applying the ointment and a dimple appeared as the girl smiled. "I'll have my candy now," she announced.

The princess plopped it in Gráinne's mouth with a chuckle. Then she tucked another into the pocket of her tattered skirt. "For later. Because you're so brave."

"Thank you, Lady Princess."

Essy frowned. It was the first time Branwen could remember that her cousin didn't appear pleased with her title. Essy pressed the doll to Gráinne's heart.

"Since we have a mutual friend, you may call me Princess Essy." Assessing the state of the doll, she added sweetly, "It seems as if your Eseult is in need of a new dress. Would you allow me to sew her one?"

"Oh yes!" Gráinne replied instantly, throwing her arms around Essy's waist but careful not to hurt her palms. Branwen smiled, although she knew she would end up sewing the dress; the princess detested needlework.

Keane had edged closer throughout the exchange. He lifted his eyebrows at the sun climbing through the sky. They had several more villages to visit before nightfall.

"We need to go now, Gráinne," Essy said, kissing her cheek. She drew herself up to standing. "Never forget that your princess loves you."

"I won't," Gráinne promised. She waved the doll excitedly as Essy and Branwen returned to their mounts.

Just before the princess hopped on to her palfrey, she said, "I will never forgive the Kernyveu for this. Not ever."

A fist closed around Branwen's heart.

RIPPLES

ESSY CRIED HERSELF TO SLEEP on Belotnia Eve, littering her bed cushions with golden strands. While the princess had been providing relief to the victims of the attack, King Óengus decided her marriage could no longer be delayed and proclaimed that a Champions Tournament would be held at the late summer festival of Laelugus for her hand. Suitors were to be given three moons to travel to Iveriu from all over the known world.

The Festival of Lovers came and went, and Lord Diarmuid didn't ask Essy to be his wife. He sent no more love letters or tokens of esteem. In fact, he'd absented himself from Castle Rigani altogether. Branwen suspected his father had ordered him to stay away. Lord Rónán's ambitions didn't trump his sense.

Branwen had cried on Belotnia, too; but for an entirely different reason. She wished she could confide in her cousin who was, after all, her best friend. No, it wasn't safe, she'd decided. She couldn't implicate the princess in her betrayal.

A welcome breeze tickled Branwen's damp brow. An unusually hot summer had begun with Belotnia and showed no signs of abating for the past three months.

Oxblood smoothed over the ebbing tide, casting deep shadows on the water. Branwen allowed herself one last look from the castle gates before heading to the south tower to prepare the princess for the champions' welcome feast.

Tomorrow, the tournament would begin.

She walked up the twisting stairwell apprehensively, taking her time. Essy had been in such a foul temper of late that she hadn't noticed how much more quiet and withdrawn Branwen had become. The only person who noticed, she thought, was Keane.

Last night, the princess had purloined far more elderberry wine than was wise from Treva's private stock, and Branwen spent the wee hours holding back her hair as she retched into a chamber pot. Guilt weighed on Branwen that she couldn't heal her cousin's wounds— neither those she could see nor those she could not. Caring for Essy after her parents died had relieved some of the grief that threatened to crush Branwen from within; she was the first true love Branwen had known. Before Tantris, the only time she felt she truly belonged— anywhere—was at Essy's side; now that he was gone, it was true once more.

When Branwen reached the landing, Keane was posted outside the princess's apartments. "Beautiful night for a walk," he said. "Late summer evenings are my favorite."

"Mine, too," she admitted. The midnight sun wasn't so very far north of Iveriu and this summer Branwen sat up strumming her harp longingly.

Keane's continued gaze was an invitation.

"What is it you do on the beach by yourself every day, my lady?" he teased, but he also seemed genuinely mystified.

Branwen smiled in a way that was perhaps a touch flirtatious. "Look at the waves, of course." Tantris and the sea would forevermore be wedded in her mind.

Keane sighed and muttered something low under his breath as he closed the door behind her. Branwen had received a token from him on Belotnia Eve, but she had declined to dance; he never pressed her about it.

"Branny!" the princess squealed as she entered. "Come here right this instant!" Clapping her hands together, Essy said, "Tonight, I want to look like a queen!"

Branwen's eyebrows shot toward the ceiling. This was not the same red- and puffy-eyed girl she'd left nursing a headache earlier. She hadn't seen her cousin in such good spirits since before the Champions Tournament had been announced.

"I thought you didn't want to be *trussed up like some roasted boar*," she reminded Essy, tone blithe.

"Tosh."

"No, I'm pretty sure you told your mother to just stick an apple in your mouth and be done with it."

Essy waved a hand in the air. "I never said that," she protested, laughing. Hope sparked in Branwen that the princess had resolved to put her people before herself. She had spoken often about Gráinne and the other children along the Rock Road, after all. Then, with a sudden burst of urgency, her cousin swiveled toward Branwen and clasped her sweaty hands on Branwen's forearms.

"Diarmuid is coming!" she exclaimed. Branwen's stomach dropped. So *that* accounted for Essy's dramatic shift in mood. "He's going to compete in the tournament." Pride, hope, and fear swirled in her voice. "Just like in a ballad!"

"Your life isn't a ballad, Essy," said Branwen, unable to keep the frustration from her voice. Her cousin wasn't the only one who'd barely slept.

"Why shouldn't my life be a ballad?" Her eyes burned into Branwen's. "I want you to make me a love potion, Branny. For me and Diarmuid."

"You already seem bespelled to me." Branwen had hoped the infatuation would fade as the others had, but her cousin only seemed more enamored.

"Fine. For Diarmuid, then."

"I thought you wanted a lover who loved you for you, Essy—not because of a spell."

Her face crumpled. "You *would* use my own words against me, cousin."

"Oh, Essy, I can't," she told her. "Even if I wanted to, I don't know how."

She'd heard of Otherworld-touched healers who had the natural magic to make love potions—or, at least, aphrodisiacs—but she wouldn't know where to start. Queen Eseult had never taught Branwen anything remotely resembling a love spell, and she doubted her aunt ever would. The queen was always saying that the duty of a healer was to help nature along, not pervert its course.

"If you really wanted me to be happy, Branny, you would at least try," Essy shot back. "I know Diarmuid's the one." Branwen bristled.

Her cousin sounded brash and a tad petulant. Exactly like the day she challenged Branwen to leap from a waterfall. They'd been visiting one of the king's vassals in Conaktir. His son was the same age as Essy, just turned eight, and he declared that no girl was brave enough to take the plunge.

Outraged, Essy told him she wasn't a girl, she was a princess. Branwen could still hear the water rushing in her mind. She showed Branwen a fierce smile and jumped.

Watching her cousin fall, she'd never felt so helpless. The splash as Essy hit the river below was louder than a punch. Her cousin survived with only a broken arm, and she wore the sling like a badge of honor.

Weren't you scared? Branwen had asked Essy afterward.

No, I was flying.

Branwen could see how much her cousin longed to fly again.

"*Please*, Branny." Essy's grip began to chafe. "My father's a coward, but maybe if he sees how in love we are, he won't make me marry somebody else."

"Essy! You can't speak about the king that way. It's *treason*."

"I don't care, it's the truth. The *king* is selling me to the highest bidder to protect his own crown." Something flared in Essy's eyes that Branwen had never seen before. Something she couldn't quite name—and it was dangerous.

Branwen placed her hands firmly on Essy's shoulders. "You do care. I know you do. You wouldn't ask your people to sacrifice their lives so you can marry your sweetheart."

"I'm going to be Lord Diarmuid's queen and we'll rid Iveriu of the Kernyveu together," insisted the princess.

"He has to win first." This time Branwen did intend the edge to her voice.

"You're just jealous you don't have a lover of your own!"

Unbidden, a single staccato laugh burst from Branwen. If her cousin only knew.

"You can't really be that selfish, Essy."

The anger in her cousin's eyes cooled and hardened. "Lady Branwen, please leave me alone with my thoughts."

"What about your hair?" she said. The princess had never dismissed her like this. Not even in her childhood tantrums.

"I can take care of myself." Essy sounded every inch the queen and, for the first time, Branwen thought it might be true. "Mother may need your help," she added, "but I do not."

Branwen stared at her cousin, debating whether or not to really leave. Both of their emotions were running high. Yes, she'd give Essy space to simmer down.

The princess caught her wrist as she turned to go. Branwen expected to feel a familiar shape traced on her skin.

Instead, Essy said, "Take this to Lord Diarmuid when he arrives."

Her cousin withdrew a handkerchief from her bodice. She had embroidered it herself. The stitching was sloppy, childlike. But there was no mistaking the pattern: an interlinked D and E.

Branwen gasped. "Essy, no. King Óengus would be furious!"

"That is no concern of yours," Essy told her. "A princess is allowed a champion."

"Not in the Champions Tournament! You can't show favoritism among Iveriu's potential allies."

The princess bolted to her feet. "This isn't your life, Branny. It's mine. I'm so sick of you telling me what to do—of *everyone* telling me what to do!" she yelled, raking a hand harshly through her tresses. Branwen lurched backward. Essy shoved the handkerchief into her hand, tears pricking her eyes. "You will do as I say. As your princess, I command it."

Shock rendered Branwen speechless.

The last time Essy had commanded her to do something, Branwen had scaled an apple tree to fetch the reddest one right at the top. She had slipped and fallen, spraining her ankle quite badly. Essy felt so guilty that she'd cried harder than Branwen, and Branwen never did tell Queen Eseult why she had climbed the tree in the first place.

Slowly, deliberately, she tucked the token for Lord Diarmuid into the belt cinching her gown. Casting her eyes down, Branwen performed an excruciatingly precise curtsy.

"As you command, *Your Highness*."

The night felt keen-bitten and barren as she exited her cousin's bedchamber.

Keane stepped toward her, scouring her face. She didn't want to meet his inquiring eyes. He'd surely heard the cousins fighting.

"Are you crying, Lady Branwen?" The tenderness in his voice took her aback.

She shook her head.

"All right," he said softly. "Just let me know if you want my company to not weep a little more."

"Thank you, Keane," she said, and she meant it.

Branwen raced down the steps of the south tower while she could still maintain her composure.

Giving the handkerchief to Lord Diarmuid could be interpreted as an act of treason, working against the interests of the Ivernic crown. At the very least, the deed would imperil Essy's honor—and that was tantamount to the same thing. And yet, her cousin had asked—no, *demanded*—that Branwen risk her life to perform it.

As her princess, Essy had commanded her, and as her loyal lady's maid, Branwen would obey. She tried to tell herself it was just the stress of the Champions Tournament taking its toll on her cousin. Essy suffered nightmares after seeing the vanquished villages: The strain of her duty must have been warping her heart. Family and ruler, Princess Eseult would always be; whether the princess remained her friend—that was one of the only choices Branwen could make for herself.

Unthinkingly, she used the illicit handkerchief to dab away bitter tears. They were unwelcome. As was this errand. So very, very unwelcome.

Branwen crossed the inner ward, making her way toward the feasting hall. It was illuminated from within by hundreds of beeswax candles. A jaunty tune from a boisterous *kelyos* band filled the air.

She stopped just outside the entrance and practiced smiling a few times. It wouldn't do for any of the guests to notice she was upset. She might not be a princess, but the queen was her aunt and the King's Champion was her uncle.

On this night, among their potential friends and enemies, Branwen represented Iveriu, too. She would do her best to bring honor to Castle Rigani. She would honor her parents—and Tantris—by making friends of enemies.

The token in her hand itched and burned. It was a loose spoke that could derail an entire wagon. Branwen considered not delivering it, but she feared Essy might do something even more rash.

The ground shifted beneath her feet. Almost literally. She glimpsed the fox on the ramparts, bobbing and weaving between the severed heads. There was a hideous beauty to them in the shaft of moonlight.

The creature scurried off and Branwen ducked surreptitiously into the feasting hall. The fractured panes of stained glass glowed in the firelight, and tonight the images seemed to her entirely whole. She could scarcely make out the lines that separated them.

She trained her eyes on Lord Diarmuid, capturing his gaze. He furrowed his brow, seemingly put out, and then followed her to a secluded spot.

"Lady Branwen, you look beautiful."

"Give me your hand," she said, and it was nearly a snarl.

Lord Diarmuid lifted his eyebrows as Branwen pressed the handkerchief between his fingers. Looking at him hard, she said, "I think you know what this is and whom it's from—and why you shouldn't accept it."

"Then why did you deliver it?"

"Why do you think?"

"You have a sharp tongue, my lady." Lord Diarmuid chuckled but it was mirthless. Tucking the token into his pocket, he said, "A thousand apologies for your trouble."

Branwen didn't believe he was sorry at all. She was about to supply him with a few more choice words of her own when Lord Diarmuid shot her a warning glance.

"Good evening," he greeted someone over her shoulder. "Lady Queen."

She flushed with shame and fear at having almost been caught in the act of treason by a woman she loved so much.

"There you are, dear heart," Queen Eseult said, tapping her on the shoulder.

Branwen gave Diarmuid a glare to let him know that like a fish, he hadn't wriggled off her hook just yet. She painted on a smile, and spun around to greet the queen.

And then her heart stopped.

A ripple of sunlight on the water.

Tantris.

ESEULT THE FAIR

THE EVENING EXPANDED AND CONTRACTED around her.
All the noises of the feasting hall faded to nothing. Branwen
must have been dreaming. But was this a dream or a nightmare?

Tantris was surrounded by his enemies—by Branwen's kinsmen.
Her uncle Morholt would think nothing of taking another Kernyvak
head. The poet was going to get himself killed.

What was he doing here? Why had he come back?

Branwen couldn't speak. Not even to scream at Tantris to run.

Queen Eseult only smiled at her. Why was the queen smiling?
There was a Kernyvman in their midst.

"Allow me to introduce you to Prince Tristan, nephew of King
Marc of Kernyv."

Branwen's fingers tightened around the velvet sash at her waist.
She shifted her weight, trying to remain steady on her feet.

Tantris—her Tantris—was alive, and he was standing right in
front of her in the middle of Castle Rigani. Only he *wasn't* Tantris.

And he wasn't hers. It had all been lies. Her heart churned with a familiar wildness, livid and roaring.

Suddenly it struck Branwen that *this* was why the Old Ones had wanted her to save him. He was a prince. If a Kernyvak prince died on Ivernic soil, there would never be peace. She had saved Iveriu by saving the poet. Yet the knowledge did nothing to quell the tempest inside her.

Tantris smiled at her, too, exuding the same easy confidence as if they were alone together at the cave.

"This must be the fair Eseult, whose beauty is so renowned," he said. He spoke in Aquilan, as everyone at court would tonight, and he obviously hadn't learned it because he was a *poet*.

The tempest became an ice storm. Branwen thought she might be ill. Tantris thought she was the princess. He thought she was *Essy*. Was that why he'd returned?

He's not Tantris, she scolded herself. *His name is Tristan and he's a Kernyvak prince. A prince who wants a princess.*

Tantris—no, *Tristan*—Tristan took Branwen's hand in his. He pressed it to his lips gently, as gently as if she were a starling. He held her gaze throughout the brief kiss, and she hated the way his touch made her feel wondrously alive. He was worse than a pirate.

"Prince *Tristan*." Branwen swallowed the name, unable to wipe the stunned expression off her face as she performed a requisite curtsy.

The queen regarded her, eyebrow raised, then spared a glance for the Kernyvak prince.

"My niece is most fair," she said, also in Aquilan. "But her name is Branwen."

Tristan's eyes roved her face. Eyes she had longed to see again. Eyes she had come to trust that now belonged to a stranger.

"Lady Branwen is more than fair. Although she looks more like an Emer to me." His grin deepened. "The bravest of Ivernic heroines."

Branwen's lips went flat. The fox may have led her to Tristan to prevent a war, but she'd been a fool to fall for him. As impulsive as Essy—who was wisely avoiding her. Well, Branwen had fulfilled her mission. She was done. She was done with this two-faced Kernyvman. No matter how appealing a face he had.

Queen Eseult's gaze moved slowly between them. "You know our legends, Prince Tristan?" she said.

"Oh yes." He focused his attention on Branwen as he spoke. "I recount 'The Wooing of Emer' daily."

"I'm surprised Prince Tristan can recount his own name," Branwen snapped.

Her aunt inhaled a short breath through her nose. Lord Diarmuid, whose presence Branwen had utterly forgotten, coughed loudly. Tristan merely smiled.

"It's true," he conceded, a wry note in his voice. "In the presence of beautiful women, my tongue—and my heart—gets stitched up in knots."

Branwen tensed. She couldn't believe he would joke in this way in front of the queen. She had risked her life for him, betrayed her family for him, pined for him—and he was *jesting* with her. Now that she knew Tristan's true identity, Branwen doubted she knew him at all.

"In any event," began Queen Eseult, casting a critical glance at her niece. "King Óengus and I are greatly relieved that your uncle no longer believes the Iverni kidnapped you, Prince Tristan." The queen was an astute woman; she knew she was missing something.

All joviality fled Tristan's features. "I am terribly grieved about the misunderstanding, Lady Queen. As is King Marc."

Lord Diarmuid couldn't refrain from a chortle. "A misunderstanding? Your uncle's men pillaged half the eastern coast looking for you."

Queen Eseult shot the young lord a barbed stare. For once, Branwen agreed with him. The day of the attack on the castle, when she'd given Tristan a sword to defend himself against her own people, he had looked so guilty. Because it *was* his fault.

"Words cannot convey how much your losses trouble me, Lady Queen," Tristan continued, ignoring Diarmuid. "I feel them as my own."

Branwen could tell her aunt believed him. Branwen wanted to believe him as well. The man who risked himself to help an injured animal would mourn each death. That was the man who had won Branwen's heart. But was that man anything more than an illusion?

"I am King Marc's only nephew," Tristan said to the queen. "I'm sure you would raze Kernyv to the ground if you thought we'd taken Lady Branwen hostage."

Her aunt looked at her, smiling warmly. "I would, Prince Tristan," she said, and Branwen was overwhelmed with a surge of love for the queen that momentarily tempered her anger.

"Nor would I blame you, Lady Queen," Tristan agreed. "I imagine anyone with a lick of sense would fight for Lady Branwen like the Hound did for Emer."

Branwen didn't dare glance in his direction. If she did, she might demand to know how he could possibly claim he would fight for her when he hadn't esteemed her enough to tell her the truth. Scores of Iverni had died because of his secret.

A tiny wrinkle appeared between the queen's brows.

"What *did* befall you exactly, Prince Tristan?" she asked.

"Yes, tell us of your adventures," Lord Diarmuid interjected, his voice laced with derision. Branwen didn't know what game he was playing, but if Diarmuid wanted to be the queen's son-in-law, he needed to play the part of diplomat this evening. She found herself wishing he would, for Essy's sake.

Tristan cleared his throat. "I was tossed overboard during a storm and washed up on Ivernic shores. A beautiful mermaid rescued me from the waves."

Branwen and Tristan locked eyes. "How very lucky for you, Prince Tristan."

"I don't believe in luck, Lady Branwen. I believe in fate."

Dry lightning crackled between them. Could everyone else feel it? She'd never wanted so fiercely to kiss a man, or to beat him over the head. She wouldn't let desire betray her. This wasn't Tantris. He never had been.

At that moment, the *kelyos* band reached a thunderous climax accompanied by shouts and cheers.

When Branwen didn't reply, Tristan frowned slightly. *Good.* If he thought he was going to charm her twice with sweet words alone, he was sorely mistaken.

The music died away, and Queen Eseult returned her focus to the nephew of Iveriu's greatest enemy. "The royal musicians are gifted, are they not?" she said, still clapping.

Tristan showed an effortless grin. "Very."

Branwen refused to smile in return. "In fact, the prince was just telling me what a talented bard *he* is," she told her aunt. "He adores spinning fantastic tales out of whole cloth."

He quirked an eyebrow at her. She tried not to fixate on the tiny scar she'd long found so endearing.

"Is that so?" the queen said, and she seemed genuinely interested, which was a particular talent of hers. "Perhaps you will share a song with us after the tournament."

"I could never resist such a request."

"Wonderful." The queen nodded. "We are delighted that you could join us for the Laelugus festival."

"King Marc wishes friendship with Iveriu. *I* wish it." Tristan peered at Branwen from the side of his eye. "Laelugus is the Festival of Peace. That is why he has sent me to win the Champions Tournament."

Branwen's chest grew tight. What if Tristan *did* win Essy? Could she watch her cousin marry the first man she'd ever kissed? She exhaled a shaky breath.

It shouldn't matter. She had kissed a shipwrecked poet. This was a prince of Kernyv. They were no longer Tantris and Emer. She had no claim on him.

Lord Diarmuid raised his chin and sneered at Tristan. "I wouldn't count your chickens before they're hatched."

Branwen disliked agreeing with the northern lord on anything— and twice in one evening beggared belief—but she said, "Yes, Prince Tristan. You will have to fight my uncle, Lord Morholt, in single combat. He's the King's Champion. And he's undefeated."

Tristan's smile brimmed with challenge. "As am I." He glared at Lord Diarmuid as he said it, and Branwen spied the Iverman's hand move toward the *kladiwos* blade at his hip.

So did the queen.

"Lady Branwen," she said to her niece, "won't you take Prince

Tristan onto the dance floor and provide him with some refreshment?" Queen Eseult touched Branwen's elbow and she sensed the urgency in her squeeze. This conflict needed to be diffused before it got out of hand.

"Of course, Lady Queen."

Branwen's own conflicted feelings at being assigned Tristan's chaperone swirled in her breast as she curtsied.

"That sounds like an excellent plan, Lady Queen," Tristan said, the muscle in his jaw relaxing. "Thank you for your generosity in sparing Lady Branwen from your company."

He bowed deeply. More than was strictly necessary for a foreign prince. He was purposefully honoring the queen by bending at the waist and showing deference. A traitorous part of Branwen's heart was pleased it might be for her benefit. Then Tristan added, "I'll see you on the field of combat, Lord Diarmuid."

"Looking forward to it, Prince Tristan."

Branwen traded another glance with the queen. The music swelled once more.

"Won't you follow me, Prince Tristan?" she said in a cloying tone.

Tristan offered her his arm. Branwen had no choice but to accept. She could no more disobey her queen than she could the Old Ones.

A raging fiddle could be heard over the drumming and the pounding of the dancers' feet as she led him toward the long tables where Treva had laid large vats of red ale. She spied Keane across the hall, prowling among the foreigners, his expression menacing. Branwen's lips lifted into a small crescent when she spotted Saoirse twirling beside Dubthach, her limp scarcely perceptible. Once Saoirse had recovered, Queen Eseult offered her a position in the castle infirmary because she had nowhere else to go, and she'd been happy to accept.

Branwen felt Tristan's eyes on her, and he was smiling because she was smiling. Instantly, she smoothed her features.

"It seems I'm to be your keeper," she grumbled into his ear. "Again."

"I have no objection to being kept by you." He pressed her closer, speaking in her native tongue, and Branwen's body sizzled just like on the day she'd found him lifeless on the raft.

"And I have no choice in the matter," she replied in Aquilan. She needed the distance of a foreign language.

Tristan halted in his tracks, stepping in front of her. "You would not choose it?" he said, switching back to Aquilan, the first crack in his confidence appearing. "I thought I had a friend in Iveriu."

"*Tantris* had a friend." She scoffed even as her pulse raced. "He led me to believe I'd saved a poet, not a pirate!"

"I *am* a poet. I'm *not* a pirate. But I'm also a prince."

As he gazed down at her, Branwen felt small and vulnerable. She couldn't allow it. She wouldn't. "Either way, you're a liar, *Prince Tristan*," she retorted. "Washed overboard my foot! Did the waves cut you from stem to stern?" And her honor was still tied to keeping him alive until he returned the favor. *Curse the Kernyveu!*

"I'm no liar. My ship *was* attacked by pirates like I told you. And I *was* thrown overboard in the skirmish." His breath tickled her hairline. "Although you lied to me, too, *just plain Emer*. And you speak more than a few words of Aquilan, it would seem." Tristan pressed his palm to his heart. "But I still carry your handiwork on me at all times—and I wouldn't have it any other way."

She inhaled sharply. "Why didn't you tell me who you really were?"

"For the same reason you didn't tell me."

"Not the same reason. I was afraid you might use me against King Óengus somehow. You're a *prince*, for Otherworld's sake!"

"I don't see what difference it makes."

"The difference between night and day. You knew the Kernyveu were looking for you. What did you think they would do to my people until you were found?"

Tristan's expression darkened. "I suspected, yes, that Marc might send a rescue party," he said, remorse staining his tone. "I should have left Iveriu sooner than I did, and I regret that but I . . . I—"

"You *what?*" Branwen demanded.

He lifted his gaze to hers. "I found a reason to stay."

His words hit her like a boulder. Her hand flew to her throat.

"Then you were incredibly selfish, my prince." Branwen willed away tears as a vision of Gráinne clutching her battered doll filled her mind. "There are many new orphans in Iveriu because you stayed. And if you stayed because of me—" She paused, fighting to keep her voice from breaking. "I'm equally to blame."

Could people really have died because Emer and Tantris had been falling in love? A love based on lies was no love at all. Branwen couldn't live with that. She just couldn't.

Tristan's brow pinched. "Branwen. Branwen, please—"

She whirled on her heel, drawing on all her strength to force down a sob. She would not embarrass the queen by losing her composure in front of all the foreign dignitaries. "Come," she said to Tristan, manner brusque. "Queen Eseult bade me to offer you refreshment." She couldn't believe she'd jeopardized her aunt's trust for this silver-tongued Kernyvak prince.

He followed her in silence.

The vats of frothed crimson ale on the buffet tables glowed in the candlelight, making her think of blood. It was disconcerting. Branwen didn't care for it herself, but legend held that red ale was the drink of kingship. King Óengus was honoring his guests by sharing it with them.

As Branwen glanced around the hall, she saw noblemen from Dyfed and Meonwara, and as far afield as the Frisii Lands. All of these men were here to win Essy's hand. More importantly, they were here to win an ally for their kingdom. Essy's male issue would be the legitimate heirs to the Ivernic throne and whoever won the Champions Tournament tomorrow would alter the course of history, bringing power and prestige to his land.

Tristan stood quietly by her side as Branwen sloshed ale from the vat into a bronze goblet. Somewhat violently, she offered it to him. A few drops splashed across both of their hands. The red starkly contrasted against her pale skin.

"Thank you." Tristan brushed the errant drops from her hand as he accepted the cup. She did her best to disguise a shiver. Bringing the goblet to his mouth, he remarked, "In Kernyv, Laelugus is the festival for handfasting."

Branwen gulped, darting her eyes away, and poured herself a cup of ale. Handfasting was the ceremony that began the engagement period before marriage. She didn't know what Tristan was driving at. Didn't want to know.

He watched her so closely as she took a drink that she nearly choked on the ale. Squinting, he said, "The symbol of Laiginztir."

She ran her fingers over the harp-shaped grooves in the cup. She'd used these goblets so many times that she didn't even notice the insignia anymore. Funny the things a stranger could see.

"You *are* from Laiginztir, then," Tristan said, sounding pleased, as if he'd solved a riddle. "See, I do know you a little."

"Hardly at all." She dismissed him by taking another sip. Everything they had shared—all of it was half-truths. Wisps of nothing. "Queen Eseult is from Laiginztir," she relented after a minute. "These were part of her dowry. The finest blacksmiths crafted these goblets for her wedding feast."

Tristan touched a finger to the harp emblazoned on his own cup. "You told me that Laiginztir was your mother's birthplace."

"My mother—Lady Alana of Castle Bodwa—was the queen's younger sister."

His lips pursed. "That makes Princess Eseult your cousin."

"My only cousin."

"Your uncle Morholt has no children?"

"Lord Morholt is a warrior, the King's Champion. He has no time for family life."

One corner of Tristan's mouth twitched and a sick feeling gripped Branwen. She'd known her uncle had slain his father, and yet she'd concealed the truth—she'd had to. She'd been protecting Iveriu. But . . .

All secrets came out eventually.

"As it is with King Marc," Tristan said with a sigh, not belaboring the issue. "That's why he needs me to win tomorrow."

"Of course. You're here to win yourself a princess."

"No." He lowered his lips to the tip of her ear. "I'm here for *you*."

"Then you've got the wrong cousin. I'm not a princess."

"You're right. You have the heart of a queen."

"Your charms are growing stale, Prince Tristan." She would *not* succumb to his flattery.

"I swear it, my lady. When I arrived back in Kernyv, there was news of this tournament. I knew you were highborn—even if I didn't know your real name—and I was hopeful you would be here. Destiny has not yet led me astray."

"Wait." Branwen shot him a glance that could have pierced any armor. "How did you know I was highborn?"

A canny grin. "Your clothes were too fine for a castle servant," he said. "Your hands too soft." Branwen swallowed at the memory of running them over his chest. "But, mostly, Lady Branwen, it was the hazelnuts," he said with a laugh.

"Hazelnuts?"

"In Kernyv, hazel trees are sacred and belong to the king. Cutting them or stealing their fruit exacts a stiff penalty. I presumed the same was true in Iveriu; therefore, you must be highborn."

She frowned. A clever deduction. It hadn't occurred to Branwen that a castle servant probably wouldn't have access to hazelnuts. Not wanting to admit he was right, she pointed out, "I could have been a thief."

"Your heart is far too noble for thievery," he said in earnest.

Noble or not, she disliked the way he pulled so easily on its strings.

"If you suspected I wasn't who I said I was, Prince Tristan, why didn't you say anything?"

He leaned in. "Because I knew everything that mattered."

"We're enemies." The proclamation escaped without permission, a threadbare sound. "Your father died at my uncle's hands. My parents, they . . ."

"I told you," Tristan said, his gaze penetrating, "I could never be your enemy, and I meant it."

His answer shouldn't taste like such sweet relief. He was a liar. A talented, beautiful liar.

Reaching under his collar, Tristan pulled something from beneath his tunic. A golden chain glittered in the low light. Dangling from one end, her own Rigani stone winked in the light.

Tapping the dazzling green, he said, "Sometimes fate needs a push."

Fear crashed over Branwen. She wrapped her hand around the pendant, concealing it. "Are you so eager to flaunt my betrayal?" she whispered. "Have my head on a pike! Announce to my family that I hid their enemy from them?"

Her words were underscored with anger, but beneath that anger lay hope. Hope that Tristan had really come back for her—Branwen—and not the Ivernic princess. For the first time, she understood her cousin's dilemma: how desperately Essy wanted to be loved for herself, and her bitterness that she would never truly know if she was.

Branwen realized that no amount of gold or jewels would make her trade places with the princess. She was deluged by sympathy and guilt over their quarrel. Instinctively, she scanned the room for her little cousin, whom she glimpsed at Lord Diarmuid's side. Keane stood a pace behind, wary.

Her eyes met the bodyguard's at the same moment as Tristan clasped his hand firmly over hers. "*Odai eti ama,*" he rasped in her ear. The touch of his skin on hers made her feel totally naked. The Rigani stone in her fist was cold and yet she swore it also burned.

Alarm registered on Keane's features.

"You've already used poetry to gain my trust," she told him. "It won't work a second time."

"Then what will?" He traced his pinkie along her knuckles and a tiny lightning bolt of exhilaration shot down her spine.

Before Branwen could answer, Tristan was wrenched away. A hand clamped on the Kernyvman's shoulder, jerking him backward. Keane loomed behind him, his demeanor hostile.

"Unhand the lady now," he ordered in a lethal tone despite fumbling with the Aquilan words.

Tristan reached for his sword. Branwen should have realized sooner why he'd seemed so comfortable with a blade that day on the beach, and with battle. She shook her head at him and he released his weapon—begrudgingly.

Keane pushed Tristan another step away from Branwen and came to stand between them. "Did the Kernyvman hurt you, my lady?" The anxiety in his voice was clear.

"No, not at all. Thank you, Sir Keane. And he's not a Kernyvman. He's a Kernyvak *prince*."

As royalty, Tristan had the right to demand blood or gold from King Óengus as recompense for being manhandled by one of the Royal Guard. Branwen needed to avoid a scene, and she also felt an urge to protect her countryman.

"I don't care what his title is," Keane spat.

She widened her eyes in warning. He was usually so unflappable. She'd never seen Keane lose his self-control quite like this.

"Sir Keane," Tristan spoke up. "I would never hurt Lady Branwen. I'm sorry if I caused any offense."

"Kernyvmen are good at causing offense."

"*Keane*," Branwen said, low.

Both men eyed her curiously. She shouldn't have addressed Keane without his title at a formal occasion. It implied either intimacy or disrespect. Branwen could tell Tristan was trying to figure out which she'd intended.

"Begging your pardon, Lady Branwen," Keane said as he sneered at Tristan, "but I would rather lie down with dogs than make peace with the Kernyveu. At least beasts have honor."

"*Enough!*" Branwen exclaimed. This time her voice was several octaves higher. Keeping Tristan safe from the pointed end of an Ivernic blade this evening was proving an almost insurmountable task.

Fury flared in Tristan's eyes, but it didn't twist his words. "Sir Keane, I hope to show you how honorable the Kernyveu can be in battle—and then I hope you might accept our friendship."

"That is a very gracious offer," Branwen began, directing another glare at Keane. "The High King of Iveriu and his court look forward to your display of prowess, Prince Tristan."

Keane snorted. Branwen could barely contain the urge to elbow him in the ribs. Challenging the honor of Kernyv, of its prince, could part a man from his head.

"I'm also formidable with a harp," said Tristan as he cast Branwen a knowing smile. Heat seared her cheeks.

Seeing Branwen and the Kernyvak prince exchange something that excluded him, a vein jumped above Keane's eyebrow. He turned toward her, showing his back to Tristan, and said, "Lady Branwen, I would ask you for a token so that I might wear your colors as I represent the Ivernic crown at the tournament."

Branwen's shoulders went rigid. Maybe he hadn't forgotten about the discarded Belotnia trinkets after all. Maybe he'd been more serious than she realized.

She clinched her hands together. To refuse his request could be construed as a rejection of the king. She deeply wished that the princess's lady's maid was also prohibited from showing favoritism at the Champions Tournament. Sadly, she wasn't.

Branwen decided that the best thing for everyone would be to agree. She couldn't risk Keane insulting Tristan even more this evening. It's what Queen Eseult would want. Besides, Branwen couldn't deny it might be thrilling to make Tristan jealous.

"It would be my honor, Sir Keane," she pronounced. With quick fingers, she picked apart one of her plaits and pulled loose an emerald-colored ribbon. Ceremonially, she placed it in Keane's open palm.

"May the Old Ones smile upon you and upon Iveriu," she said.

Keane's blue eyes ignited with victory as he tied the length of cloth to the hilt of his *kladíwos* blade. "One Iveriu forever."

"One Iveriu," Branwen echoed. After a moment, she said, "Sir Keane, would you see if the princess is quite well?"

His cheeks went a ruddy color. Keane was neglecting his official duties. He was sworn to protect Essy, not Branwen.

"Yes, certainly, my lady." He pivoted slowly and disappeared back into the crowd.

"That's some guard dog you have there," Tristan said with uncharacteristic acerbity.

"I believe it's the Hound who was the guard of Uladztir."

"I recognized his voice." Branwen crinkled her nose as Tristan elaborated, "Our last night together. The man who followed you to the cave—that was Sir Keane."

"What if it was?" Branwen looked him dead in the eyes. "You didn't ask for my colors."

"Let the Iverman have your ribbon. I already have your colors stitched into my heart." Tristan moved to touch her cheek but then stopped himself. Branwen held her breath. Not an hour ago she knew his—or Tantris's—colors were stitched into her own.

"And I intend to keep the promise I made to Emer," he said with determination. "I promised to bring peace between our peoples."

Their bodies swayed toward each other as if pulled by an invisible cord.

"Emer wanted peace with words," she countered. "Not steel."

Tristan brushed her wrist discreetly with his thumb. "First steel, then words."

"In that case, I'm sorry I'm not a princess."

Without hesitation, he declared, "I'm not."

"And why's that?"

"Because I'm here to win the Princess of Iveriu for King Marc."

An airy feeling spread through Branwen's body, followed by a jolt of indignation for Essy's fate. "Why are you winning the princess for your uncle?" she demanded to know. "You're a prince—shouldn't you be competing for yourself?"

"My heart is set on someone else," Tristan said, holding Branwen's gaze until she couldn't breathe. "But, more than that . . ." He sobered as he continued, "Marc is a young king, only twenty-seven. He was my mother's baby brother. His reign is still new. It's only been four years since he took the throne. The kingdom needs an heir for stability."

"Aren't you his heir?" Branwen asked.

A shadow skimmed his face. "If anything, I'm his biggest problem."

"I don't understand."

"When my mother married, she was gifted the territory of Liones, the southernmost tip of Kernyv. Liones is under the protection of Kernyv—and I have no desire to rule—but, technically, it's independent."

"Technically, it's independent," Branwen repeated. Realization hit like a tidal wave. "Meaning, technically, you're the *King* of Liones?"

"In a manner of speaking."

"In a manner of speaking? I don't think being king is a half measure."

"It's quite small, really. Liones would never survive without Kernyv," Tristan hastened to add. "It was more of a gesture—since my mother was the oldest but Kernyvak law prohibits a woman from inheriting the throne."

Today had been too full of the unexpected. Tantris was not only a poet or a prince but a king! If she'd let him die, two kingdoms would have waged war against Iveriu.

Eyes round, Branwen sputtered, "Is there anything else I don't know about you, *King* Tristan?"

"Don't call me that," he told her, voice tight, putting a finger to her lips. He seemed more afraid than when she'd told him the Royal Guard was trooping.

Her mind raced with political calculations. She removed his hand.

"King Marc sees you as a threat," Branwen discerned.

"Not Marc." Tristan shook his head. "We were raised as brothers. I pledged my fealty to him at sixteen, upon his coronation, and became his Champion. I'm happy for Kernyv to administer Liones. Governing doesn't interest me."

"But until King Marc has a child, you *are* next in line to the throne of Kernyv, as well as your own in Liones."

"I would *never* betray Marc." His nostrils flared. "Marc knows that. And yet, there are those who don't trust my intentions, who don't trust my . . . mixed lineage." Sadness shaded his last statement. "I will win Princess Eseult for Marc, and put to bed any question of my loyalty."

Branwen had always viewed Kernyv as a singular enemy of Iveriu; she hadn't stopped to think that the kingdom must have its own internal conflicts. As understanding dawned, she said, "You need to win tomorrow to ensure peace for the people of Liones as well."

"Yes." He nodded, face grave. "Like Emer wanted." So much was riding on Essy's marriage—more than just peace for Iveriu.

Another thought crossed Branwen's mind and she went eerily still. "If I were the princess, would you still hand me over to your uncle?"

Doubt clouded Tristan's eyes. "Marc is a good man. Far more honorable than some of the other so-called noblemen competing in the tournament."

The affection with which he spoke of King Marc inspired hope in Branwen that he might make a good husband, but all she could think was that her little cousin might be forced to marry one of those other so-called noblemen. Essy would be sacrificing her happiness for the good of Iveriu; Branwen feared her cousin wasn't strong enough for the burden. She wished there was a way to ensure her cousin's future would be full of joy.

Tristan misinterpreted her silence. "Lady Branwen, I swear to you, it would pain me beyond reason to win you for someone else. But to keep you safe, I would do it. Even if that meant being tormented by your presence every day and never being able to show you my heart."

He curled his pinkie around the sleeve of her gown, and Branwen was overwhelmed by need—both hers and his.

"I'm glad that's not the case, however, my lady," Tristan said in a deep voice.

"And if it were the case?"

He leveled her with his gaze; her limbs became entirely weightless.

"Peace above all," he said.

THE RIGHT FIGHT

THE LOVERS REACHED OUT TO Branwen in her dreams. They were shadows of fire. Liquefying flames that engulfed her. She was at the very center, and she knew she was the one who had started it.

Branwen woke up gasping for air.

Her night-shade locks were wet, matted against her forehead. She clutched the sheet to her chest and found that it was drenched. Even her skin was hot, florid.

What were the Old Ones trying to tell her? The last dream as vivid had warned Branwen to get Tristan to safety. She'd always been so certain that the lovers in her dreams were her parents, but they were long dead. She couldn't help them.

Wiping the sweat from her brow, Branwen slipped out of bed. The stone floor was cool and refreshing against the soles of her feet. Morning sun streamed through the window of the turret, golden and reassuring.

Was Tristan awake yet? Preparing for the Champions Tournament?

She still couldn't believe that he'd survived, that he was alive, and that he had returned to Iveriu. That he was *here* at Castle Rigani. Branwen had daydreamed about it a thousand times, but when it happened it wasn't at all like she'd imagined it.

As a rule, Branwen didn't believe in second chances. Her heart wasn't nearly robust enough. Still, the briefest touch of his hand was thrilling—that was as sure as breathing. Yet she also couldn't ignore the reality that Tristan was a prince and a ruler with many reasons for returning to Iveriu. Being starry-eyed would gain her nothing. Despite his claims to the contrary, Tristan might one day want a princess for himself.

Fireflies buzzed in Branwen's chest as she performed her morning rituals, mentally preparing herself to face Essy and ready the princess for the tournament.

She couldn't remember an explosion of this magnitude between them even as children. Both cousins had said things that couldn't be unsaid. Picturing Lord Diarmuid's smug expression as she gave him the handkerchief, Branwen wanted to punch a wall. Or, maybe his nose. At the same time, the way the foreign fighters eyed Essy—not as a person but merely a prize—made Branwen want to punch another wall. Or, maybe *all* of their noses.

A knock came at her bedchamber door. Her heart skittered. For a moment, Branwen hoped it might be Tristan. She clucked her tongue. He would never be allowed into the south tower—nor should she want him to be. It was probably Keane.

Opening the door, Branwen's lips parted in surprise. It was neither.

"Morning, Branny." A contrite smile spread across her cousin's face. She couldn't recall a single occasion when the princess had roused and dressed herself before Branwen yanked her out of bed.

Branwen curtsied, a splinter of anger still chafing inside. "Good morning, Your Highness." She never curtsied for Essy.

"Oh, Branny. *Don't.*" The princess held out a bouquet of honeysuckles and other wildflowers.

Only then did Branwen notice Essy's eyes were watery. Her sloppily braided hair was missing its usual luster. She looked like she hadn't slept. "I picked them for you," she said.

Branwen tried to hold herself firm even as her heart melted.

"Branny, I'm terrified." Her voice cracked. She scratched her head. "I'm *terrified* about who will win today." And Branwen couldn't blame her—even Tristan viewed the princess as the solution to a political problem. Bottom lip quivering, Essy said, "*Please*, Branny." She pressed the bouquet into Branwen's hands. "Please, let's just forget what happened yesterday. I *need* you."

Branwen accepted the bouquet. She raised it to her nose, dew tickling the tip, and inhaled the sweet scent of honeysuckle. The aroma was forever linked with her cousin. She took another deep breath. Perhaps she feared giving Tristan a second chance because Essy took up so many—but Branwen couldn't deny her another one. Not today.

"They're lovely, Essy," she said. "Thank you."

The princess gave her a wobbly smile. Branwen opened her arms and her cousin dove into her embrace. She stroked Essy's lopsided plaits as the princess cried into the crook of her neck.

"Hush," said Branwen. "I'll be right by your side."

"Promise?" Essy lifted her gaze, searching her cousin's face.

"You're the only person in the whole world I can really trust. Promise me you won't go anywhere."

Tears pricked her own eyes.

"Never."

It would be easier to tear out her own heart.

✠ ✠ ✠

Royal tents dotted the clearing that had been converted into a temporary battleground. Vats of red ale for the competitors lined either side of the pitch. Cheers and claps, jeers and hisses, echoed in the balmy afternoon.

Branwen perched on the edge of her seat beside Essy in the Queen's Tent. Directly opposite, on the other side of the field, lay the King's Tent, where her uncle Morholt waited for the final combat. As the King's Champion, Morholt would duel with the last man standing among the suitors. Whoever was to marry Essy would have to beat their uncle first, and he was a terrifying foe.

"It's a little exciting, isn't it?" Essy whispered, tugging on Branwen's sleeve, as the first contest got underway. The eight men who were victorious in this round would be paired off for single combat and fight one another until only one victor remained.

Branwen forced a tepid smile for her cousin, thinking Lord Diarmuid stood very little chance. The princess had regained her self-possession before the tournament thanks in part to the calming water mint tea that Branwen had served with breakfast. Branwen had also dabbed a soothing ointment of juniper berries on the red blotches dotting Essy's scalp, arranging her plaits to conceal them.

She spotted King Óengus, flanked by guardsmen, walking deliberately along the length pitch. He shook the hand of each contestant before returning to the King's Tent to join Lord Morholt and other Ivernic noblemen.

As Branwen watched the competitors warm up, she recalled her one fond memory of her uncle. She'd been maybe eight years old and Dubthach was chasing her through the castle, pulling her hair after one of Essy's pranks. He didn't dare to take his revenge against the princess.

Morholt caught Dubthach by the scruff of his neck, boxed him once about the ears, and the boy promptly peed himself, much to Branwen's delight.

"Thank you, Uncle," she'd said in a small voice as Dubthach ran off.

"Don't thank me," Morholt had replied. "Defending Iveriu is my duty and my honor—and that means you. But I won't always be here to defend you against your enemies." Then he'd crouched down to meet her eye, adding, "When your enemy has you cornered, fight until you can't."

The next day a wooden practice sword was delivered to Branwen's chamber. It was the only present her uncle had ever given her.

Now she darted a glance at the King's Tent. She hadn't thought of the sword for years.

Essy inhaled as Queen Eseult dropped her handkerchief to signal the charge to the fighters. Anyone who struck his opponent before the cloth reached the dirt would be immediately disqualified.

This tournament was, above all, a test of honor. Rule breakers would not be tolerated. By tradition, it was always the queen rather than the king who arbitrated the contest. The queen represented the Land—the Goddess Ériu herself—and therefore, only she was sovereign over the men competing to be her new king. She was the kingmaker: The goddess of the Land would choose a new Champion through feats of honor and bravery. It had always been thus.

Branwen held her breath as the finely embroidered silk was enveloped in a small plume of dirt. A moment later came the first ferocious clashes of steel, like the baying of feral animals. Fear clawed at the back of her mind.

Where was Tristan?

Essy grabbed Branwen's hand, locking their knuckles tight. "Do you see him?"

She turned to her cousin with alarm. Did Essy know whom Branwen was so desperately seeking with her eyes?

"Diarmuid," the princess said under her breath. "Do you see Lord Diarmuid?"

Oh. Branwen's shoulders relaxed. "Not yet."

"You thought I meant Keane," Essy said, an impish grin alighting upon her face. "I saw him this morning." She leaned into Branwen. "He was bearing your token."

Branwen blushed. "He asked for it."

"And you didn't say no." Essy laughed. "I should have guessed it was Keane," she mused. "I knew you had *someone* special in mind, Branny. You're always so secretive."

"Keane is just a friend. Honestly."

Essy arched an eyebrow at her cousin. "Whatever you say." The queen had gone very still, clearly following their conversation. Essy turned toward her mother and said, "Well, at least Branwen gets to *choose* a husband."

Queen Eseult extended a hand toward Essy, concern stippling her brow.

"The Old Ones are choosing your husband," she told her daughter. "They will choose wisely, I swear."

Essy pulled back from her mother's reach with a "*Pffft*," and the queen returned her gaze to the field of play. The clearing was awash with brilliant colors and the winking of sunlight on steel as swords bit into armor.

The foreign champions could be identified by the color of the tunics they wore and the beasts on the standards they bore. They fought together in a terrifying mass of men before the individual combat commenced. No mortal wounds were permitted but everything else was fair game. The din of fighting swarmed around them, quickening Branwen's pulse.

She still couldn't spot Tristan.

Part of her hoped he wouldn't compete; she didn't want him to get hurt—and not solely because her honor was tied to his well-being. Given what she knew of him, however, he wasn't one to run from a challenge. Tristan might be a poet, but he was also a warrior.

A sudden roar rose above the other cries. Several men toppled to the ground. Branwen recognized the Duke of the Frisii Lands and the Prince of South Jótland among them. A shield bearing three blue lions and nine red hearts splintered and fell into the dust. The fighters spilled from the center of the field like ants marching, smaller skirmishes erupting on every inch of soil.

In the very middle of the pitch, Branwen at last spied Tristan. His dark curls glistened with sweat against his bronze skin. From this distance, she couldn't see his eyes but she could *feel* how intense they were. She half wished she couldn't; still, she heaved a sigh of relief.

It was short lived. Tristan appeared to be fighting six men single-handedly.

Branwen spotted Havelin, the eldest son of King Faramon of Armorica. Its coastline was equally beset by Kernyvak pirates. If Essy were to marry Crown Prince Havelin, Iveriu and Armorica could form a strong maritime alliance against Kernyv.

She glanced at her cousin, who watched the fight avidly, wondering if the princess was thinking along similar lines. And then Branwen caught herself. She realized she was regarding Essy as a pawn to be moved in a great game—exactly as King Óengus did, as all the competitors did. She felt a stab in her heart that Essy's family was trading her happiness for peace.

Branwen could no longer maintain any illusions about what they were doing. What *she* was doing. She gave her cousin's hand a squeeze. "Prince Havelin is fighting bravely," she said. "I hear he has a sister a year or so younger than you. Also named Eseult. Maybe you'll be friends."

"He has an enormous nose," Essy complained. "And it's *crooked*."

Indeed, it looked as if the Armorican prince had broken his nose as a child and it had set very badly. Queen Eseult cast Branwen a sidelong glance, followed by a bland smile.

Essy pulled a half-embroidered piece of cloth from a basket at her feet. She had been working diligently, if somewhat ineptly, on the trim for the doll's dress she'd promised Gráinne. The stitches were all skewed; Branwen would pull them with her hook and rework them later. But it warmed her to see her cousin trying so hard to please the orphan girl. Branwen only wished Essy would stick to sewing dolls' dresses rather than clandestine handkerchiefs.

A thunderclap reverberated through the tent. Prince Havelin collapsed to the ground, his spear broken in half. Defeated. Once disarmed, the combatants had to exit the competition.

Essy's gaze flew up from her stitching and she let out a victorious harrumph. Havelin and Armorica were now out of the running. Branwen scoured the throng once more for Tristan.

Instead, her eyes snagged on Keane. His green tunic was splashed with what looked like elderberry juice. Only she knew it wasn't juice; it was blood.

He lifted his *silomleie*, a blackthorn wood cudgel, in defense against a duke from the kingdom of Logres on the east coast of Albion. The *silomleie* was a weapon favored by members of the Royal Guard because the blackthorn was said to be native to the Otherworld.

"Ooh! There he is, Branny," Essy said, pointing at Keane with her needle.

The queen followed her daughter's sight line. She squinted and then said, "What a lovely ribbon Sir Keane has tied to his *silomleie*."

That was the extent of Queen Eseult's commentary. Branwen's nerves zinged. Did her aunt think she wished to be matched with Keane?

He wouldn't be a bad match. He just wasn't the match she wanted.

Emer and Tantris existed out of time, beyond the stars. Tantris was her heart's desire—but he was a fantasy. Branwen and Tristan belonged to the world as it was.

Could she ever learn to trust Tristan, Prince of Kernyv and King of Liones? With all of the duties he had to his king and his kingdom?

The question would be moot if Iveriu and Kernyv remained at war.

Branwen tapped the brooch fastening the emerald sash at her

shoulder. Her forefinger pricked on the silver thistle-like needle that secured the cloth through the round, enameled clasp. The brooch had belonged to her mother. Lady Alana was wearing it the day she died.

Branwen's last memory of her mother after refusing to say goodbye was of candlelight glinting off silver. Queen Eseult had the heirloom returned to Branwen, although she'd refused to let her see the body. *Remember Alana smiling*, she'd said.

On the underside of the brooch was engraved the motto of Castle Bodwa: *The right fight.*

Branwen traced the ridges of the language of trees that her ancestors had used and hoped they were guiding her hand. Maybe from the Otherworld. Queen Eseult reached out to steady her niece's fingers.

"Don't forget to breathe, Branny." She laughed kindly.

At that moment, a fast-moving blur of purple and red charged Keane from behind. Branwen recognized the Parthalán crest. It was Lord Diarmuid. He assaulted his fellow Iverman with all his might.

Essy let out a gasp, casting her needlework aside to clap her hands. The queen lifted her eyebrows. Thankfully, the northern lord wasn't so imprudent as to display the princess's token outwardly. As she glanced at her aunt, Branwen felt another twinge of guilt for delivering it.

She had been complicit in compromising the honor of Iveriu last night. Essy had given her an order, but Branwen had followed it. That choice had been hers. Had she chosen wisely?

The trumpet sounded. The crowd fell silent. There were eight men left.

With a jolt of panic, Branwen scanned the field.

Queen Eseult dropped another handkerchief.

Tristan, Keane, and Lord Diarmuid were advancing to the next round.

Iveriu was one step closer to an allegiance with Kernyv. Tristan was on the verge of turning Iveriu's greatest enemies into friends. Deep inside, Branwen knew what the Old Ones were telling her to do—to *choose*: the right fight.

BLACKBIRDS

RED ALE WAS SERVED ALL around. The royal minstrels played heartily as the servants readied the tournament pitch for the first bout of single combat. Branwen's entire body thrummed with anticipation as she watched Tristan take a few practice sweeps with his broadsword.

The lots were cast for the opening match. The champion from the Kingdom of Míl, the peninsula from which the ancestors of the Iverni were storied to have emigrated, would face off against one of the princes of Langazbardaz. There were so many duchies on the southern continent that it was hard to keep track of them, and the boundaries were constantly changing. The Aquilan Empire had fragmented beyond repair: Its ruling class now tussled with each other for scraps.

The fighters presented themselves before King Óengus, and then Queen Eseult. As the combat began, Branwen was distracted by what sounded like the musical call of a blackbird. It echoed from the back of the Queen's Tent. She whipped her head around. So did Essy.

A hand beckoned. Branwen glimpsed Tristan on the edge of the pitch, still shadow-dueling with the breeze. Next to him stood Lord Diarmuid. Who was it, then? She and Essy shared a glance.

"Go on," whispered the princess, giving Branwen a nudge with her shoulder. "Wish our Sir Keane good luck. But not too much. I shouldn't like to be married to my cousin's lover."

Branwen flushed scarlet. "Keane isn't my *lover*."

The hand waved again. Another trill of the blackbird.

"Maybe not, dear Branny." Essy shrugged. "But he *is* keen on you." The princess gave Branwen a playful shove toward the back of the tent. Branwen sighed. She needed to see what Keane wanted.

According to the tournament rules, competitors shouldn't interact with the princess or her retinue until the end. But, Branwen supposed, Keane's fellow members of the Royal Guard had let him slip through. With extreme reluctance, she dragged her eyes away from the Kernyvak prince.

Swords clanked in the background. She slid stealthily through an opening between the tent flaps. Keane shot Branwen a quivery smile as he caught sight of her. He fingered the ribbon that dangled from his *silomleie*.

"Lady Branwen." He tipped his head. The afternoon light shaded his profile just right, enhancing his finely whittled cheekbones.

"Sir Keane."

The corners of his mouth flattened. "You don't normally call me *Sir* Keane."

"No." She swallowed. "I suppose I don't."

He stepped closer. Branwen spied bits of flesh speckled with blood across his tunic.

"I didn't know you were so fond of blackbirds," she said.

"The blackbird's song is believed to transport you to the Otherworld—it reminds me of you."

She gave him a measuring look. "Is that so?"

"*Branwen*," he said, running the tip of his tongue over his dry lips. He'd never been so familiar, or so bold. "I know you're angry with me."

"You do?"

"And I know why you're angry."

She arched a dubious eyebrow. "Do you?"

"Yes. That's why I came to find you." Their eyes met. Whereas Tristan's twinkled like the night sky, Keane's were as blue as the deepest part of the sea. "I'm not competing for Princess Eseult." He raised Branwen's ribbon to his lips and kissed it as if the sliver were beyond priceless. Goose bumps prickled her body—but it wasn't Keane's lips she was picturing.

"I'm only competing because King Óengus asked me to thin the herd," he continued. "Make sure only the most worthy champions advanced from the charge."

Branwen sucked in a breath. "King Óengus is fixing the Champions Tournament?"

"Certainly not!" Keane rankled at the suggestion. "It's simply a precaution. This is still a test of honor."

"I would never question King Óengus's honor," she assured him. "Nor yours."

In truth, she thought it was a clever gambit. King Óengus needed to guarantee that he formed the most beneficial alliance through

Essy's marriage. What better way to do so than to dispose of the less interesting prospects with his own men?

"And what if you win?" she challenged.

Keane's eyes darted around them, checking to see if they were being overheard. "I won't win."

"You might."

He shook his head. "I'm no match for Lord Morholt."

Branwen wasn't sure if any of the champions were a match for her uncle. Could it be that Morholt had instructions to lose to the right winner?

"And this is what you wanted to tell me?" she puzzled aloud.

He brushed the edge of the ribbon against the back of her hand. It tickled.

"I wanted you to know. Before my bout."

She was uncertain how to respond to what he was implying. Her life would be so much simpler if she could fall in love with the Iverman.

"Thank you for telling me," Branwen said.

His lips thinned. "You're still angry."

"No." She shook her head once. "No, of course not. You could never deny your king."

"Good. I'm glad you understand. I know that's the only reason you were so gracious to that deceitful Kernyvman."

"Tristan isn't deceitful!" Branwen protested, her response reflexive. "His desire . . . for an alliance is sincere." Of that, she was convinced.

"Tristan?" Keane made the name a curse.

"*Prince* Tristan," she stammered. She'd forgotten herself.

He took her hand in his and wrapped the ribbon around them

without asking. "Pardon me," he said in a much lower voice. "I don't like seeing another man's hand in yours."

"You don't have a say in the matter."

Keane stroked the pad of his thumb along the ribbon. "But I'd like to have a say."

A trumpet blared, and Branwen jumped. Their hands fell apart.

"Queen Eseult will be missing me," she said. "And you should prepare for your combat. May the luck of Iveriu be upon you."

Preempting anything else he might say, Branwen dashed inside the tent, head swimming. It had been wrong to use Keane's interest to needle Tristan last night. Unlike Essy, she had never yearned to have men compete for her heart.

The princess lifted her eyebrows expectantly at her cousin when she returned. "How was your tryst?" she whispered behind her hand.

"It wasn't a *tryst*."

Essy didn't look convinced. "If you insist."

"I *do*." After the tournament, perhaps, she would need to insist to Keane as well.

The trumpet sounded again. Branwen was saved from further prying by her cousin as Lord Diarmuid took to the field. He was paired with a warrior from Reykir Island, to the north, which lay in the middle of the Winter Sea, at the edge of the Dark Waters.

Like the inhabitants of the Skáney Lands, Reykir Islanders worshipped a one-eyed god adorned with ravens. They drove their ships farther and farther south each year. This Reykir Islander was as tower-tall as he was stout. His hair was long and the color of rushing water. He seemed not quite of this world at all.

Queen Eseult's eyes darted from the champions awaiting her signal to her daughter. Essy was visibly perturbed as she took in the sight of the Reykir Islander.

"He's going to *kill* Diarmuid, Branny." The princess shot her a look that could only be interpreted as despair.

"*Shh*. He'll be fine." In truth, Branwen thought Lord Diarmuid would need the favor of Goddess Ériu herself to defeat such a giant.

The queen gave Essy a pained smile and dropped her handkerchief.

"Shall I refill your glass?" Branwen asked her aunt. Their nerves were growing frayed, and her cousin's most of all. She could see the princess barely resisting the urge to pick her scabs, fiddling anxiously with her embroidery.

"Thank you, dear heart."

"Mine, too," said Essy, crossing her arms over her chest and sinking back against plush goose-feather cushions. Branwen traded glances with the queen; the queen nodded.

She rose swiftly and busied herself with refilling their goblets from the decanter on the makeshift side table. *Who would Tristan fight?* she wondered. The Mílesian champion had defeated the Langazbardaz prince easily, leaving the Prince of Rheged, or the King of Ordowik, which bordered Kernyv.

And, of course, Keane.

"Branny!" Essy exclaimed. "Branny, he's won!" A series of squeals and delighted giggles escaped from the princess as a cheer erupted from the crowd.

Branwen was astonished. She couldn't fathom why the Otherworld would be on the side of the arrogant northern lord; at least it meant she wouldn't be shipped off with Essy to a land blanketed in darkness half the year.

Returning with the goblets, she served Queen Eseult first. Her aunt didn't even acknowledge her. The queen's eyes were fixed on the King's Tent, a grimace etched on her face. In that moment, Branwen understood that the King and Queen of Iveriu would never let their daughter marry Lord Diarmuid.

"I told you my token would bring him luck, cousin," Essy whispered gleefully, pulling Branwen close. Her expression of pure joy cut Branwen to the bone.

The next champions took their places and she felt as if the blackbirds had enchanted her, stealing her voice, as her countrymen believed they could.

It was Tristan. He had been paired with the King of Ordowik. The Ordowikan people hated the Kernyveu as much as the Iverni did. Maybe more. Not only Tristan, Branwen realized, but King Marc needed this alliance as much as Iveriu.

Tristan bowed before Queen Eseult and lifted the Rigani stone from around his neck. His eyes fastened on Branwen as he kissed the stone. She shivered.

The queen dropped the handkerchief.

Tristan struck first, wielding his broadsword with breathtaking grace. Certainly, he took Branwen's breath away.

Essy gulped her ale, still glowing from Diarmuid's victory. "The Kernyvman has a pleasing face," she remarked.

Yes, a very pleasing face, thought Branwen. *Unfortunately.* She could tell the queen was waiting for her reaction. She gave none.

Tristan moved with fluid motions, like the sea itself. It was almost impossible for her eyes to keep up with him. He seemed to be everywhere at once.

A duck, a somersault, a whooping war cry and it was over.

Queen Eseult signaled the end of the bout. The Ordowikan king looked genuinely stupefied, as if he couldn't quite understand what had just happened.

Both men bowed. Again, Tristan grabbed Branwen's gaze.

"The Kernyvman fights well," her aunt said flatly, betraying no emotion.

"And fiercely," Branwen added in a hush.

Keane shouldered past Tristan as he walked onto the battlefield with a force that would certainly leave a bruise. He crossed his double-headed ax and his *sílomleíe* in the air, the summer sun bringing out the green of Branwen's ribbon.

Essy gave Branwen's hand an encouraging squeeze. "May luck be upon Sir Keane," she said.

Keane's opponent, the Prince of Rheged, rattled his own weapon with a flourish three times.

"May luck be upon him," Branwen echoed as they began to clash. She didn't mean it. She prayed to the Old Ones that Keane wouldn't meet Tristan in battle.

The Otherworld wasn't listening.

Keane won his first round and bested the Mílesian champion in his second. Only two other contestants now remained, and Keane would fight whoever won the next match: Lord Diarmuid—or Tristan. The pounding in Branwen's ears grew louder than a blacksmith's hammer.

She feared for Tristan if he beat Lord Diarmuid. She feared for Iveriu if he lost.

With all of the defeated foreign champions milling around the throng, Branwen saw how acutely Iveriu needed an ally from across the sea. Iveriu was a proud island, a proud kingdom—but she was small. If she remained isolated, she would fall. If not to the Kernyveu, then to the Reykir Islanders or someone else.

Queen Eseult looked increasingly uneasy as the bout commenced. Essy slipped her hand beneath her braids. Branwen snatched it loose.

"Tell me when it's over," she pleaded. The princess wrapped her hand around Branwen's until her knuckles bulged and she closed her eyes.

The sun disappeared behind a cloud, gray light raining down on the fighters. Lord Diarmuid substituted his *kladíwos* blade with a broader *fálkr*, designed for hacking blows. As the tip whistled past Tristan's ear, Branwen's stomach leapt into her throat. It only missed his handsome visage by the slimmest margin. Diarmuid's next sweep was too wide and the Kernyvak prince saw his opening.

Tristan hooked Diarmuid's ankle and the northern lord fell toward the earth, losing his grasp on the *fálkr*. A tiny smile ripened on Branwen's lips. Tristan had once performed that exact same maneuver on her. Too readily she recalled his body pressed against hers, the feel of his weight.

Hisses punctuated the general rumbling of the crowd.

"Is it over?" Essy asked.

"It's over."

The princess peeked up timidly. Tristan had his boot on Lord Diarmuid's throat and the tip of his sword thrust against his chest.

Tears bubbled in Essy's eyes. Her body trembled.

"It's over," Branwen repeated.

THE CHALICE OF SOVEREIGNTY

THE PRINCESS STRUGGLED FOR A shallow breath as Lord Diarmuid bowed before the queen, accepting his defeat. Essy's hand shook in Branwen's.

"Lord Diarmuid brought honor to the Parthalán name today," Queen Eseult said to her daughter. She patted her knee in a conciliatory gesture.

"You don't care if I'm ever loved, Mother," Essy spat, tears leaking from her eyes. "Don't—don't pretend that you do." Her teeth began to chatter and she swiped snot against her sleeve. "All you care about is being queen!"

"Essy, dear heart," her mother said gently. "That's not true."

The trumpets blasted again. Keane and Tristan stepped onto the pitch. Branwen was torn between comforting her cousin and watching the bout. The Iverman and the Kernyvman were fighting for honor and glory, yet she had stoked their ire. The sensation was exhilarating, almost addictive. Definitely ill advised.

Essy clutched at her chest with one hand, her breaths coming faster and faster, as she gripped the edge of her seat with the other. Branwen's focus returned to the princess, concern mounting. Queen Eseult touched her daughter's cheek.

"You will be a queen, too, Essy, and when you are, you will understand. You will thank me," she said.

The princess batted her hand away. "I will never thank you, *Lady Queen*"—Essy rasped a breath, her speech becoming more clipped—"for taking away my chance—my *one* chance at love!"

"Don't be so dramatic," said the queen, tone weary.

Branwen rubbed her cousin's back as Essy's shoulders began to heave. She didn't think the princess was just being dramatic. Her eyes were unfocused, and Branwen could see genuine panic glistening in her tears. Why couldn't her aunt?

Another braying of horns jolted the princess. "Duty calls," Essy hissed at the queen. Branwen had rarely heard such venom in her cousin's voice.

"Yes," agreed Queen Eseult. "Yours and mine." She dropped a handkerchief. Essy pulled at her bodice as if it were smothering her.

The moment the cloth landed in the dirt, Keane and Tristan circled one another like wolves hunting the same prey.

"*Your* duty, Lady Queen. Not mine." Essy leapt to her feet. Her face was red and splotchy, and she seemed unsteady.

In her peripheral vision, Branwen spied Keane wheel around, his double-headed ax a terrifying scythe. Tristan jumped deftly over the sweep of the blade. How could she ever have believed he was a poet rather than a warrior?

"Sit back down before you make a spectacle of yourself, *Lady Princess*," seethed Queen Eseult. Nobody but her daughter could so rile the monarch. Branwen was glad neither her cousin nor her aunt was armed.

"You—you only care about what other people think—" Essy tottered. Branwen sprang up to brace her.

Queen Eseult's eyebrows lifted, appalled. "And you're *drunk!*" she accused, but Branwen didn't think Essy was drunk. She'd carefully monitored the ale today.

This was a different kind of inebriation. Sometimes her cousin was the most fearless person she knew; other times, fear conquered her completely.

"You are not my mother!" the princess shouted as she ran from the tent. For a moment, Queen Eseult looked indescribably bereft. Then her face turned to stone.

More than anything in the world, Branwen wanted to stay and watch as the two men fought over her future, but her cousin needed her. She curtsied to the queen and sprinted after Essy.

Edging her way through the crowd, Branwen tried to remain discreet. It wouldn't do for the Ivernic princess to be seen shirking her duty—even if that wasn't quite the truth. King Óengus needed to display his strength before the foreign emissaries. If he didn't appear to be able to control his own daughter, they might presume he couldn't control his kingdom, and that would be very dangerous for all of them. There were no shades of gray in war. A weak king never remained king for long.

The spectators jostled Branwen as she continued toward the battlefield. Keeping one eye on the pitch, she scoured the throng for Essy's blond head. When they were children, her cousin would flee to the hazel tree whenever she was upset. Today, Branwen was fairly certain she'd fled to Lord Diarmuid's side.

These attacks had plagued her cousin for as long as she could remember. Sometimes the cause was obvious; sometimes not. Thankfully, the episodes didn't last long. In the midst of them, however, Essy said it felt like forever, as if she were being crushed inside Treva's great winepress. Branwen was usually the one to soothe her cousin, but she was still surprised, and a little disappointed, that the queen hadn't recognized the signs. Perhaps the pressures of her own duties were affecting her aunt more than she let on.

All at once, the audience put their hands together in what seemed like a stampede of cattle. Branwen's eyes dashed to see the source of the commotion. Then she wished she hadn't.

Dawn-red blood trickled from Tristan's temple. Keane had clipped him with the butt of his *silomleie*. Tristan stumbled. His sword fell uselessly into the dirt.

Keane lunged.

Then Tristan did something unexpected. He dropped to the ground, tucked his knees into his chest, and rolled to his left. Keane lunged again. Tristan rolled in the other direction. Branwen forced her gaze to the Iverman, who vibrated with rage.

She pushed her way forward. The compulsion to protect Tristan was almost overpowering. *Stop.* She was supposed to be looking for Essy. The next moment, Tristan bashed Keane's forearm with his shield, and the gallowglass tumbled to the earth. Branwen stood frozen in her tracks.

The shouts of the crowd swelled until they became a deafening hum.

Keane stared at Tristan in wonder before his eyes tripped over Branwen. She was now only a few horse strides away, covering her mouth. Tristan followed Keane's gaze and when he found Branwen, his expression softened. Keane noticed it, too.

The Iverman canted his head at her. He smiled as he drew a small dagger from his waistband. Branwen tried to call out a warning but no sound came out. Burning waves crashed in her mind.

Fingers interlocked with hers. *Essy's.* Her cousin's breath was still a wheeze, but the cadence had slowed. She gave Branwen's hand a little pulse.

Branwen could barely squeeze back. She saw the true beginning of her life in Tristan's eyes—as well as its end. The unmistakable shriek of steel tearing flesh howled in her ears.

She blinked. Only for a moment.

A moment was all it took for the world to change.

Tristan pivoted on his heel, took hold of Keane's wrist, and turned the blade back on him. "Look away," Essy murmured in Branwen's ear as Tristan stabbed the Iverman in the thigh.

Blood flowed from the wound. The *silomleie* fell from Keane's other hand. Tristan grabbed it and raised the weapon above his head with a cry of victory. Keane clutched his wounded thigh.

Queen Eseult dropped the handkerchief. Tristan had won. Kernyv had won.

"It seems both our sweethearts are losers today, Branny," the princess said sullenly. "I couldn't find Diarmuid anywhere."

Branwen swallowed hard. Tristan raised the Rigani stone once more to his lips. His eyes sought her out in the crowd.

Maybe she really was his Emer?

Glancing in the direction of the Queen's Tent, Branwen said, "We need to get back," tugging on her cousin's hand. The princess refused to budge.

"No. I'm sick of taking orders from *her.*"

"Then do it as a favor—for me," she entreated.

After another glimmer of hesitation, the princess took a step toward the tent and linked her arm with Branwen's. "I didn't mean for you to miss Sir Keane's match," she said. Yet Branwen had seen enough. Essy blew out a breath and it seemed easier than the last.

Pushing one of her cousin's plaits behind her ear, Branwen told her, "I'm sorry you were so upset." Essy's angry words the night before were simply the flip side of a terror she couldn't control; Branwen would do her best to forget them.

"At least that Kernyvman won't relish his victory for long," said Essy, trying to lift her spirits.

"What do you mean?"

"Uncle Morholt—he'll make quick work of King Marc's nephew." The princess laughed a little cruelly.

Morholt. For one blissful moment, Branwen had forgotten. Tristan would face her uncle in the Final Combat.

There were only two ways it could end: death or dishonor. Morholt would never concede defeat. Either Tristan would kill her uncle, or he would be killed. His choice was to slay the man who felled his father or be slain by him.

Was this what the Old Ones had foreseen when they'd bade Branwen to save him?

There was no answer. She expected none.

She closed her eyes and listened to the blackbirds sing.

✠ ✠ ✠

Tension strangled Castle Rigani like a noose. Essy had returned with Branwen to the Queen's Tent without further complaint. While her aunt's back was turned, Branwen took a rather unladylike gulp of ale.

Queen Eseult stood to address those assembled, noble and commoner alike. The outcome of this last battle would affect them all. The result of the Final Combat would change what was written in the annals of history.

Her aunt's self-possession was more than mortal. It might have been only the harsh late-summer sun, but Branwen swore she was glowing. Her eyes gleamed as brilliantly as the finest Rigani stone. She knew the queen represented the Goddess Ériu at the tournament, yet in that moment, Branwen could believe she *was* the goddess.

She caught a glimpse of ancient power. It radiated from Queen Eseult. Understanding crested in Branwen that the Old Ways weren't something that could be taught—they were something you carried inside. She hoped her aunt was right and that, like the other women in her family, she could also master them.

Branwen cast a sidelong glance at Essy, who had abandoned the healing arts. Nevertheless, she and the princess shared the same blood, and her cousin was to be queen. The Otherworld must be guiding her in different ways.

Queen Eseult raised a bronze goblet heavy with red ale. She stretched her arms out toward the competitors. Both Tristan and Morholt sweat from heat and anticipation.

Tristan was also bruised. Even if he didn't show it, surely he was worn out from a day of fighting. Branwen thought it was distinctly unfair that her uncle should take the field fresh and well rested. But he was the King's Champion, and this was the custom.

"Who would drink from the Chalice of Sovereignty?" the queen asked, her voice dark and sweet.

These were sacred words. Branwen was sure they resounded throughout all the verdant valleys of Iveriu.

Lord Morholt stepped forward and bowed on one knee. "I would," he said.

Queen Eseult lowered her eyes from the red ale to the champions.

"As the sun must conquer the moon each morning, so, too, must the High King of Iveriu fight for peace each day." She set the sparkling vessel to her lips. "Only a man who possesses the Truth of the Ruler may drink from my cup."

A knot twisted Branwen's belly, yet she also felt a strange warmth there.

"The Land needs a Consort who is brave and honorable. It is *she* who makes kings. It is *she* who wields death," the queen continued. "The Final Combat can end only in death or dishonor. As the Goddess Ériu declares it, so will it be done."

Tristan had lied to Branwen. Was it possible his deception would cost him the competition? Tingles erupted all over her skin. Not quite painful, not quite pleasurable. Or, was the Truth of the Ruler a different truth, where sometimes lies were necessary?

Queen Eseult drained her cup. It would only be refilled at the end of the match—for the winner. Its emptiness symbolized the barren land and fallow fields of a kingdom without a rightful ruler. Branwen had never witnessed the ritual with her own eyes—it hadn't been enacted in her lifetime—but she knew all the details from the histories and songs of the bards.

The fighters took their places in the center of the field. A circle only two horse-lengths wide had been drawn in the dirt. The Final Combat was always performed in very close quarters. There could be no running away. Dueling in such proximity required dexterity and cunning. The victor also had to display more mental agility than his opponent. This contest was a test of strength in every sense.

A true king must know when to attack, when to pull back, and when to feint.

Each warrior was entitled to only one weapon. In her uncle's hand was the Balu Gaisos, a spear passed down from King's Champion to King's Champion. It was reputedly carved from the bone of a sea monster and given to the Hound of Uladztir himself by Skathak when he completed his training at the Fort of Shadows.

Tristan withdrew a sleek length of steel. A *misrokord*. Branwen clutched her skirts between her hands tight enough to draw blood. The long, narrow knife seemed flimsy compared with the size of Morholt's barbed javelin.

"Don't worry, Branny," Essy told her, resting her head against Branwen's shoulder. "Uncle will prevail. We won't be sailing away to Kernyv anytime soon." The princess spoke flippantly, as she often did to mask her embarrassment after an attack; although, her cheeks remained rosy. With more spite, she added, "The Kernyvman's pathetic excuse for a sword can't possibly defeat the Balu Gaisos."

That was what Branwen feared. Still, she trusted Tristan must have a reason for selecting the *misrokord*. Normally, the blade was only employed to deal a quick death to a warrior suffering on the battle-field. Master Bécc had taught Branwen the name meant "mercy" in the Aquilan language.

Her uncle took several practice throws with the Balu Gaisos. The Kernyvman didn't even blink. With a yawn, he simply dusted off his heart-shaped shield as if he were bored, teasing a few raucous snorts from the defeated foreign fighters ringing the pitch. Morholt's eyes blazed with enmity. They complimented his sash of plaited saffron, silver, and gold: the colors of Laiginztir and of the Royal Guard.

Queen Eseult's face remained completely serene as she released the embroidered cloth. To Branwen, it felt as if an earthquake shook the castle. But it was only the force of her knees knocking together.

"No need to fear so much for me, dear cousin," Essy assured her.

Seagulls screamed in Branwen's ears. Only it wasn't seagulls. The screech of metal against metal grated on her last nerve. A gale howled through her heart.

Shields held high, the proud lion of Iveriu roared and charged against the sea-wolf. Branwen had always abhorred the hybrid beast of Kernyv that the Iverni believed populated its waters. Against a blackened sky and a white horizon was painted a ferocious wolf head atop a scaled fishlike body. Before she met Tristan, Branwen had indeed considered Kernyvmen to be the wolves of the sea.

The tip of the Balu Gaisos whistled past Tristan and met squarely with the jowls of the sea-wolf. Enraged, Morholt spun around fast. It seemed almost as if the lion on his shield had reached out and swiped Tristan with its claw. Blood speckled the white of the poet's sash like rubies.

Tristan ducked the next blow of the Balu Gaisos and landed one of his own along Morholt's torso. The Iverman grunted and parried.

The two men moved as if they were dancing, dancing with death, and Branwen could almost hear the beat of the *kelyos* band from last night, the incessant, seductive slapping of palms on drums.

On the sidelines, she spotted Keane's glowering visage. Branwen could tell he still wanted a piece of Tristan for himself. Thankfully, he would never dare interrupt the sanctity of the Final Combat. And if Tristan won—*when* he won, he *had* to win—he would effectively become Iveriu's new Champion. Keane couldn't touch him then.

She hoped.

Essy rocked back in her seat, spilling some ale on Branwen's gown. "Cousin," she breathed.

Morholt had faltered. There was a loose Rigani stone in the dirt. Branwen squinted—it was attached to a chain. It was her gift to Tristan. Could it be bringing him luck, after all?

"Oh no, Branny!" cried Essy.

Their uncle's spear had plunged tip down into the ground, lodging deeply. Utterly useless. Branwen fought the smile bowing her lips, although she did still fear for Morholt's life. They had never been close but she didn't want him to die—especially not because of his own pride. And she didn't want Tristan to be the one to kill him.

Branwen recalled what Tristan had told her about Morholt stealing Kernyvak children. About Tristan's own father dying to protect them. But Kernyvak pirates also abducted Ivernic children.

That was why Tristan had to win: to stop the bloodshed. To stop children from being taken from their parents, and parents being taken from their children. Morholt must have seen that.

The two men began to grapple, clouds of red earth rising around their tormented forms, and Branwen understood why Tristan had chosen such a slight weapon. The Balu Gaisos was designed for immediate victory but it was heavy and cumbersome. Tristan had danced around her uncle until the Iverman had lost his footing.

Branwen dashed a glance at Queen Eseult. If she was concerned for her brother, she did not betray it. She only winged her eyebrows. Branwen thought the queen was impressed with Tristan's ingenuity, and she felt a pride she tried not to show.

The fighters tore at each other, wrestling in the dirt. It looked to Branwen as if Tristan was trying not to overly injure his opponent. They flipped on top of each other several times but Tristan had the upper hand. Then Morholt elbowed him in the face, and blood spurted from his nose.

The Ivernic spectators cheered, including Essy. Branwen did not. And her aunt noticed.

Morholt wrapped his beefy hands around Tristan's neck and began to choke the life out of him. Branwen couldn't breathe, either. What a fool she had been to think that names mattered! Tristan, Tantris: He was the same man and her heart knew his heart.

Could the lovers in her dreams have been Branwen and Tristan all along?

The warmth in her belly and tingling sensation along her flesh returned, consuming her. She thought she would retch all over the Queen of Iveriu.

Out of the corner of her eye, just skirting the field of combat, Branwen saw the fox weaving between the feet of the foreign fighters. Flesh, or illusion? She didn't care. The creature must have been there to protect Tristan. The Otherworld had heard her prayers.

Tristan rammed his knees into Morholt's sternum with all his might and the Iverman lurched, toppling backward. Tristan dove on top of him, drawing his *misrokord* and pressing it to her uncle's neck in one elegant motion. Morholt grabbed for the Balu Gaisos but the spear was just out of reach. His fingers scrabbled over the earth in vain.

The *misrokord* cut into Morholt's throat as Tristan prepared to dispense mercy. This was it. The sea-wolf had triumphed over the lion. The Final Combat was over.

Tristan had won. All that remained was Morholt's choice.

A hush settled over the crowd like a glacial mist. Essy gripped Branwen's hand, pulling her to the edge of her seat. Queen Eseult turned to her niece.

"Bring me the red ale," she instructed.

Branwen swayed as she retrieved the waterskin. She felt drunk herself.

The queen rose from her chair and stepped to the front of the tent. Morholt struggled beneath Tristan's blade. Branwen passed her aunt the ale.

"Who would drink from the Chalice of Sovereignty?" Queen Eseult intoned. She beckoned Essy to join her and handed the bronze goblet to the princess.

"On behalf of King Marc, King of Kernyv, I would," Tristan called back. As nephew of King Marc he was of the same bloodline and could consent as a proxy.

Branwen's pulse quickened. Nobody else dared to speak. Nobody dared to draw breath.

"Son of Kernyv," her aunt proclaimed. "Would you be my Consort?"

"I would."

She uncorked the waterskin and poured the red ale with great reverence into the chalice that Essy was holding.

"Son of Kernyv, would you promise to care for the Land above your own life? To turn Winter once again into Spring?"

"I would," Tristan asserted.

Queen Eseult slanted her gaze at her brother. "Lord Morholt, Champion of King Óengus, Son of Iveriu." She drew in a deep breath and, for the first time, Branwen spied a crinkle of worry on her aunt's brow. "You have failed to defend the Land this day. What is your choice: death or dishonor?"

Through clenched teeth, Morholt ground out, "Death."

The queen's shoulders fell minutely before she nodded. The

Land had chosen. It wasn't within her aunt's power to save her brother's life.

She nudged Essy forward with the chalice. "Come, Son of Kernyv. Iveriu embraces you," Queen Eseult told Tristan. "Drink from me."

The princess proffered the chalice in his direction as if she were doing something distasteful. She turned her face away, not wanting to watch the killing. Branwen positioned herself just behind her cousin in case she fainted. She would always be there to catch her if she fell.

From over Essy's shoulder, Branwen's gaze locked with Tristan's. He seemed to be pleading with her. He didn't want to do this. Even though Morholt had been responsible for his own father's death, he didn't want to rob Branwen of her only uncle.

But that wasn't Tristan's choice.

Morholt had fought his enemy until he couldn't, as he'd instructed Branwen to do so many years ago. Her uncle could never see the Kernyvman as anything more.

The Land had made her choice. The Otherworld had made its choice. And Morholt had made his.

Tristan was the tool, the implement. He raised the *misrokord* for the mercy blow. One rapid, razor-sharp strike was all it would take. His gaze remained focused on hers. Branwen grimaced, closed her eyes, and waited to hear the reaction of the crowd to her uncle's death.

She heard nothing.

Branwen opened one eye, and then the other.

Tristan had lowered the *misrokord*, refusing to deal the deathblow. Instead, he offered Morholt his hand in friendship.

Her uncle's eyes went wide with hatred. For a second, he was too stunned to move. Suddenly he howled, "You won't steal my honor from me, you dirty Kernyvak sea-wolf!"

Faster than the Hound of Uladztir himself, Morholt reached for the Balu Gaisos, hefting it loose with all his might, and thrust it at the defenseless Tristan. Branwen screamed without even realizing it. The spear pierced Tristan's shoulder so completely that the tip was visible from the other side.

"Treachery!" called a voice from the crowd. "Treachery!" shouted another foreign fighter. And another.

With supernatural grace and speed, Tristan returned the assault. His blade split Morholt's throat from ear to ear. This time, it was Essy who screamed.

The chalice tumbled from her hands and the red ale spilled on the ground.

Castle Rigani was watered with sovereignty and blood.

WHITETHORN

TRISTAN FELL TO HIS KNEES, a putrid black pus spewing forth from his shoulder.

"Treachery!" howled Havelin, the Crown Prince of Armorica, taking an angry step toward the King's Tent.

Branwen bolted from her seat, running as fast as she could to Tristan's side without a thought for her uncle or the queen or Iveriu. She just had to be near him.

Only one thing could turn a wound against itself like that so quickly. Poison. Venom.

And not just any venom. The deadliest kind—from the fangs of a destiny snake.

Dropping down beside the Kernyvak prince, Branwen went a wintry kind of calm. All of Castle Rigani held its breath. Her uncle Morholt had met his destiny now and it seemed he'd been intent that Tristan should meet his. What Morholt had done was beyond dishonor; no wonder the Land hadn't chosen him.

If Tristan died, the Land would be without a Champion, without a future.

"Emer," he choked out, the venom already confusing his mind. "We have to stop meeting like this."

Branwen refused to let destiny take its own course today. "Hush now, Tantris," she whispered, showing him a half smile through silent tears. "Save your strength so I can heal you."

"You healed me the day we met." Tristan's eyes rolled back in his head and his body convulsed. Black tentacles spread out from the wound toward his heart.

No, no. Not like this! Only the sound of swords being drawn pulled Branwen back from the terror swirling inside her. Lifting her eyes to the crowd, she saw the foreign warriors raise their weapons in the direction of King Óengus. His bodyguards closed in protectively around him.

The king held his ground, expression black.

"We came here for a fair contest!" Havelin cried.

"Not some Ivernic trickery!" added the prince from South Jótland with a growl. The sentiment was echoed by the duke from the Frisii Lands and the Mílesian champion.

A clash of steel resounded as the Royal Guard raised their arms against the foreigners. If they believed King Óengus had lured them from across the Ivernic Sea to be slaughtered, there would be a riot. A pitched battle at the heart of Rigani—without rules this time.

"Poison is not a warrior's death!" hollered the duke from Logres. A fresh round of hisses and jeers ensued.

Someone jerked hard on Branwen's shoulder, trying to pull her away from Tristan.

"Come with me," Keane said harshly, eyes anxious. She shook her head, wrenching herself from beneath his grip, and he surprised her by dropping to one knee. "Branwen, you aren't safe here." He nodded at the increasingly agitated mob.

"I'm not going anywhere."

Keane flicked his gaze from her to the wounded prince and back again. "The Kernyvman isn't worth your tears."

Anger rippled along Branwen's brow. "I'll decide who deserves my tears." She didn't have time to argue with him. The din from the malcontent warriors grew louder. "Either help me, or leave me alone, Sir Keane."

She focused her attention on the spear protruding from Tristan's shoulder. The hideous black vines of poison coiled themselves tightly around the wound. The longer the Balu Gaisos remained lodged in his body, the faster the toxins would spread through his bloodstream, rotting Tristan from the inside out.

If Branwen removed the spear too precipitously, however, Tristan might bleed to death where he lay. What should she do? *What should she do?* She couldn't lose him again.

She was decided. She yanked. The Balu Gaisos fought her stubbornly.

"What are you thinking?" Keane barked. "He's your enemy."

"If you want a man to remain your enemy, then treat him as such," she retorted, not even glancing up. "Iveriu needs friends."

"Well said, my niece."

Queen Eseult loomed over them, her golden hair gleaming like the sun itself. Instead of seeing her aunt, Branwen saw the Land. And the Land was dismayed at the agony of her Champion.

"Don't remove the spear just yet," the queen cautioned. She narrowed her eyes at Keane. "Sir Keane, Sir Fintan," she said, turning to the bodyguard at her side. "Carry the Prince of Kernyv to the infirmary as carefully as possible."

Keane's lower lip twitched but he wouldn't defy his queen. A grim expression settled over his features as he linked his arms through Tristan's. Fintan placed one arm dutifully beneath the Kernyvman's knees and the other under his ankles. Together, Fintan and Keane raised him off the ground.

The queen's gaze veered from Tristan to the representatives of Iveriu's friends and rivals. A shocked silence fell upon the crowd, waiting for her pronouncement.

"The Land cries out for her wounded Champion. The Goddess Ériu will heal the Son of Kernyv."

Branwen clasped her hands together, pressing them to her chest, and realized they were once again covered with Tristan's blood.

She burned with renewed rage.

Only the King of Ordowik dared to challenge Queen Eseult. "You say the Land will heal Prince Tristan. But the Land didn't protect him—from your own brother."

Glancing up at the queen from where she had huddled on the ground, Branwen noticed a single cord of her aunt's neck jump.

"Lord Morholt dishonored himself and disgraced his kingdom. The Land no longer acknowledges him. He will receive no Champion's burial." There were several gasps from among the Ivernic nobles.

Queen Eseult's brilliant green eyes dulled as she spat on her brother's body. "He is no longer my blood. From this day forth, I will not speak his name. No child in Iveriu will bear his name. He will only live in infamy."

Dead silence.

Then a raucous chorus of cheers. Her aunt had appeased the foreigners. The queen betrayed no reaction; Branwen heaved a sigh of relief.

"Dear niece, there isn't much time. If Prince Tristan dies, King Marc will invade our shores." There was little doubt about it. "You must go quickly," she told Branwen.

"Where, Lady Queen?"

"Whitethorn Mound."

"Whitethorn Mound?" she repeated, disbelieving.

"Prince Tristan will surely die without Otherworld magic. We need the whitethorn bark." Branwen's heart skittered. "And we need to make an offering. To the Old Ones," Queen Eseult said gravely.

"What should I offer them?" Branwen asked.

Discreetly, Queen Eseult withdrew a crescent-shaped knife from her skirts. "They will want blood, my niece. The blood of a natural healer. *Your* blood."

✛ ✛ ✛

Branwen slipped through the east gate unnoticed by the rabble. King Óengus had instructed the servants to bring out roasted suckling pigs and several more vats of red ale to sate the appetites of the foreign champions. In the commotion, Branwen spied Essy at Lord Diarmuid's side and Keane bundling her off to safety in the south tower.

She couldn't worry about her cousin right now. Branwen sprinted through the woods, struggling to keep up with the fox, who had reappeared at the castle gate. The creature led her farther and deeper into the forest than she had ever gone.

All Ivernic children were taught to be wary of Otherworld dwellers, not to trespass on their territory lest they be stolen into their world forever. Some were less than benign. Although Branwen had doubted the truth of the stories, she'd avoided *ráithana* and *lesana* all the same—the hills and ring-forts where the Old Ones were meant to reside.

Her heart pounded and her breath whistled through her teeth like the howl of a Death-Teller, presaging her demise. The Otherworld women who foretold death were the most feared. No, there would be no more death today. She would give the Old Ones whatever they wanted—even stay in their world—to save Tristan.

Not just because Iveriu needed the Kernyvak prince to live. But because Branwen's heart would be homeless without him. She had watched him leave her once. She wouldn't let the man she loved slip away again.

Branwen tripped over her skirts as she ran up the hill to catch up with the fox. The creature made an annoyed barking noise. She unfastened her outer tunic and threw it to the ground so it wouldn't slow her down.

Whitethorn Mound came within view. The burning summer sun turned the branches surrounding the hill into a sea of white flames. The branches were supposed to be imbued with powerful magic. *Skeakh*, they were called.

Cutting one of the *skeakh* was certain death for whoever performed the act. It was worth the risk. She needed the bark of the whitethorn to save Tristan.

Treading carefully, Branwen approached the edge of the mound. She wasn't here to steal from the Old Ones; she was here to offer an exchange. A blood price. Her entire body grew taut as she prayed they would accept.

She lagged behind the unnaturally red fox as it ascended the mound. The gleaming branches parted for Branwen, almost as if they were welcoming her. Apprehension warred with curiosity. Then they closed around her again, forming a ring on top of the hill, a glistening white wall.

The sweeping views down over Castle Rigani, of the leafy coastline, and out across the Ivernic Sea were astounding. From up here, everything was more vibrant. Each color held an almost painful clarity. It was as if Branwen were seeing her homeland for the first time. Her senses heightened. The beauty of the Land provoked fresh tears. Awe suffused her. Was this how Iveriu looked from the Otherworld?

Was Branwen *in* the Otherworld? Had she crossed through the Veil?

The fox trotted anxiously around her legs, nipping at her heels. *Hurry*, it urged. *How?* she wanted to ask. Branwen should have asked the queen how and when to perform the sacrifice. As if in answer, a gust of wind came out of nowhere, tangling in her hair and forcing Branwen to raise her arms above her face.

Chills ignited down her spine. Her grip on the blade Queen Eseult had given her tightened. The fox snarled.

Branwen focused on the knife. She had only ever seen it in the possession of the queen. Her aunt called it the moon-catcher. She knew the blade was deeply rooted in the magic of the Old Ways, but she didn't know the details.

She'd rejected magic so obstinately after her parents died that now, when she needed it the most, she didn't know how to wield it. She flexed her knuckles around the mother-of-pearl handle until they were also a translucent white.

Every moment that Branwen hesitated, Tristan was one moment closer to death.

How could she give the Old Ones the sacrifice they required if they didn't tell her what they needed?

Sunlight glinted off the smooth, curved blade.

Trust. Queen Eseult would tell Branwen to trust her instincts. She'd spent so long spurning them, preferring herbal recipes and well-tested remedies to gut feelings—feelings she couldn't control. *What if her instincts were wrong?*

Shaking and unsure of herself, she lifted the moon-catcher above her head.

"I have come to ask for the bark of a sacred *skeakh.*"

A screaming gale tore at her eardrums. Her limbs grew numb as she stood her ground. "The new Champion of Iveriu is dying," she yelled into the wind. "The Land embraces him, commands that he be healed. The Goddess Ériu wills it!"

The wind slapped Branwen in the face. Her fingers began to freeze around the iron crescent. Icicles formed in her veins as if she were being frozen solid. Her heartbeat grew slower, lethargic. She was dying, slowly, like Tristan. Only he was dying swiftly.

Trust. This time it wasn't her own voice Branwen heard. It was a voice she never thought she'd hear again. *Trust yourself.*

Lady Alana had been a natural healer, too. She wouldn't have wanted Branwen to turn from the Old Ways, to turn from her own power—power that could help others. Healing was an act of love, she realized, and her mother would want her to share her magic. Branwen had been too angry at losing her to see it until now.

Trust. She had to relinquish control and embrace the unknown.

She had to trust she was strong enough to brave whatever storms might come.

Using every last bit of energy, Branwen sliced open the center of her palm with the moon-catcher, right across her heart line.

"This is my body! This is my love!" Branwen hollered, the muscles in her throat constricting. "I give it to the Land. I offer you everything I am!"

Blood like the darkest wild berries gushed forth. Branwen was too numb to feel the pain. Red rain showered the whitethorns. The fox leapt excitedly, brushing her knees with its bushy tail. She could barely feel that, either. She feared she was petrifying.

A small whirlwind consumed Branwen, lapping up her blood. From inside the tempest, she heard moans of delight and satisfaction. And then the biting vapor grew hot, steaming hot, thawing her frozen body, her ice-like heart.

Branwen had never felt so uncontrolled. So free. So powerful.

Beads of sweat like diamonds glittered across her whole being. These new puffs of wind were like a warm bath: welcoming, accepting.

She had trusted the Old Ones so they were trusting her. They were appeased.

And Branwen was exhilarated.

The fox scurried toward the edge of the whitethorn ring and clamped a *skeakh* branch between its teeth. She gazed into its ebony eyes. Branwen understood the message. She approached the fox respectfully, raised the moon-catcher, and brought it down in one fluid motion.

Grasping the whitethorn with her bleeding hand, she gripped it with the heart line she had cleaved in two.

And then, something even more extraordinary happened. The white bark of the *skeakh* took root in her palm, infusing her wound with its magic. Heat jolted Branwen to the core. Delicate, translucent blossoms flowed down the length of the branch.

Branwen understood why the offering had to be the blood of a natural healer. The Land itself flowed through her veins; her blood had quite literally caused the branch to flower. It wasn't the bark itself that Branwen needed to cure Tristan—it was the magic, and the Old Ones had filled her with it.

The fox pulled the whitethorn branch from her hand and Branwen saw that a single perfect white elderflower bloomed in its place. She needed to bind her wound to Tristan's so her magic could destroy the poison. Her muscles spasmed as the magic coursed through her. The intense heat subsided, replaced by a floating sensation.

She would never again doubt that the Old Ones were listening to her supplications. The whitethorn barricade vanished. Branwen was alone once more with the fox on the hillside. As she glimpsed Castle Rigani, its magnificence had dimmed slightly. She had crossed back into her own world.

Branwen tucked the blade at her waist and cradled the blossom between her hands. The fox exhaled a frustrated breath. She smiled. The same power that forced buds to wake in frozen earth was alive inside Branwen, fueling her.

"Let's run like the wind, my little friend," she said.

And they did.

THE STARLESS TIDE

QUEEN ESEULT STOOD VIGIL AT Tristan's bedside. Alone. She looked up at her niece expectantly as she appeared in the doorway of the infirmary. Branwen stretched out her hand.

The queen took in a short breath. Her gaze traveled from the bloodstained bodice of Branwen's gown to the nearly healed flesh of her palm. The skin shimmered, a silver sheen glowing in the dusk.

The elderflower had melted in her grasp, leaving behind this glittering, milky residue.

Branwen glided across the room toward Tristan. Queen Eseult had stripped his tunic from him and removed the spear tip. His bare chest was tattooed with black swirls, ribbons of hate.

Over his heart, she recognized her own love-knots. The poison from the destiny snake was dissolving the remnants of her stitches like acid. She glanced sideways at her aunt, fearful she might recognize the embroidery that she herself had taught Branwen.

The queen's features gave no hint of it.

"I have given him *derew* root to ease his suffering" was all she said.

Branwen nodded, relieved. The wound on her palm tingled as if the magic knew where it was needed. She leaned over Tristan's handsome face, his sweaty curls matted like a crown around his forehead. His eyes darted back and forth beneath their lids. There was disquiet in his soul.

A rich voice rumbled through Branwen's mind. Female. Imbued with authority and love.

"I am the Land," Branwen said, repeating the words being spoken from the Otherworld. "With my blood, Son of Kernyv, I heal you."

She pressed her heart line directly against the gaping wound in Tristan's shoulder on instinct. Branwen gasped as shuddering waves of pearlescent light flowed forth from her being into his. Extreme pressure mounted in her veins, clamoring for release. She feared she might literally burst from beneath her skin.

The pressure was followed by a heat so intense that Branwen was certain she had been dipped into a boiling cauldron. It was more than burning. It was melting.

She sank her palm deeper into Tristan's wound and her essence blurred into his. His body convulsed, as did hers. The weeping midnight veins across his chest began to retreat.

Just as Branwen had watched a smelter pour liquid fire into a mold, so the Otherworld magic traveled the venomous byways of Tristan's body, consuming the toxins in its path. The inky swirls converted into white, translucent strands; darkness succumbed to light.

Tristan's eyes blinked open, hazel flecks bright. He bolted upright, reaching for her, and let out a tortured cry. The world lurched around Branwen. Her hand spasmed.

Tristan reached for her again as she doubled over in pain. Too weak, he fell back harshly against the bed. She was in too much agony to scream. Climbing up from her arm was the poison Branwen had taken from Tristan. It traveled up to her neck, constricting her like a snare. Obsidian thorns flowered.

The Land had saved her Champion by devouring his pain. Now she had to bear his burden for him.

Branwen's ankles wobbled; her knees gave out. She crashed onto the unforgiving stone tiles. Years' worth of grief and hate surged up her throat. Scalding black bile spewed forth. The Land took the worst parts of the human heart and transformed them into something good. Then she had expelled the rest.

"Branny!" Queen Eseult exclaimed.

Branwen collapsed in a perspiration-soaked heap at Tristan's side. Someone called her name from far out at sea.

She was carried away.

✣ ✣ ✣

Branwen drifted, drifted among sweet black waves. Had she returned to the Otherworld? Would she be able to find her parents here? Were they calling her?

A new vortex encircled her, made of sea and death. Death promised to reckless strangers, death too good for mercenary raiders. Castle Rigani became nothing but a collection of jagged shadows, gravestones lining the shore. And Branwen was losing sight of it.

The frothing waters became tentacles, forbidding her to swim, holding her immobile. Toxic strands that strangled her very being. The Ivernic Sea wanted Branwen to watch. She needed to cut her way free. She whirled an arm wildly for the moon-catcher in her pocket.

A spray of surf slapped her in the face, laughing. Another swell knocked the moon-catcher from her grasp. The violaceous light of a tempest winked off the blade as the tide carried it away.

Pain and vengeance wanted to consume Branwen whole.

The whirlpool sucked her under.

Branwen was falling, falling through the sea, falling through time. She saw herself on the day her parents died, building a castle in the sand. She saw Essy destroy it in a fit of giggles.

She sank farther into the abyss-shaded waters.

Farther through time, even past her own birth.

Waves turned from black to red.

Screams like Branwen had never known shredded her ears. The Land was bleeding. The shore was her body; the sea was her blood. Branwen floated at the very heart of the Goddess Ériu.

She writhed, foaming at the mouth. The Land felt everything—every death, every violation. War raped the Land.

Now Branwen felt it, too. The agony of her people overwhelmed her. Did Queen Eseult carry this burden at all times? Branwen tried to shut her eyes against the savagery of burning fields, a fire that danced along her skin, even in the middle of the sea. Salt water splashed her eyes, scratching, forcing them open.

By poisoning Tristan, her uncle Morholt threatened to revisit this misery upon the kingdom. Branwen couldn't stand for it. The sea began to boil, the bubbling cauldron from which Iveriu was born.

Leagues below, the sea floor cracked, revealing rivers of liquid fire that raged beneath the earth. In its veins. Destruction. Enough to renew the world or extinguish it.

A terrible thunder resounded below the surface. The earth quaked. Fire like shooting stars sped toward Branwen, then fizzled out of existence.

If peace could not be found, this would be Iveriu's fate. Truly, it was more lethal than a destiny snake.

It was her duty to prevent this—to protect Iveriu at all costs.

Otherwise, all that would remain of her beloved homeland was ash floating on a starless tide.

Branwen stopped fighting. She let the venom infuse her. If she saved Tristan and the Land, the black waves would be sweet—sweet, indeed.

TONGUE OF HONEY, HEART OF BILE

WHEN BRANWEN AT LAST REGAINED consciousness, the castle was quiet. A damp cloth was draped on her brow. Her cousin stood by her, silhouetted by a somber wash of gray.

Essy immediately fell upon her with kisses. The princess's tears were hot against her cheeks. Branwen's mouth felt dryer than the desert plains in the Kingdom of Míl. She tried to speak, but her tongue was cracked.

"It's all right, Branny. Don't wear yourself out." Essy pulled away, and dipped the linen cloth into a pail. She dabbed Branwen's brow and a trickle of fresh water wended its way to her lips. She licked it eagerly.

Their eyes met and the princess understood what her cousin needed.

"Keane!" she called out.

No. Essy hadn't understood at all. Branwen's heart twisted at the mention of his name. She recalled how they had argued at the

Champions Tournament. The memory was fuzzy, a bad dream. How long had she been asleep?

Keane's head popped out from around the doorjamb. His face was etched with worry, and he looked as if he had aged a few years. Branwen cast her eyes toward the floor. Glancing slowly around her, she realized she was in Essy's bed.

The princess scooted next to Branwen on top of the plush quilt. Imperiously, she ordered Keane, "Fetch Lady Branwen a jug of fresh mint water! And ask Treva to send up platters of candied venison tarts from the kitchen." For once, Branwen didn't mind her cousin's haughty tone.

Keane panned his gaze across Branwen, but she refused to meet it. She heard him cough uncomfortably, then reply, "Of course, Lady Princess. Sir Comgan will be just outside in my absence."

Essy released a snort and waved a frustrated hand in the air. Turning back toward Branwen, she said, "Father hasn't allowed me a moment's privacy since the Champions Tournament. And the foreigners have all gone home already."

Every fiber in Branwen's body grew taut. She tried to speak. Only a croak came out. Essy's expression immediately shifted from annoyed to gentle. She pressed the cold cloth against Branwen's mouth.

Sucking down a few more drops of water, Branwen managed to rasp, "*All?*"

Had Tristan left her without a second thought?

"No, not *all* of them," the princess huffed, blowing out a large breath and feathering her bangs. "That bloody Kernyvman is still here."

Princesses shouldn't say *bloody* but Branwen was too bleary to admonish her. She swallowed a few more times, the soreness of her throat beginning to ease.

"Is he well?"

She counted the seconds until her cousin replied.

"Oh yes, he's well enough." Essy crinkled her brow. "And it seems he won't be going home without me." Anger bloomed on her features. "I'll never forgive him for killing Uncle Morholt or making you so ill, Branny. He nearly took you away from me."

New tenacity gleamed in the princess's eyes. "Once you're feeling better, I'll scold you, too, for risking yourself like that," she promised. "Over a bloody Kernyvman!" Branwen tried to laugh. It still hurt. "You burned with fever for two weeks," Essy told her. There was fear behind her words. "If you had died, I would have exacted vengeance on Kernyv myself."

Branwen sucked a little more on the edge of the wet cloth. "I— I'm not important, Essy. The alliance is what matters."

"*Stop*," Essy commanded. "You're more important than any alliance."

Tears pricked at Branwen's eyes. Her cousin's love was a force of nature. To Essy, she might be more important than the alliance between two kingdoms. After what she'd seen, what the Land had shown her, Branwen knew that wasn't true.

She reached for Essy's hand, her movements still clumsy. "Kernyv will be your home," said Branwen. She began to trace the hazel symbol. "You will grow to love it."

Essy shook her head emphatically. "You're my home, Branny. Castle Rigani is my home. Not that Otherworld-forsaken land of pirates!"

"Hush, my dear daughter," Queen Eseult chided as she swept effortlessly into the bedchamber. Her voice was warm. Saoirse followed behind and it heartened Branwen to see her stride was steady.

"Welcome back," the queen told her. She walked around to the opposite side of the bed and stroked Branwen's brow. "I'm sorry I wasn't here when you awoke, dear heart."

"As am I." Saoirse's eyes glistened as she smiled, positioning herself at the foot of the bed.

"We've changed places," Branwen said. "I hope I've been a good patient?" She coughed a laugh. How strange to be the one needing care.

"Of course," Essy insisted, answering for Saoirse. She dabbed Branwen's forehead again. "Only you would worry about that."

Branwen nearly told her to stop fussing, but she remembered how her father would say that the strongest people knew when to accept help. She smiled at her cousin. Of the queen, she asked, "Prince Tristan has fully recovered?"

"Like magic," her aunt said. "I'm certain the Kernyvak prince will also be most disappointed not to have been here when you opened your eyes."

"He's been visiting?"

"Every day." There was something shrewd in the queen's gaze. "As soon as he could stand," she added. Had her aunt recognized the love-knots, after all?

"Keane, too," Essy said.

"Our Branwen is indeed well loved," the queen agreed. "Iveriu owes you a great debt, my niece." Heat returned to Branwen's cheeks.

Her journey to the Otherworld and healing Tristan were like a disjointed dream. She couldn't tell what was real and what had been a fantasy. Surely, an elderflower couldn't really have blossomed on her hands? And the sea. The rage boiling in the blood of the Land made her shudder.

The queen brushed her knuckle along Branwen's cheekbone. "Alana would be proud of you." Her eyes watered.

She was there. Branwen had heard her mother's voice—hadn't she?

"It was the Land," she protested. "It wasn't me."

"You are the Land and the Land is you," Queen Eseult said solemnly; Branwen knew that truth intimately now. Her aunt placed a hand on Essy's shoulder. "As are you, daughter."

The princess stiffened. "I'd rather be a healer than share a marriage bed with some old king."

Branwen almost noted that twenty-seven wasn't so old, but she held her tongue for her cousin's sake.

Her mother cut Essy with a glance. "The Land has chosen our roles for each of us." In a lower voice, she said, "We won't discuss this matter now, when Branny has only just returned to us from a fever."

For once, the princess appeared thoroughly chastened, fingers skittering over her scalp. "Of course. I—" She cast Branwen a plaintive look, and Branwen lifted a corner of her mouth. "I'll go see where that water is," Essy said. Her neck flushed. "I'll be right back."

"Thank you, cousin."

Essy studiously avoided eye contact with her mother as she exited the chamber. Branwen wondered what had passed between them while the fever gripped her. Saoirse traded a brief glance with Queen Eseult before muttering, "I'll help" and slipping out behind the princess.

When they were alone, Branwen told her aunt, "I'm sorry I haven't been able to help with the preparations for the voyage to Kernyv, Lady Queen." She ran the cloth across her chapped lips once more. "There's so much to be done."

"Oh, dear heart, please don't fret. You've already done enough."

Queen Eseult sighed. "Your healing talent has surpassed my wildest imagination, Branny. I wish I could be your teacher, but I know the Otherworld will supply you with a new one. When the time is right."

Branwen was rendered speechless; warring emotions surged in her heart. She wanted to tell the queen what she had seen, yet no words came.

Her aunt continued, "I noticed that Prince Tristan has nearly lost his heart before. It was stitched precisely and tenderly back together."

Their eyes locked and Branwen raised the cloth to her mouth.

"The hand that tied those love-knots, my niece, must have been guided from beyond the Veil. And I think that you may have your own reasons for journeying across the Ivernic Sea."

So the queen had guessed. Her aunt knew that she had saved Tristan from the waves and hidden him from her own people. Why wasn't she angry?

Seemingly reading the question in Branwen's eyes, Queen Eseult said, "The Land has chosen her Champion."

"Thank you." She was grateful and mystified at her aunt's reaction.

"But, perhaps, it might be wise to let Essy settle into Kernyv before telling her of your . . . attachment. She has a trying time ahead of her."

Branwen nodded, a tendril of shame threading around the knowledge that Tristan was safe and alive, like the honeysuckle and the hazel. The queen might not think her a traitor, but she didn't think her cousin would feel the same. Not now. Not when the unknown stretched before her. Essy had been the first inhabitant of

Branwen's heart; there would be time enough in the future for her to learn to share.

Keane reappeared in the doorway with an earthenware jug, knocking lightly. He bowed before the queen and quickly set about pouring Branwen a glass of water.

His eyes shone miserably. Their fingertips touched over the brim of the cup. "Lady Branwen, I prayed to the Old Ones every day for your recovery," he said.

A different kind of guilt bubbled up in her chest. "Thank you for your good wishes, Sir Keane."

"They're the best. I always bear you the best wishes, Lady Branwen."

She buried her face in the cup, the minty water cool and sweet. Her cheeks burned, but her thirst was sated.

Keane stood above her, trailing his gaze longingly along her brow. Branwen could tell he wanted to touch her. Fortunately, he would never take such a liberty in front of the queen. She also noticed that he favored his left leg. He had been wounded in the Champions Tournament, too. Branwen had scarcely paid attention. She'd only had eyes for Tristan.

"Is that better?" Keane asked, an unwarrior-like quaver to his voice.

She nodded and he looked immensely relieved. "We should leave you to rest, dear heart," said Queen Eseult, warming her with another smile. "I'll keep the princess occupied so you can sleep."

Heavy footfalls raced toward the door and the queen looked up from her niece with alarm. Keane spun on his heel, drawing his *kladiwos* blade. Branwen's emerald ribbon dangled from its hilt.

"*Tristan*," she whispered.

He was out of breath, his dark curls wild, and his tunic untucked. But, by the Old Ones, he was glorious. A tiny shiver that had nothing to do with any fever flitted through her body. And her heart.

"Branwen."

There was something so raw about the way he said her name that it made her shiver all over again. Queen Eseult narrowed her eyes at the Kernyvman.

"*Lady* Branwen," Tristan corrected himself. Then he bowed from the waist. "Lady Queen."

"Prince Tristan, I see that good news travels fast," said her aunt. "All of Castle Rigani is elated that Branwen's fever has broken."

Staring at the Kernyvak prince, Branwen wasn't sure her fever had broken at all.

"If Lady Branwen had lingered in the Otherworld any longer, I would have ventured there to retrieve her myself," Tristan declared.

Keane glared at the Kernyvman as if he could disembowel him with only his eyes. The tension in the room grew thick like sludge, and a vein thrummed in Keane's neck.

"It is heartening that the people of Kernyv will consider my niece such a treasure as we do," Queen Eseult told Tristan. "Branwen is indeed my second daughter. But I have found that men who possess tongues of honey often possess hearts of bile."

Keane couldn't refrain from a smirk at the queen's remark.

Tristan dropped dramatically to one knee at Branwen's bedside. "My heart was indeed full of bile until my fair lady purged it from me." He moved to take her hand, then stopped himself—catching the impropriety. Branwen herself shrunk back, thinking of the queen's warning. "Lady Branwen will have all of Kernyv's gratitude, always," Tristan proclaimed. "More than even Emer knew from the Hound when she saved him from himself."

Finding her voice, Branwen said haltingly, "Prince Tristan, Iveriu is your friend. And the Land always protects her friends."

"I am certain that you always protect your friends, Lady Branwen," he said.

When their eyes met, the rest of the world fell away. They floated in a glistening blue sea of sky, on the other side of the Veil.

Straightening up, Tristan turned toward the queen. Keane stood stiller than a statue but Branwen sensed he was prepared to launch an attack.

"Lady Queen, I want to assure you that if we are fortunate enough to have Lady Branwen accompany Princess Eseult to her new home, she will also be afforded King Marc's protection," Tristan said. "She will be as dear to him as your daughter. To all of us."

Keane gritted his teeth even more noticeably. He cast a glance at Branwen and she looked away.

"I would expect nothing less," said the queen. She rose abruptly. Keane and Tristan stood at attention. "Come, my charming prince, escort me to my chamber and let us at last leave my niece to regain her strength."

"It would be my pleasure," he said. "Lady Branwen must be hearty and hale for the voyage across the sea to her new home."

"I will stand watch," Keane said, enunciating each word with a hard edge. The queen hesitated for a moment before nodding her assent.

Tristan proffered his arm to the queen, gazing back over his shoulder at Branwen. "Until the Old Ones grant us leave to meet again," he said. "Or tomorrow morning. Whichever is sooner."

Branwen failed to conceal a look of delight. Her heart winced as he disappeared from view.

Keane hung back a beat.

"Iveriu is your home," he said. As Keane exited the bedchamber, he touched the ribbon attached to his blade. She could still feel his presence outside the door.

Castle Rigani was her childhood home, but Branwen had ceased to be a child. The Land needed her to make Kernyv her home, to bring the alliance to fruition.

The only way to protect Iveriu was to leave it.

ECHOES

"**O**H, BRANNY, IT'S WONDERFUL."

Her cousin held the doll's dress up to the window. A soft, daffodil-colored light streamed into Branwen's sitting room. Early autumn glowed inside and out.

"Gráinne will love it," the princess declared. As Branwen suspected she would, Essy had grown frustrated with the needlework for the doll's dress she'd promised the orphan.

"I'm so glad."

Running her finger along the clover embroidered on the collar of the dress, Essy beamed a smile brighter than Branwen had seen for weeks. The strain of Branwen's illness had left marks on her cousin's body, and demeanor, that she deeply regretted.

"I can't wait to see her face," said the princess, and the expression on hers was all the thanks Branwen needed. Essy had invited the children who lived along the Rock Road to a small celebration at Castle Rigani before her departure.

Although the event meant more work for Treva, who was forever running from the kitchens to the granaries, ensuring there were enough oatcakes to serve the Royal Guard, honored guests, and key members of the allied clans at Essy's Farewell Feast—Queen Eseult declared it a marvelous idea. It certainly provided an excellent distraction from the impending voyage.

"Thank you, Branny," breathed her cousin, pressing the dress to her chest. Glancing toward the window, she exclaimed, "Oh! I almost forgot. I have an appointment with Noirín."

Noirín, Dubthach's mother, and the other castle seamstresses were working night and day on the trousseau Essy would bring with her to King Marc's court, at Monwiku. Emerald dye, freshwater pearls, and homespun lace had grown in short supply.

Branwen leaned back into her chair. "Run along, then."

"Only if you promise not to do any more work this afternoon." Essy shot her a stern glare. Branwen laughed. Her cousin had become extremely protective during Branwen's recuperation, guarding her as closely as Keane did the princess, and she saw in Essy a queen as kind and munificent as her mother.

"I promise, cousin." The care with which Essy nursed Branwen had brought them closer, although sometimes it was hard to be on the receiving end of orders to rest.

The princess released an unconvinced "*Hmph.*" Then she said, "I'll bring you some water mint tea when I'm done," and exited, clutching the dress for Gráinne tight.

As soon as Essy was out of sight, Branwen reached behind the chair for a basket she kept carefully hidden. She scooped up the shimmery material from the bottom, gathered it into her lap, and threaded a needle. She wanted this to be a surprise and she didn't really consider it *work*.

Branwen preferred complete quiet while she sewed. She liked to listen to the rhythm of the stitch, the prick and slice of the needle as it slid through the smooth silk. The pearl-gray would set off Essy's fair complexion.

While the castle seamstresses prepared the rest of the princess's wardrobe, Branwen had asked Queen Eseult if she could be the one to embroider the mantle her cousin would wear on her wedding night. The tunic had a much lower than usual scalloped neckline adorned with scabbards. The swords were drawn. Blooming garlands for fertility. The pearls fastened in between them represented virtue and innocence.

She pulled loose a string that had gone awry and embroidered the tip of a *krotto* harp on the train of the dress. When Essy slipped into her gown, she would become a symbol of peace, hope, and bounty. Now that Branwen had experienced the Land's pain, it simmered constantly beneath her flesh. She prayed King Marc would understand the intentions of the message she had so painstakingly crafted. She wanted him to see her cousin as powerful, magnificent—give her the respect she deserved.

Music rose from beneath her window. An enchanting, doleful cry. Then it was gone.

Ever since Branwen had journeyed to Whitethorn Mound, she'd started catching glimpses of things that weren't there, echoes of songs that weren't real. Not in her world. Was this what it meant to be Otherworld-touched? The Old Ones had let Branwen cross over and part of her seemed to have remained.

Maybe that was the hidden cost. Could healing Tristan the way she did be the reason not a second went by that Branwen didn't think of him? No, that had started long ago. When she believed him to be Tantris the shipwrecked minstrel. Branwen couldn't help but wonder what her own First Night might be like with him.

Distracted, she pricked her finger. A storm-red sun welled to the surface and fell upon the gown. Her chest pinched. She sucked the splotch of blood until it was gone. *Breathe*. No one would ever notice it had been sullied.

Another high-pitched trill. A blackbird. Branwen rested her forehead against the diamond-shaped panes, craned her neck farther.

Down below, in the somewhat secluded garden of the south tower, Essy sat beside the hazel tree. Sunlight transformed the locks ringing her companion's face into a dazzling golden mane—like one found on a lion in Master Bécc's bestiaries.

Panic lanced Branwen. The princess was ensconced next to Lord Diarmuid. She must have given Keane the slip.

Branwen dropped the gown and it flowed toward the floor like rippling water. She was out of her chair in a flash, bolting through the door and down the twisting stairs. What could Essy have been thinking? Her cousin knew how much Branwen had endured to ensure the peace between Iveriu and Kernyv.

Was Essy truly in love with the arrogant lord?

Granite slabs slid under her feet as Branwen ran faster and faster. And then she slipped. She flew through the air and spilled into a sturdy pair of arms.

"Tristan."

Branwen pulled herself free of his grip, slamming back against the hard stone wall of the stairwell.

Tristan sucked in a short breath, intrigue teasing his brows.

"Careful," he mocked her gently. "Where are you off to in such a hurry?" He reached out to her. She caught a distinct whiff of candied apples. Tristan must have been raiding Treva's larder. And beneath that scent lay the sweetness of the sea. The freshness. Her pulse immediately sped up at the idea of tasting it. "You shouldn't run while you're still recovering," he said. "Whatever you require, I will fetch it."

How could Branwen tell Tristan that she was trying to stop Essy from compromising her virtue with Lord Diarmuid before wedding his king? If he ever suspected an indiscretion, he would be honor bound to report it and the alliance would be broken. She couldn't put him in that position. She couldn't ask Tristan to choose between her cousin and King Marc. Her mouth tightened with anger that Essy was making Branwen choose between peace and love.

Unconsciously, she felt for the brooch at her shoulder. She had worn it every day since the Champions Tournament. She was certain her mother had been guiding her through the Otherworld, and Lady Alana's presence had been stronger since she'd visited Whitethorn Mound. Somehow Branwen had forgotten that, as a little girl, she used to talk to her mother on the beach and that the waves had talked back.

And then, one day they brought her Tristan.

Tristan's gaze dipped to the brooch. "It's lovely."

"It belonged to my mother."

He pursed his lips, staring at her intently. Outside, the sky had faded as autumn took hold. The green leaves were turning to gold, falling. But in Tristan's eyes, all Branwen could see was an endless summer.

"We haven't had a moment truly alone since you saved my life," he said from deep in his throat. "Again."

"No," she agreed. Queen Eseult's counsel had kept Branwen from acting rashly. "Not that I'm keeping a tally." It came out breathless. Branwen should be preventing Essy from committing her own rash acts—*right now*—but the way Tristan was looking at her rooted her to the stone.

He leaned closer and slipped one finger between the brooch and the flimsy piece of cotton covering her shoulder. The breath hitched in Branwen's throat as he ran his fingertip along the grooves, just above her heart.

"What does it mean?" he asked.

"Don't you know the language of trees?"

He shook his head, taking another step toward her.

She gulped. "The right fight."

Tristan brushed her cheek with the back of his hand. A tide of yearning washed over her and she sorely wished they were back at the cave.

"I was afraid I'd failed," he said, a grave look crossing his face. "I thought I'd failed to bring peace." His gaze penetrated her. "When I awoke, but you didn't—I thought I'd failed you."

The anguish in his voice drew Branwen's hand to his cheek in return. She couldn't resist tracing the line of his jaw. "You didn't fail, Tristan." Words tumbled from her mouth. "You could never fail me."

The admission was a revelation. Tristan had found a fissure in Branwen's heart, too, when she discovered him on that raft. He had worked his way in, burrowing deep, and healed the rupture.

Tristan framed her face with his hands. "There *is* no peace for me without you, Branwen." Then his lips found hers.

Time lost all meaning in the darkness of the stairwell. Branwen gave herself over to this new hunger clawing at her. Craving. She had spent so much of her life fighting against the longing left by loss. But as she kissed Tristan, she stopped struggling. She let both her pain and love consume her. His hands slid down her sides until his callused fingers encircled her wrists.

Her breathing grew ragged. Branwen was entrapped like an animal. Only she didn't want to escape.

The promise of a different kind of peace lay between his arms.

A lament tore through her mind. The blackbird's lament.

Branwen jerked away. She darted her eyes through the slit in the turret toward the garden. If she didn't separate her cousin from Lord Diarmuid this very instant, there would be no peace for anyone.

"Branwen, what's wrong?" Tristan watched her carefully, concern radiating from his eyes.

She couldn't answer. She didn't want to lie to him. The blackbirds had carried off her voice again.

"Was I too bold?" he said. "I thought you'd forgiven me. I thought you felt the same way."

Did she ever. But she had to go. Branwen couldn't let Essy feel this—this . . . release with Diarmuid or all would be lost.

She shook her head, willing her gaze to communicate all that she couldn't say, and fled from Tristan, his kiss still on her lips.

Essy squealed in delight as Branwen entered the garden. Presumably at some sweet nothing that Lord Diarmuid had whispered. Her own ears were still burning from the ones Tristan had just bestowed upon her.

The princess laughed again. She didn't notice Branwen from behind the hazel tree. Jealousy pricked her that not only had Essy lied to her, but she'd brought the northern lord to *their* tree.

Lord Diarmuid spotted Branwen first. He straightened up and stepped a few paces away from the princess. He shoved a handkerchief speedily back into his pocket—the one Essy had forced Branwen to give him.

"Lady Branwen," he said, running a finger under the collar of his tunic.

Essy wheeled around. The look of sheer joy on her face made Branwen pause. Who was she to deny her cousin love? What gave her the right to forbid Essy the wonder that she herself experienced with Tristan?

The smile on the princess's face turned to ashes.

"Branny . . . it's not what it looks like."

They both knew she was lying. She didn't put much force behind her protestation.

Branwen angled her shoulders toward Lord Diarmuid. He slumped like a little boy expecting a scolding he didn't think he'd earned.

"I didn't realize you had returned to Castle Rigani," she told him.

"Only just. King Óengus summoned my father, and I accompanied him." Which explained Essy's sudden lighter spirits.

"I see. Would you allow me a moment in private with my cousin?" Branwen pronounced each word precisely, and each syllable had teeth. "I'm certain you would prefer it if Lord Rónán didn't learn where you had absented yourself to."

His jaw tensed. Diarmuid feared his father, even if he didn't fear her. Lord Rónán would surely banish him back to Talamu Castle if King Óengus didn't have his head first.

The northern lord bowed deep and low. He regarded Branwen in a new way, as a true adversary. When it came to defending the honor of Iveriu, that's exactly what she was. It was the mission with which she had been charged; the part she had been chosen to play.

Lord Diarmuid vanished behind the hazel tree. Carved into its trunk were Branwen's and Essy's names.

Her cousin's eyes grew incandescent with anger, and Branwen reached out to snatch the tears leaking from their corners. The princess reeled back.

"Essy, you know this is forbidden." Her voice was soft, and yet still rock hard.

"Are you my warden, Branny?" she demanded.

A blackbird swooped between the cousins and perched on the lowest hanging limb. Its beady midnight eyes were trained on Branwen. This time its call was desolate. The princess didn't appear to hear or see it.

Branwen inhaled. "The Land has chosen her Champion, dear heart."

"Sod the Land! You sound exactly like my mother." Essy balled her hands into fists. "Sometimes I think you forget that she is *my* mother—not yours."

Branwen winced. The words sliced through her heartstrings just as the princess must have known they would.

"You can live happily ever after with Keane," Essy continued ranting, "while I'm shipped off like cargo to a loveless prison!"

"I'm not going to live happily ever after with Keane," Branwen ground out. "And Kernyv is not a prison."

Her cousin scoffed. "For me, it is. Why should you get to choose your sweetheart and not me?"

Branwen was a hypocrite, and she knew it. Tristan had almost made her forget herself. She couldn't let that happen again. She *wouldn't*. Rubbing Lady Alana's brooch, her resolve strengthened.

"Because, Lady Princess," Branwen replied, "Queen Eseult *is* your mother, and *you* will be Queen of Kernyv. And one day *your* son will be King of both Iveriu and Kernyv!"

Fury further reddened Essy's cheeks. "I don't care!" She yanked at her hair. "I don't care about being queen!" she yelled. "I don't care!" Golden hairs like feathers were caught by the breeze. The princess had always raged as fiercely as she loved.

"Stop it, cousin. You are the Land, and the Land is you."

"Then the Land chose unwisely, because not even magic could make me stop loving Diarmuid!"

The blackbird cawed again, with a piercing trill.

Branwen grabbed her cousin's forearms before she could do herself more damage. "Essy! Stop!"

The princess wrenched from her grasp and Branwen stumbled on one of the roots at her feet. "Leave me alone, Lady Branwen!" Essy commanded.

She took one step toward her cousin. The princess thrust out her hand.

"By the Old Ones, *please*, leave me alone." Tears rinsed her cheeks. "You don't listen to me anymore but you listen to them."

"*Essy*—"

"No, you're on their side. You and the queen. Not mine. Diarmuid is the only one who really loves me."

Branwen's jaw dropped.

The blackbird's cry was practically a howl. The princess left Branwen in stunned silence in the dark shade of the tree. Withered leaves crumbled beneath her feet.

The sun disappeared and a light rain began to fall.

Magic. *Magic*, Essy had said. Not even magic could make her forget Lord Diarmuid.

She glanced up at the blackbird. Its wings were glazed with a purple sheen in the drizzle. If the Otherworld was truly guiding Essy toward Kernyv, then the Old Ones must want her to be happy there.

Branwen would ask for their help.

Magic: That's what she needed—what Iveriu needed—now.

LIKE A FORTRESS

HER HEART POUNDING AS SHE made her way from the garden to the west tower, Branwen paused to tap the harp on the green keystone. She sighed, steeling herself, and it resounded up the spiral staircase leading to Queen Eseult's chambers. She spared a brief glance at the east tower, the one her uncle Morholt had occupied, and took the first step.

Morholt's tower was empty now. All of his belongings had been destroyed immediately following the Champions Tournament. Burned. There were to be no remnants of the disgraced King's Champion at Castle Rigani.

Branwen still possessed the sword he'd given her as a girl, however. No one had thought to look for it. She wasn't sure why she had kept it: a vestige of the man who had tried to steal Tristan from her forever. And yet, she couldn't part with it.

Fintan looked tired as he greeted her, his barrel chest more cumbersome. Everyone in the castle was worn out from making preparations for Essy's journey. Branwen knew her aunt wasn't sleeping much, which meant her bodyguard wasn't, either. He was her most constant companion.

"Miserable weather," he muttered before announcing her. Branwen managed a wan smile in return.

The queen was framed against the beveled window by heavy brocade curtains, gray light slipping through her braids. Her eyes were closed, her brow smooth. She looked like she was asleep except she was standing upright.

"Lady Queen?" Branwen said, feeling guilty for disturbing her. She swallowed down the metallic taste on her tongue.

"Branny." Her aunt's eyelids flipped open. "You're all flushed."

Branwen's hand moved to her mouth. Was she? Could the queen tell she'd been recently kissed?

Queen Eseult gave her an assessing look. Now that she was here, Branwen wasn't sure how to ask for what she wanted without betraying her cousin. The queen crossed the room toward her.

"You're working yourself too hard." Her aunt's voice was shaded with affection.

Branwen shook her head, threading her fingers together. "Not at all. Essy's First Night gown is nearly finished. It's just . . ." Why couldn't she find the right words? "Do you have a moment?"

"Always for you." She motioned for her to be seated in a leather armchair beside the window. Walking over to the court cupboard, the queen picked up a carafe and began to pour two small glasses of citrine-colored spirits. "Tell me what weighs on your heart."

"Allow me to serve you," Branwen said instantly, hovering above the seat cushion.

"Dearest, I am perfectly capable of serving myself." Queen

Eseult's face turned pensive. "It's important to remember that some-times we have only ourselves to rely upon."

"Of course." She sank into the chair.

Her aunt presented Branwen with the glass. Taking a sip from her own goblet, the queen settled into the opposite seat, gazing out at the gathering clouds. "There's going to be a storm," she said absently.

Branwen stared down at the golden liquid infused with dried Clíodhna's dust. In small doses, it had a relaxing effect. Queen Eseult must have more worries than she showed.

Her aunt waited for her to speak. "Lady Queen," she began, "it is a matter of the heart that concerns me—but not my own." The queen afforded Branwen a weighted look and invisible bees stung her chest. "Or, rather, it's the taming of a heart that preoccupies me."

"The taming of a heart that is not your own?" said Queen Eseult, sipping from her cup. "That can indeed be a difficult task, my niece. The heart is an unruly beast."

"Yes." Branwen was all too aware.

"Does this heart belong to a Kernyvman, perchance?"

Gooseflesh prickled Branwen's neck and crawled down her chest to her belly button. "In part," she said. Her aunt puzzled at her, lifting her eyebrows as an indication that she should continue. Branwen felt a tickle at the back of her throat.

"I'm also afraid for Essy's heart, Lady Queen."

The queen went still and Branwen feared she'd made a terrible mistake. The edges of her aunt's mouth turned downward. "As am I," she confided. Her shoulders heaved as she exhaled a large breath. "Since the day she was born, I have wanted nothing more than to entrust Essy's heart into safe hands." Unfamiliar regret stained her words. "Yours, too, Branny."

A thud came at the window as the blackbird crashed against it. The queen didn't startle. "We must trust that the Land has chosen a worthy Champion," she continued. *Did she not see the bird?*

"I do, Lady Queen. Only—" Branwen gripped the stem of the goblet harder. "Only I'm afraid that Essy will never know love." And she was afraid her cousin might destroy herself in the process of trying to know it.

"There are many forms of love, Branny."

"True love," Branwen said more forcefully. Then, almost in a whisper, she repeated, "True love."

The queen's eyes, so like her mother's, glinted in the dull light. "My daughter has your love, and I know it to be the truest kind."

Overwhelmed by the compliment, Branwen persevered, fingering her brooch.

"She will have it always," she promised the queen, adding, *No matter how she rages*, in her mind. "But I'm not speaking of the love between cousins, I—I mean what exists between . . . lovers."

Queen Eseult set her goblet down on a side table.

"And this is something with which you have experience, Lady Branwen?"

Tristan's face glimmered in her mind and wildfire scorched her skin. Her eyes blinked rapidly.

The queen listed her head, lips twisting to one side. "In that case, you and the Kernyvak prince will have my blessing—once you're in Kernyv."

"*Th*-thank you, Lady Queen," said Branwen, deluged by gratitude, swearing to herself she wouldn't squander the queen's understanding by giving in to her passions again on Ivernic soil, "but, that's—"

"Not what you came here to discuss," the queen finished for her. She leaned forward, eyes avid. "Branny, please, speak plainly. I believe it was I who explained how children are conceived when you began your monthly bleeding."

Her aunt's laughter was echoed by a shrill descant from the blackbird perched on the window ledge. It almost sounded like a warning yet Branwen couldn't break her course. She had cared for her little cousin's heart since before she could walk.

"Essy asked me once to make her a love spell. I don't know how." Branwen cast her aunt a nervous glance. "I think you do."

"Branny, no." She steepled her fingers tightly together. "It's too dangerous."

"It was dangerous when I healed Tristan," she said, jutting out her chin, surprised by the strength of her own words.

Her aunt also seemed taken aback. "I would never have asked you to risk your life if all of Iveriu had not been at stake."

"I know—I know, and I believe all of Iveriu is still at stake." Branwen couldn't bear to find any more matted clumps of hair on her cousin's pillow, stained with blood. "Iveriu is relying on the princess to ensure peace and happiness. The princess needs us to ensure her happiness, too."

"I see." The queen drummed her fingers on the table; the nails were brittle, unfiled. "It is my daughter's heart you wish to tame."

Black wings rattled against the windowpane. Again, her aunt took no notice. The bird must be another Otherworld echo.

"Yes—and that of King Marc." Branwen never would have

believed she could be so bold. But love made a person do bold—sometimes inconceivably stupid—things. And Branwen loved her cousin.

Silence washed over the room, cold and salty. Finally, Queen Eseult said, "True love is like a blossom. It must spring naturally. Forced fruit is almost always bitter."

"Almost," Branwen said, half question, half prayer. "We owe Essy—" The queen raised a finger, and she bit off her own words.

"I'm sorry, dear heart. My answer is no. The risk is too great. Essy will find her own way with King Marc, as I did with Óengus. We built our love like a fortress, stone by stone."

"Fortresses are built to keep people out."

Her aunt glanced at her owlishly. Branwen had never spoken to the Queen of Iveriu with such audacity. She clasped a hand over her mouth.

"Perhaps it's *your* heart that needs taming, Lady Branwen."

She ducked her head, shame hot on her brow. "Forgive me, Lady Queen." Renewed silence scratched at Branwen's ears. Then she heard the queen drawing in a long breath through her nostrils.

"If you agree to forgive me as well," said her aunt, and Branwen peered up through her lashes. "I know you speak from love, and I am overweary." Queen Eseult fell back against the soft cushion of her chair. "Essy will have you to defend her happiness in Kernyv." She reached for her goblet. "And you are a most determined Champion."

The blackbird launched itself from the windowsill and took to the sky.

Branwen gulped. The queen winked. "It will have to be enough."

She nodded, smiling weakly, but as she descended the steps of the west tower, the truth bit Branwen deeply.

It wouldn't be enough for her cousin. *She* wouldn't be enough.

✠ ✠ ✠

As if the princess already found her lacking, she'd spoken to Branwen as little as possible since she'd been interrupted mid-tryst. Branwen refused to apologize for doing her duty. Essy most likely also blamed her for the fact that King Óengus had charged Lord Diarmuid with preparing a report on the readiness of Ivernic lighthouses, which kept him away from Castle Rigani, although Branwen had no hand in it. So far, the stalemate had lasted half a moon.

The cousins worked together wordlessly to string garlands of autumnal flowers, rosebay and white yarrow, for the children's celebration. The castle servants no doubt remarked on the nippy silence when they were out of earshot.

It was protocol that Tristan, as the winner of the Champions Tournament, should escort the princess on official duties. Essy neither smiled at him nor reciprocated his attempts to befriend her. Their kingdoms had made peace, but the princess waged her own private war.

One afternoon she'd insisted on going riding and rewarded her escort by having her mare relieve herself on his boots. Keane had enjoyed that moment in the stables immeasurably. It pained Branwen more than she could speak aloud. Her cousin's disdain for both of them was already clear as day.

Imagine if she knew the truth about how Branwen felt for the Kernyvman.

Crumbled leaves, toasted brown, crunched beneath her feet as she hurried through the south tower garden after retrieving the present for Gráinne that Essy had forgotten in her apartment. The little girl would arrive any minute. Branwen suspected her cousin had mislaid the doll's dress on purpose to be rid of her lady's maid as she greeted the village children. Excited, apple-round faces had begun filing into the feasting hall, eager hands swiping at Treva's delicious spiced buns.

Although there was a chill in the air, the atmosphere among the coastal villages, and throughout Iveriu, was less desolate than it had been this spring. Peace—and hope—was nearly tangible.

Branwen's gaze flickered to the hazel tree. She curled her lip.

"How has that tree offended you, my lady?"

She swung around at the voice. Tristan took a cautious step out from the shadow of the archway. Something in Branwen's core pulled tight. Light shone through the scattered leaves clinging to the branches above, dappling his warm brown skin.

"I'm afraid, perhaps, that the tree is not the only one to have offended you," he said. Tristan drew nearer, stopping a couple paces in front of Branwen, and planted his feet. He raked a hand through his mop of curls. "You've been avoiding me."

So many explanations, answers, excuses rushed through her mind that she couldn't choose the right one. She clutched the doll's dress against her chest. Tristan scanned it quickly. "The frock would look fetching on you," he said, cracking a quarter smile. "But it seems a tad small." She couldn't quite laugh.

"Branwen?" Tristan made her name sound like a riddle. "Lady Branwen," he corrected himself. "If you regret the kiss, please accept my sincerest apologies." Devastation tipped his words.

She couldn't stand it. "*No*. I mean, I don't—" Branwen stepped closer, and lowered her voice. "I don't regret it." Suggesting otherwise would be a lie. Relief loosened Tristan's stance. He lifted a hand to touch her cheek. Branwen caught it in midair.

"We can't, Tristan."

"What did I do wrong?" His shoulders sagged, swaying in her direction.

She wanted to tell him that nothing he could do was wrong. That nothing had ever felt more right.

"It's Essy," she said. His eyebrows shot up. "She's beside herself about the voyage, about becoming queen, about King Marc—"

"He will be a good husband to her," Tristan interrupted. "I swear to you, Branwen."

"I believe you, it's not that—it's . . . I don't want to throw my happiness in Essy's face." Branwen pointed at the names carved into the bark of the hazel, and Tristan followed with his gaze. The names would remain, etched into the trunk, etched into time, long after she and the princess had been forgotten.

Tristan nodded, seeming to understand. "Then . . . I make you happy?"

Her face must have betrayed her because a smile broke out on his so glorious it could turn night into day. A ray of midnight sun. Before she could speak a reply, however, "Lady Branwen!" called a familiar voice. It sounded like the sharpening of knives, and she flinched. She and Tristan broke apart.

Keane fingered the emerald ribbon on his *kladiwos* as he strutted toward them. Her ribbon. Despite their quarrel, Branwen didn't dare ask for it back. She hoped Tristan would understand.

"You're a difficult woman to track down," said the bodyguard.

"That's the way I like it, Sir Keane." Branwen had also averted any possibility of being alone with Keane since her fever broke. She knew it couldn't last forever.

"*Prince* Tristan," Keane acknowledged with a glare, as if he were spitting out nettles. His gaze shifted between them. "The princess was asking for you, Lady Branwen," he said. "The children have all arrived."

"Thank you," she told him politely. "I'm on my way."

"As am I," said Tristan. He held out an arm. "I would be delighted to escort you."

Keane wrapped Branwen's ribbon around his pinkie like he wanted to choke the life out of it. "Princess Eseult sent *me* to collect her cousin."

Tension coiled more tautly around the threesome than the honeysuckle around the hazel. Branwen knew which of the two men was more likely to bend than break.

"Prince Tristan," she entreated. "Would you mind giving this to the princess?" She held out the doll's dress and glimpsed Keane smirking. "Save me a spiced bun?"

Tristan visibly swallowed. Branwen argued with her eyes, like the night Keane had nearly discovered him in the cave.

With a cordial bow, Tristan declared, "It would be my distinct pleasure" and strode through the archway into the inner ward.

Keane watched him leave, sneering all the while. "The Kernyvman shouldn't attend the celebration," he said, voice rough. "The children don't need one of his kind to remind them of everything they've lost."

"Prince Tristan is the nephew of King Marc, and you would do well to remember it. Because of him, Ivernic children have the chance at a peaceful future. And, despite the indignities he's suffered on our shores—including an assassination attempt—he still willingly extends his hand in friendship."

"He certainly wants to be *your* friend, my lady."

Branwen seared him with a poker-hot glance.

Keane made a disgruntled noise in the back of his throat. "Ah, Lady Branwen, you put me on the back foot. Why is it I can never say what I mean?"

"I don't know, Sir Keane. Why is that?"

Red stained his cheeks. Sighing, he offered her his arm. Branwen wanted to gallop away faster than her palfrey. Instead, she accepted it. A brisk breeze tousled her hair as they processed toward the feasting hall.

Branwen hunted for Tristan across the courtyard, but all she saw were leaves falling against the sky. Taking in her wistful expression, Keane stopped short in the middle of the ward.

"Why did you give me your token, Branwen?" His voice was strained: menacing, but mostly hurt.

"Because you asked for it."

"Was it given unwillingly?"

His eyes were as uncharted as the Dark Waters, to the west of Iveriu. She cast her own to the cobblestones. "I didn't say that." Keane was a warrior of her homeland. She would never seek to dishonor him. But, but . . .

"Ask for it back, then," he said. It was a challenge.

Her gaze snapped back to his. "If that's what you want."

"Of course it isn't what I want!" His bottom lip quivered. Only once. "Unless there is someone else on whom you wish to bestow your colors?"

Keane nodded toward the great hall as if he were shooting an arrow straight at Tristan's back. Branwen said nothing, only pressed her lips into a line.

"Stay." He reached a gloved finger to her cheek. "Stay in Iveriu, where you belong."

Her heartstrings tightened. Even if there were no Tristan, her other true love was journeying across the sea. "The colors of my heart will always be Ivernic," she told him. "But I belong with the princess."

Keane furrowed his brow. "You love your cousin that much?" he said.

It was a question Branwen had posed to herself more than once in recent weeks. The answer leapt from her lips. "More than anything."

He nodded. Branwen's shoulders began to sag in relief and exhaustion.

"What if I asked to be assigned to accompany the princess to her new home? I know King Óengus is on edge about entrusting her safe passage to Kernyvak hands." Keane took a short breath. "Would that please you?"

She gripped her skirts. This was not a complication she had foreseen.

"The Kernyveu would take it as an offense," Branwen said. "Besides, you could never bear to live among your enemies."

"I would bear it if you asked me to, Branwen."

Keane leaned forward, his eyes fixated on hers. He meant to kiss her. And not on the cheek.

Branwen flinched. He paused, their faces an awkward distance apart. It was the only answer he needed.

He garbled something she didn't quite catch, before saying, "I see. You have an Ivernic heart. But you don't want *this* Ivernic heart."

Bristling, the guardsman brushed past her, speeding toward the feasting hall as if he meant to wage war. Numbness spread through her, leaving Branwen strangely bereft, but she didn't call him back. Keane's love would be like a fortress keeping others out—and trapping her inside.

It was not the kind of love Branwen wanted.

THE LOVING CUP

ESSY TWIRLED IN A CIRCLE, ringed by dancing children. Sweet, breathy voices filled the hall, singing a silly round about an Ivernic hero who steals a goat from the Otherworld. Aureate light swathed their faces and crowns of wildflowers bounced atop their heads.

The sight gladdened Branwen beyond measure. She hadn't seen her cousin smile so genuinely since their fight beneath the hazel tree. Keane and Tristan flanked the princess from behind the singing children, shoulders taut, more likely to strike each other than anyone else.

Branwen edged her way around the dance floor to join Queen Eseult. Her aunt watched the merriment from beside one of the tables that had been laid with sacks of pork rinds and other staples from the castle larders. Hearth-baked bread scented the air. Treva, Dubthach, and Saoirse were on hand to distribute the provisions to the children's guardians. Hopefully, the supplies would help the villagers as winter descended.

"Lady Queen," said Branwen, curtsying in greeting. Her aunt smiled and kissed her cheek.

After a final chorus about the antics of the Otherworld goat, the little dancers erupted in giggles and the ring dissolved as they filled their faces with more of Treva's confections. Branwen spied a child with a ruby head, hair gathered into pigtails, darting gaily between the other children toward the princess.

When Essy's gaze landed on Gráinne, her face lit up. Branwen felt lighter as well. "Who is this?" the queen asked.

"One of Essy's most devoted subjects," Branwen replied, and her aunt laughed.

"Princess Essy!" Gráinne exclaimed gleefully, barging her playmates out of the way. She seemed far less frail than when they had first met. "That was fun!" She hugged the princess fiercely.

Winking at the little girl, Essy said, "I believe I promised your Eseult a new dress, didn't I?" Gráinne's beloved doll had been tucked under her arm as she danced and she brandished it enthusiastically.

When Essy beckoned Saoirse forward, Gráinne burbled and squeaked.

Using golden thread, Branwen had stitched rolling waves along the trim of the dress's pleated skirt. Just below the collar she'd embroidered a brooch that resembled her own. Essy's face fell slightly as she caught Branwen's eye, and the princess swallowed audibly.

"It's so lovely, Princess Essy." Gráinne clapped her hands, grabbing the dress brusquely from her grasp. The girl stripped her doll and discarded its ruined dress like yesterday's fish.

Tristan chuckled as he ambled to her side. "A princess should have a dress that suits her station," he said approvingly, dashing the girl a smile.

Gráinne went stock-still. A ribbon of fear creased her brow. An Ivernic child would recognize a Kernyvak accent anywhere.

Essy speared Tristan with her eyes and stroked Gráinne's brow until it smoothed. Branwen felt Queen Eseult go rigid beside her, ready to intervene, but it wasn't necessary.

"There's no need to fear, dear heart," Essy assured the girl. "Prince Tristan is no longer our enemy." The queen relaxed at Branwen's side. Did her cousin believe her own words?

"But he's a Kernyvman!" Gráinne protested, her fright giving way to a scowl.

"Indeed," the princess replied. "Here, let me help you."

While Essy slipped the new dress over the stuffed cotton shoulders of her namesake, Branwen kept an eye on Tristan. The shame that washed over his features lashed her heart.

Would Kernyvak children fear *her*? Branwen wondered.

Sweeping his arm dramatically to the side, Tristan dropped to one knee and bowed before Gráinne. "The Kernyveu love your princess, too," he said directly to the girl. Her gaze pitched between him and Essy. "She is to be our queen. Come, won't you be my friend?"

Gráinne admired her finely attired doll. "My princess is beautiful and kind. She deserves the best prince in the world!"

"Quite so," Essy agreed. "Every girl deserves the prince of her choosing." She stared the queen straight in the eye and the double-edged meaning stabbed Branwen deep, as she imagined it did her aunt.

Tristan rubbed his throat. "Your princess is in need of a crown, I believe, little maid."

Nimbly, he plucked a few stray petals from the stone floor and knotted them together.

Gráinne tittered, smile widening as Tristan crowned the doll. She pecked him on the cheek, then scurried off to present the new and improved Eseult to her band of friends. There was no girl alive whom Tristan could not charm. Except, perhaps, for Essy, who looked considerably less impressed.

Her cousin's expression soured as soon as the children were no longer looking. She approached Branwen and her mother, selecting an elderberry tart from one of the pewter platters on the table.

"You have a way with children," Queen Eseult told her daughter, smiling broadly. "You'll be a wonderful mother."

The princess released a short, caustic laugh. "I'm not even wed and already you would have me with child."

"Essy, don't twist my words." Emotion stretched Queen Eseult's voice. Surveying her daughter's face, she said, "The ribbons in your plaits look lovely" in an obvious attempt to diffuse Essy's temper.

The princess popped the tart in her mouth and chewed. She touched her braids. "Branwen chose them for me: green for Iveriu, black and white for Kernyv." Essy narrowed her gaze at her cousin; Branwen's heart thumped. "I am more symbol than woman, Lady Queen. And *she* is nothing but your puppet."

Branwen staggered back as if she'd been run through with a sword. Tristan immediately moved in her direction; she shook her head. He would only make matters worse.

"Princess Eseult," snapped the queen. "I didn't raise you to be unkind."

Essy squared her shoulders. "Indeed, you raised me to fix your mistake. I am nothing but a failure."

"You're not a failure," she said more softly.

"No, I'm *your* failure, Mother. You failed to produce a boy, to give Iveriu the male heir it needed. I will spend the rest of my life paying for your shortcomings."

Queen Eseult sucked in a breath as her eyes began to gleam.

"Fear not, Lady Queen," Essy added. "You didn't raise me to be unkind. If I give King Marc a girl, I'll ensure she doesn't live to regret being born as I have. I am not as callous as you."

Branwen blinked, stupefied. The princess couldn't truly mean her words.

With a satisfied smirk, Essy stalked back toward Gráinne and her other adoring subjects, leaving speechless the two women who loved her the most. Queen Eseult squeezed Branwen's hand and excused herself without another word. Fintan followed her out.

Tristan crossed to Branwen, coming as close as he could without touching. Keane exchanged one glance with her, then looked away as if he would murder thin air.

"What happened?" Tristan whispered from the side of his mouth, still smiling at the children, and Branwen recognized that he'd also been raised at court.

She couldn't tell him. Much as she might want to. Threatening the unborn heir to his uncle's throne, even in the heat of anger, might endanger the alliance. Branwen dug her fingernails into the heels of her hands.

"Nothing," she said.

"Branwen—"

"*Please.*" It was a rasp.

"Can I do anything to help?"

She tilted her gaze at him. "Just stand by my side."

"Always."

✛ ✛ ✛

Branwen lay sleepless in her bed; the candle in the window burned near to the wick. Essy's accusation tormented her.

The memory of the look on her cousin's face riled her anew.

I am not a puppet.

Throwing a cloak over her nightdress, Branwen looped her curls into a bun at the base of her neck and exited her chamber with a furtive glance down the corridor. She didn't lift the hood of her cloak, because while she wanted to avoid notice, it would be dangerous to be confused for an intruder. The castle was quiet as she slinked through the starlit courtyard toward the west tower, but it was a false quiet—the kind that comes in the middle of a heated exchange. Until the princess was wed, the alliance could still fall apart.

Fintan looked less surprised than Branwen had expected as she approached the door to Queen Eseult's apartment. The guardsman observed much though he said little.

"Up late, Lady Branwen?" Shadows from the torchlight gave his pitted cheeks a mottled appearance.

"Is the queen awake?"

"She is." He reached for the door latch and Branwen spied concern in his eyes.

"Lady Queen?" she called as she entered. She pushed her unkempt locks behind her ears, adjusted her cloak.

Her aunt looked up from where she was seated by the window.

The queen's own plaits were somewhat unkempt, her expression careworn. It was after midnight, yet she hadn't changed from the gown she'd worn to the children's celebration. She seemed utterly drained.

"Forgive me for disturbing you at this hour," Branwen said, joining her by the window. Candlelight wavered between them: a thin, pulsing rhythm at their feet. The queen's hands were clasped together. She ran one thumb over the other, back and forth, back and forth.

"Please, sit. Take off your cloak." Branwen unfastened her mother's brooch and Queen Eseult raised an eyebrow at the nightdress peeking out underneath. "What do you need, Branny?" she asked. Her aunt usually seemed so unshakable—not tonight. Lowering herself into the opposite seat, Branwen noticed an untouched plate of cured meats and cheeses on the side table. A goblet filled to the brim.

"I wanted to see how you were," she said. "After—after what happened earlier."

The queen sighed. She glanced out the window, then back at her niece, smiling with something close to chagrin.

"Alana must have ingested an ancient creature when she was pregnant with you." She spoke with affection as she touched the silver brooch that gleamed against Branwen's shoulder. "You're an old soul, indeed, my niece."

Many a bard sang about pregnant women swallowing supernatural creatures and giving birth to them. The Hound had supposedly come into the world this way. "I don't know if that is so," Branwen demurred.

"Ancient or not, you are wise beyond your years. I thought

devising an errand to keep Lord Diarmuid away from the princess would suffice. . . ."

She met her aunt's gaze. So, the queen had been responsible for the sudden need to inspect the lighthouses. And, by extension, so had Branwen.

"I have never seen Essy grow so attached," her aunt admitted. Branwen leaned forward. "Lady Queen, I beg you to reconsider the spell. I fear for Essy without it."

Queen Eseult chewed her lip. She rubbed the inside of her thumb almost raw, and the evidence of the queen's vulnerability unnerved Branwen a little.

"My mother—your grandmother—warned me against using primordial magic. But"—the queen paused—"with my daughter's heart, it seems I am not as strong."

Blood roared in Branwen's ears. "You're saying—"

"Yes. I'm saying yes. The Loving Cup," Queen Eseult said in a hush, although they were alone.

"*Thank you*. Thank you, Lady Queen."

"Branny, there are always consequences," she said.

"I will bear them."

"*Unintended* consequences."

"I am strong, Lady Queen." Branwen had proved as much on Whitethorn Mound, and she couldn't bear for Essy to ever again look at her the way she had today. "I have already given the Land my blood."

Queen Eseult pursed her lips. "That was healing magic. This is something different."

"I want my cousin to know love," Branwen declared. "What do I need to do?"

"We must wait for the Dark Moon."

Anticipation raised the tiny hairs on her arms. "When will that be?"

"In a month's time. The night of the Farewell Feast." The queen paused. There was only the sound of a flickering candle. "Maybe it is fated, after all."

Branwen thought of Tristan, and how he said he believed in fate not luck. Fate had brought them back together.

"I think it is, Lady Queen. I think it is."

TRAITOR'S FINGER

THE MOON WAS HIGH AND bright as Branwen crept out of the castle, slipping under the noses of the Royal Guardsmen. Everyone in Iveriu was breathing a little easier now that the alliance with Kernyv had been agreed. And Branwen intended to keep it that way.

Tonight she would fetch the final ingredient for the Loving Cup.

Grass and pebbles crunched under her feet as she followed the path that led to her cave—Tristan's cave. *Their* cave. Only that wasn't her destination. She turned a sharp right and began climbing up a steep hill, scrambling over roots and fallen leaves.

The silver glaze cast by the moon was enough to light the way to where Branwen was headed. A secret place. A forbidden place. Only Queen Eseult knew the precise location, and now so did she.

The traitor's grave. Uncle Morholt's grave. Fintan had moved the body in a wheelbarrow, but her aunt had blindfolded him so he wouldn't be burdened with the knowledge. The queen had buried her brother's body by herself with no ceremony but the binding spell to ensure his ignominy.

Ironically, to ensure fidelity, the key ingredient of the Loving Cup was a traitor's bone. When the queen had told her that, Branwen had understood that this spell was the deepest magic. As difficult as turning the tide. For, indeed, the heart was vaster than the Dark Waters.

Uncle Morholt had been stripped of his Champion's ring before being interred. That was the finger she was after. The one that symbolized fealty between a knight and his lord, a man and his betrothed.

Branwen lifted her skirt, bunching it between her hands as she ascended the rocky slope. The hem was soggy from trailing over ground still wet from earlier showers. Now the skies were clear and the air fresh. If the ship didn't set out for Kernyv soon, the seas would become too treacherous and they would be forced to wait until winter had passed.

Queen Eseult was determined that the alliance should be settled as quickly as possible, before the New Year festival of Samonios; which is why they would set sail in ten days under the Dark Moon, even though it was thought to be inauspicious. Branwen remembered the fishermen at Castle Bodwa refusing to take their boats out during the Dark Moon because they said they'd only catch Otherworld creatures and it wasn't worth angering the Old Ones. Killing an Otherworld creature brought down their wrath.

Only since meeting her fox had Branwen come to share their beliefs. What would have happened if Tristan hadn't rescued him from Keane's trap?

The yowl of a night predator tore through the air, causing Branwen to shudder. She reached for the moon-catcher her aunt had given her. The curved blade seemed an unimposing weapon compared with the fanged jowls of the wolves that stalked these woods.

Branwen scratched the gooseflesh erupting on her arms and carried on. She thought of Essy, and of Tristan, and she resolved to keep going. She wanted peace and she wanted her cousin to be happy. She also never wanted Tristan to be forced to choose between his honor and his duty to his king.

Selfishly, Branwen didn't want Tristan to have to choose between her and his kingdom, either. As long as Iveriu and Kernyv were friends, Branwen was free to love Tristan—and he her. She would do this for all of them.

The ethereal light illuminating the forest grew stronger as Branwen reached the top of the hill. She stopped to catch her breath, glancing around her. The silhouettes of naked trees against the sky resembled fearsome raiders. Another tingle zipped down her spine. But they weren't flesh; they were just bark.

No one had followed her.

What Branwen was about to do was expressly proscribed by the ancient laws of kingship. But sometimes it was necessary to break the law in order to keep the peace.

A screech of air rushed in her ears. Unnaturally yellow eyes met hers. The blackbird was back. It cawed so shrilly that Branwen thought her ears might bleed. The creature clipped her with its shimmering wing and flew off.

Queen Eseult had warned her she would be tested. Branwen had never felt as close to her aunt as she did that night in her chamber. She was so honored that the queen had listened to her; she was treating Branwen as a woman, an equal.

Branwen wished her mother had lived to share such secrets with her. An ache welled in her chest at the notion of it—of what had been stolen from her, and what she didn't want to be stolen from any other girl in Iveriu or Kernyv.

Jamming her lips together, Branwen took thirteen paces to the northeast. Even in the darkness, she could see that the ground was shriveled around the spot. Nothing would ever grow here again.

There were no tales of denouncing a King's Champion. Branwen hadn't thought it possible, yet Queen Eseult had repudiated her own brother to a traitor's grave to preserve the peace. The only fate worse, perhaps, was being claimed by Dhusnos. The Dark One. He who birthed the Ivernic people but slighted the Goddess Ériu. For his offence, she drowned him, condemned Dhusnos to rule the Sea of the Dead. Those claimed by the Dark One spent eternity under his yoke.

Branwen sank to her knees on the barren dirt, raised the moon-catcher, and began to dig.

While Queen Eseult never said as much, Branwen knew it grieved her aunt to condemn Lord Morholt. She had seen both her brother and sister laid to rest. She must wonder why she had survived when they had not. Branwen had wondered the same thing about her parents—until the day she met Tristan. That was the day everything began to make sense, slip into place, like the stained glass in the feasting hall.

Earth, chilly and coarse, slid between Branwen's fingers and lodged beneath the nails. Her arms grew sore, her breathing shallow.

The Loving Cup must be prepared in total secrecy, the queen had instructed her. *Its true purpose must never be revealed.* Not to Essy, and certainly not to King Marc. Using magic on a foreign king would be considered an act of war.

At last, the feel of burlap spread between her hands. The freedom of the spirit, the chance to return to one's kinsmen in a different form—to try to right the mistakes of the previous life—was one of the most dearly held beliefs in Iveriu. It was a gift given by the Land to her people.

And the Land could take it away.

Queen Eseult represented the Goddess Ériu to her people, sacred magic flowed in her veins, and she had used her power to bind her brother's spirit to his body so that he could never be reborn. That was a traitor's fate. With her denouncement, he lost the gift of rebirth. Iveriu didn't want traitors returning from the grave.

The queen explained she couldn't ever touch the vessel that contained her brother's spirit or the binding spell would be undone. But they needed something from him. Branwen had to be the one to take it.

To preserve the honor of Iveriu, Branwen had to do something dishonorable. Beneath her closed lips, her teeth chattered. She probed along the rough sack for the seam. In order to trap a man's soul in his body, it was necessary to enclose him—seal him off forever—before laying him in the ground.

Branwen hoped Tristan wouldn't think less of her for what she was prepared to do. But then, he would never know. He *could* never know.

A bone-cold hand slid beneath her grasp. Her heart raced erratically. She clenched her jaw to stop the chattering and her eyes darted around her. The sliver of moonlight crossing her forehead suddenly felt sharp.

She pulled her uncle's decomposing hand through the slit she'd made in the sack.

"I'm sorry," she whispered.

Queen Eseult had assured Branwen that if she worked hastily and accurately, Morholt's spirit wouldn't be able to escape. For a moment, and only a moment, Branwen contemplated releasing it.

Then she shook her head and peeled Morholt's ring finger from the flaking flesh surrounding it. As the finger caught the light, it glowed in a most terrifying way. His skeleton poked out from beneath his skin.

Branwen covered her mouth, squashing a surge of nausea.

She lifted the moon-catcher and it lived up to its name. The blade burned a blinding white. Branwen lowered her eyes, and she took a swing.

Whoosh. Crack. Plop.

Morholt's severed finger fell into her palm. It was frigid, slimy as a slug. Revulsion curdled in Branwen's stomach and she swallowed down a rush of red-hot bitterness.

Forgive me.

Tucking the broken finger into the pocket of her tunic, she retrieved a needle and thread. Her own fingers quivering, she threaded the needle and began to repair the traitor's vessel as skillfully as she could. Tiny sparks scorched Branwen from within. She winced. Her uncle's spirit was fighting her, wanting to fly away.

She gritted her teeth. *No.* Sweat beaded along her brow in the crisp autumnal night.

You can't be free, Uncle Morholt, Branwen told him. *Or none of us ever will be.* She didn't know if his spirit was listening.

The last stitch popped several times. With a more determined motion, she made an awkward, unseemly cross-stitch. It contrasted greatly with the fine love-knots beside it. Branwen recognized Queen Eseult's artistry. She had honored her brother—if only a little.

It was done. Morholt's spirit was sealed for eternity. Panting, Branwen scooped the dirt in her hands like a plow and threw it over the body. By the time she was done, her tunic was filthy and her face streaked with earth and sweat.

Pain pulsed throughout her joints as she slowly, stiffly, got to her feet.

She turned toward Castle Rigani, which looked black against the starry midnight-blue sky. The waves crashing on the beach below seemed nothing more than a sea of shadow. A thousand strands of mermaid's hair effervesced on the sand.

Branwen sighed deeply.

Susurrations filled her ears as she walked home. The Old Ones knew what she had done. She couldn't be certain when or where they would exact their price.

A scurrying in the undergrowth set each of her nerves alight. Amber eyes. The fox growled and launched itself at her, barking and whining.

She started to run; the fox chased after her, snapping at her ankles. Once again, shrieking noises filled her ears.

Covering them with her hands, Branwen stumbled. She couldn't brace her fall. She crashed face-first into a puddle, choking on the grimy water. Drowning.

How could she drown in a puddle?

Branwen jerked her head up and the surface of the dark water came to life. It was spitting and hissing. Boiling. The water was on fire. Figures emerged in the flames, a strange shadow play.

She wanted to look away, but she remained entranced. Those

gifted with Otherworld sight were believed to scry the future on the water's surface; it had never occurred to Branwen that a puddle would suffice.

The fox circled, yapping. At either edge of the shallow pool, she glimpsed an image of Essy. The princess was wearing her First Night gown, a crown upon her head.

Her cousin had become Queen Eseult of Kernyv. Two likenesses of her cousin walked toward each other, toward the center of the puddle, where a pyre burned. Embers crackled and glowed. An angry mob surrounded the two Eseults on every side. There was no escape. No breath. Only smoke.

Both versions of her cousin marched steadily in the direction of the fire. Branwen tried to yell but she could only rasp. Men she didn't recognize ringed the blaze, their faces obscured by flickering specters.

Eseult stepped into the bed of flame and it exploded like a star. Everyone was annihilated. Stark white and then—nothingness.

The surface of the puddle stilled. Branwen lifted her face from the water, spewing out the gulps she had inhaled. The fox yipped beside her, almost apologetic.

He seized her gaze and flames burst in the creature's eyes. Another test, perhaps.

Well, Branwen had survived. She had succeeded.

She patted the skeletal finger in her pocket and spat out the rest of the rainwater.

Queen Eseult had told her she was a healer. True healers healed kingdoms. Branwen would heal the rift between Iveriu and Kernyv even if it was her last act.

THE LAST NIGHT OF THE WORLD

Essy sat quietly as Branwen braided finely spun gold through her hair. It made her already flaxen tresses appear burnished, thickening her mane so that no one could perceive the illusion. Even without a crown, the top of her head sparkled.

Tonight was the Farewell Feast for which all of Castle Rigani had prepared so diligently, and tomorrow they would set out for Kernyv. One life would end and another would begin. Branwen's body vibrated with expectation. So did her cousin's, but of a different kind. Essy tapped her foot incessantly, taking short breaths, not meeting Branwen's gaze. Beneath her silent veneer, the princess was furious.

Branwen pretended not to notice. Tonight was significant for a reason her cousin could never discover. Before they could embrace their new life, in that place between endings and beginnings, lay the task that Branwen had ahead of her. The Dark Moon was here, the moon of magic and death. Unseen, a void in the night sky, it was the most potent time for spellwork, Queen Eseult said.

The traitor's finger—her uncle's finger—was wrapped in thick velvet and secreted beneath Branwen's bodice. Her aunt had prepared a jar of beetles in the infirmary to strip the flesh from the bone: an efficient if morbid solution to the stench of decay. For ten days and nights, Branwen had carried the bone on her person at all times lest it be discovered. Strange dreams had plagued her since she unearthed the grave, but at least the fox and the blackbird had ceased their constant shadowing.

Branwen didn't know if she should be grateful or disconcerted.

She lived in apprehension of the price the Old Ones would ask for the Loving Cup. Still, she was resolved. She had yet to fail their tests. She hoped her mother would be proud of the woman she was becoming, like the queen seemed to be. Yet Branwen hadn't felt Lady Alana's presence since that night on the hill. Would the sacrifice required for the spell be never feeling her mother's spirit again?

At the thought, she pulled Essy's hair too tightly.

"*Ouch*," the princess grunted. It was the first word she had spoken this evening.

"Sorry," Branwen said, and resumed braiding. Her cousin barely glanced in her direction, which was a small mercy because each glance since the children's festival had been more pointed than a spear.

Dexterously, she wove the golden thread into Essy's scalp to disguise the bald patches, where clumps of hair were missing. Heaviness pressed on Branwen's chest. Lord Diarmuid had returned from his lighthouse survey but, to her immense relief, the northern lord kept himself at a distance from the princess. She sighed. While Branwen was relieved, the fresh scabs dotting Essy's head evidenced that she was not.

Once her cousin had shared the Loving Cup with King Marc,

Branwen was confident Essy would know true happiness and all of this unpleasantness between them would sink to the bottom of the Ivernic Sea. Nor would the princess have a reason to further harm herself. She just had to hold on until then.

Essy began humming under her breath. It was Étaín's song. A wistful ballad that narrated the demise of the Ivernic heroine and her cursed love. "*I did not ask for the love I was given: the love for which I must be forgiven.*" In the princess's sweet soprano, the melody became so haunting it would bring a Kernyvak raider to his knees.

Branwen stopped herself. Those Kernyvak raiders were now their allies, or they would be, she reminded herself. She had done everything within her power to make sure they turned from enemies into friends, and yet it was still difficult to shake lifelong prejudices.

"*Do not believe this life is what I wished,*" sang her cousin in a lilting soprano. "*A thousand years, sealed with a kiss.*"

How would the Ivernic noblewomen be received at Monwiku? Branwen wondered. King Marc might order his court not to treat them as enemies but, besides Tristan, would they ever have any friends?

The princess broke off mid-chorus and turned her vivid green eyes on her cousin. They were shining. "You seem almost more disconsolate than me," she said. Her voice was barely a whisper and Branwen was surprised at the tenderness behind it.

Essy craned her neck to meet her gaze. Branwen stilled like quarry caught in a hunter's sights, afraid to provoke the princess's ire anew.

"I don't know what you mean, cousin."

Was that how Branwen appeared? Her stomach pinched. She'd been preoccupied by the Loving Cup, to be sure. She hoped Tristan didn't think she was having second thoughts about joining the princess in Kernyv. Branwen hadn't dared be alone with him since that stolen moment in the garden. The following day, however, she'd discovered a missive wedged under her bedchamber door. It was inscribed with the words: *Odai eti ama*. It wasn't signed. It didn't need to be.

Should she have reciprocated?

"That's what I mean—that faraway look in your eye. As if you're through the Veil in the Otherworld," Essy said, fear and annoyance comingling in her voice. "I think maybe you've never truly returned to us, Branny. To me."

Branwen exhaled an enormous breath. The princess had no idea how close she might be to the truth. "I'm here, cousin. There's just so much yet to do before tomorrow morning." She brushed Essy's jawline with the back of her hand and Essy trapped it there.

"Branny . . . Branny, I—I don't want you to come with me to Kernyv." Shock drenched Branwen's nerves like a freezing bath and she tried to pull away. The princess held her firm. "I don't want you to leave Iveriu—leave Keane—just for me." Tears from her cousin's eyes trickled down their clasped hands, warm and sticky. "I don't want to take away your choices because mine have been taken away."

Guilt spread across Branwen like poison ivy. "Oh, Essy," she said, swiping at the tears with her thumb. In her heart, she knew she wasn't solely journeying to Kernyv out of duty. How could she not follow Tristan across the waves?

"I've been more snappish than an Otherworld goat for weeks, I know," said Essy, choking on a sob. "I thought it would be easier to leave you if you hated me. But it's not."

Branwen crouched down to meet Essy's eye and tears threatened to spring from her own. The princess hadn't been pushing her away out of spite—she'd been trying to set Branwen free.

"Essy," she said gently. "I'm going with you because I *want* to go with you. You are as dear to me as any sister ever could be."

Tears continued streaming down the princess's face. "Now I wish I'd paid more attention when you tried to teach me about herbs, that we'd spent these last weeks together."

"There will be plenty of time for that in Kernyv."

Essy tugged at one of the golden threads near her hairline. "What about Keane? I don't want you to hurt him because of me. Even if I hate having a bodyguard, he's been like a brother, and broken promises smart."

"I never made Sir Keane any promises, Essy." And it wasn't because of the princess that she had hurt him.

"You gave him your token for the Champions Tournament," persisted her cousin. "And you didn't see how grief-stricken he was while you were ill. He was heartbroken. He still is—it's obvious. I don't want to take you away from a man who loves you." Another wave of tears launched an assault. "I'm so sorry."

Branwen quieted Essy's fingers. "Cousin, this is my choice. I choose you. I won't let a man come between us."

A gasp, a strangled kind of laugh-cry escaped from Essy at those words, and she buried her face in the arch of Branwen's neck. Her swallow-like body heaved. The traitor's finger shifted against Branwen's breast, lying in wait, as she shushed her cousin. The bone of the betrayer would ensure nothing came between the cousins again.

After a few moments, the princess settled. "There now," Branwen said, lifting Essy's face toward hers. "The tints on your cheeks have all smeared. Let me fix them before the banquet begins."

Essy scrubbed her face with her hands. "All right, Branny. You always take such good care of me." She hiccupped. "I'm sorry if I don't thank you often enough."

A smile teased the corners of Branwen's mouth as she grabbed a piece of silk from the sideboard and began soaking up the crimson splotches of berry tint from Essy's cheeks. Her cousin had a good, kind heart and Branwen was right to protect it. She'd lashed out from fear, but she meant no harm. Essy twisted her skirts between her hands as Branwen reapplied the rouge.

When she was finished, the princess said, "Now let me do you." Branwen hesitated. She didn't think her cousin knew how to properly apply beeswax or crushed berries. Essy sensed her resistance and lowered an eyebrow. "Branny, I've been watching you for years. I've learned a thing or two."

"For you, anything," Branwen acquiesced as they changed places. She took an apprehensive seat on the wooden stool and Essy plucked a pot of wheaten flour powder from the vanity.

The princess dusted it lightly over Branwen's face. "There, you look like a lily flower."

"So long as I don't look pale as a Death-Teller," Branwen replied. A shiver ran down her spine, and she wished she hadn't mentioned that. Speaking the name drew one near, particularly on a Dark Moon.

Essy patted Branwen's face with rosewater to make the powder stick. The scent was delectable. Under her breath, the princess hummed the verse where Étaín falls in love with her husband's brother. She selected a sky-blue tincture and began applying it liberally to Branwen's eyelids. *Do not blame him, do not blame me—it was preordained.*

"Not too much," Branwen interrupted, "or I'll look like a court jester." She pictured presenting a garish visage to Tristan at the feast and swallowed hard.

"Hush." Essy swatted at her playfully. "Sir Keane won't be able to resist you."

Branwen stiffened as the princess wielded a fine-tipped horsehair brush and dipped it in a lavender-blue pot of beeswax before outlining Branwen's eyes. It was cool and delicate. "We're leaving in the morning, cousin. I think it'd be better if he *did* resist."

Essy put a hand on her hip. "You have tonight."

A thousand lightning bugs tickled Branwen's skin, but she said nothing. Essy always lived for the present.

The princess dabbed her lips with a poppy-colored stain. She clapped her hands together merrily, pleased at her handiwork. "You're so beautiful, Branny!" she exclaimed.

For a moment, Essy seemed as young and carefree as when she was a little girl. Like the day she wrecked Branwen's sandcastle. Branwen's heart stuttered.

"Look!" Essy said, turning Branwen to face the mirror.

Branwen's reservations vanished as she peered into the looking glass. The contrasting light and dark blue tints brought out her eyes, and her pale skin glowed beneath the rouge. A few freckles glinted.

Her lips were curved like butterfly wings, a kissable carmine. Yes, Branwen looked distinctly kissable. Thinking of herself like that made her blush, but she wanted Tristan to see her that way as well—even if they couldn't act on it.

"See," said the princess leadingly and Branwen indulged her with a smile. "Now tell me you don't want to dance with Keane like it's the last night of the world!"

She didn't reply. If it were the last night of the world, Keane would not be the partner she chose. Her cousin's triumphant expression began to wilt.

"Branny," she said. "I need you to do something for me." There was an urgency to Essy's tone that frightened Branwen. "Diarmuid won't talk to me."

Choosing her words with precision, Branwen said, "Men aren't masters of saying good-bye. I imagine he's trying to spare you a bittersweet departure."

"Right now, it's only bitter. There's nothing sweet about it." Her voice broke. "Remember how Master Bécc said that if you strip the bark from the hazel that the impression of the honeysuckle remains?" Branwen nodded. "Diarmuid is under my skin, too, and I need to know if I'm under his—whether I was truly loved at least once in my life. To know I had something truly my own. Before I'm given to a husband I've never met."

Pity overflowed inside Branwen. If only she could tell her cousin about the Loving Cup. She was willing to risk the retribution of the Old Ones because Essy had made her impression on Branwen's heart long ago.

"What is it you want me to do?" she asked.

Essy opened the jewelry box beside the mirror. "Give Diarmuid this." Withdrawing a small scroll, she pressed it into Branwen's hand.

Branwen sucked in a breath. "This is dangerous. Not just for you—for me."

"I won't order you to do it. Not like last time." Her lower lip trembled. "I'm *asking* for your help. Do this for me and I'll leave for Kernyv without protest," pleaded her cousin. "I'll die happy."

Branwen clutched at Essy's shoulders. "You're *not* going to die."

"I might as well," said her cousin, the fervor leeching from her words. It was replaced by something colder, deader. Branwen shuddered. They were close—*so* close—to laying the foundations for a lasting peace.

The din from the guests arriving at the castle gates transformed into the swell of the surf. The sea was speaking to her; Branwen tried to listen.

She leaned back, turning over the scroll with her fingertips. "I'll deliver your message, Essy," Branwen told her. "I hope Diarmuid gives you the answers you seek."

The princess threw her arms around Branwen. "I love you, Branny," she whispered. "Never forget."

"We should get to the feast."

Essy leapt to her feet, eyes bright with hope, and extended a hand. Branwen secreted the scroll in her skirts. She forced a smile as she escorted the princess down the stairs. Whatever was contained in the letter was tantamount to treason, Branwen had no doubt—not just against Iveriu, but Kernyv, too. Words could bring war faster than a blade. As if excited by the prospect, the traitor's bony finger itched against the underside of Branwen's bodice.

She had come too far to let Uncle Morholt win.

SEALED WITH A KISS

LANTS OF BURNT-ORANGE LIGHT FELL over the feasting
hall. The victories of Iveriu's legendary heroes were frozen and
dark in the paneled glass. Branwen realized she would never see them
again in the golden afternoon light. She would never see Castle
Rigani or any of its inhabitants again.

Branwen had chosen a gown of flushed pink for the farewell celebration, the color of cheeks on a winter's morning. In between her
plaits, she had tied tiny acorns painted gold. Her right shoulder was
adorned with her mother's brooch.

Vats of red ale glistened in the candlelight. Would King Marc
serve his subjects red ale at Monwiku? Branwen's brain buzzed with
questions about her new home. Well, she would have the entire voyage to quiz Tristan about their destination. Even if the tides were
with them, the journey would take two weeks. Maybe more.

After Branwen had greeted King Óengus and Queen Eseult, she
retreated to a quiet alcove. Essy stood with her parents in the center

of the hall, ringed by representatives from the Mumhanztir clans, which included Lord Conla, her previous infatuation. If the Champions Tournament had been announced a season earlier, would she have pinned her hopes on Conla rather than Diarmuid?

Keane and Fintan stood sentry behind the princess and the queen, their *kladiwos* blades jangling against their hips. Tonight, the Royal Guard sported the emerald-green tunics of peacetime. Their sleeves were trimmed with saffron-colored piping, however, to denote that war was only ever a dice throw away.

Branwen's ribbon was still attached to Keane's sword. She presumed that after she'd made clear she didn't reciprocate his feelings, he would have gotten rid of it.

"Why are you hiding, my lady?" Tristan asked, sliding into place beside her.

Her chest tightened as she realized how much she wanted him to touch her again. Hope and fear bit her heart, deep and sweet.

Breathlessly, Branwen answered, "I'm not hiding. I'm used to fading into the background."

Tristan frowned. Oh, he was gorgeous when he frowned. He wore leather trousers and an ecru-colored tunic trimmed with black velvet—the royal Kernyvak colors. Ever so faintly, she could make out the muscles of his torso beneath the tunic. His dark locks had been tamed with beeswax this evening, although they were longer than when he had arrived for the Champions Tournament. Branwen liked it.

He leaned into her. "Is that why I've seen so little of you?"

Branwen inhaled deeply, finding it hard to utter a verbal response. Her eyes skimmed his features. Candlelight from the chandeliers warmed his bronze skin in the most alluring way. Belatedly, Branwen wondered if Tristan felt uncomfortable in a sea of pale faces; not that he seemed anything but confident. The Aquilan Empire had given up its campaign to conquer Iveriu before it had begun and their island received few merchant ships from the southern continent. Would Monwiku be comprised of more diverse courtiers?

Tristan's gaze dropped to his chest, where the Rigani stone pendant used to dangle. "I'm sorry I lost your promise to me, Branwen. I scoured the entire tournament pitch for it, I assure you."

"It doesn't matter. The amulet served its purpose."

"Yes—it brought me back to you. We've come a long way from the cave." Lowering his voice, he added, "*Emer*," and her body sizzled with panic and something else, something akin to yearning. The whole of Castle Rigani could have been illuminated by the energy that coursed between them.

Branwen saw Keane regarding them from the center of the festivities. He always observed his surroundings vigilantly. It was doubtless why he was selected as a bodyguard, yet it unnerved her. She took a step away from Tristan. Glancing over her shoulder, he twisted his lip as his eyes settled on the Iverman's leery stance.

"Sir Keane watches you closely," he said. *Too closely.*

Anxiety spooled through her. "Out of duty."

"Nothing more?"

Surreptitiously, Branwen reached out and took his hand, pulling it behind her back. She slid her sweaty fingers between his, even though it was unwise. The compulsion to touch him was stronger than her sense. Tristan closed his eyes for a beat and sighed.

"The memory of that darkened stairwell keeps me up at night," he said in gravelly voice. "I hope the princess realizes how lucky she is to have as concerned and loyal a cousin as you." Branwen felt a tickle in her heart at the words, followed by the urge to squirm. Essy's letter to Diarmuid burned a hole in her skirts. No matter what she did, Branwen always betrayed someone she loved.

"Prince Tristan!"

Queen Eseult raised her goblet from across the hall, beckoning him over. Branwen immediately released Tristan's hand and her palm ached for the feel of his skin. The gossiping quieted to a dull roar as Tristan processed toward the queen. No one in the kingdom doubted her authority, or that she and King Óengus ruled the land together, as partners. Branwen prayed King Marc would defer to Essy in the same way.

She followed Tristan, keeping a step behind, her cheeks and chest tingling. The queen had asked her to be circumspect, after all, yet she burned not to be. Essy smiled at Branwen as she joined the guests at the front of the hall, then compressed her lips at the Kernyvman.

When Queen Eseult was satisfied she had the attention of her subjects, she said, "Prince Tristan, in addition to being a warrior, I've learned, is a poet. He promised me a song when he first arrived in Iveriu."

"I always keep my word, Lady Queen," Tristan said, inclining his head.

She flicked her wrist in one precise motion. Fintan instantly materialized holding a *krotto* harp between his meaty palms. Recognition flashed in Tristan's eyes.

"This *krotto* belonged to my sister, Lady Alana of Laiginztir—Lady Branwen's mother. It has been passed down for generations, and now I gift it to you on the eve of your voyage," the queen declared.

Essy released a small gasp, annoyed on her cousin's behalf. Queen Eseult would always be queen before mother or friend, as the princess would learn to be. She didn't need Branwen's permission. Lady Alana's harp was the queen's to gift. Still, Branwen inferred a deeper meaning.

Tristan's eyes skittered to Branwen, uncertain whether to accept the token. To rebuff the hospitality of a regent would be a huge offense. And yet, he sought her permission. She gave a small nod.

"I am honored, Lady Queen," he said.

Queen Eseult looked from Branwen to Tristan. "The honor is mine." This was as close to a public blessing as her aunt could give them, whether Tristan realized it or not. The queen clapped her hands together once, reminding Branwen of Essy. "Now, the song."

Tristan accepted the *krotto* from Fintan. Another servant brought him a stool. Seating himself, he set the harp upon his lap, plucking at the strings and tuning each one methodically. Unbidden, the image of Tristan plucking the laces of her bodice with the exact same precision skipped through Branwen's mind.

He scanned the faces of the crowd, smiling archly. "Do the ladies have any requests?" he asked.

"Étaín," Essy said, a croak in her voice. "Étaín's song." A little louder now.

The queen scowled. "That is such a sad tale."

"It's what I'm in the mood for," her daughter replied. A pinkish mustache of frothed ale adorned Essy's upper lip. Branwen had to refrain from wiping it away out of habit.

King Óengus folded his arms across his chest, glaring at his only child. Étaín's name meant "jealousy." If the bard was anyone other than Tristan, he might take it as a slight against his king and his people.

Tristan smiled a tad more nervously. "'The Wooing of Étaín,'" he said, stroking a chord. "A wonderful choice, Lady Princess. Let's see if we tell it the same way in Kernyv. Maybe Étaín will get a happy ending."

"None of us gets a happy ending," Essy countered, glancing in Diarmuid's direction. Branwen had seen him arrive late and position himself as far away from the princess as he could. She flashed her cousin a smile that was sympathetic yet tinged with warning.

Strumming the first few notes, Tristan said, "Maybe tonight we can change our fates, Lady Princess."

Essy responded by rolling her eyes. Tristan caught Branwen's gaze as he expertly teased the strings. She swallowed. "*Étaín—in jealousy was I born and named,*" he began in a mellow baritone. Branwen was immediately entranced, as was the rest of the audience. "*Étaín—destined to bring my lovers pain.*" The elegy was usually sung by women, but the timbre of his voice captured the heroine's plight completely. An exquisite despair. The rough, masculine edges to his words hinted at the violence that jealousy provoked.

Branwen flicked a glance at her cousin. She was utterly still, as if she were paralyzed, and her eyes were wet with tears. The queen watched her daughter, too.

"*How could I have known my heart's true home lay with another?*" sang Tristan, studying Branwen's face, calling back her gaze, and her pulse hurtled toward the stars. Beneath his ready smiles, she glimpsed the deep sorrow he kept buried. He couldn't prevent it from staining the melody.

"*For love of me, his own heart he refused to tame.*"

Although all the revelers knew how Étaín's story would end, they clung to Tristan's every verse, hoping this time the outcome might be different. Even Keane looked stirred. A low gasp escaped Essy as the wife of Étaín's lover cursed her to become a fly, then conjured a storm to blow her away.

Branwen's attention drifted to Lord Diarmuid. She picked a sliver of skin along the bottom of her thumb, red and raw. He looked handsome enough in a pale blue Uladztir tunic, but he certainly wasn't worth the peace between two kingdoms. She winced as the cuticle tore.

"I did not ask for the love I was given: the love for which I must be forgiven."

While the other guests were distracted, Branwen melted back into the crowd. This would be her best opportunity to speak with the northern lord.

"Lord Diarmuid," she whispered, sidling next to him. He startled, confusion on his face. "Follow me."

Diarmuid hesitated. "*Now*," she said. And he did. Branwen's stomach turned over several times as she led him through a passageway concealed by a tapestry depicting the ancient Queen Medhua of Conaktir.

"Fate-tossed, far and wide was I blown." Tristan's dulcet voice rang in her ears, lamenting how Étaín was lost among the mists of time. *"A thousand years, sealed with a kiss."* That was normally where the tale ended.

Branwen heard Tristan pluck the strings for another verse as she snuck into the courtyard beside the hall, Diarmuid at her heels. She was too far away to make out his words. Without the moon, the only light in the quadrangle came from the banquet. Strange tawny shadows were cast over the night. The presence of the Otherworld was palpable, ready to be unleashed.

But first Branwen had to deal with Lord Diarmuid.

"Where are you taking me?" he said, tone arrogant. She felt his breath on her back as he exhaled. "I've left Essy alone and I'm not in the humor for another scolding."

She stopped short, whirling toward him. "There's nothing funny about this, and she is *not* Essy to you, Lord Diarmuid," Branwen reminded him harshly. "Princess Eseult is your sovereign—and nothing more."

Diarmuid's shadow flickered as he shifted his weight. "If that were true, we wouldn't be here right now."

Branwen wanted to knock the smugness right out of him. Her eyes whizzed around the courtyard. She couldn't hear or see another living soul. On the ramparts, a few grisly skeletons glared down at them.

"Alas, Lord Diarmuid, you are not altogether wrong about that." She threw her shoulders back. "Your princess requires that you return the token she gave you for the Champions Tournament."

"The handkerchief? Essy wants it back?"

Branwen heard the hurt in his words. Maybe Diarmuid did have real feelings for her cousin. It didn't matter. Nobody was worth a war.

"Your *princess* wants it back," she said.

In the darkness, she sensed their gazes collide. Branwen could just about make out the whites of his eyes. Then he blinked. There was a rustling of cloth as he retrieved the handkerchief from a pocket.

Essy would hate Branwen if she discovered what she had done. She hated herself a little. "Do you truly love my cousin," she demanded, trying not to touch his fingers as she accepted the handkerchief, "or simply her crown?"

Diarmuid swallowed loudly enough for her to hear it. A strange wheezing sound. Branwen asked because Essy wanted to know, but she needed to know, too.

"Would you lay down your life for her love?" Branwen tucked the handkerchief away. He seemed at a loss for words. "Would you abandon your lands and titles if she asked you to?" she prompted.

He coughed, hard. "I love the Lady Princess Eseult as a vassal loves his lord," he said, after another lengthy pause. "As is only right."

It was done then. Diarmuid was relinquishing his claim on Essy's heart now that he could no longer have her crown. The Loving Cup would bring her cousin greater love than she would have known in Iveriu.

"In that case," Branwen said, straightening her spine, "may the Old Ones watch over you."

"And you, Lady Branwen." Torchlight moved like a pendulum across his brow. "Please give the princess a kiss good-bye for me." Diarmuid planted a firm closed-mouth kiss on her cheek. He smelled of roast pork and too much ale.

"Farewell, Lord Diarmuid."

Branwen turned on her heel and walked away, leaving her cousin's fair-weather lover in perplexed silence. She would burn both the handkerchief and the letter, and there would be nothing left of the affair but smoke and ash. He never could have been the lover Essy desired.

Just as she was about to rejoin the celebrations, a hand shot out and pulled Branwen roughly into one of the servants' stairwells. Down below, she heard the jangling of pots and pans from the kitchen. The pungent aroma of sow's milk filled the air.

Branwen found herself pressed against a cold, slick stone. Condensation tickled her neck. Excitement pulsed through her body that Tristan might have followed her to steal another kiss. It was quickly replaced by dread that he might have seen her with Diarmuid.

The damp of the stairwell seeped into her pores as her eyes adjusted to the scant candlelight.

"Three darknesses into which women should not tread," Keane rasped in her ear. "The darkness of mist. The darkness of a forest. And the darkness of night. You've ventured into all three, *Lady* Branwen." He sank his body into hers. "You're not a lady at all."

Keane reeked even more strongly of spirits than Lord Diarmuid had. Angrily, she pushed him away. In his inebriated state, he stumbled back against the other wall but regained his footing in an instant.

"What's wrong, Branwen?" He sneered. "It seems I'm the only eligible bachelor at Castle Rigani you *don't* tryst with."

On impulse, Branwen raised her hand to slap him and he caught it, gripping it tight. "You don't know what you're talking about!" she whispered furiously.

Keane had seen. Keane had seen her with Diarmuid. He thought they were *trysting*.

"Does your bastard Kernyvak lover know you also enjoy a good, stiff northern breeze?"

Branwen's jaw tensed. His spite could ruin everything. "Prince Tristan is a friend," she protested, breath ragged. "Soon to be family."

Keane's laugh was so hateful it made her skin crawl.

"Until this moment, I thought it was only the Kernyvman who wanted to be more than your friend. Your expression tells me you want it, too. Are there any lines of decency you won't cross?"

Incensed, she tried to strike him with her other hand. Keane caught that, as well, and pinned both of them over her head, jostling her back against the wall. A new kind of terror struck her.

"Keane, you're drunk." Branwen tried to reason with him. "*Let me go.*" He made no move to release her and dread slithered around her like a creeping vine, stomach roiling at his touch. Desperation colored her voice as she said, "This isn't you, Keane," and she hoped she was right. On the Rock Road, Branwen had sensed the rage inside him as he spoke of his murdered parents, but she'd had no inkling it might be turned against her.

"Please, stop. Release me," she said, "I thought we were friends." Her voice strained on the final word.

He grimaced at that. "*Friends?* Like you are with the pirate? Branwen, you were never my friend. You were playing me the whole time. You never intended to keep the promise you made me," Keane fumed. "I am drunk—a drunken *fool*. And it's your fault."

His anger crashed into her, a rabid beast. Branwen did genuinely regret leading him on when she knew her heart was spoken for, but it didn't justify his behavior. His grip was tight on her wrists as she tried to placate him.

"I'm sorry," she said in a quiet voice.

Keane shook his head in a violent gesture. "I've watched you for a long time, Branwen. Waited. Made sure you were safe—I would have given you everything I had. But then the joke would have been on me."

She stared at him. "Safe?"

"Yes, *safe*. Who do you think was watching over you when you would sneak out to your cave? I know it wasn't only a fox you met there." He snorted. "I heard you speaking with a man. I didn't want him to take advantage of you."

Renewed terror numbed her. Could Keane have realized it was Tristan? Branwen's throat went tight. "Why protect me, Sir Keane, if you think me so without virtue?"

"Because *I* wanted to be the lover you invited to your cave," he said miserably.

Untold relief flooded Branwen that Keane had only guessed what she did at the cave, that he didn't know anything certain about Tristan. She would protect him with her life, and her honor. Branwen had already made that oath when she placed the *kladíwos* blade in his hand to fight her own people.

Keane's eyes bored into her. The noise of the carousing next door filled the space between them. After a few more tense moments, he said, "Maybe creed doesn't matter to you. Is that it, Lady Branwen? I'm just not highborn enough for you?"

"Love doesn't care about a noble birth, only a noble heart," she said, her voice deepening, becoming more authoritative. "Which is why you'll never have mine. Now release me."

He looked as dazed as if she had punched him square on the nose. Keane relinquished his hold on her, and Branwen thought he was coming to his senses. Then, brutally, he forced his mouth onto hers, parting her lips heatedly with his tongue.

In that fraction of a second, Branwen knew the exact taste of anguish. Life had crimped Keane's heart, made it greedy and unyielding, but she hadn't realized it had also twisted his soul. She beat against his chest with her hands while he roamed the outline of her bodice with his. Vitriol flowed through her veins.

His fingers tripped across Essy's love letter, tearing it from the folds of her dress.

"No!" she exclaimed. In her mind, Branwen saw a world on fire.

She tried to snatch the scroll back but Keane kept it out of her reach. He broke the seal. "This must be from one of your many lovers," he said mockingly. The tiny ripping sound ricocheted in her ears.

Keane unraveled the missive, and that's exactly how Branwen felt. Her world was coming undone.

"*My darling Diarmuid,*" he began reading aloud. "*Tomorrow I am to be set adrift, abandoned. Without you, my life is jettisoned from me.*"

A flutter came at the window, high above in the turret. The blackbird trained its eyes on Branwen. Once more, she tried and failed to grab back the letter from Keane.

"*This world, Iveriu, means nothing to me compared with you. I am ready to leave it behind if I can't have you.*"

Disbelief permeated Keane's entire face, rancor in his voice. He began to shake.

"*Come for me, my love,*" he continued, "*Rescue me. I will follow you anywhere. I value my crown less than the weight of its gold. Let us follow our hearts rather than the designs of others.*" A soul-shattering pause. "*Your devoted lover, Eseult.*"

Branwen bit the inside of her cheek and tasted blood. This was so much worse than she'd imagined. She pictured Essy as a little girl beside the waterfall, only this time all of Iveriu was on the ledge with her.

Keane dropped his hand to his side, crumpling the scroll with his fist, sighing heavily. Thank the Old Ones she hadn't delivered that letter.

Thinking of how her cousin wanted to make amends before the feast, a red streak of anger sliced Branwen to the bone. Essy wasn't setting Branwen free, she wasn't giving Branwen back her choices—she was running away and leaving her behind. For half a second, Branwen considered abandoning the entire project of the Loving Cup. *No.* She couldn't. Queen Eseult was counting on her, as was the Land. And she was a healer first.

When Keane raised his eyes to Branwen again, there was no light in them.

"My princess is a slut, and you, *Lady* Branwen, are nothing but a whore."

Crack. Branwen's hand collided with Keane's cheek like a thunderbolt. The force of it reverberated through her, made her teeth ache. Fury had replaced her fear. Keane rubbed the red mark she'd made and scoffed.

Totally calm, he said, "I have wasted my whole life in the royal service. And for what? To make peace with my enemies?" A muscle tightened in his jaw. "No, the spirits of my family will not rest until they have a thousand Kernyvak heads."

Branwen would have preferred it if Keane fulminated. His self-possession terrified her more.

"I will show this letter to your dear, sweet Kernyvak prince, and then he will have no choice but to tell his uncle that the Ivernic princess is defiled."

"Essy thinks of you like a brother, Keane. Would you condemn her this way?"

Hesitation flickered on his brow, before transforming into an ominous smile.

"You can't choose your friends, only your enemies—and I have chosen mine."

Panic bloodied her. Peace could be lost by a few swirls of ink, the princess's pen mightier than any sword. The blackbird pierced the veil of stars with a plaintive cry.

"I can't let you do that," she said.

He snarled a laugh. "You don't have a choice."

Keane had been far more broken by pain and war than she'd known. Branwen had believed herself to be broken by her parents' deaths. Now she understood the love of her aunt and cousin had held her together. But there were more broken warriors like Keane—too many—who would like nothing more than another fight.

The right fight. Branwen tilted her head toward the window. Had the blackbird spoken? It sounded so much like her mother.

"I do have a choice," Branwen told him.

With more strength than she knew she possessed, she grabbed the *kladiwos* blade dangling at Keane's waist, holding tightly to the ribbon, and pressed the edge to his throat.

He scoffed. "You won't do it."

"Give me the letter."

The face Branwen had once found pleasing had become a hideous mask. "I don't believe you," Keane said.

"You have no idea what I would do for peace."

Her words gave him pause. He regarded her oddly, as if he were seeing someone else entirely. A nerve twitched repeatedly above his eyebrow. With a grunt, he extended Essy's letter toward her.

As Branwen reached for it, Keane yanked her forward, snaking the sword from her grasp and knocking her chin against his collarbone with a thud. *No,* it couldn't end like this. She couldn't fail now.

Mother, Father, help me. By the Old Ones, help me!

Light brighter than day, brighter than the Belotnia fires, erupted in the confined space. Keane stared at Branwen in horror. The flames were sprouting from Branwen's palm, rippling along her heart line.

Fury consumed her and she watched from outside herself as she pressed her palm to Keane's heart.

He seized and shook like a man hit by lightning. Steam surrounded them. A fine, glimmering mist.

Keane tried to speak, to cry out, but he could not. Life drained from him.

Her hand on his heart, Branwen told him, "One Iveriu. Forever."

The blackbird flew away and took Keane with it.

THE IN-BETWEEN

BRANWEN STARED DOWN AT KEANE'S tortured body. Her mouth fell agape as she returned from afar. She doubled over and vomited the entire contents of her stomach onto the stone beside his head.

And then she ran. She ran faster than any Otherworld creature. She reached the opposite side of the castle before reason began to prevail. She couldn't let Keane's body be discovered by the Royal Guard. He was Essy's bodyguard; someone might think a plot had been hatched against her life—that peace with Kernyv was only a charade.

Choking back her rage, Branwen tried to catch her breath. She had murdered a man. She had killed Keane to protect Iveriu; but, if anyone knew, it might also destroy any chance for peace. Was Keane the price the Old Ones demanded for the Loving Cup?

Branwen needed to think quickly. The muscles in her neck

tensed and jumped. There was only one person she could trust to keep this secret.

Tristan could never know; how could he love her if he knew she had taken a life? If he had seen what she was capable of? And Essy . . . Essy thought of Keane as a brother. She couldn't find out he'd been willing to destroy her reputation for a personal vendetta.

Barking came from the ramparts. The fox. *What? What do you want to tell me?* More futile whimpers. Sweat pooled in her palms and Branwen smeared it along the sides of her gown.

She strode toward the nearest torch and set Essy's words of love ablaze. The love that had cost Keane his life. They were followed by the handkerchief. The clumsy stitches smoked and blew away.

Only one piece of evidence remained.

"On behalf of King Marc of Kernyv, I gladly accept this Seal of Alliance," Tristan announced to King Óengus, and all those assembled, as he signed his name to the treaty he would bring home with him across the Ivernic Sea. "The son born from their union will unite our peoples forevermore as rightful heir to both kingdoms."

Thunderous applause and cheers rocked the feasting hall. Branwen smoothed her plaits behind her ears, trying to conceal her untamed appearance. Queen Eseult's eyes found her straightaway, as if her niece's heart had called to her own. Branwen tipped her head toward the antechamber and the queen nodded. Then she slipped back into the darkness.

Terror pinched Branwen's chest harder with each passing second.

Hopefully, Tristan was too preoccupied with the king to notice her prolonged absence. Essy, she was certain, would have seen Diarmuid return. She could only pray that her cousin didn't come looking for her; she didn't think the princess could bear the weight of such a secret. Of death.

Branwen forced her eyes shut as she waited, pretending she hadn't just killed a man. She tried to picture Keane as he had been at the Champions Tournament, strutting across the battlefield. But all Branwen could see was his withered, tormented face—as if he had been burned alive from the inside out. And that smell, the stench of singed flesh.

She doubled over again, shivering, and crumpled to the floor.

"Branny?" the queen said kindly. A warm hand rubbed up and down her spine.

Full of shame and tears, Branwen barely dared to look at Queen Eseult.

"What's happened? Tell me," her aunt implored her.

Blubbering, and wiping the snot from her nose, Branwen gathered in all the air she could. As much as she thought it might take for her to burst. For a moment, all she wanted was to disappear, evaporate. Explode.

Haltingly, she said, "I've done a terrible thing."

Her aunt crouched down beside her. "Whatever it is, Branny, we'll remedy it."

"Not this." She gasped another breath. "Not this."

Queen Eseult framed Branwen's face with her hands, her gaze insistent.

"It's Sir Keane. He, *he* . . ." Branwen's voice faded to nothing. Senseless garbles.

"He what?" The queen's tone held a shred of fear.

How could Branwen explain to her aunt what Essy had asked of her? She didn't want Diarmuid's blood on her hands, too. The queen would be within her rights to ask for the feckless lord's head on a platter for trysting with the princess after she was betrothed to King Marc. At the very least, he would be exiled. Branwen didn't want that, not for Essy, not after what she had done to prevent anyone from finding out.

Clasping her shaking hands together, Branwen told the queen, "He doesn't believe in peace."

"I see. And where is Sir Keane right now?"

"In the servants' stairwell. Only—"

A sharpened eyebrow. "Only what, Branwen?"

"He's dead." She paused. "I killed him."

No response.

"It was an accident. I didn't mean to, I swear I didn't!"

The queen's gaze clouded over briefly; she pulled a loose thread from the hem of her sleeve. A boisterous tune spilled out from the feasting hall, accompanied by Tristan's melodic baritone. Branwen glanced toward the shafts of honey-colored light that stretched from the hall to the antechamber. It seemed such a different world from hers. She didn't belong there anymore. She could barely breathe as she waited for her aunt to speak.

Finally, Queen Eseult said, "How? How did you kill him?"

Branwen's face broiled under the queen's scrutiny. "I don't know, Lady Queen. I was scared. He threatened me. He wouldn't listen to reason—" The words became stuck in her throat and they scratched her like a claw. Her chin wobbled so furiously that her teeth chattered; the *clack-clack*ing resounded in her mind. "I . . . I pressed my palm to his heart and he began to burn. It all happened so fast."

The queen's lips parted, shock momentarily fracturing her composure, an unreadable look in her eye.

Fresh tears rolled down Branwen's cheeks. "I killed Keane, Lady Queen. It wasn't my intention, but I did."

She hadn't meant to kill Keane, she was sure she hadn't. She just needed him to stop. Branwen had only wanted him to stop. And yet, beneath her horror squirmed some new, dark exhilaration.

Queen Eseult touched a hand to her mouth as she inhaled. "The Hand of Bríga."

Confusion knit Branwen's eyebrows together. *The Hand of Bríga?* She'd never heard of it. Worrying one hand over the other rapidly, her shoulders lifted even closer to her ears. The queen reached for Branwen's right hand, quieting her excessive fidgeting. With reluctance, Branwen let her take it, and she turned it over to examine the heart line.

After Branwen had healed Tristan with the white magic of the *skeakh* bark, the scar had turned a lustrous silver—like a tear in a veil of lace. It was the seam between her and the Otherworld. Now, the tiny ridges of her palm were an angry crimson, as if she had been the one scorched.

"The Hand of Bríga," her aunt repeated. "From the same source comes creation and destruction. It's been generations . . ."

Foreboding skirred through Branwen's being. Before she could ask the queen what she meant, her aunt commanded, "Fetch Sir Fintan immediately. Take him to Keane's body. I will meet you there after I procure something from my chamber."

Branwen was about to protest but the fierce certainty in the queen's eyes silenced her. "I'll always protect you, Branny." Queen Eseult held her hand a beat longer. "As long as it's within my power."

"Thank you." Branwen curtsied, still in a daze, and skulked back into the hall.

Luckily, Fintan was standing at attention just outside the door, ready to protect his mistress with a fist or a blade.

"Sir Fintan," she said in a low voice, slightly breathless. "Queen Eseult has need of you. Quite urgently. Please follow me."

His brow arched in suspicion. Branwen caught a glimpse of how terrifying Fintan could appear to his enemies. She hoped he would never count her among them.

Hand closing around the hilt of his *kladiwos*, he said, "Lead on, Lady Branwen. Lead on."

Keane's back was turned toward them as Branwen and Fintan approached, his knees folded into his chest.

"*Oi.*" Fintan sighed gruffly when he spotted him. "Too much ale, lad?" he muttered, half in amusement, half in chastisement. "Get up, Keane!"

But the soldier didn't stir.

More annoyed, Fintan said, "No sleeping on the job! Can't hold your mead? You give the Royal Guard a bad name." He shoved Keane with the toe of his boot.

Still, the bodyguard didn't move a muscle. Branwen watched the scene unfold, heart slamming against her rib cage. Part of her brain tried to delude itself that Keane was only asleep. That it would only take a bucket of water to rouse him.

"Move your arse, man!" Fintan exclaimed, squatting down beside him. His joints groaned. One hand on his blade, the old soldier yanked Keane's shoulder toward him.

As his eyes fixed on Keane's contorted visage, Fintan drew his *kladiwos* and sucked down the phrase, "Otherworld protect me."

Branwen's shoulders began to heave. Keane looked far worse than he had only ten minutes ago. Now he didn't just look withered, but shriveled—the husk of a man. Skin sagged from his cheeks, loose like the lard Treva used to make soap. He was melting, liquefying. It was truly gruesome.

And Branwen had done that. Branwen had destroyed this man. She had wrought a terrible death.

Fintan grabbed her elbow roughly. "What happened here, Lady Branwen?" he barked. Stress bled through his eyes.

The stone stairwell pulsated with the echoes of shouting and dancing from the revelers. Chanting and a chorus of *From the northern wilds, I found myself many a bride!* jarred harshly with the grisly fate of the warrior curled at their feet.

Fintan shook her again. "Sound the alarm, Lady Branwen. Kernyvak bastard. We're under attack!"

Before Branwen could explain, a majestic voice cut through the confusion. "There is no attack, Sir Fintan," said Queen Eseult. "Keane suffered from a wasting sickness."

Her bodyguard pushed to his feet and bowed his head. "But, Lady Queen, this is some kind of Kernyvak treachery. Keane was as healthy as Queen Medhua's bull not half an hour ago." He jabbed Keane's thigh with the end of his sword and a chunk of flesh fell to the ground.

Branwen covered her mouth with her hands. There was nothing left in her stomach so only acid bathed her throat.

"Sir Fintan, Kernyv had no part in this—"

"Lady Queen, how can you be sure?" he interrupted. "We must get you to safety. And the princess." Branwen had never known Fintan to speak over the queen. The wizened warrior looked truly afraid, afraid of whatever could do that to Keane.

Would Tristan be frightened of her, too? The thought was a thousand tiny razor cuts in her heart. Like Keane, Branwen was bleeding from the inside out.

"*Fintan*," the queen said severely. "The Land commands you to remove Sir Keane at once and never to speak of this again."

The guardsman went completely still. In the murk of the corridor, Queen Eseult glowed with an ethereal light. No one could doubt that she spoke for Iveriu, for the Goddess Ériu herself. She was not to be questioned. Fintan bowed reverently from the waist.

"Come, Branny, take Sir Keane's feet," she commanded. "Fintan, his head."

As Keane and Fintan had once carried Tristan, Branwen and Fintan now lifted Keane. His face smeared like grease in the soldier's hands. The queen didn't balk at getting her hands dirty—or bloody. She held Keane's abdomen as the three of them carried his body through a secret passageway that Branwen hadn't known existed.

The procession seemed agonizingly slow, but before long she found they were on the beach below the castle. Despite the moonless night, in the glow of the mermaid's hair and the stars that glittered like snowflakes upon a midwinter garden, Branwen could just about make out the mast and sails of the ship that would ferry her to Kernyv, bring her new life: the *Dragon Rising*. It was well named; its hulking great frame was monstrous, indeed. Branwen grimaced as she realized that she wasn't so very different from a dragon of legend—they both breathed fire.

"We will give Sir Keane back to the waves, Fintan," Queen Eseult instructed.

"He deserves a proper burial, Lady Queen."

"Sir Fintan, there soon won't be enough of his body left to bury."

Branwen thought she might die right then. Keane had survived the Skeleton Beach massacre as a boy. Now the same watery grave awaited him. Perhaps fate could not be changed—only delayed.

Fintan acquiesced with a nod. The three of them continued plodding toward the sea. Branwen's arms ached and her knuckles chafed against the leather of Keane's boots. Freezing water soaked her skirts as they set the body down amidst the sea foam and the strands of turquoise light.

He floated for a few moments and began to sink. Only Branwen's emerald ribbon bobbed along the surface of the water.

The wind whipped up the sea spray, coating her cheeks with a fine mist, and swallowed what was left of Keane. Silhouetted against the sky, illuminated by the haze of mermaid's hair, the blackbird cried. Two kinds of salt crystallized in winding trails down Branwen's face.

Fintan recited the Royal Guardsmen's oath. "From Kerwindos's Cauldron was I born," he intoned in a scratchy bass. "I serve the Land against all those who seek to harm her. Until I return from whence I came."

Queen Eseult bowed her head in respect as the last bubbles, like desperate breaths, stilled on top of the water. Turning toward her bodyguard, she said, "I don't believe Sir Keane has any family."

"None living, Lady Queen."

"In that case, it falls to you to drink the Final Toast, Sir Fintan," the queen said. She withdrew a small oblong flask from beneath her cloak. The silver glittered in the aqua glow of seaweed.

Fintan nodded grimly. He uncorked the flask and put the lip to his mouth. Branwen had seen this ritual performed many times. Far too many. Each time a man died in the service of Iveriu.

She had watched her uncle Morholt perform it for her father. The Final Toast was always drunk by the closest male relative to the fallen man or, barring that, his lord or master. Fintan was Keane's superior in the Royal Guard, so it was right and proper that he should imbibe the first drink Keane would taste in the Land of Youth.

Branwen had always thought it distinctly unfair that they didn't have such a tradition for the women who died for Iveriu.

The elder guardsman swigged the entire contents of the flask without taking a breath and wiped his mouth brusquely with the back of his hand. "Lady Queen, we should return to the feast. There might yet be Kernyvak pirates patrolling our shores."

"Just another moment of silence for Sir Keane," she answered in a tone that brooked no compromise.

Branwen licked the sea salt from her bottom lip, willing her hands to stop shaking. How could she keep this secret that already dragged on her heart like a deadweight—the heart she wanted to share with Tristan? Now Keane would always have a piece of it, a piece that was shadow-stung.

A strong gale rolled off the sea and whistled between the mourners. A hard, mucus-laden cough rattled Fintan's chest. Queen Eseult canted her head in his direction.

"You must return to Castle Rigani, Sir Fintan," she said.

"At once, my queen. After you."

"No, Fintan—just you. Tell King Óengus that I have cloistered myself in my chamber with a dreadful headache and that I'm not to be disturbed." She placed a hand on his shoulder. "When you wake tomorrow, you will remember none of this."

To Branwen's great astonishment, the bodyguard didn't protest. "If that is what you desire, Lady Queen" was all he said.

288

She nodded, taking the flask from his grasp. The shadows of light playing on Fintan's haggard face revealed eyes dilated as wide as vats of ale. Branwen sucked down a short breath.

The guardsman bowed from the waist and took his leave. Her aunt's gaze slid from Fintan to the water to Branwen. Branwen looked back with anticipation.

"Queen Medhua's tears," the queen explained. Branwen knew that the ancient queen was called the Intoxicating One. "I blended *derew* root, loverswort, spirit-fire, and a few other herbs to influence Sir Fintan's mind."

"Is it safe?"

Her aunt lowered an eyebrow. "Quite safe enough, when mixed correctly." It was true that Branwen wasn't in any position to question the queen's methods. "I prepared the dose before the feast so we could slip out unnoticed to brew the Loving Cup." She suspected it distressed the queen to interfere with Fintan's mind, but she always did what needed to be done.

Queen Eseult clamped one hand on Branwen's arm and stared into her eyes. "We just needed the draught a little sooner than I expected."

"Yes, Lady Queen." The words scraped the inside of her throat.

She regarded Branwen a long moment. The crashing tide competed with the blood in Branwen's ears to deafen her. "Do you still want to go through with it, my niece?" the queen asked. "The spell?"

"Of course." It was Branwen's knee-jerk reaction. She was amazed at the ease and vehemence with which the words popped from her mouth. But Branwen had already sacrificed too much to turn back now. "Yes, my queen," she repeated. Against her chest, the traitor's finger grated. "I do. I have already paid the Old Ones' price."

Queen Eseult rubbed her widow's peak, loosening her plaits like she really did have a headache. She pressed her lips together as if she wanted to say something, but then thought better of it. Her aunt resembled Dubthach's mother, the seamstress, when she pinned Branwen's skirts, needles clasped between her teeth.

A sigh as thick as fog. "Then let's begin. The Dark Moon is at its zenith and waits for no woman."

From far out at sea, Branwen caught the Death-Teller's song on the wind.

✦ ✦ ✦

She focused on the *clip-clop* of Queen Eseult's boots along the rocky shoreline to drown out the drumming of her own heart. Branwen skidded on the slippery stones several times but always managed to catch her balance before tumbling to the ground.

"We're here," the queen announced. She took Branwen's hand and slid it along the roughened cliff face. The stone came to a point. She pressed the flat of Branwen's palm against it and the rock retreated like a lever, a small crevice springing open. Amber light streaked out from the sliver. The passageway was so narrow Branwen had to turn her hips at an angle.

She shielded her eyes as she followed her aunt into an atrium that had been carved into the rock. The Rigani stones of this particular cave were so bright and clear that they were practically translucent. In the center of the room, a great cauldron boiled, oak and rowan branches crackling. Directly above the hissing pot, perhaps a thousand handsbreadths in the air, was a smudge of sky. A tiny opening. Right where the Dark Moon was perched on its canopy of clouds.

"Is this Kerwindos's Cauldron? *The* cauldron?" Branwen asked, awestruck. The Iverni believed all life sprang from here—even the Old Ones.

"Perhaps." The queen raised a shoulder. "Truth is always obscured by time. This is a place of in-between—neither our world, nor the Otherworld. The power we need to harness is strongest here."

Branwen nodded because it was the first thing all night that made any sense. In order to steer the course of fate, one must be neither wholly within it nor outside it. Her eyes darted every which way, scouring the cavern, enthralled.

Queen Eseult's eyes pierced hers. "You do understand." Another sigh. "I thought you would." She envied her aunt's composure.

"You have the traitor's finger?" she asked. Branwen inclined her head. "Show me."

Branwen plucked at the laces holding closed the side of her gown. Immediately, it made her think of Tristan's fingers dancing over the harp strings, how she wanted him to play her, too. Something deep inside tightened as her bodice loosened. Did she deserve that kind of joy now that she had taken a life?

She held out the finger to her aunt as an offering. Queen Eseult shook her head. "I mustn't touch it." Of course. How could Branwen have forgotten? Without noticing her move a muscle, the queen sidled up next to her. "Lady Branwen of Castle Bodwa," she said, tone unwavering, calm. "You must silence your mind. You must empty it so that it can be filled with the Loving Cup."

Branwen cast her eyes to the rocky floor, embarrassed. The firelight bounced off the willow-colored stone.

Queen Eseult placed a finger under Branwen's chin, lifting her head. "The Dark Moon has risen," she said. Branwen sensed it, too. "We need to harness the power at its peak to infuse the potion." Withdrawing her moon-catcher, her aunt pricked the tip of her forefinger. "Mother of Creation, I am the Land. Your daughter calls on you."

One cardinal drop rushed forth and leapt from the queen's finger into the cauldron.

Boundless silence. Followed by a roar from the cauldron.

She gestured for Branwen to cut her finger as well. "Mother of Creation," her aunt continued, "who created this world, the Otherworld, and everything in between. We offer you blood for love." Life pulsed in her voice.

Branwen splashed a drop into the tumultuous concoction and a yowl ricocheted through the cave, mightier than that of any Death-Teller.

"The blood of the Hand of Bríga will set alight even the coldest of hearts," Queen Eseult proclaimed to the sky.

A glorious energy invaded Branwen through the prick on her finger, exploring her mercilessly. A sensation both ecstatic and numbing. It seared her veins, searching for her heart. What precisely was the Hand of Bríga? Had her aunt known all along?

She tried to follow the queen's advice, keep her mind empty so that she could be filled to the brim with—with whatever *this* was.

The sounds of wind and fire were replaced with harmonious singing and lapping water. She recognized the voice. Tristan sang to Branwen's very soul.

The Hound of Uladztir bites and hisses,
Longing for Lady Emer's sweet kisses.

Vines of scorching energy curled around Branwen's rapidly beating heart. In her mind's eye, Tristan's youthful face faded and was replaced by the distinguished crags of battles fought and won.

By his side perched a slender woman with night-rich hair that had turned to snow. Branwen recognized herself in a snatch of laugh lines. This was her future—her future with Tristan. A future full of love. Despite everything, it was still possible.

Through her shimmering vision, Branwen's attention focused once more on Queen Eseult. A strangely solid presence, immovable as any mountain, against which her dreams were projected.

"To ensure love and loyalty, we offer the bone of a traitor conceived in perfidy," the queen declared. "Blood and bone, forged by fire, we beseech you for the truest of desires."

Branwen dropped Morholt's finger into the scalding brew without prompting and words flowed from her mouth unbidden.

"Mother of Creation, I am the Land," Branwen said. "We women of Iveriu make life with our bodies, make peace with our bodies. Now let us make love."

A screaming storm, like a ravening horde, gnawed inside her mind. The gentle old warrior and his wife broke apart, splintered and fractured. One cast adrift in the sea, the other tied to a pyre. The tune was changing.

I did not ask for the love I was given.

Branwen watched from a frozen, darkened sky as crops burned to dust and babies wailed.

Do not believe this life is what I wished.

This could be the future—a traitor's future—if the Loving Cup didn't succeed.

A thousand years, sealed with a kiss.

Kerwindos's Cauldron existed outside time and space. Both visions were possible, Branwen realized. All that stood between peace and fire was her.

"Mother, I give you my love for peace."

The Dark Moon began its descent.

THE HAND OF BRÍGA

A TRAIL OF LIGHT SUGARED BRANWEN'S eyelids. They fluttered, opening one at a time, as she sat up in bed groggily. Her entire body ached. She tried to stretch her arms above her head but she felt so weak, frail. She didn't feel nearly powerful enough to have killed a man. A man who was now at the bottom of the Ivernic Sea.

Not wanting to look but needing to see it, she turned over her right hand. In the center of her palm, bisecting her life line, ran a long purple welt. The skin was puckered along her heart line, deep violet surrounded by a reddish hue. The burn was healing but she would be forever marked. The life she took would never be forgotten.

All she wanted to do was crawl back under the covers and hide, sleep for a thousand years. But today was not a day for granting wishes. Today the future grabbed Branwen and embraced her, whether she was ready for it or not.

Tentatively, she swung her legs over the side of the bed and prepared to take her first steps toward Kernyv.

The door burst open. "Branny!" Essy cried, her alarm peppered with anger. "Keane is missing, and I couldn't find you . . . and I thought you had run away together," she said in a hurried jumble of words. "I thought you'd left me—left me to sail for Otherworld-forsaken Kernyv all by myself!"

Panic, barbed and rusty, twisted in Branwen's gut. Rage flickered. "I would never do that, cousin." Her words came out strident. If Branwen hadn't burned the letter, Essy would have been the one to run off and leave a broken kingdom in her wake. "What do you mean Keane's missing?" Branwen played up her confusion.

"He didn't report for duty this morning. In fact, nobody's seen him since last night."

She tried very hard not to be sick.

"I overheard Fintan saying he's probably sleeping off his drink between the bosoms of a buxom serving maid," Essy continued, crossing the chamber toward her. "But I didn't believe it. I know Keane wants only you."

The princess pushed her hair behind her ear, tugging at plaits that were horribly askew. "I saw him follow you and Diarmuid—but I had no way to warn you."

A kernel of fury frizzled and popped in Branwen's heart. Keane was charged with defending the princess but he'd been willing to betray her. Branwen had had no choice. No choice at all.

"I'm sorry, Branny," Essy said, her tone doleful. The princess hung her head, plopping down on the bed beside her. Several loosened strands fell to the quilt.

"Keane and I parted in anger," said Branwen, sighing, which wasn't entirely a lie, although the truth was so much worse.

"Is it my fault?"

Yes—and no. She shook her head. "I couldn't love him the way he wanted." A bead of sweat trickled down her spine. No one should love that darkly.

Essy's hand was clammy as she threaded it through Branwen's. She wanted to resist. She was still furious about everything that had transpired, but she was also exhausted and her cousin's touch felt like relief against her feverish skin.

"I'm sorry," the princess repeated. "I'm so sorry you've given up your chance at love. Otherworld knows you won't find any among the Kernyveu."

But she had. Branwen had found love, and she couldn't tell the princess. Nor could she reveal that she knew the contents of Essy's letter. Too many secrets thrummed between them—between all of them. Once Essy and King Marc drank the Loving Cup there would be no more need. She would breathe freely again.

The princess stroked Branwen's heart line unwittingly and she yelped. She wished she hadn't. "Oh no, Branny." Her cousin examined the wound more closely. "What happened?"

"Nothing." She shrugged it off. "I touched one of Treva's saucepans." Essy narrowed her eyes at Branwen, unconvinced. "Really, it's fine," she insisted.

The princess raised Branwen's hand to her mouth and kissed the cooling scar. Essy's mouth was soft and tender. Branwen was so moved by her cousin's small gesture that she snatched her hand away. She cast her eyes toward the quilt, fighting back tears.

Essy gaped at her. How could Branwen explain her reaction? She couldn't. Not even to herself. She was heavy and hollow at the same time. Even though she'd killed Keane in self-defense—in defense of her kingdom—part of her had died, too.

Innocence: the girl who had never harmed another soul. Now Branwen was a woman who knew what it was to steal a life.

There was no going back.

Refreshingly mild fingers wended along Branwen's forehead, through the fine hairs surrounding her temples. She felt a tiny pressure on her scalp and then Essy brandished the hair she'd just plucked.

It was white.

The image of Branwen as an old woman sitting contentedly at Tristan's side rose in her mind. Had it already happened? Had she visited her future in Kerwindos's Cauldron? Or maybe she was simply aging. Could that be the cost of magic?

Essy twirled the colorless strand around her pinkie and laughed anxiously. "You really have been working too hard, cousin." She unwound the hair and let it float away on the draft. Then she looked up at Branwen, eyes round.

"Did you deliver the letter?" she asked. Branwen hesitated. If she had, did Essy intend to flee the castle—did she even have a plan? Branwen exhaled to calm the fire in her veins. The princess zigzagged her finger along her thigh, expectant.

"Dear heart," Branwen began, unable to look at her directly. "He wouldn't accept it. Lord Diarmuid asked me to give you a good-bye kiss on his behalf." She kissed her cousin fondly, on the cheek.

"*No.*" The princess began to quake. "No, it can't be." She clutched at her heart like it was an open wound. "He wouldn't give me up so easily."

Branwen felt a pang in her chest as Essy's breathing grew shallow. Her cousin's actions had been rash and dangerous, but they were done out of desperation: the desperation to be loved. She stroked Essy's back, trying to soothe her.

Her cousin's shoulders jerked up and down as if they were on a string. "I don't believe you. Diarmuid said I was his Étaín." Her eyes shone in the morning light. "He won't just let me sail away without a good-bye."

"He's said good-bye, Essy."

"No, he'll come—" she forced out between pants. "He'll come . . ."

"Breathe, Essy." Branwen rubbed her cousin's arms; contact usually helped steady her. "*Breathe.*" Tears watered the bedclothes. The princess had placed her faith in a man incapable of fighting for anyone but himself.

"Essy!" Queen Eseult exclaimed from the open door. Branwen and Essy snapped their gazes in her direction. "Dear heart, what's wrong?" The queen rushed over to the bed, crouching at her daughter's feet.

"Don't act like you care, Mother! You've already sold me to Kernyvak pirates!"

Her aunt wore a blank expression. "Essy, don't say that," Branwen snapped.

"Why not? It's true!" Essy hurled the accusation at her mother. To Branwen, she said, "You always defend her!"

Branwen opened and closed her mouth. She had witnessed last night just how fiercely her aunt loved. She only wished her cousin could see it.

"I love you more than you'll ever know," pleaded the queen, staring up at her daughter.

"You're right." Essy scrubbed at her cheeks. "I'll never know because I'll never see you again."

Her mother flinched. The princess launched to her feet, a barely restrained tempest. "Get out of my way," she told the Queen of Iveriu, who straightened to standing and reached for her daughter's cheek.

"Please, Essy. I'm losing two daughters today." Queen Eseult looked older this morning, bereft. A few more gray hairs graced the top of her head. "Let there be peace between us."

Essy stared at her mother as her breathing slowed. "You can have peace for Iveriu or peace with me. You can't have both." The finality in her cousin's voice stunned Branwen. The princess removed the queen's hand from her cheek and pushed her from her path.

Pausing in the doorway, she looked from Branwen to her mother.

"You're mistaken, Lady Queen. You've only ever had one daughter to lose—and it isn't me."

Essy vanished down the corridor as Queen Eseult sank to her knees. Branwen was instantly at her side. The queen's flowing wild silk gown gathered around them like waves. Branwen wrapped an arm around her aunt as she wept silently.

"Oh, Branny," she said. "I came to comfort you and you've ended up comforting me."

"It's my honor."

The queen looked at her, a woeful smile on her face. "I pray that Essy will come to realize that what I've done, everything I've done, is for her—and for the Land. The Land must think of all her children, every soul in Iveriu."

"She will," Branwen said quietly. Queen Eseult took Branwen's right hand in hers, stroking the back, then flipped it over, scrutinizing the welt.

"You and I have always been kindred spirits, my niece. I believe the Old Ones brought us together. I've tried to raise you as Alana would have wanted."

A lump formed in Branwen's throat. "I'm so grateful."

"*I'm* grateful, Branwen, for the privilege of watching you grow into such a strong, fearless woman." She touched the healing wound. "A leader."

"I'm not fearless." At this very moment, Branwen was afraid of countless things—not least herself. There were no books she could study, no recipes she could follow, to understand what was happening to her.

"You *are*." The queen covered Branwen's palm with her own. "You are a brave and fearless young woman. You have Alana's spark. It's why you were chosen to bear the Hand of Bríga."

"What is it?" she asked, almost childlike, sagging against the queen. The older woman smelled of cloves. For an instant, Branwen closed her eyes and the tumult in her heart abated.

Queen Eseult rested her head against Branwen's in return. "It's a blessing, but some might see it as a curse. There are two sides to everything in creation, dear heart."

"I still don't understand how I did—" she broke off, her memory lingering on Keane's contorted body, "*what* I did."

"Death is a heavy thing. I wouldn't wish you to carry it, my niece, but the Land has chosen your path for you. Sometimes the way of a leader runs with blood."

Branwen shivered. "I didn't do it on purpose," she said, and she never wanted to repeat what she had done to Keane.

"The power must have been dormant. When you felt the Land under threat, you awakened it." The queen held her gaze and, in that moment, she would have told her aunt anything she wanted to know. Branwen couldn't breathe.

After another beat, Queen Eseult said, "There are three aspects to the Goddess Bríga, as I assume Master Bécc taught you." Branwen nodded slowly, gratitude rushing through her. Maybe the queen didn't want to know how Keane had threatened the peace. Branwen certainly didn't want to break faith with her cousin. Sometimes it was better to leave things unspoken.

"When you healed Prince Tristan with the *skeakh* magic," continued the queen, "I realized you had been blessed with the Fire of the Hearth: Bríga's healing powers. As your mother had been."

Branwen parted her lips slightly, bursting with questions, but her aunt gestured for her to remain silent. "Last night, when Prince Tristan sang for you—yes, for *you*," Queen Eseult insisted without letting her argue, "I saw you possessed the Fire of Inspiration. Like our goddess, you are a poet's muse."

She blushed such a furious vermilion that she felt it beneath her skin.

"But," Queen Eseult cautioned, "you also embody the Fire of the Forge—Bríga's most powerful aspect. The Old Ones would not have granted it to you lightly. I have not heard of a woman possessing all three aspects since the great Queen Medhua herself." Their eyes met. "One needs all three to form the Hand of Bríga."

She was too astounded to respond. The queen traced a finger along Branwen's hairline and discovered another newly whitened strand.

"Using the Hand of Bríga does not come without its toll," she told her. Queen Eseult twisted one of her own gray hairs. "I will admit to you, my niece, and please never repeat these words, that

I have wondered why the Old Ones chose Essy to be queen—and not you. Now their intentions have become clear."

Branwen pulled at her shift, waiting for her aunt to explain how the Old Ones chose her to kill a man.

"We are sending two Ivernic queens to Kernyv today," Queen Eseult declared in that confident, nearly divine tone of hers. "One for this world, and one for the Otherworld. Together, you will defend the Land." She inhaled. "The Old Ones have chosen you as their protector across the sea, Branwen, and they have imbued you with Bríga's powers so that you may guide mortal affairs."

"But who will guide *me*?" The plea leapt from Branwen's mouth before she could capture it. She had been wandering farther and farther away from this world since her visit to Whitethorn Mound. Was she becoming less human?

"The Old Ones are always guiding you," her aunt said more gently. "You must believe in yourself, my niece, as I do. I am trusting you to protect the interests of Iveriu above all."

The queen reached into the pocket of her voluminous skirts. She presented Branwen with a small golden vial. No larger than her pinkie finger.

"The Loving Cup," she breathed. Branwen had no memory of finishing the spell.

Seeming to pluck the thought from her mind, the queen said, "The Hand of Bríga fueled the magic. You were both *here*, and *not here*. The memories should return, I believe. But you are now far more of an adept than I."

Branwen folded her hands around the Loving Cup. This was her burden, her responsibility. She secreted the vial between her breasts, next to her heart.

Queen Eseult embraced her with tremendous force. "Just a few drops in their wine on the wedding night should be enough," she instructed, urgency bolstering her words. "It's in the best interest of Iveriu—and Kernyv—to have a legitimate heir as soon as possible."

Branwen rubbed her palm, thinking of Essy's accusation at the children's celebration. "This will bring the princess love?" Her voice hitched up at the end so that the statement became a question. "Happiness?"

"The love between a man and a woman is a storm. The love of a mother for her child promises a new dawn. A way forward for both kingdoms." The queen cupped Branwen's cheek. "There are many kinds of love, my niece, and many kinds of happiness. The Land wants all her children to be happy."

Branwen saw the love, and determination, in her aunt's eyes. She trusted her implicitly. She would trust in her wisdom as she had always done. "I understand, my queen," she said, and she hoped Essy would, too.

Someday.

A shadow darkened the queen's face. "I must also warn you to keep your newfound powers to yourself. The Kernyveu are not so fond of the Old Ways as we Iverni. The leaders of the New Religion do not deem women worthy of their Mysteries." The corner of her mouth edged skyward. "But we women have mysteries of our own."

Trepidation made Branwen's stomach lurch. How could anyone question the sanctity of the Land or that women embodied the bounty of Goddess Ériu?

"I will be discreet, and I will do whatever is necessary to keep Essy safe."

Queen Eseult nodded. "The princess is as much your sister as you are my daughter, Branny. Always." She kissed her on the bridge of her nose. Her tears fell upon Branwen's cheeks. "We must prepare you for the voyage."

"But . . . but . . . there are still so many things I need to ask—need to *know*."

She laughed softly. "You will be given the answers when you need them. Trust in the Old Ones." The queen pulled away, drying her eyes. "There *is* one last thing you can do for me, Branny."

"Name it."

"Call me Eseult. We are all queens now. Three queens for Iveriu like in ancient times."

Branwen was rendered speechless. She cloaked her aunt in an embrace. "Thank you, Eseult," she said, testing out the name. "Thank you for giving me a home."

"You will always have a home in my heart."

Branwen inclined her head, renewed fortitude coursing within. "One Iveriu."

DRAGON RISING

THE *DRAGON RISING* WAS ANCHORED in a cove known as Blackford Harbor, not far from Branwen's cave. Its great sails were a terrifying pair of wings. Branwen had readied herself hastily after the queen—her aunt, *Eseult*—had departed from her chamber.

Branwen was so honored to call the queen by her true name. Even if she had a hard time believing she could ever be a queen herself. She worried her fingers over her mother's brooch as she strode along the beach below Castle Rigani. She had wanted to walk to the ship alone. Her steps were sluggish not solely because she was bone-weary.

This was the last time she would gaze upon the Ivernic Sea from the shores where her parents' spirits dwelled. Would they be able to watch over her in Kernyv? Did the same Otherworld exist beyond the Veil from the island of Albion?

An enormous shadow scudded across the line where the sea met the horizon. Branwen shivered despite her woolen cape. Much as the depths called to her, she had never traveled upon the waves for more than an afternoon of pleasure sailing or fishing. She wasn't entirely certain what to expect.

The deep indigo waters were as dangerous as they were hypnotic. And Keane would lurk forever beneath the surface. What would happen when he failed to return to the Royal Guard? Branwen didn't doubt that Queen Eseult would handle the situation, yet she hated making her complicit. Her heart throbbed. Perhaps a leader's path did run with blood. Could Branwen abide more of it on her hands?

She rubbed the singed heart line beneath her right glove.

The Old Ones were trusting her to protect Iveriu in a foreign land, and she had to trust them. Before she met Tristan, she had never put faith in things she couldn't see. Love changed things. She no longer doubted that the fox had led her to Tristan's raft to start their kingdoms on this journey toward peace.

Branwen wasn't merely accompanying the princess to Kernyv. She had a mission of her own. She could easily imagine the road her life in Iveriu would have traveled had she never met Tristan. Now she was sailing into the unknown. Kernyv wasn't the Otherworld, but it was a *different* world—a world she would need to learn to navigate. The challenge was daunting. And, she couldn't deny, thrilling.

With a sigh, Branwen touched her chest. Beneath her cloak and tunic, secured in her breast bindings, lay the Loving Cup: the drink of peace. As soon as they arrived in Kernyv, everything would be set to rights.

A leather satchel hung diagonally across Branwen's body. It bounced against her hip as she trudged through the sand. The bag contained her most precious possessions: a strand of dried mermaid's hair she'd kept from the day she first met Tristan, a waterskin of

Treva's elderberry wine that the cook had pressed into her hands with gleaming eyes, and a beautifully carved miniature *fidkwelsa* set—her favorite game of strategy—that had belonged to her father.

There was also the moon-catcher the queen had insisted Branwen keep, the wooden sword Morholt had given her, and a fine shawl of Ivernic lace that Noirín had spun for her as a parting gift. The shawl was nothing compared with Essy's exquisite trousseau, but it made Branwen feel like a princess, if not a queen.

Saoirse had kissed Branwen on both cheeks at the castle gates, her own cheeks damp, and Dubthach himself gave Branwen a surprisingly hearty hug good-bye. Maybe it shouldn't have come as such a surprise. He'd been her childhood playmate and they were unlikely to meet again in this life. It made Branwen hopeful to see Dubthach and Saoirse arm in arm. The world seemed on a better course than it had a few seasons ago.

She was glad that Queen Eseult had bestowed her mother's harp upon Tristan. He would surely make better use of it than Branwen, and she would enjoy hearing him sing. It was a gift for both of them.

Regardless of what her aunt had said, Branwen could never take credit for Tristan's talent. Not that she would mind being his muse, especially if that meant feeling his breath on her lips, the cadence of their hearts beating as one, like when he serenaded her as Emer.

Her gaze returned to the sea, skipping along the waves as the surf crashed against the rocks.

The world went black. Terror quickened her heart, incited her fire. A pair of gloved hands shuttered her eyes. She was once more prisoner in Keane's grip.

Branwen screamed.

The hands spun her around, releasing her; sunlight blinded her. Blinking furiously, she tried to catch her breath.

"Tristan?" She squinted at the silhouette of windblown curls. Her hands were balled into fists.

"Branwen," he said. "I didn't intend to scare you. Forgive me." Concern stippled his brow. His eyes surveyed her up and down. "I only wanted to surprise you. You looked so lovely framed against the sea and sky."

"Remember what happened when you surprised me in the cave?" she said, lowering an eyebrow, as her dread melted away. "My bite is worse than my bark, I assure you."

Tristan laughed and stepped closer. "There are no more raiders coming to your coast. I promise." In an instant, he snaked an arm around Branwen. Her entire body tingled. It was too familiar a gesture for an unmarried couple. Anyone who glimpsed them together would assume they were lovers.

"Tristan," she warned, although her traitorous lips ached to force his open.

He peered down the length of the beach in either direction.

"Nobody's around," he said. The hazel flecks in his eyes winked like stars.

"That's because they're at the dock—where *we* should be," Branwen told him. It was hard to want to be anywhere other than right here, however, welded against him. "Why aren't you on the ship?"

"I was looking for you." Tristan dipped his forehead against hers. She should break their embrace. She should. His mouth was treacherously close. "I've been looking for you since last night," he said. The statement was subdued.

A bolt of panic shot through her. "Why?" she whispered.

"I wanted you by my side when I accepted the Seal of Alliance." He pressed a palm to her cheek. "It's as much your victory as it is mine."

Guilt smothered Branwen. Tristan was generous and noble, treated her as a partner—and she had killed a man. The vision she'd had of them in the in-between, growing wrinkled and white-haired together: Did Keane have to die to make that come true?

"I'm sorry, I didn't mean to worry you. I think I had too much ale," she said. "I went to my bedchamber to lie down, and I fell asleep."

Tristan removed his hand from her face as a scowl seized his own. "You weren't in your rooms," he said tonelessly.

"What? You came to my bedchamber?" she accused, surprising herself at how tart she sounded when she was in the wrong—just like Essy.

His expression softened slightly, cheeks coloring. "I know it isn't proper." Tristan took a deep breath. "You vanished. And then Sir Keane did, too. I went to check on you. You weren't there." The wariness of a well-trained warrior lingered in his eyes.

"There is absolutely *nothing* between me and Keane." There was nothing left of Keane at all.

"Where were you, Branwen?" The question was rough. Lost.

"Perhaps Sir Keane isn't the only one who watches me too closely. You're not my bodyguard, Tristan." Her cousin's words surfaced in her memory: *Are you my warden, Branny?*

Tristan winced with his whole body. "I don't want to be your *bodyguard*, Branwen." He raked a hand through his hair. Blowing out a long breath, he lifted his eyes to hers. "I just want to love you." His jaw ticked. He reached for Branwen's right hand.

"Last night, as I was singing to you, I realized I had never spoken the words aloud. I love you, Lady Branwen of Castle Bodwa. I came back for you and I won't leave Iveriu without you."

Her heart kicked. Until that moment, Branwen hadn't known that one syllable could cut so deeply. *Love.* Bloody and sharp.

His dark gaze drilled into her as he waited for her response. She found it difficult to form words. Not because she didn't feel them. Because she felt them too much.

Tristan's face began to crumple, a tinge of regret at the corners of his mouth. Every nerve pulled tight inside her. This time *she* had to be the one to jump off the waterfall or she might lose him.

"I love you, too, Prince Tristan of Kernyv and King of Liones."

A masculine laugh of sheer joy echoed on the waves. "Thank goodness. I feared I was less attractive as a prince than as a minstrel," he said, his jest holding a shred of fear.

"I *do* love your ballads."

"I'll sing to you every night."

"Only at night?" she teased.

He looked at her through hooded lids. "Whenever you want. I don't know how long I can resist showing my affection," he said. She nibbled her lower lip. "I want all of Iveriu and Kernyv to see what you mean to me. That I belong to you entirely."

Branwen stiffened as her heart sighed. Their first kiss had taken place on this beach. "I've been yours since the day we met," she admitted, even though she hadn't known it at the time. But Essy—Essy needed her now more than ever.

Deciphering Branwen in his uncanny manner, Tristan said, "You deserve your own happiness, my love."

My love. The breath caught in her throat. Did she? With power to destroy flowing through her? "My *love*," he repeated with a growl. She was his, and he was hers. This time when Tristan towed her closer, she didn't resist. Her knees were too weak.

He tugged on her hand and the glove fell to the sand.

"What happened?" Tristan's eyes had gone wide, a hint of anger pulling at his features. "You didn't have this wound at the feast."

Branwen sputtered. She tried to draw back. He threaded his fingers through hers. "The way you reacted just now—did someone hurt you?" The question was a roar. She knew it wasn't directed at her but she still froze. "Was it Keane?"

He tried. She shook her head. Tristan's expression said he didn't believe her.

"If you're in trouble, let me help you."

Another vigorous headshake. "I don't need you to fight my battles." Shame and embarrassment wrestled inside her.

"You don't let me do anything for you. *Please*, tell me where you were last night. Tell me how you injured your hand."

Branwen's eyes burned. She loved this man with her entire being but she also loved Iveriu. Too much was riding on her being strong enough to bear this secret alone.

"I promise to understand," he said. Tristan spoke as quietly as an assassin's blade but his words were twice as lethal. He might be able to understand about Keane. He would not understand about the Loving Cup. He already believed King Marc would be a good husband to Essy. Branwen had to be sure.

"It was an accident. I'm *fine*. I'll heal." She hoped at least her last statement was true.

"I thought you didn't want any more secrets between us."

"I don't. But I still can't tell you." Branwen pulled him toward her. "Do you love me enough to trust me? Trust that everything I do is for peace?"

The apprehension on his face transformed into resolve. "Branwen, you made me believe in peace. And in love. I will always believe in you."

She smiled, then, and filled the space between them with kisses instead of lies.

✠ ✠ ✠

The princess threw Branwen a forlorn look from where she stood on the bow of the *Dragon Rising*. She sucked her lips together when she saw Tristan at her cousin's side, turning her back on them, and yanking on her braid. On the dock stood the king and queen; they were surrounded by a retinue of Royal Guardsmen, servants, peasants, and courtiers. It seemed like all of Iveriu had descended upon Blackford to see the princess off.

All of its dreams of peace were being spirited away on the back of a dragon.

Near the gangway, King Óengus was speaking with an older gentleman whom Branwen didn't recognize. His skin was a deeper brown than Tristan's with wind-whipped wrinkles. Charcoal whiskers sprouted from his nose and ears in addition to his overgrown beard.

"That's Morgawr—he's a tough taskmaster, but the best captain I know," Tristan said, pointing in his direction. "Kartagon, of course." From the captain's daunting appearance, Branwen well believed

Morgawr could battle sea monsters. The Kartagons were as famed for their sailors as their warriors. Morgawr looked like both.

She arched her eyebrow. "A pirate?"

Tristan's grin made an appearance. "Depends on whom you ask." He laughed. "No, he's part of the Royal Fleet. Don't worry, you're in safe hands."

Discreetly, Branwen squeezed his and smiled. "I know I am."

His grin deepened. "Come on, let me introduce you," he offered and, although she knew all the reasons it was impossible, Branwen wished Tristan could introduce her as the woman he loved.

As they approached Morgawr and King Óengus, Branwen caught a snippet of their conversation. "It's ill-omened to sail under the Dark Moon," the captain groused to the king, his bushy eyebrows all awry. She noted that his accent in Ivernic was thicker than Tristan's. "But if the Horned One wills it, we'll reach Monwiku before Samonios." At the mention of the Horned One, Morgawr lifted the piece of bone—no, antler—that dangled from a leather cord around his neck and kissed it.

Branwen's right hand twitched inside her glove. How much credence did Tristan put in the New Religion? She stole a glance at him from the corner of her eye. What would he think of the Hand of Bríga? Could he accept that Branwen was made of both creation and destruction? She drew in a steadying breath.

King Óengus clasped the captain's shoulder. "Iveriu and Kernyv are counting on you to deliver the princess safely."

"I'm aware, Your Highness," Morgawr replied, meeting the king's gaze.

Tristan smiled as he greeted the men, his charm contagious. He'd won over everyone at Castle Rigani except for Essy and Keane.

Branwen lurched as she thought of the bodyguard, but she pushed the gnawing emptiness away.

"Morgie here isn't giving you too much guff, I trust, King Óengus," Tristan said cheerfully, slapping the old sailor on the back.

"Not at all," said the king. "Simply going over the details."

"Allow me to introduce you to Lady Branwen, Captain Morgawr," Tristan said, presenting her to the elder Kernyvman.

"I'm one of the details," she said.

Morgawr belly laughed, and bowed. "It'll be my pleasure to serve as your captain for the voyage across the Dreaming Sea."

Branwen wrinkled her nose. "The Dreaming Sea?"

"You didn't think we called it the *Ivernic* Sea in Kernyv?" said Morgawr with another chuckle.

"No, I suppose not." She flushed. Many things would be different in Kernyv. Turning to the king, Branwen curtsied. "Good day, Your Highness."

"Branwen." King Óengus hinted at a smile despite his habitually stern countenance.

Morgawr caught the king's eye. "We should set sail while there's still some daylight left, sire. The crew gets antsy if we depart after dusk." He tapped the antler.

Tristan laughed. "Sailors and their superstitions."

"Prince Tristan, the sea is like a woman, fickle and feisty. If you break her rules, there's no telling what she'll do."

"Captain Morgawr," Branwen interjected, "a woman treats a man the way the man treats her."

He roared again with laughter and patted his stomach. "You'll be a very welcome addition to King Marc's court, I daresay, my lady."

"I'm sure she will," King Óengus concurred. "Lady Branwen always makes Iveriu proud."

Her jaw nearly dropped. The king was a reticent man and he rarely spared any speech for her. She had doubted he spared her a thought, either.

"Thank you, Your Highness. I will do my best."

"A king may rule, but it is his subjects who keep him in power," he said, capturing her gaze. Her nerves zinged. Did he know about the Loving Cup? "A wise man told me that once." There was a note of affection in his voice. "Lord Caedmon."

Branwen took a small gulp. Perhaps the queen confided in her husband more than she had realized. How hard must it be for a monarch to acknowledge that the stability of his rule rested on somebody else's shoulders?

"My father was indeed wise." And for the first time in her life, Branwen didn't see King Óengus as practically a god. He was a man, with his own flaws, who had accepted his limitations and was doing what he thought was right for his people. Her father must have liked and respected him very much.

"Good-bye, my niece," he said.

She curtsied, one last time, low and graceful.

"Good-bye, my king." Over his shoulder, she spied her aunt. She smiled at Branwen and mouthed, *Otherworld protect you.*

The wind snapped and blew Branwen's tears away. She left Tristan to say a formal good-bye to the king and mounted the gangway. One foot and then the other, her last feel of Ivernic soil. Deep within, she knew she would never set foot in Iveriu again.

But she would protect it always.

✢ ✢ ✢

The cabin Branwen was to share with Essy had been elegantly appointed with thick draperies of burgundy velvet sewn by Noirín, but it was a bit small. It had been designed for one passenger, not two. Essy's trunks had already exploded in the compartment. Branwen found a tiny space to make her own.

Another sailor, maybe twelve years old, ducked his head in the door. "We're about to push off, my lady." He glanced at her anxiously.

"Pardon?" Branwen asked, not understanding what he'd said. It sounded like he was talking through a mouthful of potatoes, even though he was making the effort to speak her language.

The freckled Kernyvman's pale complexion instantly pinkened. He possessed an oddly strong nose. "We're pushing off," he repeated.

"Thank you." She summoned a smile. "What's your name?" she asked.

"Cadan."

"Thank you, Cadan," Branwen said, launching to her feet. "How do you say *thank you* in Kernyvak?"

"*Mormerkti*, my lady," he replied, a shy smile creeping across his face.

She returned it. "*Mormerkti*, Cadan."

The boy bowed, still smiling, and disappeared up the creaking stairs to the deck. Branwen loped after him, not wanting to miss her final glimpse of the Ivernic coast.

She found Essy standing at the far end of the deck, facing away from the shore, watching Cadan scuttle up the rigging like a squirrel.

The tide was coming in and the sun was fading. Just below the surface, mermaid's hair eddied. Branwen dropped another scarf along her cousin's shoulders with a kiss.

"Are you so eager to turn your back on Iveriu?" she asked.

Without glancing in her direction, Essy said, "I prefer the open sea. Iveriu has already turned its back on me."

"That isn't true, cousin."

"You're the only one who's never abandoned me, Branny. I know that now." She drew in a long breath through her nose. "He didn't come. Diarmuid didn't come for me."

Branwen had known that he wouldn't, and yet she still ached for her cousin. She wanted to soothe her hurt, tell her that in a few weeks she would be happily married and not even remember Diarmuid's name.

"I'll never be Étaín," Essy lamented.

Branwen pulled the princess close. "Étaín wasn't happy with her fate."

"At least she got to choose."

Before Branwen could respond, a great *crack* ripped through the sky. An enormous jet-black sea-wolf ascended as the sail unfurled: the royal crest of Kernyv. The little girl who lost her parents to Kernyvak raiders would never have believed she could see the standard against the horizon with anything but fear in her heart.

The ship rocked from the force of the wind trapped by the sail and Essy tumbled into her arms. Instinctively, Branwen angled the princess toward the coastline. Her cousin would miss her homeland even if she couldn't admit it.

"The hearts of men are changeable," she said. "The heart of

the Land is not." As she spoke the words, she felt her right hand growing hot.

Branwen glimpsed the fox on the cliffs above. She had been perturbed by the creature's absence of late. It barked noisily but no one else noticed; only she could see him. He dwelled in the Otherworld. Branwen had come to understand he could take a corporeal form and reveal himself if he chose, but the mortal world was not his home.

Farewell, little friend.

"It's *my* heart that's unchangeable, Branny," Essy replied, her breaths coming in jerks. "You are my only love now, cousin. My only family. Not Iveriu. Not some faceless Kernyvak king. You're the only one worthy of my love."

"And I do love you, Essy," Branwen said, choking up. "So very, very much."

She could never tell her cousin how much in words. Only in deeds. She had killed for her happiness, and the princess could never know. She intertwined their fingers. Essy drew the symbol for hazel on the back of her hand and Branwen added the honeysuckle.

A cherry-red sun slid toward twilight, casting the cliffs in shadows of pink and lilac. Branwen inhaled deeply, smelling the rosemary in the air—her mother, the Land.

"We'll be happy in Kernyv, Essy. I swear it."

Her cousin's mouth tilted into a smile that was baneful, and—for the first time—regal.

"It's just you and me now, Branwen. Just us against the world."

The hush of evening held them close as the darkening waves lapped effortlessly against the hull.

"You and me, Essy."

PART III

THE
DREAMING
SEA

DEAD CALM

BRANWEN THRASHED. THE WAVES ROSE above her head. Salty. Winter-bitten.

Water surged up her nose. Clouds, chasm black, amassed on the horizon like wild horses about to stampede. *Float, Branwen.* That had been her father's first swimming lesson. *When your strength gives out, let the current take your weight.*

The current was too strong. Seawater stung her eyes, burned her throat. Overhead, an enormous bird circled, a spiteful set to its beak.

Branwen was nothing more than carrion to the beast.

Far below the waves, something caught the silvery light of the storm. Arching her back, Branwen dove beneath the churning surface.

Gold glittered, a thin chain undulating like seaweed.

She squinted: Dangling from the end was a Rigani stone. Branwen reached out, her fingers just missing her prize—the prize she'd once gifted Tristan.

Long black tentacles tangled around her ankles as if the sea itself had grown fingers. Tiny, ticklish hairs clamped onto her like suckers, and she felt herself go limp.

A dark shape moved toward her, prowling through the choppy water. As it grew closer, Branwen distinguished two white, water-logged eyes. Half the flesh was sloughed from one side of the corpse's bloated face.

The monster had been a man once.

He arced around Branwen, swimming lithely, his brown hair gliding like a fin.

A skeletal figure accused her. Veiny blue eyes confronted her. *Keane.*

He stretched Branwen's green ribbon between his hands. He meant it as a promise. Watching realization dawn in her eyes, he wrapped the ribbon around Branwen's throat as the tentacles held her immobile. She clawed at his bony hands.

She could not scream. She could only watch the Rigani stone drift farther and farther out of reach. On the brink of death, Branwen quailed as Keane pressed his pale, puffy lips to hers.

This time, he wouldn't let her get away.

Branwen stroked the base of her throat rhythmically, unconsciously, as Essy waited for her to take her turn at *fidkwelsa*. She was safely aboard the *Dragon Rising*. She wasn't drowning. Keane was dead. She touched her neck again. No ligature mark. She exhaled a shallow breath. Keane could only haunt her, not hurt her.

The princess grunted and flipped over one of the pieces on

Branwen's side of the board. "Stop that!" said Branwen, swatting at her cousin.

"Go already." She tapped her foot. Ever since they were children, Essy had lacked the patience required for the game.

Branwen fingered a tiny wooden horseman painted silver. Her gaze darted toward a shimmer on the tide. She shook her head, dispersing the image of Keane's ghoulish visage behind her eyes.

The princess crossed her arms. Branwen had to admit her own concentration was frayed at the moment. "We don't have all day," her cousin complained.

"I think you'll find we do."

The *Dragon Rising* hadn't moved for hours. Scarcely any progress had been made since they'd departed Blackford nearly two weeks ago. It was as if the sea had turned to tar.

Leaning forward, Branwen reviewed the players at her disposal. Knights, squires, and horsemen were positioned defensively on squares around their queen; the kings were marshaling their troops. The object of the game was to see who could get his queen to safety first and eliminate as many of his opponent's pieces as possible in the process.

Branwen picked up a miniature squire, carefully concealing her scarred palm, and moved it one space closer to her queen. A minor kitchen injury should have faded by now; she didn't want to rouse her cousin's suspicions. Tristan hadn't mentioned it since Branwen had asked him to trust her, but she noticed him eyeing the mark whenever he thought she wasn't paying attention.

Essy slapped her thigh. "Ugh, Branny, you made me wait all this time for that—*that*! You didn't *do* anything."

Squires had very little power on the board but, used correctly, they were excellent in a counterattack. Branwen bit down on a victorious smile.

"Good afternoon, ladies," Tristan said, strolling toward them, a fishing pole over his shoulder. He pulled a stool over to their table.

"Caught anything interesting?" Branwen asked him.

His answering smile was smug. "Perhaps." She saw the unspoken *You* in his gaze and the knot of disquiet in her chest unfurled.

The princess barely acknowledged Tristan as she said, "Did we invite you to sit with us?"

"*Essy*," Branwen scolded and yet, truth be told, she was cheered by her cousin's irritation. The princess had been too heartbroken to leave her cabin for the first few days of their voyage. She'd lain listless on her bed, staring at the ceiling, not even pulling at her hair. Since then her melancholy was only punctuated by vexation, and no one vexed her as much as Tristan.

Undeterred, he swung his pole toward Essy and said, "May *I* invite *you* to fish with me?"

"Noblewomen don't fish," Essy retorted. "Not in Iveriu."

Barely holding back a laugh, Branwen tucked a loose curl behind her ear and, with horror, discovered another white strand; she plucked it with a vicious tug and let it fall. There was no breeze to carry it away.

Tristan pursed his lips. Nothing evaded his notice. She folded her hands together in her lap, unable to avoid rubbing her blemished palm. She wanted to tell him about her abilities but she was afraid— afraid she would repulse him. Branwen forced a smile and he resumed his attempts to curry favor with the princess.

"What are you playing?" Tristan asked her.

"*Fidkwelsa*. I'm sure it's far too complicated for a pirate's mind."

He laughed. "I'm familiar with Little Soldiers."

"I suppose that's an accurate description of the Kernyvak military."

"They call *fidkwelsa* Little Soldiers in Kernyv?" Branwen asked, trying to keep the conversation civil.

"Yes, King Marc taught me," he said, angling his shoulders toward her. "He's a fanatic."

"In *fidkwelsa*, the queen is more important than the king," Essy said snidely. "He's only her lowly manservant."

"That is often the case." Tristan grinned, and Branwen knew that grin was for her. She raised a hand to conceal her own smile. "But the king can still take the queen with one move," he said.

There was a sneaky maneuver known as the Western Gambit in which a king could seize his opponent's queen. It was hard to accomplish but Branwen relished the challenge.

"Well, I suppose *you're* the expert at taking queens against their will, Prince Tristan," said Essy. "In fact—"

An enormous billed bird landed with a thud on the mast, distracting the princess. The beast bellowed, making a hideous racket, but it didn't sound like a bird, more like a bleating lamb. Branwen gasped. The creature from Branwen's dream. She fought the sensation of salt water clogging her airway.

Rustling its night-colored feathers, the creature stretched its wings and settled onto its perch. From tip to tip, the bird's wingspan was larger than a toddler. The crimped skin of her heart line tingled.

"*Oi!* Off with you!" Captain Morgawr hollered, charging the bird from the helm. The creature stared at the hulking Kernyvman, impassive. Branwen took some comfort that others could see the bird, that it wasn't an Otherworld illusion, yet the sound filled her with dismay.

Morgawr gritted his teeth and drew his sword, rattling it in the air. "Cursed *kretarvs!*"

Essy raised her eyebrows. "*Kretarvs?*"

The captain didn't respond at first, keeping his eyes fixed on the winged beast. It seemed to Branwen that Morgawr and the bird were having a staring match. Her heart rabbited. How could she have seen this *kretarv* in her dream when she didn't know it existed? The beast dug its talons into the mast. They were as big as a woman's hand and looked deathly sharp.

"Carnivorous seabirds," Tristan explained quietly, but Essy pretended not to hear him.

Morgawr swiped the underside of the *kretarv*'s belly with his blade and the animal let out another grating cry before taking flight. The lament sounded almost human. The princess visibly shuddered. Morgawr touched the antler he wore around his neck to his lips, then using two fingers, he made two diagonal slashes in the air that intersected.

"You hale and sound, Lady Princess?" the captain asked, sheathing his sword and walking over to them. "Lady Branwen?"

"We're fine, Morgie," Tristan assured him. Branwen didn't feel particularly hale. She brushed her knuckles lightly across the curve of her neck. She had thought the nightmares of Keane were guilt, plain and simple. What if it was something more?

"Never should have set sail so close to sundown," grumbled the captain. "Unlucky."

Tristan shook his head, lifting his shoulders with a kind smile, and twirled the fishing pole against the grain of the deck. Branwen knew precisely what he was thinking. "Your prince doesn't believe in luck, Captain," she told him, composing herself.

"My lady, I would die for my prince," he replied. He toyed with the mangy end of his beard. "But in this matter, young Tristan is misguided. *Kretarvs* on the mast are an ill omen." He clutched his antler shard.

Essy rubbed her hands over her arms, hugging herself close. "Why do they make that wretched noise?" she asked.

"They're predators, Lady Princess," Morgawr said. "They mimic the call of whichever prey they're after. Maybe they're hunting for comely Ivernic maidens today."

Essy laughed nervously; Branwen didn't respond. In her dream, she'd sensed the *kretarv* waiting to make a meal of her. Her mouth grew dry as Keane's invisible hand tightened the ribbon around her throat.

The captain bounced his eyes between them, making sure he had their full attention. Branwen got the impression he was the kind of man who enjoyed telling stories at the tavern. "Many a seaman has been lured up to the deck by the light of the moon, sweet nothings from his ladylove being whispered in his ears. And then—"

Morgawr slapped his hands together like the crack of a whip. "The *kretarv* swoops down, grabs the careless mariner with its talons, and dives back into the depths below with a tasty treat in tow."

"That's not true," Essy protested, curt and prim.

"'Tis so, my princess. But we'll keep you safe."

Tristan dashed a glance first at Essy, then at Branwen. "Very safe," he said.

Again, Essy ignored him. Branwen knew he would try—but how could Tristan protect her from a creature that stalked her dreams?

The captain straightened up, recognizing that he'd frightened his audience a little too well. "Better go see about finding us another tack," he said, and returned to the helm.

"Lovely weather we're having," Tristan said to Essy, restarting the conversation. His efforts to befriend her were tireless.

Languidly, she turned her gaze on him. "Yes, lovely weather for a nap. I'm suddenly quite tired. Your presence is quite tiresome."

Branwen opened her mouth to reprimand her cousin but Tristan caught her eye, asking her to let him handle it. They had grown well versed in each other's expressions.

"Princess Eseult," Tristan implored. "We are to be family— cousins. Is there nothing I can do to make us friends as well?"

Across the deck, Branwen noticed Cadan watching them as he mopped. She had learned the boy was an orphan, like her. There were far too many orphans along the coasts of the northern seas.

The princess pushed to her feet, regaining Branwen's attention. "Prince Tristan, I have no family save Branwen—nor will I ever. And you and I will never be friends."

Before she or Tristan could respond, Essy had fled the *fidkwelsa* board and rushed down the steps toward the royal compartment. Tristan sighed, and Branwen read the distress on his brow.

"You'll win her over—eventually." Discreetly, Branwen placed a hand on his knee beneath the table. "You did me."

The creases above his eyebrows instantly disintegrated. He covered her hand with his own. "At least we get a moment alone." Branwen scrutinized the crewmen going about their daily tasks. "As alone as possible," Tristan corrected himself, flashing her a wicked grin. Heat flared from their entwined hands. She saw him wince, almost imperceptibly, and snatched hers back.

Had Branwen almost seared Tristan like she had Keane?

Tristan edged his stool closer and cupped Branwen's cheek. "You've gone pale." His dark eyes glowed with concern. "Does your injury pain you?"

"It's healing," she said, tone clipped. She feared her injury might pain *him*.

"Then what is it?" He trailed his thumb along her jaw. "You've been skittish since we set sail. Are you homesick?" Tristan's lightly callused fingertips made Branwen's body liquefy. His touch banished the dread that constantly held her in its grip. At least for a little while.

"When we reach my homeland, I'll take you to my favorite spot in Monwiku. You'll love it," he promised. "You can see from there to forever."

"I'd like that," Branwen said. Here, in the vastness of the sea, she could already see forever. She was so insignificant by comparison. The flat surface made her ill at ease.

"Tristan," she began, hesitant. "Do you think the *kretarv* is a harbinger, like the captain said?"

He chuckled. "Sailors love to tell tales. Is that what has you rattled?"

Branwen seesawed the squire on its square. She'd wanted him to laugh it off, to tell her there was no such thing as waking nightmares. Still, she shifted on her stool, unsettled.

"But the ship has hardly moved for days," she countered.

"We'll get there, Branwen. Trust me." Tristan attempted a placating smile. "We'll get to Kernyv, peace will be secured, and then—" He curled one of Branwen's midnight locks around his finger. "Maybe you'll finally relax?"

She blushed deeply. "Maybe." She grazed her hand over the

center of her chest. The Loving Cup was fastened securely against her heart. Like in a game of *fidkwelsa*, Branwen knew she had the winning move. Perhaps Tristan was right, perhaps she could afford to let down her guard.

He held her gaze and it took more than human strength to withstand the pull of his lips. Desire pulsed between them. Branwen imagined they glowed like an orb of sunlight. Tristan twisted and untwisted the strand of her hair, then coughed into his hand.

"Shall we finish your game?" he asked, pointing at the gilded pieces Essy had abandoned.

If they stayed this close together, thighs practically touching, Branwen might do something hasty. "Would you mind checking on my cousin?" she said.

Tristan quirked the corner of his mouth. "As my lady commands." If Branwen didn't know he was such a gentleman, she might interpret the lip twitch as a sign of exasperation.

"Wish me luck." He stood, collected the fishing pole, and saluted her as if she were sending him into a wolf's den armed with only his wits.

"I thought you didn't believe in luck?"

He spread his hands. "I'll take what I can get." Tristan cast Branwen a look that was somewhere between hungry and forlorn as he headed belowdecks. A look that nearly made her abandon all restraint. The sea was like Kerwindos's Cauldron, Branwen mused, neither Iveriu nor Kernyv. Out of time, out of place. Under other circumstances, she might savor the freedom of being . . . nowhere, everywhere. Especially with Tristan.

Not on this journey. They needed to reach Kernyv as soon as possible. Her mission depended on it. Consumed by her thoughts,

Branwen rose from her seat and scanned the skies for any lingering *kretarvs*. Queen Eseult had said her memories of the in-between would return. Could she have seen the lethal creatures during the spell? What exactly did they portend?

"Lady Branwen," said Morgawr as she joined him at the helm. His eyes crinkled as he greeted her. "Not fretting over my story, I trust."

"I was curious—do you see those birds often?"

The captain peered at her sidelong. "Often enough."

"When you chased it away, you made this sign—" Branwen repeated the two diagonal lines. "What does it mean? Does it frighten *kretarvs*?"

Morgawr pivoted to face her. Keeping one hand on the wheel, he lifted the antler pendant with the other. "I wear this as a reminder of the Horned One's sacrifice. He died so another might live. I invoked his protection."

"And the sign?"

"You know how he died?"

"Tristan—*Prince* Tristan told me. Impaled."

Morgawr nodded. He cut the air with his fingers. "This represents the stag's antlers," he said, and Branwen felt queasy. "It was a painful death, but a good death."

"Prince Tristan also said your god is called the Lord of Wild Things. Is the *kretarv* not one of his creatures?"

The captain lowered an eyebrow and Branwen instantly regretted her question. "The Horned One sees the best in all of his creatures, believes we're all capable of redemption. I'm just a man. I'm not so forgiving."

"Oh."

He barked a laugh. "Are you without faith, my lady?"

"I believe in the Old Ones." She stuck out her chin.

"Faith is faith, I suppose. You pray to your gods and I'll pray to mine that we make this crossing safely."

Fear pebbled Branwen's chest. "Are we in danger?"

Morgawr's gaze slid over the side of the hull. A fresh scowl gripped his face.

"See there, Lady Branwen . . ." He motioned toward the water. A dark shadow—shaped like the kites Branwen used to race along the Ivernic coast—darted terribly fast in the wake of the ship. She curled her hands into fists.

It's not Keane. It's not.

"Sharks know when a storm's coming," the captain said. He mumbled something low in Kernyvak that must have been a curse. Raising his voice, he called out, "Storm! Storm's coming!" At Morgawr's bellow, Cadan and the other shipmen immediately stopped what they were doing and scrambled to secure the rigging.

Branwen swung her gaze from the murky shape pursuing them to the endless blue sky. "There isn't a cloud in sight," she said, confused.

"That's when the worst storms hit, my lady. The ones you don't expect." A worried gleam appeared in his deep-set eyes. "And on Samonios Eve. Unlucky, unlucky. Better get yourself below. Tell the prince and princess to stay put."

Branwen turned to comply with his order. Hesitating a beat, she asked the captain, "Why do you call it the Dreaming Sea?"

His mouth twisted as he appraised her. "All sailors are dreamers. Otherwise, we wouldn't live our lives fate-tossed by the waves.

Sometimes we find what we're looking for. Other times, we just get lost."

Branwen felt her stomach plummet. A wave broke against the hull and her knees buckled. Bunching her skirts in her fists, she righted herself.

"Hurry to your cabin, Lady Branwen," urged Morgawr. Taking in her wan complexion, he added, "Never fear, I haven't lost a ship yet!"

If the *Dragon Rising* perished, it was much more than a ship that would be lost. She felt for the Loving Cup once more. Racing down the stairs to find the princess, Branwen couldn't shake the feeling that something—or someone—didn't want them to reach Kernyv.

THE BITTERNESS OF THE SEA

RAIN LASHED THE SHIP FOR three days as if the Old Ones themselves were crying before a lull came in the waves. Branwen held the princess in her arms as her pallor turned from moon white to pond-scum green and back again. Essy muffled her whimpers in the curve of Branwen's neck, seeming genuinely afraid of the storm.

Fate-tossed, Captain Morgawr had called them, like the verse from Étaín's song, which seemed a fitting description. Yet, unlike her cousin, Branwen found the storm invigorating. She sensed the lightning before it struck, almost as if the flames inside of her called to those that speared the sky.

Tristan had checked on Branwen and Essy every few hours during the worst of the squall, although he ignored the captain's command to stay belowdecks. He wanted to be with the crew, battling the storm. He wasn't built to let others risk themselves while he hid from danger. Branwen also thought he looked frustratingly handsome with his curls dripping dark drops from the torrential downpour.

"This infernal rocking is making me sick," Essy moaned, peeling away from Branwen in the bed they shared and flopping her head against the goose-down pillow. She rubbed circles against her forehead.

The swaying motion had become familiar to Branwen, comfortable even. She suspected it would be more difficult to find her feet again on land.

The princess released another lengthy sigh. "Is there any more of that elderberry wine?" she asked.

"I don't think wine will make you feel any *less* sick." Branwen ruffled Essy's hair. "Shall I read to distract you?"

"No more false love stories," replied Essy. The despondent tint to her words tugged at Branwen's very core. So often she'd wished her cousin would abandon the romantic foolishness of the Ivernic ballads. Yet the princess's resignation was even harder to stomach. Every fiber of Branwen's being itched to reassure her cousin that she would soon know true love.

The princess closed her eyes and gripped the bedcovers as if she could stop the ship from rocking through sheer force of will.

"Do you remember that rhyme Master Bécc taught us, Branny? From Armorica—a land that hates Kernyv as much as we do." When she didn't reply, her cousin recited, "*L'amar de la mar est amare.*"

"The love of the sea is bitter." Branwen snorted. "Very funny. Master Bécc isn't fond of boats." Although he did love puns in the Aquilan language.

"The Armoricans have as much right to be bitter about the sea as we do."

But Branwen wasn't bitter about the sea. The sea had brought her love. The sea had brought her Tristan. She turned onto her side and stroked Essy's furrowed brow. One of her earliest memories was of watching the princess sleep in her cradle. Then, like now, her cousin seemed so vulnerable. So delicate.

The ship lurched suddenly and Branwen knocked against the princess, bashing her nose.

"Oof, Branny!" she complained. Essy's eyes lit with mischief. Something Branwen feared she wouldn't see again. "So *that's* how you keep your nerves so steady!" The princess reached forward with greedy fingers, trying to wrest the golden vial from between Branwen's breasts. "Is it Clíodhna's dust?"

Branwen slapped her hand away, panic bursting in her heart. She had loosened the bindings of her underclothes while they were huddled in the cabin. Too much, it seemed. She flattened her palm over the Loving Cup. How much longer could she keep it a secret?

Essy scrunched up her face. "It's not nice not to share—especially when the world won't stop spinning." She pressed a hand dramatically to her brow.

"On second thought, a thimbleful of elderberry wine might quell your nausea."

"No. I want whatever you're having."

Branwen recognized her younger cousin's stubborn face. It was the same one Essy wore as a child, refusing to leave the table without another slice of apple cake.

"*Essy.* Treva made this especially for the wedding toast and entrusted it to me for safekeeping," she lied. "You'll enjoy it then." Branwen tapped the princess's nose as if she were a bad puppy. "But not before."

"Ah, yes, my *perfect* wedding." Essy sneered. Branwen tucked the vial farther down the front of her bodice. "Maybe a *kretarv* will put me out of my misery before I set foot in Kernyv!"

Branwen inhaled through her nostrils. "Tristan assures me that King Marc is a loyal and kind man," she replied in a level tone.

"Of course he is. Pirates are known for being courteous and steadfast!"

A nervous cough interrupted the cousins. Cadan loitered in the doorway. "Pardon me, Lady Princess, Lady Branwen," he said, licking his lips and keeping his eyes pinned to the floor.

"What is it?" Essy demanded, not bothering to mask her temper.

"It's . . . it's . . . ," the boy stuttered. "It's only that there's a rip in the sail. Captain Morgawr sent me to ask if you might have a spare piece of cloth." His cheeks turned brighter than Treva's wild strawberry tarts.

"Finally, a use for all your dresses," Branwen teased the princess, attempting to lighten the mood.

"Give them my First Night gown, Branny. I'd love to have a reason not to use it."

Cadan flexed his knuckles taut against his trouser pockets.

"*Hush,*" Branwen reprimanded. Poor Cadan. His Ivernic was apparently proficient enough to glean Essy's meaning. He had no idea where to look or how to react to the mention of her marital bed by the lady who would be his queen. Taking pity on him, Branwen said, "I'm sure we can find something."

"Thank you, my lady," he answered, concentrating very hard on the floorboards.

"I'll be up in a minute, Cadan."

He raised his eyes in alarm. "The deck is still slippery. Unsafe."

At that moment, Branwen wanted nothing more than a fresh

gulp of salty air. Essy was looking for a fight and, after three days in the cramped cabin, Branwen might have been, too. She felt like a hunting dog caged in the kennels beneath Castle Rigani.

"I'll be up in a minute," Branwen repeated. She would not be dissuaded.

Frowning, the cabin boy nodded and retreated down the corridor as Branwen hopped off the bed and began rummaging through the princess's many leather-bound trunks. She selected a ruby-colored gown that she knew her cousin didn't particularly favor. A winter dress cut from thickly woven wool.

Bundling the heavy garment in her arms, Branwen crossed the compartment, seeking out Essy's gaze, not really asking for permission. The princess twisted a sun-bleached tendril around her forefinger. Tight. "Please be careful, Branny," she said. Her eyes had rounded. "You're all I've got."

Branwen shot her a comforting smile. Her cousin's irritation had been replaced by genuine concern, but they both needed some time apart.

"Don't worry. I've found my sea legs." And, hopefully, Essy would lose interest in the golden vial while she was gone. "Why don't you try reading something? Everything will be right again soon."

The princess's voice carried after Branwen as she made a brisk exit, although it was no more than a whisper.

"Nothing will ever be right again."

✠ ✠ ✠

An overcast sky hung above the mast when Branwen reached the top of the rickety staircase. The saltwater-warped wood creaked like an old man's bones. She spied Tristan talking with Morgawr on the bow, their backs to her. Their discussion was animated and they didn't notice her approach from behind.

"I know every star above the Dreaming Sea, my prince," the captain was saying to Tristan. "I don't recognize any of these."

"I have faith in you, Morgie."

He grunted. "Your father was the only navigator better than me. Hanno could see his way through fog without a lantern."

Tristan clapped the older man on the back. "We're only a few days late."

Branwen halted mid-stride, alarm streaking through her. "Have we been blown off course?"

Both men swiveled toward the sound of her voice. They exchanged a brief glance. "Only a delay," assured Tristan, taking a step in her direction. Surprise stenciled on his face, he dropped his gaze to the bunch of cloth.

"For the sail," she said.

Captain Morgawr scowled. "I sent the boy for that." Grumpily, he took the dress from Branwen. "*Oi!* Cadan!" he hollered in an ornery tone. "Where're you hiding?"

"Don't scold the boy, Captain. I insisted."

Tristan cracked a grin. "Lady Branwen can be quite insistent." His eyes were warm like a summer's night.

"I doubt any of your crew is as agile with a needle as I am," Branwen said to Morgawr.

"The lady's work *is* unparalleled," Tristan vouched to the captain. He placed a hand to his heart and glanced at Branwen. "I'm intimately acquainted with it."

"Suit yourself, my lady. After you." The captain carried the dress to where the damaged sail had been stretched against the deck, hovering over Branwen as she used a small knife to open the crude stitches one of his men had made. Morgawr watched a few more minutes before regarding the horizon like a friend he had once known well but hadn't seen for years, then walked away.

Tristan squatted beside her. He handed Branwen an ungainly needle threaded with leather cord. "You must be freezing," he said, concerned.

The wind whorled her dark hair, unbraided for once, around her shoulders. She should have been cold. She'd forgotten her cloak. She wasn't. Ever since the night she'd killed Keane, Branwen had been consistently, uncomfortably hot.

She shrugged. "The captain seems jittery."

"That's his job." Branwen canted her head, holding Tristan with her gaze. "Sailors spook easily," he deflected.

"But you don't. Spook easily?" It was only a fraction of the question she wanted to ask him: *Could you accept my magic? Could you accept me?*

"No, Branwen. I don't." Covertly, he caressed her cheek. She didn't dare press for more of an answer.

Focusing on the task at hand, she said, "Hold the flaps straight if you want to help."

"As you wish." Tristan smoothed the burgundy slip of fabric between the folds of salt-bitten white. He was quiet as Branwen began to sew the first strips together.

Over, under; over, under. Loop, cross; loop, cross.

"Morgawr knew your father?" Branwen asked leadingly. She saw Tristan nod from the corner of her eye.

"They joined the Royal Fleet together, as young men. A lot of

Kartagons do. My father met my mother at a ceremony for new officers."

Branwen's head bobbed rhythmically with each prick and entreaty of the tide. "That sounds like the beginning of a ballad," she said.

"Everyone says they were very much in love—it wasn't a politically advantageous match." She slid her gaze toward him, urging Tristan to carry on, as her hands flew over the sail. "The Aquilan legions never fully conquered Kernyv as they did other kingdoms on the island of Albion," he explained. "When the empire began to crumble, some of the Kernyveu wanted the peoples whose ancestors had originated on the southern continent—Kartagons, and others— to leave. But, like my father's family, they'd been in Kernyv for many generations. They'd only seen Kartago on a map."

Tristan went quiet for a moment. He lifted his gaze to the clouds, which effervesced a purple gray as twilight usurped the sky.

"It's been nearly a hundred years since Great King Katwaladrus decreed that the southerners could remain. Still, some of the Kernyvak nobles resent them, especially the wealthy and influential families. And to marry a princess?" He scoffed. "I see my grandmother's hand. She's strong like you, Branwen. She told me my father was the only man in Kernyv worthy of her daughter, and that was that." Affection underscored his tale. "I can't wait for you to meet her."

Branwen glanced up sharply. "Meet her? She's *alive*?"

"Yes?" he said, befuddled.

"But—back at the cave, you told me it was just you and Marc?"

Tristan grimaced. "We were both dancing around the truth then. I'm glad we don't have to do that any longer."

Branwen's face softened even as her chest constricted. She swallowed, eyes trailing back to the sail. "The raids on Iveriu started under King Katwaladrus," said Branwen. The Iverni didn't call him Great. "Do you think he sent the Kernyveu to fight us so they wouldn't fight each other?"

Tristan laid his hands on top of hers, pausing Branwen mid-stitch.

"This sail is like the wound between Iveriu and Kernyv. Together, we have healed it." Goose bumps lifted on the nape of Branwen's neck. *Not yet.* Tristan tipped his forehead against hers. "Kernyv will love Iveriu as much as I love you," he promised.

He lowered his mouth to hers, gathering her bottom lip between his teeth. Branwen dropped the needle. She gasped as he bit her with exquisite tenderness. Tristan tasted sweet and fresh as he whispered her name, and Branwen scrabbled at his chest with yearning. Her pulse pounded in her ears, reaching for the stars. *Surrender.* This was what surrender felt like.

A light drizzle tickled the crown of her head. She forgot where they were—when they were—everything but the need to know him, feel him, make him hers. Strong arms encircled her, pulling her closer, bleeding into her.

Branwen. His voice was rough like the sea. *Branwen.* His voice was deep like the sea. *Branwen.* She would follow him to its very bottom.

"Branwen!"

Her eyes snapped open as if from a trance.

"Already embracing our new homeland, I see."

Essy.

CHOICES

ONE MOMENT OF WEAKNESS. WAVES smashed against the hull, buffeting Branwen's heart. She gurgled a breath. The phantom ribbon tightened around her throat.

"Princess Eseult," said Tristan, his tone remarkably steady despite his startled expression. He met her gaze, head unbowed.

"I'd thank you to take your hands off my lady's maid."

Essy spoke with a cold rage, thin as the ice that covered the rivers of Iveriu on winter mornings. She loomed above the lovers, radiating a disapproval that perforated Branwen like a thousand flying knives. With the bleak, silver horizon thickening behind her, the Princess of Iveriu incarnated the Goddess Ériu in her death guise: the destroyer of unfit kings.

Tristan removed his arms from around Branwen's waist. He skimmed his hand along her cheek, undaunted.

"Lady Princess—" he began, and Essy silenced him with an outstretched finger.

"I don't care to hear any Kernyvak lies today." Her voice shook with fury. She peered down her nose at Branwen, expression deadening. "At least now I understand why you're so eager to hand me over to our enemies," she said. "You were the one person I trusted, *cousin*. I thought you were so selfless, giving up a life in Iveriu for me. But you're just like everyone else—you've betrayed me for your own gain."

Branwen lurched back as if her mare had kicked her straight in the chest. She wanted to scream that it was *Essy* who had planned to desert *her*, to forsake two kingdoms for a callow crown-chaser. *No,* she wouldn't. Branwen pressed the heels of her hands against her eyes. She wouldn't betray the princess. Not even to defend herself in front of the man she loved.

"You're as big a hypocrite as my mother," Essy charged. Branwen's hands fell to her sides, curving like claws, fingernails chiseling into her skin. "No wonder you always defend her. So pious, so dutiful. Both of you use the Old Ones as an excuse to get what you want!" she continued, pummeling Branwen with her words. "How dare *you* tell *me* whom to love when you've given yourself to our enemy! You *disgust* me."

"That's quite enough." Tristan launched to his feet. "Don't speak to Branwen that way. You'll regret your words when your temper abates."

Essy's laughter tinkled like icicles. "I'll speak to my lady's maid however I see fit. The only regret I have is not seeing through her deceit sooner."

Branwen remained on her knees, tethered to the spot. She grasped at the Loving Cup beneath her shift. If only Essy knew. She couldn't tell her. She *couldn't*. Branwen had to brave her cousin's scorn. The Old Ones had placed their faith in her.

"Your cousin loves you," Tristan told the princess when Branwen still found no words of her own. She could only stifle a sob.

"I was wrong when I told you Branwen was my only family, Prince Tristan. I have no family. I love no one and no one loves me."

Warm, not-quite pleasant tingles erupted on Branwen's palm, burning away the shock, reminding her of what she had already done for love.

"You know that's a lie," Branwen ground out, meeting the princess's stare. She rose to standing.

"Do I? *You're* the liar!" Essy shouted. "You said you'd never let a man come between us." Her teeth clacked together. "You said you were choosing me—coming to Kernyv for me." She thrust a finger at Tristan, skewering him with a spiked glance. "You were choosing *him*."

"I wasn't," said Branwen. At her side, Tristan stiffened. "I would follow you anywhere, Essy." She flung a pleading look at Tristan as she took a step toward her cousin. "I didn't want to hurt you. I've loved you since the day you were born. Hurting you is the last thing I would want."

The princess's breath came in fits and starts, her shoulders hitching toward her ears. Raindrops spattered her cheeks, mixing with the tears that streaked from her eyes. "All you do is hurt people, Branwen. You hurt me. You hurt Keane." She lifted her chin. "He knew, didn't he? That's why you parted in anger."

Tristan balked, back straightening in surprise. He looked to Branwen for confirmation. Essy laughed, and it was a discordant sound.

"You didn't know, though, did you?" she said to Tristan. "It's comforting that I'm not the only one Branwen keeps secrets from. And she keeps so many."

347

Anger exploded in Branwen's chest. "Essy, you don't know what you're talking about." She pictured Keane in the stairwell, dying at her hand, dying to protect her cousin's secret. "You don't know *anything*," she growled.

"If I don't know anything, it's because you never *tell* me anything!" The princess's gaze wavered between Tristan and Branwen. "What I do know is that you're a traitor. You chose your enemy over your own blood."

"*Essy*—"

Her cousin's shoulders deflated inward. She trembled where she stood. An avenging goddess no longer, she resembled a child lost in a wood. Branwen reached out to soothe her as she had done all her life. Essy backed away.

"Don't touch me!" Her pitch was high, hysterical. Savage. "You might think you've won. That I don't have any choices left. But I do—I *do*!"

Essy wheeled around, plum-colored skirt billowing like a bruise, and fled toward the other end of the ship. Wet wood squelched beneath her boots, her leather soles skidding several times.

"Let her go," Tristan said to Branwen in a tired voice. Consternation stained his features. Branwen tunneled her fingers through her damp locks. She welcomed the rain, fresh on her face. How could she have let the princess discover them? They should have arrived at Monwiku by now; then she wouldn't need to hide her heart.

Never before in her life had Branwen looked at the sea and seen an enemy. Never had the waves made her feel trapped. This ship was her floating prison.

"Your cousin is wrong," Tristan said. "About so very many things."

"She's young." Branwen defended the princess out of habit, standing there eviscerated as she was. She swiped at her eyes.

"She's going to be Queen of Kernyv."

Branwen slanted her gaze to his, and she saw misgivings there. "She'll grow into it."

"You're the most loyal person I know." He crossed to her side and took her hand, his smile rueful. "And you deserve to be happy. If your cousin loves you, she should want you to be happy, too."

"I *will* be happy, Tristan," she said, defiance sparking in her heart. The *later* didn't need to be said aloud. He read it in her stance.

"Happiness indefinitely postponed is no happiness at all." His thumb grazed the back of Branwen's hand, pleasure fluttering through her and, somehow, it did feel traitorous. "You also have a duty to yourself," he said. Shivering a breath, she jerked away and Tristan nailed her with a question: "Unless you *are* ashamed of me?"

"*What?* How could you think that?"

"What the princess said—about Keane. Is it true? Did you part in anger?"

"Yes," she replied carefully, crafting her thoughts. She pressed her palm against her skirt. "He wanted more from me than I could give." Looking Tristan square in the eye, she said, "I couldn't give him my heart because I had already given it to you."

His jaw went slack. He loosed a breath. "It's not your fault you're so easy to love," he said, voice tender, but Branwen was no longer sure it was easy to love anyone. "Why didn't you just tell me?" Tristan asked.

"Because it's done. It's over. And I've come across the sea—with *you*."

His lips twitched. "You would have come across the sea without me." It wasn't a question. "The princess is wrong about that as well."

"She is."

The rain began to fall harder, pattering against the deck.

"You're as fierce as any warrior, Branwen."

She sighed. The war with Kernyv had made her fierce. Being orphaned at six years old had made her fierce. She thought of Gráinne clinging to her doll when they first met on the Rock Road, prepared to defend the charred toy with tooth and claw. Gentle people did not survive in the world as it was. Branwen wanted to make a better one.

"If you weren't a prince, Tristan, what would you do? Who would you be?"

His eyebrows shot up. Whatever he'd been expecting Branwen to say, it wasn't that. "I would explore, I think. See what lies beyond the southern continent. Sail to the edge of the map—maybe beyond."

Branwen's snort gave way to a chuckle. "Become a pirate, after all?"

They shared a grin. "What about you?" he asked.

"I don't know." She glanced down the length of the ship. She should find Essy, try to mend things.

"Wait." Tristan squeezed Branwen's elbow. "Wait here in the rain with me for a bit."

They breathed together, watched the water fall on each other's lips. They waited. Together. Until lightning forked through the sky.

✦ ✦ ✦

Tristan insisted on accompanying Branwen to her compartment. She worried the sight of him might send the princess into another rage,

350

but she couldn't deny the solace of knowing he was there, at her back, feeling his body heat in the spindle-like passage. With a tentative step, Branwen approached the threshold.

Although the door was slightly ajar, she knocked. She heard no noise coming from within. Above, thunder cracked.

"Essy?" she said. Another knock, gingerly. Maybe her cousin had cried herself to sleep. "Essy?" A chill slithered down Branwen's spine. Tristan tensed at her inflection.

Branwen shoved the door in a brutal gesture. It banged open and she heard a moan. "No!" She sprinted inside.

Branwen's hands flew to her mouth. A cry more anguished than any *kretarv* ripped from her throat.

The princess lay sprawled on top of the bed, unmoving. Her blond hair feathered around her like rays of sunshine. Branwen rushed to her cousin's side, clenching her jaw to suppress another scream. Essy was whiter than a Death-Teller, the skirt of her dress hitched up on the left side to reveal her thigh. Fiery blood spurted from her leg onto the sheets.

A dagger-sharp length of sewing scissors protruded from the fleshy part of Essy's upper thigh. The blades were each as long as a forefinger.

Branwen lowered her face above her cousin's. She was still breathing. At the foot of the bed, Tristan sucked in a gulp of air.

"*Essy*," Branwen rasped as she scanned the princess's injured leg with a healer's eye. The stab wound was almost precisely where Queen Eseult had told Branwen to avoid when she cauterized Saoirse's shadow-stung flesh with the fire-poker.

Her stomach roiled. Essy had been there, too. Essy had heard those instructions. *Could she . . . Could she . . . ?*

"Cousin, talk to me." Fear frayed the ends of Branwen's words.

"Branny?" the princess mewled, disoriented.

Branwen dropped to her knees beside the bed. The blood was coming so fast. "Essy, what happened?"

Tristan hovered silently, averting his eyes from the princess's exposed flesh.

"I—I thought I might sew Gráinne's doll another dress." Essy spoke haltingly, and Branwen didn't entirely believe her. She saw no other sewing supplies.

The princess's angry words from less than an hour ago flew through her mind like shards of glass: *You might think you've won. That I don't have any choices left. But I do—I do!*

"Oh, Essy," she breathed.

She should have realized it was more than one of Essy's furious outbursts. She should have seen the depths of her cousin's despair. She should have—*Stop.* Recriminations wouldn't help the princess now.

Tristan crossed toward her, dropping a hand on Branwen's shoulder. He lowered himself to the floor beside her.

"What do we do?" he asked quietly. He worked his jaw from side to side. The blood continued to flow. Tristan must have seen men injured like this on the battlefield. The prognosis wasn't good.

"Why am I so cold?" Essy murmured.

Tristan sought Branwen's gaze; panic brimmed from his. They were alone in the middle of the sea. Her chest contracted. Branwen was the only one who could save her cousin.

"Keep her awake," she ordered him.

Tristan moved to sit beside the princess, smiling at her with the warmth of a hundred bonfires. "You won't ever be cold in Kernyv," he said.

Essy managed a sneer. "It's true. We're favored with a southerly wind from the Mílesian Peninsula. It heats the rock beneath our feet. We have flowers in Kernyv that you've never seen."

"There's nothing in Kernyv I want to see." Her scoff was faint but Branwen praised the Old Ones.

Branwen pressed her fingers around the wound. Each time Essy winced, she felt the pain as her own. *Think, Branwen.* If she removed the scissors too precipitously, as when Tristan had been gored by the Balu Gaisos, Essy could bleed to death even faster. Leaving the metal inside the princess, on the other hand, risked infection and there was no guarantee when they would make landfall.

If Essy died, the dream of peace died with her.

Branwen gritted her teeth. She would have to risk it.

"Tristan," she said. "Ask the captain for his strongest spirits. Strong enough to set on fire."

He replied with a brief upward tug of the lips. "I'm sure Morgie has something in his cabin that'll do the trick." Tristan leapt up with reflexes as quick as the storied Hound. "I'll be back before you can miss me."

"No . . . need . . . to hurry," Essy said breathily. "I could never miss a Kernyvman."

"I hope to change your mind."

Branwen pinned him with a look. *Hurry*, she mouthed as he bolted above deck.

"Don't worry, Branny," said her cousin. "I don't feel any pain."

That's what she feared. She kissed her brow. It felt waxy. "You're in shock, Essy. I'm going to make you better."

"You can't fix everything."

"I can try."

She tilted her face so Essy couldn't see the tears streaming down her face, then pushed to her feet, careful not to jostle her patient.

"Where are you going, Branny?"

"Nowhere. Gathering my tools. Keep very still." Tamping down on her nerves, Branwen assembled fine needles and thread from her healing kit. She could stitch up the surface of Essy's thigh but there was nothing she could do about the internal damage. She wondered, only for a second, if the Seal of Alliance Tristan carried back to Kernyv would be just as useless in binding the wound between their two kingdoms.

She ransacked the trunks with bloody, frantic fingers. Why hadn't she thought to include Clíodhna's dust among her belongings? What Branwen wouldn't give for a *skeakh* branch!

Please, she beseeched the Old Ones. *We've come so far. You can't let her die. Not my Essy.* Branwen couldn't imagine a world without her cousin—didn't know who she would be without her.

Tristan burst back into the cabin clutching a blue-tinted bottle.

"Morgie calls it Seahorse Piss. Guaranteed to put hair on your chest."

"Just what I nee—" Essy slurred.

Tristan dropped down beside the princess on the side of the bed closest to the door. "Who doesn't like a princess with a bit of chest hair?" he said.

Essy grimaced, too weak to laugh. Nodding at the bottle, Branwen said, "She needs more than a dram," and Tristan set the bottle gently to the princess's mouth. Essy spluttered but swallowed several healthy swigs.

"Save a little for my implements," Branwen teased her, attempting to keep both herself and her patient calm. Queen Eseult had taught Branwen to clean her tools with strong spirits in the absence of fire. *Please let this work.*

She knelt once more beside the princess and released a shuddering breath. Wordless, she used a small knife to cut away the rest of Essy's skirt. Tristan kept his gaze planted firmly on the princess's face. Seeing his king's bride in such a state was nearly treason, but these *were* exceptional circumstances.

Dousing her tools in the Seahorse Piss, Branwen told Tristan, "Position yourself directly above Essy's head." He shuffled to where she flicked her glance. "You need to hold her down."

Her heart hiccupped as he seized Essy's wrists, clamping them to the bed. For a moment Branwen didn't know if it was the ship that rocked. The recollection of Keane helping her with Saoirse rattled her bones.

"This is going to hurt," Branwen warned as she poured the stinging spirits onto the open wound. Essy flailed, hissing like a destiny snake. Branwen didn't allow herself tears. She watched as Essy's eyes caught on Tristan; he smiled down at the woman who would be his queen.

"I'm here," he promised. "I've got you."

To Branwen's utter astonishment, Essy stopped squirming.

"On three," she directed.

Tristan shifted his smile to her. "On three." They were a team, like Queen Eseult and King Óengus. Always.

Tristan began to sing, something soft and soothing in Kernyvak. Branwen didn't understand the words but they gave her courage.

"Three," she breathed.

Essy's scream tore at something deep in Branwen's soul as she removed the scissors.

And then there was blood. So much blood.

Tristan blanched. Essy's eyelids opened and closed more rapidly than a starling's wings before closing altogether.

Branwen had chosen wrong. The Princess of Iveriu was going to die and it was all her fault. Iveriu was dying. The blood in Branwen's veins began to simmer.

The fire wanted to escape. *Oh. Oh.*

"Tristan," she commanded, her voice not quite her own. "Fetch another blanket."

He furrowed his brow but he didn't question her. He kissed the crown of Essy's head, whispering, "Be strong" and left to do as he'd been asked.

Branwen looked down at her hands: The center of her right palm glowed like an ember. As if being guided from beyond the Veil, she pressed it to Essy's shredded flesh. An orange glow surged across her cousin's leg and she convulsed. She convulsed again. Fear gripped Branwen that she'd kill her cousin like she had Keane and she retracted her hand.

Control it. She closed her eyes. *Control.* She imagined the fire as a single shaft of candlelight.

What would Queen Eseult do?

Steeling herself, Branwen tried again. This time Essy sighed, still unconscious, but not from pain. The sparks of flame entered her bloodstream like fireflies.

Branwen watched with bewilderment as the blood began to clot. The flesh wove itself back together as if it were upon a loom. Her aunt's words echoed in Branwen's mind.

From the same source comes creation and destruction. She could use her power to protect life as well as to take it. For the first time since

356

Keane's demise, Branwen actually saw the Hand of Bríga as a blessing rather than a curse.

Before Tristan returned to witness her handiwork, she grasped the bedsheet, tore off a strip, and tied it tightly around Essy's thigh. When she awoke, Branwen would try to explain, beg her to keep her secret.

Tristan rushed through the doorway with Cadan at his heels. "I've got the blanket," he said, suddenly looming above her. Lanced by panic, Branwen hid her fingers, which dripped with fire and blood. But his attention was focused squarely on Essy's bound thigh.

"You stopped the bleeding?" She nodded. "You truly are a wonder." Tristan's voice shook with equal parts disbelief and admiration.

"I hope so." Branwen grabbed the bottle of Seahorse Piss to wash the blood from her hands. All of a sudden, the blood and spirits began to blur in her vision. Light-headedness cascaded over her. Branwen staggered backward, groping for the wall, the bottle slipping from her grasp.

She heard a *crash*.

Darkness descended as Branwen slumped to the floor.

TRUE COLORS

R OSEMARY TICKLED HER NOSE. BRANWEN hugged herself close. *Home.* She gazed down at Castle Rigani from Whitethorn Mound. Chills erupted all along her body. She turned around slowly. The trees were no longer lush, overflowing with flowers like snow. The petals were withered, graying. The branches were nearly bare.

A familiar bark attracted her attention. The fox's gleaming red coat had become muddied, lost its luster. Ears pinned back, the creature growled at Branwen, accusing. It swished its tail, then scurried down the hill.

She tried to follow but the wall of branches ringing the hilltop refused to part for her. She slapped her hands against the invisible barrier. Pounded with all her strength.

What do you want? Branwen cried in her mind, her limbs benumbed.

Three great *kretarvs* circled the mound. She was hemmed in. They were predators and she was their prey. There was nowhere for

Branwen to run as the first dove toward her, its beak wide like a bestial smile. Followed by the second, and then the third.

The first of the gruesome birds sped toward her again. It slashed her chest just below her right breast with its beak and began to feast. The two others attacked her hands and feet. Agony savaged her body so that she called out for death.

In the distance, a gigantic tidal wave crested on the Ivernic Sea, heading straight for the coast. Taller than any tower Branwen had ever seen, the wave would decimate anything in its path and it was on a direct collision course with Castle Rigani. As it surged toward the shore, Branwen saw faces appear from the black depths, poking at the surface.

The faces of the dead. Restless, unburied souls—like Keane.

Horror drenched her; bile rose in her throat. Branwen could do nothing but whimper. Flame flared from her heart line and fizzled. Smoke swirled mockingly in the air.

Death spilled onto the beaches of Iveriu and washed Castle Rigani out to sea.

✢ ✢ ✢

Heart beating rapidly, Branwen blinked her eyes open. Callused fingertips stroked her wet cheeks. It was dark save for the flickering light of a lantern.

"*Shh*, Branwen. You were crying in your sleep."

She scrubbed her eyes, Tristan's face coming into focus. Where was she? On Whitethorn Mound. No, that wasn't right. Branwen skimmed the length of her body. No wounds. No blood. "Am I still dreaming?" she said.

359

Tristan laughed softly. "No. Although I have often dreamed of having you in my bed."

His bed? Branwen jolted upright. Her gaze swerved around the darkened space. Tristan perched at the edge of the narrow cot on which she rested. How did she get here? In the corner of his densely packed quarters, Branwen spied her mother's *krotto* harp.

With a sigh, Tristan touched her arm. "You're all right," he said as if he were trying to convince himself. "I brought you here so you could properly recuperate." Her heart twinged at how weary Tristan seemed. Branwen's mind had scattered to the winds. She had to call back her thoughts from very far away.

Her muscles were stiff and her head throbbed dully. Meandering her gaze down to her hands, "Essy?" she gasped, remembering.

"She's well. Asleep. Incredibly," he assured Branwen. Tristan pursed his lips, penetrating her with his stare. "Cadan is standing guard. I wanted to be with *you*." Contrition belied his relief. His primary duty was to the princess, and they both knew it.

Branwen rolled her shoulders. "What time is it?"

"Just before dawn."

She had slept a long time. Unconsciously, Branwen rubbed her palm. She needed to see Essy, prove to herself that the Hand of Bríga had saved the princess. In her dream, the flames had sputtered to useless smoke. She couldn't shrug off the notion that Keane was no longer haunting Branwen, but *hunting* her.

She moved to rise from the bed and Tristan placed a firm hand on her knee. A blanket separated his skin from hers yet desire streamed through her, a yearning for him to touch the flesh along the inside of her knee. She hitched a breath. Guilt slammed into her as the memory of her cousin, prostrate and bleeding, flooded into her mind.

"The princess is hale. Sleeping peacefully," Tristan reiterated, more force behind his words. "You're the one who collapsed, Branwen—after you healed her." He took a deep breath. "We need to talk honestly. I've been sitting vigil for hours, listening to you breathe, hoping you would wake . . . not knowing how to help you." His agitation increased with each statement. He fiddled with the sheet.

"Tristan, I—"

"Let me finish," he interrupted. She nodded, mouth growing dry at his brusqueness. He twisted the sheet harder. "This wasn't the first time I've watched you languish. This wasn't the first time you've healed someone with more than mortal medicine. At the Champions Tournament, I felt the life leeching from my body. I was no longer there. I was somewhere else—a field of beautiful white flowers."

Branwen's shoulders jerked back. Had he seen the *skeakh*? Tristan kept his gaze steady on her. "You were there with me. I don't know where it was, but you were with me. When I recovered from the poison, Queen Eseult told me you'd been infected while tending to me. But that was a lie," he said, and there was no hesitation in his voice. That was the lie Queen Eseult had told everybody, including Essy. Branwen forced herself not to react. "At the time, I decided I'd been delirious."

Tristan shook his head and reached into his pocket. "I would be dead twice over if it wasn't for you."

Tiny lines troubled Branwen's brow as he offered her an intricately braided leather circlet. One strand had been bleached white, while the others had been dyed green and black.

The colors of Iveriu and Kernyv.

"I had this made in Monwiku. Before I set out for the Champions Tournament." He skated his thumb over the leatherwork. "I didn't think I'd find a love like my parents had until I met you," Tristan admitted. Her heartbeats grew deafening. "I've been meaning to give you this since the Laelugus feast." He sighed. "The timing never seemed right."

Their fingers brushed as she took the bracelet from him.

"This is a promise, Branwen. When we arrive in Kernyv, I will ask King Marc for permission to formally propose."

Branwen's heart cleaved in two. Tristan kissed her fingertips and she could imagine all too easily how their bodies would melt together on their First Night. Half of her wanted to sing praises to the Old Ones for sending him to her; the other half envisioned Essy, alone and afraid.

"Tristan, it's still not the right time. Look what happened with my cousin today. She's . . . she's not strong enough to see us together."

His posture tensed. "You're more like Marc than you know. Duty before love," he said, and it didn't sound like a compliment. Irritation itched at the back of Branwen's throat. Tristan had no reason to suspect that Essy's injury might have been self-inflicted— and Branwen didn't want to compromise her cousin by sharing her fears.

"Didn't you tell me that the Kernyvak barons see you as a threat to your uncle's reign?" Branwen reminded him instead. "How would it look if you returned from Iveriu with a bride of your own?"

Tristan made a disgruntled noise. "You're very skilled at inventing reasons why we shouldn't be together."

"I'm not *inventing* anything," she protested, temper ignited. He scoffed again. "*Tristan.*" Their eyes met and the sadness in his chastised her more than words ever could have. "Tristan," she said more gently. "I *do* want a life with you." She stared down at the bracelet, at the constancy it represented. "I just need more time. There are things

I need to do first. Let Essy settle into her marriage. Iveriu and Kernyv need a stable union. Why should we rush?"

"Why rush?" Her head snapped up at the crisp edge to Tristan's words. "The *rush* is I can feel this"—he gestured at the space between them—"growing vaster every day. Sometimes you feel farther away than when you were across the sea. And I don't know why. Maybe if we're handfasted, you'll trust me enough to let me in?"

Instinctively, she touched the Loving Cup. So small, and yet its weight was crushing.

"That's not a wise reason to ask me to be your wife," she said.

"No. It's not." A storm gathered in Tristan's eyes, his breathing ragged. "Tell me something true, Branwen. *Trust* me." He turned over her right hand to expose the scar. The skin was newly inflamed. "Tell me the truth about this." He traced the length of it and his touch was like a balm.

"It's just us here," he said. Shadows capered on the wall as the ship rocked. "Like at the cave."

She wanted to go back. So much. She wanted to go back to the day they met, and she wanted to go forward—to the future she'd been shown in the in-between. Branwen could do neither. She only had now.

"It started with you," she admitted. "Everything started with you, Tristan."

He ran his tongue along his lips. "Everything started for me with you, too. Everything good."

Remorse swept through Branwen. She wished it was only good things that began with Tristan. Speaking to their joined hands, Branwen told him about her mother, the Old Ones, and the trade she had offered on Whitethorn Mound: blood for magic.

"After the Champions Tournament, things began to change," she said. "For me. Queen Eseult says it's a gift from the Goddess Bríga."

Tristan edged closer and lifted Branwen's hand to his lips, tender against her wound. It was a thrilling sensation. She echoed the rumbling sigh that escaped him. Telling the truth gave Branwen an airy feeling. It was too tempting to tell him everything.

He lowered her hand to his lap. "There's a cost, though." Tristan twisted a pinkie around one of Branwen's curls. Her eyes widened: The strand was white.

"The healing drains you," he said.

She nodded. There was a cost—magic had cost Keane his life. Tristan gazed at her with adoration. He saw only the good. If Branwen told him the full truth of her powers, how could he ever look at her the same way?

"You don't need to save everyone all the time." He slid an arm around her shoulders, pulled her head against his chest. "Let me help you."

She listened to the rhythm of his heart. Tristan meant what he said, she knew, but there were some things only Branwen could do.

"Please don't tell anyone," she whispered.

Gazing down at her, he said, "What are you afraid of?"

Myself. "Queen Eseult told me women aren't allowed to take part in the Mysteries of the New Religion. Is that true?"

His embrace grew more rigid. "Only some people feel that way."

"Even so, Iveriu is depending on me to help secure the alliance. I need to be accepted at court."

"You will be." He pulled back and gathered Branwen's face between his hands. "And I will keep your secret—I will always protect you." He kissed one cheek, then the other. "Thank you for trusting me, my love."

Branwen planted her lips on the arch of his neck and inhaled his scent, his warmth. Tristan groaned as desire passed through him to her.

Between labored breaths, he said, "We'll wait as long as you want." He plucked the bracelet from the covers. "Keep it. Wear it when you're ready. It's my promise to you: You're the only woman for me." He slid his thumb along her cheekbone. "You should get some more sleep."

"You'll stay?"

Branwen didn't want to sleep alone. She didn't want Keane to find her again in her dreams tonight. Holding Tristan's gaze, she scooted to one side of the bed, making room. It wasn't something a noblewoman should do.

He jammed his eyes shut, his internal debate nearly audible.

"I'll stay," he said.

He remained above the bedclothes and Branwen below as she turned on her side, allowing him to mold his body to hers. Every part of her sighed.

Draping an arm across her waist, Tristan threaded their fingers together, pressing his palm to hers.

"Sleep. I'll be here when you wake."

And she did. And he was.

SEA-WOLF

A COLD PEACE HAD DESCENDED BETWEEN Branwen and Essy. When the princess woke after her accident, she had no recollection of how serious the injury had been. She refused to discuss how she had managed to stab herself so Branwen held her tongue as well. Essy had enough troubles—she didn't need to concern herself with Branwen's abilities.

Four days had passed in near silence as they listened to the tide lap against the *Dragon Rising*. This afternoon the princess pretended to be dozing as Branwen replaced the dressings around her thigh. Tiny blisters had appeared from the bindings. Perhaps she'd fastened them too tight. The wound itself was healing so well it would hardly leave a scar.

Pouring some of their precious fresh water from a flask into a silver bowl, Branwen mixed it with soap shavings from the castle larders. She dipped the end of a handkerchief into the water and dabbed at Essy's flesh. Her cousin made a noise as if it tickled but kept her eyes stubbornly shut. After she dried the area, Branwen tied a fresh bandage, leaving the wound more room to breathe.

She stretched her arms above her head. Several joints cracked. She collected the soiled linens and the bowl of soapy water, deciding to wash them on deck.

"I'll be above if you need me," Branwen told her cousin, knowing full well she could hear her. A smile touched her lips as she narrowly avoided crashing into Tristan in the passageway.

"Good afternoon, my lady." There was a rakish glint to his dark eyes.

Branwen had spent the night in his arms and, even though she had done nothing but sleep, she couldn't stop thinking about it. From his husky timbre, neither could he.

Her gaze darted to the *krotto* under his arm.

"I thought Emer might like the Hound to serenade her," Tristan explained, and the suggestion spun around Branwen like gossamer.

"She might." She tried for a coy smile. Casting a backward glance at the cabin, she couldn't suppress a tinge of sorrow. Branwen hugged the laundry to her chest. "But she needs to clean the bandages." With a raised eyebrow, she suggested, "A song might lift the patient's spirits."

Tristan's face fell. "A song couldn't make things any worse," he conceded. Whatever appreciation Essy had shown for the Kernyvman when she was mortally wounded had dissipated as soon as she recovered her senses. Branwen wasn't certain which of the two of them her cousin loathed more.

"*Mormerkti.*" Branwen touched his elbow. "You've always been rather brave for a poet."

"*Sekrev,*" he said. "You're welcome." As she repeated the new word, testing it on her tongue, Tristan tipped forward and whispered, "I'll sing for you later," while kissing the shell of her ear. The sensation riveted her. He winked, brushing her waist with his hand as he shimmied past and entered the cabin.

Branwen lingered in the hallway, listening to Tristan greet Essy by plucking a chord on the harp. He also failed to be fooled by her sleeping act.

"What do you want?" whined the princess. Branwen tiptoed closer.

"Can I offer you a ballad? Perhaps Lí Ban, the mermaid?" he suggested, and Branwen grinned—a real one. Lí Ban was none other than the sister of the Otherworld goddess who tried to steal the Hound from Emer. Considered a great beauty, even among the Old Ones, she survived a flood by transforming into a fish from the waist down.

"I would rather hear the death rattle of a flatulent porpoise, Prince Tristan," Essy declared. "Don't you have someplace to be?"

"Afraid not. Morgie's still looking for another tack."

Yet another one. After the storms, the ship was becalmed again. A few of the older crewmen were visibly disturbed.

Branwen heard a *clunk*—Tristan setting down the harp, she presumed.

"Princess," he tried again. "I will come back every day until we find common ground."

"You can come back every day until the end of time and I'll never have anything in common with the Kernyveu. Or with you."

"Branwen."

Did he realize she was eavesdropping?

"What about her?" said the princess.

The wood wheezed beneath his weight as Tristan paced. Suddenly, it stopped.

"We both care very deeply for her."

Essy inhaled. "You'll never be worthy of her." Branwen's heart swelled. The princess hadn't disputed caring for her. Hope kindled inside her that their relationship could still be repaired.

"You're right." Tristan gave a resigned laugh. "But I will spend the rest of my life trying to be."

The Loving Cup pricked Branwen's breast like a knifepoint. *She* was the one who wasn't worthy, who was still keeping secrets. And yet, she would try, by the Old Ones, she would try to love Tristan and the Land at the same time.

"Fine," said her cousin. "That is *one* thing we have in common."

"It's better than nothing."

Essy harrumphed. Branwen could picture her crossing her arms.

Dropping his voice, Tristan said, "You're both the bravest women I know."

"*Brave* isn't something anyone has ever called me."

"But you are. I know this can't be easy—voyaging across the sea to marry a stranger."

"No one asked what I wanted," Essy rebuked him. "*You* most definitely didn't ask."

"I . . ." Branwen heard Tristan blow out another breath. "If it's any consolation, I know Marc is apprehensive, too."

"It's not."

"You carry a mighty burden as a ruler. You must marry for duty—for peace—rather than love. To me, that is brave. A hero's sacrifice. It makes *you* a hero, Princess."

For a moment the ship was so still that Branwen could hear

herself blinking away her own tears as they spilled down her cheeks. What Iveriu needed *did* require a hero's sacrifice. Branwen should have been the one to tell her cousin so.

She also knew without a doubt that she'd done the right thing in conjuring the Loving Cup. It would make Essy's burden easier to bear, even if the secret drove a wedge between her and Tristan.

"It should be Branwen," Essy said quietly. "She would make a much better queen. My own mother thinks so—and I agree."

Branwen tasted salt upon her lips.

"I will be proud to call you my queen, Princess Eseult," Tristan insisted, and he sounded entirely sincere.

Essy coughed. A few seconds later, she said, "Sing to me of the mermaid, then."

Branwen could almost hear Tristan's smile. "With pleasure," he said.

The wistful notes of the harp flitted over Branwen's skin, raising the tiny hairs. She headed for the stairs as Tristan's baritone wrapped around her heart.

She should have been glad he had succeeded in breaking her cousin's silence where she had failed. *One step at a time*, she told herself.

Sunlight filtered down from above. *One step at a time.*

✠ ✠ ✠

Branwen found a quiet spot on the bow to launder the bandages and a few other items of clothing. She focused on the simplicity of the task, taking satisfaction in the scrubbing until her upper back rebelled. The water swirled with crimson as the bandages came clean.

Drawing in a long breath, Branwen pushed to her feet, shaking loose her stiff muscles, and leaned against the side of the ship. Out of nowhere, gliding over the waves, soared a *kretarv*. She and the vile creature locked eyes. She was unable to turn away, mesmerized.

Its gaze was darker than coal, and pitiless. Right at the very center, Branwen spied the true face of fate: disinterested yet ruthless. A chill that matched the fire of her heart stole through her. The *kretarv* was calling her name. What started as the guttural moan of a man—Keane—turned into the shrill soprano of a woman, both equally defiant and plaintive.

Mother. She took a step toward the *kretarv*. Her mother needed her. Branwen had to go to her.

Held tight in the carrion bird's eyes, a long-concealed truth was revealed to Branwen in a vision. She watched in frost-covered horror as Kernyvak raiders ambushed Lord Caedmon and Lady Alana's caravan from Castle Rigani to Fort Áine.

The arrows came first—flaming arrows shot by raiders hidden in the trees. A coward's attack. The pirates took out the horsemen at the front and rear of the traveling party. The shouts of men on fire were sickening; it was a sound that Branwen knew all too well.

A face she never thought to see again appeared before her. Her father's face. It was contorted by rage as he brandished a *kladiwos* in defense of his wife. Branwen's memories of his kindly smile diffused when confronted by his bloodlust—and it made her proud.

She also fully recognized what made Lady Alana the sister of Queen Eseult: a spine of steel. Her mother fell to her knees beside one of the burning, mutilated Royal Guardsmen; and when she discovered she couldn't save him, she put her knee on his neck and used her body weight to snap it. Lady Alana put the man out of his misery and then grabbed his sword, rushing to join her husband.

Branwen's heart raced faster, her blood nearing a boiling point. In the midst of battle, a milky-gray sun peeked out from behind a cloud and winked off Lady Alana's brooch. The same one Branwen was wearing even now. She felt for it intuitively.

The moment her fingertips brushed the ancient language of trees, Lady Alana turned toward Branwen as if she could actually see her, and her mother startled.

Lord Caedmon swung his *kladiwos* furiously against a Kernyvak pirate with one eye. But one eye was all the brute needed to slice off Lord Caedmon's hand from the wrist. The gnarled fingers and the blade crashed to the ground, spraying Lady Alana with her husband's blood.

Lady Alana dove for her husband's sword and swiped upward at the Kernyvman's belly. Her despair washed over Branwen. As well as her conviction. Branwen realized her mother knew death was imminent, but she refused to back down.

"Alana," Lord Caedmon croaked, reaching for his wife with his remaining hand. "*Go!* Run. Leave me and save yourself."

"Never, my love."

Her father coughed up bloody spittle. "Think of little Branny."

A moment's hesitation passed over Lady Alana's face before she gritted her teeth and said, "This is the right fight, Caedmon."

She looked directly at Branwen as she spoke these words. Branwen reached for her mother but she had no form; she could only watch.

Lady Alana retrieved the *kladiwos* from the Kernyvman's belly in a deft motion and brandished it in the air. Another, stockier, pirate with a scraggly dark-brown beard launched himself at the couple.

Branwen's mother turned to her husband. "I love you with my life, Caedmon. I won't let the Kernyveu have you."

And then she slit his throat.

Branwen screamed but she made no sound.

Her mother had made the right decision not to give the Kernyveu a highborn hostage, Branwen knew. But she was in awe. Would she have had the strength to do the same if it were Tristan?

Branwen didn't have time to ponder the question; an arm seized her mother around the waist. The pale forearm was tattooed with a sea-wolf surging up from the waves, but it was gangly, as if his arms were too long for his body. The new raider couldn't be older than thirteen or fourteen.

"Lady, we will not hurt you," said the boy, voice shaky. He spoke in Ivernic. "By my troth, I have no desire to harm a woman." He appeared better groomed than the other Kernyvmen, his clothes finer, yet lacking in confidence.

"There is no honor among pirates," Lady Alana spat. The raider might be younger and more wiry than the rest, but he was strong. Branwen's mother struggled under his grip, her sword useless.

"My lady, we aren't common pirates. I would let you go—return to Castle Rigani untouched—to deliver a message to King Óengus."

Her mother's gaze trailed to the spot where Branwen was hovering. She smiled wistfully. Green flames leapt in her eyes.

"I will certainly deliver a message to my king. From whom?"

"Marc," the Kernyvman replied.

This world and the Otherworld closed in on Branwen.

Marc loosened his grip slightly on Lady Alana. She wheeled around, raising the *kladiwos*, and plunged it straight into her own heart.

"This is *my* message to King Óengus: One Iveriu."

Blood sprang from her mother's breast and Branwen experienced each agonizing moment of her death. Marc stood petrified, watching, shock smoothing his face. Then he ran off, leaving her mother where she lay dying next to her husband. Drawing her last breaths, Lady Alana crawled to Lord Caedmon's side and cupped his cheek.

Fire scorched the coming evening, setting her parents ablaze. They loved while they burned; they burned while they loved.

And now Branwen understood the meaning of misery: She was giving her only cousin to the man responsible for the death of her parents.

Branwen closed her eyes and prepared for the *kretarv* to take her under.

BLOOD AND LOVE

"**L**ADY BRANWEN! LADY BRANWEN!"

Someone was shaking her furiously. It took a moment or two for her vision to focus.

"Cadan?" she said with confusion. "Cadan? What's happening?"

The look in the boy's eyes alarmed her. As he let her go, she saw the deep bloody impressions of talons on her arms. Her gaze traveled up to Cadan's face. He had two long scratches bisecting his left cheek, oozing thick blood like jam.

She touched it, unthinking, and he winced. "You saved me," she said. Guilt and gratitude swelled inside her, her fingertips tingling.

Cadan gasped in response. Branwen watched, stunned, as the bleeding stopped. The flesh began to close. *Oh no.* She'd used the Hand of Bríga to heal him without thinking about it. She looped her gaze around the deck. Relief surged. No one else had seen. How could she keep her secret if she couldn't control her abilities?

"Don't worry, my lady," Cadan breathed, recovering a hoarse voice. "I won't tell. I've never heard of anyone fighting off a *kretarv* once it's caught you in its gaze." But she hadn't fought; the beast had exploited her darkest fears to lure Branwen to a watery grave.

"*Mormerkti*, Cadan."

"The Old Ones are protecting you, for sure," said the boy.

"You believe in the Old Ones?"

He flung a glance toward the helm. "Don't tell the captain. My grandmother came from Iveriu. She taught me about the Old Ones."

"That's how you speak Ivernic so well."

Cadan blushed. "She was captured as a girl," he explained matter-of-factly because these were the facts of their world. Essy's marriage would protect children like Cadan and Gráinne, like his grandmother had been; that's what everything Branwen had done these past months had been for. And yet, if what the *kretarv* had shown her was true . . . doubt like she'd never known savaged her.

Lowering his voice, the cabin boy went on. "Grandmother didn't like the Horned One. Said there was too much that needed fixing in the world for just one god. Especially if he was a man."

Branwen rasped a laugh. "I would have liked her."

Cadan glanced once more at his captain. "The village where I was born, the fishermen believe in the Old Ones. They say the *kretarvs* belong to Dhusnos. That the birds scavenge victims for the Sea of the Dead."

Dhusnos: The name inspired a frisson of fear. The Dark One. The oldest of the Old Ones apart from Kerwindos. All Ivernic children were taught that the House of Dhusnos was a holding cell, a watery prison for the souls not permitted to pass into the Land of Youth. Shades, they were called. Souls forsaken by the Land. When livestock died for no reason in coastal villages, the Iverni blamed the Shades.

"Then I'm even more fortunate you were here to protect me, Cadan," Branwen told the boy, sounding distant even to herself. She felt her head—it pounded as if a mischievous sprite were wielding a mallet inside.

Had Dhusnos used the *kretarv* to send Branwen the memory of her parents? To what end? The Dark One wasn't known for being beneficent.

"*Mormerkti*, my lady." A heartrending smile formed on the boy's lips. If Branwen had been lucky enough to have a younger brother, she hoped he would have been like Cadan. His gaze shifted to her forearms. "You're still bleeding," he said, pulling at his lip.

Oh. So she was. Could Branwen heal herself? How she wished she'd had more time to study with Queen Eseult.

"Just a few scratches." She smiled to put him at ease, although her palms were clammy. A thunderclap rent the air and Cadan jumped.

Captain Morgawr hollered, "Oi, Cadan! Get the lady to her cabin! Another squall's rolling in!" Yet the clouds were only the palest gray.

"I can see myself to my cabin," Branwen said. The boy hurried to gather the freshly laundered linens into the silver bowl for her. She'd have to dry them in her quarters. "Thank you," she said again in Ivernic. The ship rocked sideways and she nearly lost her balance as she retreated belowdecks.

The storm that threatened the *Dragon Rising* was nothing compared with the whirlwind in her mind. Surely the Marc from her vision wasn't *the* King Marc? It must be a common enough Kernyvak name. Keane couldn't have been right all along in opposing this peace accord. This was the *kretarv*'s trickery. It had to be.

Branwen's fingers drifted to her bodice, checking for the Loving Cup in a way that had become habit. The only true cure for war: love. But how much could the spell change King Marc's essential character?

The boy who ran away while Branwen's mother bled to death simply could *not* be the same man whose power she was helping to secure. She refused to accept it. The Land would never allow it.

Tristan's voice carried down the hallway, rich like a heady perfume. The harp reached a crescendo, and a momentary smile graced Branwen's face. Sagging against the doorjamb, she listened to Tristan finish a chorus about ancient Queen Medhua's cattle raid. She clapped a hand against the silver bowl in appreciation.

"*Branwen.*" Tristan startled as he glimpsed her over his shoulder. "You're bleeding." Running his eyes up and down her body, he leapt from his seat, leaned the *krotto* against the bed, and took two quick strides to where Branwen swayed in the doorway.

"A *kretarv* caught me," she said, dismissive.

"A *kretarv*!" exclaimed Essy. Her face pinched in fright. "Oh, Branny!"

Tristan plucked the laundry from Branwen's arms, setting it on top of a trunk, then grabbed her wrists, pulling her closer.

"It's nothing," she said as he inspected the gashes left by the foul seabird.

"Healers make the worst patients." Worry laced Tristan's laughter. She brushed him off and a look of hurt crossed his face. "Let me tend you for once," he insisted. His voice was strained.

To her utter astonishment, Essy got out of bed and demanded, "Me too."

378

In a daze, Branwen directed the princess to where the salves and the last clean, dry bandage could be found. Her cousin only limped the slightest bit. Tristan guided Branwen toward the bed, brushing his hand along her jaw as she sat down. She stiffened at the casual display of affection. Essy, however, was ignoring them as she rifled through the trunks.

"What did the *kretarv* show you?" Tristan asked her. He added, "my love," in a whisper.

The question lanced Branwen. How could she possibly tell him? A macabre part of her heart had always wanted to know the details of her parents' deaths. Did the *kretarv* sense that? Or the Dark One?

"I don't know," she answered.

Tristan stroked the inside of her wrist. "Morgie has told me tales of what sailors see in the beasts' eyes." A crinkle appeared between his. "Most don't survive—to think how close I came to losing you."

His breath was hot in the small distance between them.

Branwen scoffed. "Captain Morgawr likes to spin a good yarn."

Essy interrupted any further questions. "Juniper cream," she said, holding up the jar. Tristan tried to take it and Essy moved the ceramic container out of his reach. "I can do it. She's *my* cousin."

Tristan and the princess warred with their eyes.

"Essy can help me," Branwen said pointedly, although she could scarcely believe her cousin wanted to. Reading the hope in her eyes, Tristan relented.

"I'll come back in a bit to see if you need anything." He lifted the harp under his arm and Branwen showed him a grateful smile as he exited.

"I'm sure he will," Essy muttered under her breath. She rested next to Branwen on the bed and the mattress dipped. She slathered the ointment into the lacerations the way she had done for Gráinne what seemed like so long ago. Branwen hissed.

"Sorry," said the princess.

"That means it's working," Branwen told her, repeating the explanation she'd used a thousand times when Essy complained one of her cures was worse than the disease. Her cousin bit back a smile.

The princess's hands were soothing on Branwen's skin. She didn't know how to interpret this unexpected act of kindness.

"Why didn't you tell Tristan what you saw?" asked Essy. Branwen's nerves fluttered. "I've known you my whole life. You never forget anything, Branny."

Her stomach twisted. "I saw my parents," she said. Her voice rang flat. "I saw them die." A fat teardrop trickled down her cheek. Essy brushed it away. Branwen couldn't tell her how it had happened—she couldn't tell anyone how. If it was even the truth.

"Oh, Branny," her cousin said. "Sometimes I forget how much you've lost." The gentleness ruptured something inside Branwen. All of the tears she kept so firmly under control launched an uprising.

"For a moment, just a moment, I wanted to follow the *kretarv*," Branwen divulged. "I wanted to be with them. I can't lose you, too, Essy. I *can't*." She raised her gaze to meet her cousin's, streaked with tears as it was. "Why did you do it?"

Essy went completely still. She gnashed her front teeth into her bottom lip. Finally, she said, "I didn't mean—I didn't want to die, Branny. I just . . . I had all of this anger. Fear. Rage." Her breaths became pants. "I thought I would burst from my skin. I needed release. I wanted, *I* wanted to be in control of the pain for once."

Branwen seized her cousin's shoulders. "Promise me you won't do it again. Promise me that if you want to, you'll tell me. Tell me what you're feeling."

"You never tell me what you're feeling." There was no accusation in her tone, just acceptance, and that left Branwen feeling completely bereft. "Why didn't you trust me enough to tell me you were falling in love?"

The quiet words were a punch to the gut.

"Because I know how miserable you are. I didn't want to make it worse by showing you my happiness."

"You didn't give me the chance to be happy for you, Branny. You took that choice away, too. You must think very little of me."

"No, Essy. I—I'm sorry."

"That's why it hurt so much to see you with Tristan. Because you didn't trust me. You didn't believe I could love you enough to want you to be happy—even if it *is* with a Kernyvman."

Branwen made a noise that was somewhere between a sob and a whimper. Tristan had said almost the exact same thing.

"I know no one loves me, Branny," said her cousin. "It doesn't mean I don't want *you* to be loved."

Branwen crushed the princess in a fervent embrace, not minding the pain from the *kretarv*'s talons, not wanting anything but to be near her baby cousin.

"*I* love you, Essy. I love you more than anything. Tristan will never replace you in my heart."

Essy hiccupped. "If you love him, I'll try not to hate him," she said. She heaved a breath. "He doesn't seem like the worst of Kernyvmen, after all."

"*Mormerkti.*" Branwen kissed the bridge of her nose. "That's Kernyvak for thank you."

Her cousin laughed, pulling back. "Don't expect me to learn their language. It sounds like Treva's meat grinder!" Branwen didn't quite agree but she laughed along. Essy's gaze drifted to the coverlet. "What's that?" she said, indicating the bracelet Tristan had given her. It must have slipped from Branwen's pocket.

A dart of fear whizzed through her. "It's . . . Tristan gave it to me."

"Why aren't you wearing it?"

Branwen blinked, tears weighting her lashes. "I didn't want to upset you."

Essy pinched the circlet between her fingers, admiring it. "Ivernic and Kernyvak colors," she said. She was silent a beat. Then she fastened it around Branwen's wrist. "It suits you, cousin." There was no edge to her words.

Branwen wrapped her arms around the princess and squeezed. Between Tristan and Essy, she had love and family. Despite what she had lost, the Old Ones had sent her so much good fortune. The Otherworld was love, just as Queen Eseult had explained, and Branwen was filled to bursting with it.

"*Mormerkti*," she breathed.

House of Dhusnos

WATCHING TRISTAN AND HER COUSIN as they played a game of *fidkwelsa* on the deck, nothing seemed amiss except for the fact that it was amicable. Branwen stroked the promise bracelet on her wrist. Another day had elapsed since the last storm and tension wound even more tightly around her. She should have been heartened that she and Essy had reconciled, and she was, but whenever she closed her eyes, she saw her parents die.

Again, and again.

Perhaps it had been better not to know. Even if what the *kretarv* had shown her was a lie—she couldn't not see it. She wanted to trust Tristan when he said that his uncle was an honorable man. If there was even the remotest possibility that what the *kretarv* had shown her was true, however, how could Branwen let him have custody of Essy's heart? The question burrowed deep, unwilling to let go.

Essy's laughter carried across the still sea. When the princess forgot she was supposed to hate all Kernyvmen, it seemed she might genuinely enjoy Tristan's company. Prickly thorns sprang up on the underside of Branwen's skin—not from jealousy, but regret. Tristan and Essy had no secrets between them; their budding friendship was honest, while Branwen was keeping dangerous secrets from both of them.

"Lady Branwen." Cadan's voice just barely penetrated her mental fog. "My lady, you need to eat something."

She looked down at the rock-hard walnut bread outstretched in his hand. "I'm not hungry. You have it, Cadan."

His lips quivered and he practically salivated. They had been at sea too long. Supplies were dwindling. The boy's stomach rumbled.

"Go on," she said.

Cadan shook his head. "Captain says the princess and her maid-servant eat first."

Servant. The word cut Branwen to the quick. In Iveriu, she had been known as cousin, niece of the queen, and daughter of Lady Alana and Lord Caedmon who would inherit a castle of her own. In Kernyv, was she to be known merely as a servant?

"I insist," Branwen told the boy. She couldn't stand the idea of him going hungry while she had no appetite. "And if the bread is truly mine, then I can do with it what I please." Cadan nodded. "I'd sooner you eat it than a *kretarv,* but I'll feed it to a *kretarv* if I must."

Not needing any further encouragement, Cadan sunk his teeth into the small, tough loaf. It made a distinct *crunch, crunch* sound, like stepping on the mulch in the castle gardens.

As he ate, Branwen noticed the scratches made by the *kretarv* were completely gone. Her own injuries were healing at a normal rate. Most likely she would have small scars.

Catching her eye, Tristan beckoned Branwen over with a wave of the hand. She couldn't deny that she'd been more distant with him since the *kretarv* attack. She wanted to inquire how often King Marc took part in raids, but she didn't know how to pose the question without eliciting further questions. Besides, thirteen years ago, Tristan was only a child himself. With a small exhale, Branwen lifted the hem of her skirts and walked over to the *fidkwelsa* board.

Her cousin squealed with glee as her horsemen surrounded Tristan's queen. She beamed like when she'd pulled off a particularly good prank. Usually something involving poor Dubthach.

"It's such a shame your squires aren't better equipped, Prince Tristan," Essy told him.

"Ah, Lady Branwen." Tristan smiled languorously. "Would you like to lead my men? I seem to be failing them as a general. Perhaps you'll fare better." From his tone, Branwen wondered if he was letting the princess win.

He patted the empty stool beside him and Branwen obliged. Essy looked between them, seeming unperturbed. "Branny's never lost to me, but . . ." She smirked. "There's a first time for everything."

As Essy contemplated her next move, Tristan dropped a hand to Branwen's beneath the table. When he felt the smooth leather peeking out from beneath her sleeve, he shot her a questioning look. Branwen's lips parted in an unhurried smile.

It was enough of an answer. He squeezed her hand. The flecks in Tristan's eyes glinted brighter than the sparks from any blacksmith's anvil. *Soon*, they promised. Branwen ardently wished they could disappear belowdecks without being missed.

"Hurrah!" declared the princess. "I'll take your queen in two moves."

Tristan zipped his eyes to the board, then back to Branwen. "A little help?"

"Two on one is cheating." Essy folded her arms, mouth pinching into a sulk. "You'll lose to me fair and square."

Captain Morgawr's shadow fell over the board before Tristan could take his turn.

"My prince," he said. "May we speak in private?" The captain pulled on his beard.

Essy's gaze latched on to Branwen. Something was wrong.

"Speak freely, Morgie," Tristan replied. He gave Branwen's hand another squeeze. "I'll have no secrets."

She bit the inside of her cheek.

"Very well." Morgawr panned a skeptical gaze across the noblewomen. "As you know, the first storm hit on Samonios Eve. No one knows where the Veil lies in the sea, and it's thinnest that night. I think we were blown straight across."

"What do you mean?" Essy demanded. "We're in the *Otherworld*?" She paled beneath the rouge she'd wanted to apply this morning, which Branwen had taken as a sign she was getting back to her usual self. "That's not possible." She looked to Branwen. "Is it, Branny?"

Branwen's throat grew scratchy. There were Ivernic ballads of heroes stranded on Otherworld islands after being lost at sea. Not that she'd put much credence in them. Of course, she'd dismissed Whitethorn Mound until she crossed over. Yet she couldn't believe the Old Ones would abandon them—Iveriu—when they were so close to realizing their goal.

"Taverns are filled with tales of seamen who've sailed clear off the edge of our world." Morgawr spoke before Branwen could. He raised his substantial eyebrows in the direction of the clouds.

"However, a familiar star appeared to me last night. I can chart a course to Kernyv," the captain concluded.

Relief broke on Tristan's face. "Excellent news!" He leapt from his stool and shook Morgawr's hand. "I never doubted you."

The veteran sailor's expression remained grave.

"We will have to pass through the House of Dhusnos."

Essy gasped. "The Sea of the Dead?"

"I didn't think followers of the Horned One put credence in Ivernic gods," said Branwen hotly. Nothing motivated her so much as her cousin's fear.

The captain didn't meet Branwen's eyes, casting his gaze instead at the waves. "I've witnessed enough things on the sea I can't explain to not discount other people's gods."

"Is there no other course?" Tristan maintained a calm veneer but Branwen recognized the hesitation in his question. No laws of this world or the Otherworld governed the Sea of the Dead. After his rift with Goddess Ériu, Dhusnos was shunned by the other Old Ones—and he shunned them.

"No, my prince," said Morgawr. "Not before we starve. I don't know who's been steering this ship, but it isn't me."

Essy visibly shuddered at his response. Tristan set his mouth in a grim line. "Then we sail and may the Horned One protect us." Glancing at Branwen, he added, "And the Old Ones."

"I'll take their protection today," the captain agreed. "We should make haste." Slashing two fingers in the sign of his god, Morgawr barked a few commands at the crew. *Boom!* The sail swung around. He took a few paces toward the helm, then called back, "Hanno would be proud of you, my prince. He was a fearless leader. I see him in you."

Tristan nodded, color rising in his cheeks.

"Prince Tristan, we can't do this," said Essy in her most imperious tone, pushing out of her seat. "I'm to be your queen and I demand you tell the captain to find another route. Being from Kernyv, he doesn't understand the danger."

"I understand your fears, Lady Princess. And believe me, Captain Morgawr is aware of the risk. For the time being, however, I still outrank you aboard this vessel. I can't risk the crew starving to death—or you and Branwen."

Tristan let out a heavy breath. He would always put his people above himself. Branwen could only hope King Marc would be an equally benevolent ruler now that Iveriu was no longer his enemy.

"No." Essy grabbed Tristan's forearm, her nails like claws. Ever since they were girls, the princess was most ferocious when she was frightened. Yet Branwen had never seen her quite like this.

"I'm sorry. We must push through," Tristan said, determined.

Essy jerked him closer. "Just when I was beginning to think not all Kernyvmen were brutes!" She released his arm with a forceful shove. "Apparently, I was wrong."

Tristan pitched Branwen a beseeching look. "Essy—" she started.

"Don't. Of course you would take his side!"

She launched to her feet. "I'm not. But we don't have a choice."

"Lady Princess," said Tristan, dropping to one knee. "I swear to you that you will be safe as long as I still draw breath."

"And I told you the oaths of Kernyvmen mean nothing to me." Essy hooked Branwen's elbow, spinning on her heel and towing Branwen behind her as she strutted toward the royal compartment.

Branwen snatched a glance at Tristan from the top of the stairs. He remained on bended knee. A pallid expression drained his face.

Goddess Bríga, Goddess Ériu, protect us, she prayed.

All she could do was pray.

✢ ✢ ✢

That night passed without incident, and the following day. Wind finally gusted in the sails of the *Dragon Rising* with no storm on the horizon. Branwen began to wonder if the legends surrounding Dhusnos and the Sea of the Dead were nothing more than rumors employed to keep precocious children from swimming too far from shore at high tide.

She and Tristan watched the rose-hued sunset together while Essy refused to leave the cabin. He kissed the bare skin of her wrist beneath the promise bracelet and it sizzled hotter than the Hand of Bríga. If this was death, she thought, maybe it wasn't so bad.

Branwen didn't return to her cousin's bed until the first stars appeared in the sky.

✢ ✢ ✢

"Wake up! Branny, wake up!"

Panic propelled her into consciousness. The princess tore at her nightdress, fingers tearing at the linen.

"What is it?" she breathed. "What's happened?"

Essy's lower lip trembled, her brow drenched with sweat. "I'm scared, Branny."

Branwen pulled her cousin into her arms, making a shushing noise. "There's no need to be scared." Half asleep, she kissed the top of her golden head.

389

"It's these dreams. Since we left Blackford, they won't stop."

An ill wind blew down Branwen's spine. "What dreams, Essy?"

"Every night, I dream this great black wave is chasing the ship. Tonight, I saw blood on the sail and the wave crashed over the hull, splitting the ship in two. We began to sink. I was drowning—I couldn't breathe." She pulled at her messy hair as she spoke, her speech becoming more agitated. "I still can't breathe."

Essy's shoulders heaved in Branwen's embrace, her violent reaction to crossing the Sea of the Dead becoming clear. *You should have told me*, Branwen wanted to say, but she quashed the reproach. There was still much distance to be bridged between them.

"*Shh*, Essy. Captain Morgawr has never lost a ship," Branwen murmured in her ear. "We're all right. We'll be in Kernyv before you know it. On dry land." The promises sounded weaker than she intended. How could both Branwen and the princess be dreaming of the same great wave?

Essy continued to shake. "I can't breathe down here. I need fresh air."

"It's the middle of the night."

"*Please*, Branny."

She considered a moment. Nothing of note had happened during the past two days and sometimes walking helped alleviate her cousin's nerves before they overwhelmed her. Branwen kissed her cousin's temple. "Only for a few minutes," she said.

They dressed quickly, covering their nightdresses with woolen cloaks, and padded upstairs to the deck. It was eerily quiet. Most of the crewmen were in their quarters. Only the night watch was up top. The full moon had reached its apex over the midnight waves.

Branwen raked her gaze over the dark expanse but saw nothing out of the ordinary.

The knot pulling Branwen's shoulders together released. Linking her arm with Branwen's, Essy took a deeper breath. An admiring smile lit her face. "The stars are saying hello," said the princess.

"I think they are." Out here on the open sea, the jewel-like stars studded the silky black sky above and glistened on the water below, making Branwen feel as if she had been wrapped in a mantle of stars.

"What are you ladies doing on deck?" Tristan asked in a hush. Branwen started, then instantly relaxed—until she spied moonlight shining on the hilt of the sword that dangled at his hip. He was prepared for combat.

Essy didn't deign to answer, simply regarding him with contempt. *One step forward, two steps back*, thought Branwen. She sighed.

"Couldn't sleep," she said to Tristan, tilting half a smile skyward. "Thought we'd look at the stars."

"But I see them in your eyes," he teased. Essy snorted and rolled *her* eyes so hard Branwen thought they might get lodged in the back of her head. She pressed a finger to her lips, suppressing a laugh. Tristan winked.

"Not much sleep going around, I'm afraid." Lifting his chin, he said, "That's the Evening Star," and gestured toward the brightest star in the sky. "Navigators call it the Queen."

"Master Bécc taught us it's named Wenos, after the Aquilan goddess of love," Essy corrected him as haughtily as she could. "And her twin brother, Wenesnos, is the god of poison. Seems accurate."

"Right you are, Princess." Tristan coughed into his hand. Again, Branwen muzzled her amusement.

Essy turned up her nose. Relinquishing Branwen's arm, she strode toward the railing. "And those?" she called over her shoulder. "What do you call that small cluster of stars?"

Tristan lifted a hand to his brow, squinting. "Which cluster?"

"*That* one." Annoyance bled through her voice as Essy stabbed a finger at the blackened horizon.

Branwen narrowed her gaze at the spot and hope gushed through her. "I think they're fires. Along the coast," she said, unable to contain her excitement. "It's the fires of Kernyv!"

Tristan turned toward her like quicksilver. "That's not Kernyv."

At the same moment, Cadan called out from the rigging.

"Pirates!"

Not You Without Me

A CLOUD SLINKED AWAY FROM the moon, and all at once the other ship became illuminated. The design was unlike any Branwen had ever seen from the cliffs of Iveriu, and its sails flickered in and out of her peripheral vision. It was there one instant, gone the next, like sunlight on a spider's web.

A line of tiny fires—torches, she supposed—dotted the starboard side of the pirate vessel. Two seconds later, a fireball whizzed overhead. The pirates weren't holding torches. They were aiming arrows. Flaming arrows. The ambush of Branwen's parents had begun just like this.

Another arrow sailed through the air with a bloodcurdling hiss as it planted itself in the mast of the *Dragon Rising*.

Essy shrieked and Tristan leapt from Branwen's side, dragging the princess away from the railing and shielding her with his body from the trajectory of arrows. He did not shield Branwen. Their eyes met and a bitter taste filled the back of her mouth. Tristan was Essy's Champion. Not hers.

The specter-white ship soared across the water toward the *Dragon Rising* with incredible speed. Unnatural speed. A third volley of fire-tipped arrows riddled the bow of their ship. The conflagration sang to Branwen, entreated her to join it. The flames called her cousin.

"Get the princess to her chamber!" Tristan roared, unsheathing his sword. There was a new ferocity to his tone. Tristan was a prince but he'd never made Branwen feel she was anything less than his equal—until that moment. Protecting Essy was his most important duty.

For Branwen, too. Of course it was. Only—for less than the space of a breath—she wished Tristan would toss the princess aside and gather Branwen in his arms instead.

Great hooks, shaped like horrifying talons, caught the side of the *Dragon Rising*, hauling it toward the attacking vessel. Branwen stood, dazed, as if trapped once more by the glare of a *kretarv*.

"*Move!*" Tristan shouted angrily, yanking her by the elbow. Determination galvanized her. She wanted to fight. With Tristan at Essy's front and Branwen at her back, the three of them shuffled together like a crab toward the staircase leading belowdecks. All of the crew members who'd been asleep rushed up it, a geyser of furious men, weapons brandished.

The Princess of Iveriu was their most precious cargo. Everyone aboard would die to protect her. Could these pirates be here for Essy or did they choose this ship at random to plunder? Did they lurk in the House of Dhusnos, waiting for someone brave or desperate enough to enter?

As the attacking vessel drew closer, Branwen could spy no colors flying at the top of its mast. The sails continued to shimmer as if they weren't quite there. But the force with which the hooks dragged the *Dragon Rising* closer was all too real.

She screwed up her eyes yet she couldn't discern the forms of the men launching the arrows that assailed them. It was as if they were invisible.

The howls of the crew assaulted Branwen's ears, bleating and terrible. With each flame that landed, she felt more alive. She rubbed the inside of her palm. She would have believed she'd carried the Hand of Bríga all her life.

Too late she saw one of the pirates solidify on the deck of the other ship. Branwen clutched her throat, wanting to retch.

"They're not ordinary pirates," she rasped.

These were the souls of those abandoned by the Land, indentured to crew on Dhusnos's ships until he released them. These were his Shades.

Essy stopped in her tracks. She pulled Branwen closer, gripping her hand so tightly she thought it would bleed.

"My dreams," she said in a strangled whisper. The Old Ones had sent both cousins dreams, but Branwen had been convinced the nightmares of Keane were no more than she deserved.

Branwen and Tristan shared a heavy glance. Trepidation brightened his eyes. He must have reached the same conclusion about their attackers—they were something more than human. Or less.

Branwen didn't get the chance to offer her cousin any false assurances.

A great wave of Dhusnos's Shades crashed over the side of the ship. In her mind's eye, she saw Castle Rigani demolished. The peak of the whitecap would have been beautiful if it weren't so petrifying. The water dissolved into a sea of men—men who were part animal.

Their chests were bare and freckled with small, gaping mouths—beaks. Dhusnos had transformed these forsaken souls into half-men, half-*kretarv*. Black feathers stippled their backs and forearms. And the hungry cry of their many beaks was enough to stop a heart dead.

Tristan's fist tightened around his sword. "Get the princess to safety!" he shouted as he charged into the fray. His face twisted with a rage that had been absent even when fighting Lord Morholt. Immediately, Branwen threw Essy behind her.

Scintillating golds and pulsating oranges enlivened the scene of carnage.

Branwen watched, aghast, as Tristan swung his sword straight through one of the Shades. The Shade vaporized in a mist of blood and salt water—she could taste it on the wind. Not a heartbeat later, the Shade coalesced behind Tristan once more, unharmed.

"Watch out!" she yelled.

Tristan ducked and tumbled like he had at the Champions Tournament, narrowly averting a severed spine.

Smoke permeated the air, blurring the edges of the fighting men into ferocious shadows. *Fire and sea and fighting men.* Had Branwen been warned about this moment since childhood?

The crew of the *Dragon Rising* struggled to breathe. Essy doubled over in a hacking cough, as if her chest itself was on fire. Only Branwen appeared unaffected.

She hooked Essy around the waist, half dragging her toward the stairwell. Dhusnos had been the enemy of the Goddess Ériu since as long as anyone could remember. The Land needed Essy to arrive safely in Kernyv. Nothing would delight Dhusnos more than to ruin her plans. He must have caused the storm on Samonios Eve and becalmed the waters for weeks on end.

The Dark One drove the ship straight into his carefully laid trap.

And now he had sent his Shades because they were getting too close to securing peace. Kernyv must not be far. Essy just needed to survive the night.

What happened next seemed to take a millennium, and yet it was over within the blink of an eye.

A black-feathered arm clutched Branwen's throat from behind. The hand was more skeletal than flesh and at the center of the palm was another ravenous beak. Her jaw dropped when she glimpsed the emerald ribbon tied around the wrist. *Her* ribbon.

Gasping, she felt the greedy mouth begin to suck the life from her. Branwen had never believed the farmers' tales of their animals dying where they grazed. Now she understood. The Shades sustained their living death by stealing the strength of others. This was strangulation from the inside out. So much worse than in her dreams.

Branwen would not go easily. Resisting with everything she was, she managed to whirl around in her attacker's arms, facing him head-on. His countenance was more of a skull than anything resembling a man. As she stared into his burning eyes, the Shade's visage morphed into one she recognized. Its red eyes chilled to winter blue.

Keane smiled a viper's smile. Had Branwen truly condemned him to this living death as a half-beast? Morbid fascination compelled her to take in every feature. She almost couldn't blame him for stalking her nightmares. Almost.

He smiled wider as horror saturated her, then threw out his arm again, seizing her neck. He clenched his bony knuckles tight around her throat and wrapped his other arm around her waist, hoisting Branwen closer. The ribbon flickered in the breeze, taunting her. Keane had retained the piece of her she'd given him even in death.

It's how I found you, snarled a voice in Branwen's mind. Not Keane's voice. *The newest of my warriors, felled by the Hand of Bríga. Not seen since ancient times. How curious.*

Branwen shook her head vehemently but Keane's face wouldn't dissolve—nor would he let go.

You call out for me, Branwen of Iveriu, said the voice. She went cold all over. *You have felt my call—the wild call of the sea—since you were a babe. You are drawn to my House.*

Dhusnos. This was Dhusnos. He was using Keane to speak to her. How had Branwen attracted the Dark One's attention?

I'm sorry. She didn't have the air to apologize. *I'm sorry, Keane. Let me go.* Her vision grew spotted.

He can't hear you, Branwen of Iveriu. Dhusnos laughed. *He is little more than a beast, fueled by rage. Thank you for gifting him to me. His lust for your death allowed me to find you.*

Branwen moaned. This, all of this, was her fault. She had led death itself straight to Essy's door. To Tristan. To everyone aboard the *Dragon Rising.*

Destruction runs in your veins. When the Land abandons you, when She asks too much of you, Branwen of Iveriu—it will be time for you to join me.

Branwen was running out of air. *She won't!* she cried silently.

The Keane-creature hissed through bloody, ulcerous gums. "She will." He hauled Branwen toward the stern of the ship.

"Branny, no!" A desolate cry.

The princess charged toward her and the Shade. Branwen saw a new, steely resolve on her cousin's face. Tristan was running after Essy but he lagged too far behind. Branwen thanked the Old Ones he was still alive.

Essy released a battle cry and began to pummel the Shade with her fists. When she recognized Keane her jaw fell toward the deck. She kept pummeling. The beaks cackled. Branwen could only look on, awestruck. Essy never stopped.

Keane swung Branwen around like a whirligig, her knees colliding with Essy's sternum.

Her cousin groaned. She teetered, trying to catch her balance.

And then she was gone.

Essy tumbled overboard and was swallowed by the waves of night.

All fear fled Branwen's heart and was replaced by a rage that burned brighter than any forge. "*Essy!*" she screamed. "*Essy!*" Her little cousin had sacrificed herself for Branwen.

Branwen wasn't worth it. Branwen wasn't worth more than peace.

Keane's skeletal mouth laughed. His beaks laughed with him. Essy's dream hadn't been a warning from the Old Ones. It had been a provocation from the Dark One.

Keane's arms evaporated from around her and Branwen crashed to the deck. He reappeared, looming over her, still laughing. She swiped at his ankle, trying to trip him, but her hand cut through nothing but smoke.

He gripped the collar of her dress, yanking Branwen to her feet, and pressed the hungry beak of his left hand into the back of her neck. Once more Branwen was at Castle Rigani, Keane trying to force a kiss on her. This time it was the kiss of death.

"Branwen!" she heard someone call as if from very far away.

Hatred coursed through her. She raised her hand to Keane's hideous face and slapped him. Surprise sparked in his eyes. She had made contact.

His beak continued to feed. She struck him again.

Could the feeding make him vulnerable?

Instinct replaced thought, the Hand of Bríga taking over. Branwen placed her right palm flat against where the Shade's heart might be. She possessed a weapon of which nobody else was aware.

She smelled the now familiar odor of singed flesh, and something else—sulfurous, like rotten eggs. Keane began to glow like a lantern from within. He trembled with the force of an earthquake. Branwen refused to let go. In a horrible symmetry, Keane's features distorted and dissolved once more. He howled that same inhuman plea for mercy.

Branwen would show him none.

Piece by piece, Keane's hybrid body flaked and turned to ash. She had incinerated him whole. A great bonfire was suspended in midair.

She glanced around her and met Tristan's gaze.

He had seen. He had watched her burn a Shade alive, end his living death. Something no human should be able to do.

There was a strange combination of wonder and horror in his wide eyes. And love, Branwen told herself.

Smoke and screams and love.

They didn't need to speak. Branwen knew what he was about to do.

Tristan dove overboard into the Sea of the Dead to save the princess. He would die for Essy, Essy would die for Branwen, and

Branwen would die for them both. The three of them were inextricably bound by the waves.

Branwen would make the waves her home one day.

But not today.

✠ ✠ ✠

She collapsed to her knees as the battle raged around her. She couldn't distinguish the sea from the sky: Up or down, both paths led to an abyss. If Essy drowned, King Óengus would have no choice but to declare war on Kernyv in retaliation for losing his daughter.

Anger blew through Branwen as she stared at the hand that had decimated Keane. Death had many faces and Dhusnos contained them all. This had been his plan. Revenge on the Land and more bodies for his ships.

"Lady Branwen!" a voice called, young and afraid. Smoke was rising from the deck so thick that it bled into the stars. "Branwen!"

Cadan. The boy quaked from stem to stern. Despite the murk, she could see his complexion turning ashen as his years were drained from him. The total look of repulsion in his eyes curdled her blood.

Now wasn't the time for regret. She couldn't give up just yet.

Branwen leapt to her feet, racing for the boy. Half a breath later, an enormous Shade with only one effervescent red eye knocked her back onto the deck. Branwen wrestled with the monster, rolling together until he had her arms pinned above her head. The rows of beaks across his chest pecked at the front of her dress, trying to latch on to her like the tentacles in her nightmares.

When she felt the Shade begin to siphon her essence, she wrested free her right arm and plowed her blazing heart line against his cheek.

The vengeful Shade vaporized, an exploding star. Branwen covered her face with her hands as molten-hot sparks swirled around her, then launched into a sprint toward Cadan. Almost unthinking, she scorched Dhusnos's men as she advanced. The power flowing within her could be a vicious and elegant thing. The Dark One had been right about the destruction in her veins.

She wouldn't let the Sea of the Dead steal anyone else while she possessed the power to stop it.

A Shade had clamped Cadan to his chest from behind in a lethal embrace. The boy strained for breath. *Crunch. Pop!* His spine was cracking.

Branwen's eyes locked with those of the Shade, which were shining carmine like two harvest moons. He wasn't rushing to leech the life from the cabin boy; he was taking his time. This Shade exuded the confidence of a leader—he must be the captain of Dhusnos's crew.

Cadan went slack in the man-beast's arms and Branwen raised her palm toward the Shade, a plume of flame springing forth.

Flinching, he released his grip. The boy fell to the floor, unconscious. Branwen rushed to help him.

Holding his hands over his face in surrender, the Shade put his lips together in a piercing whistle. He backed away from Branwen, heading toward the side of the ship, and his men followed his lead.

She couldn't believe it. The captain of Dhusnos's men was afraid of her. One by one, the monstrous intruders plunged overboard, detaching the talon-like grapples and setting the *Dragon Rising* free. Branwen didn't have a moment to process what that meant before she heard a *thud* beside her and turned from Cadan toward the sound.

Tristan landed on the deck, hefting Essy behind him. He

attempted to lay the princess down softly, but panic made him sloppy. Strained breaths hissed through his teeth. Essy wasn't breathing at all.

Branwen refused to accept her cousin's death.

She met Tristan's eyes and the look in them trod the boundary between hope and despair. "The princess needs you," he forced out. "It's my fault. She begged me to find another way. I should have listened. I've killed her."

"Not if I can help it." Pushing Tristan to one side, Branwen began pounding on Essy's chest with her fist. This was *her* fault, not his. Together, Tristan and Essy filled the cavern in her heart that she hadn't believed could ever be filled. She wouldn't let it be emptied again. Branwen funneled all her love into her fists.

Slam. Her cousin's body jerked. Pinching Essy's nose, Branwen pressed her lips to the princess's nearly blue ones.

"It's . . . not . . . working," Tristan said, laboring over each syllable, his anguish complete. He fell to his knees.

Branwen kissed Essy harder, trying to force all of her life into her cousin. She pictured the little blond troublemaker who was so fond of mischief, with whom she had shared sweets and childhood secrets. The girl—the woman—who would be queen over two peaceful kingdoms.

Take my life, cousin. Take my life and finish what I've started.

Essy coughed beneath her kisses. As the princess's chest heaved, her own grew leaden. The Sea of the Dead sloshed around her heart. Branwen sat back, clutching at it hard enough to bruise. Somehow she had taken the water from Essy just as she had ingested Tristan's poison after her uncle's betrayal.

Tristan gathered the princess in his arms as she took her first breath on her own. Then he turned his intense gaze on Branwen. She was the one gasping for air now.

"*Branwen—*"

She closed her eyes, drifting in a warm sea full of stars. Lord Caedmon had told Branwen to let the current take her weight. She had no strength left. Her mother's face shimmered before her. Lady Alana was shaking her head.

And then, Branwen could breathe again. The heat of her heart turned the water to steam. Death evaporated. The Land of Youth wasn't ready for her yet.

Strong arms reached for her. Solid arms. Real arms. Tristan folded Branwen onto his lap, next to Essy. He kissed Branwen on the lips—not gently—and she felt his body sing with relief.

Essy's eyes floated open. "I love you," she murmured.

I love you, too.

Tristan helped both of them to their feet. Branwen could barely stand. The Hand of Bríga burned like ice. All of the fire she'd summoned had receded. She felt withered, a crone, a thousand years old.

The aftermath of the slaughter was harrowing to behold.

Captain Morgawr was alive and commanding the other survivors to put out the still-raging fires. The deck was congealed with blood and ash. Essy hid her face in the crook of Tristan's neck, but Branwen forced herself to look. She choked on a sob as she beheld the pallor of Cadan's visage.

She had been too late. Branwen hadn't saved him, after all.

Down below, the fine black mist of fallen men lingered. Tristan tucked Essy into bed and turned to Branwen with glistening eyes. "You're a marvel," he said in a whisper. "You've saved both Iveriu and Kernyv with your kisses."

She said nothing, but held his gaze.

Do you think I'm a monster, too? Branwen couldn't force the question to her lips. Grief was an anchor in her heart. He kissed her between the eyes. She didn't kiss him back. All this, all this death. She had brought it down upon them.

Eventually, Tristan sighed and left, closing the door behind him.

The click of the latch resounded in Branwen's mind as she stripped the princess of her sea-stained garments. She stared at the closed door for a long time before crawling into bed and nestling Essy against her. She tasted the soot on her tongue—rough, like grains of sand—and tapped the Loving Cup above her heart.

"Not me without you," Branwen whispered, tracing the first line of *hazel* above Essy's heart. Her cousin was already asleep.

Exhausted, Branwen stopped fighting the tide.

Just for a moment.

DREAMLESS

BRANWEN WOKE UP ALONE IN her bed. A strange giddiness wended its way up her body.

Land. They were close. She sensed it. Dhusnos had tried to thwart them. The Sea of the Dead had failed.

A tremulous breath loosened inside her. Branwen had enjoyed her first dreamless sleep since departing Iveriu. Despite the horror of the Shades' attack, peace remained within reach. The princess would marry King Marc and unite their kingdoms forever. No more Ivernic or Kernyvak children would be born to war.

Cadan. The cabin boy's name knifed through Branwen's mind.

She should have defended him—not the other way around. Her heart panged. She would seek out his family if he'd had any living, to grieve with them and share his Final Toast, but Cadan had no one left to remember him.

I will. I will remember him.

So young yet he'd fought so bravely. He died fighting for peace. A hero. She would honor his sacrifice every day.

Branwen stretched her arms wearily above her head. Every part of her pulsed with dull pain. The sleeves of her nightdress bunched around her elbows, revealing the *kretarv*'s claw marks. She wrapped her hand around the nape of her neck and prodded the wound left by Keane's beak, examining. She would clean it later. The scar would remind her how close she'd come to losing Essy forever.

Branwen had underestimated the hate that festered inside the Iverman. Enough that the Dark One had used him to track her across the Ivernic Sea. She'd ended Keane's life and now his afterlife, too—and that she didn't regret. What constricted her chest was the fear that there were Kernyvmen at King Marc's court as hateful as Keane had been.

With a groan, she sat up. Essy must have already been on deck, gazing upon the shores of Kernyv. If the princess were in danger, she trusted the Old Ones would alert her. Branwen was also eager to see the land that held her future. The future she and Essy had been sent so far to shape.

Her right hand smarted as she exchanged her nightdress for a simple shift. The Old Ones had gifted Branwen with the power to defeat the Shades and save the princess because the princess's body was the body of Iveriu itself, of the Goddess Ériu herself. They were all interconnected. How she wished there was some way to show Essy what she'd learned during her visit to Whitethorn Mound.

Yet worry still coiled tight inside her. Several white strands of hair remained on the pillow. Using the Hand of Bríga had drained Branwen's life force as well. And then, there was Tristan: He had witnessed the devastation she could wreak.

Would he still want to be handfasted?

Buzzing with nerves, Branwen swathed her shoulders with a fur-lined shawl and fastened it with her mother's brooch. As she tramped up the steps, her movements were stiff. The cuts on her stomach where the one-eyed Shade's beak had pecked at her chafed against the fabric of her dress.

A fall of rain had slicked the deck of the *Dragon Rising*, mulling against the blood and ash. The water between Branwen's toes was strangely refreshing. She'd forgotten shoes in her excitement to see Kernyv. Eyes racing along the dramatic cliffs that greeted them, her lips parted in a small, private smile.

The green of the Kernyvak landscape was a more unruly hue than Iveriu but breathtaking all the same. Rugged and imperious, yet welcoming. Long ago, Tristan had told Branwen their lands weren't so very different. She hadn't believed him then.

"Didn't think I'd live to see these shores again."

Branwen jumped at the sound of Captain Morgawr's voice.

"It's stunning," she said.

Morgawr grunted. She cast him a sideways glance. He stood tall, battered but proud. She could only imagine what the captain was thinking as he stared at his homeland. He would have to explain to King Marc how his men had been massacred. How he'd nearly lost the Princess of Iveriu. She didn't envy him the task.

"I owe you a debt of gratitude," he said, and Branwen grew uneasy. "The Horned One blessed us with your presence, my lady. Without you, we'd be lost."

She tucked her right hand beneath her shawl. "You don't owe me anything, Captain. And I don't believe in the Horned One."

Morgawr peered at her, bushy eyebrows high. "Not my business to tell," he said. She nodded, exhaling shortly. "All the same, the Horned One believes in you, and I give you my thanks." He kissed the antler pendant.

"See there," said the captain after a few quiet moments. He was pointing at a turret in the distance. "That's Monwiku Castle."

Branwen shielded her eyes to get a better look.

"It's on an island?"

"You can walk across the causeway at low tide." He laughed at the surprise that crinkled her face. "We'll dock in a deeper harbor. There." Morgawr indicated an inlet closer to the ship along the coast. "Port of Marghas. That's where King Marc's envoy will collect you."

Branwen had never heard of a castle built upon an island. Kernyv would hold many more wonders, she didn't doubt. This was Tristan's home and she wanted to know all of it. All of him. A spark zipped down her spine.

"Excuse me, Captain," Branwen said, breaking into a sprint.

"Careful, my lady! Deck's wet!" he called after her. "We'll make landfall in a couple hours!" She barely heard him.

They had all nearly died last night. Branwen didn't want to wait for her life to begin in Kernyv. Her bare feet pounded on the steps at the opposite end of the ship. Branwen wanted to show Tristan they were already married in her heart. *Now.* Share her body and soul, tell him her truth, make him hers in every way.

There was no more time to waste.

Branwen heard laughter—deep, masculine laughter—coming from inside Tristan's compartment. The door was slightly ajar and a shaft of buttery light spilled out. More laughter. This time, it was much higher pitched. The sound of rustling.

"A splash of water is more adventurous than you, Tristan," said a teasing voice.

Branwen's heart ceased to beat as she shoved the door the rest of the way open.

The bedsheets were twisted and tossed like a windstorm had hit the room. Essy lolled on top of them. Naked. Her long, gilded tresses were not enough to make her modest.

Had the *kretarv* returned? Either way, Branwen was held in a moment of suspended horror.

Beside the princess, Tristan lay kissing the inside of her thigh. The muscles of his bronze back and his warrior's scars rippled as he held her cousin tight. Branwen recalled how beautiful he had seemed to her that day on the beach when the Kernyveu attacked; he was even more beautiful to her today.

Was this Branwen's fault? She had encouraged their friendship. She had pushed Tristan away, time and again. Had she pushed him straight into her cousin's arms?

Or was it the fear of what she'd done to the Shades? Still, she would have thought Tristan would put honor and duty to his king before his heart. His *heart*. Hadn't he said that belonged to Branwen?

Her eyes traveled from the lovers back to the sheets. There was a deep crimson stain in the center.

A scream worked its way up Branwen's throat. All the love she contained turned to hate. It was a living thing. Hate that frothed and boiled.

"Branny!" the princess gasped.

Tristan whipped his face toward Branwen. His expression was glazed. He gawped at her blankly, as if he'd glimpsed a Death-Teller, before recognition returned to his eyes.

"Branwen." Her name on his lips was a moan. The sorrow of the seas infused it.

She didn't care. She lunged.

Branwen yanked Tristan from the bed with all her might. She was half afraid of burning him alive; the other half yearned to do it. He tumbled to the floor and the princess leapt from the other side of the bed.

Shrouding herself in the sheet, Essy slammed back against the wall of the stuffy cabin. It smelled of sweat and love. Branwen took a step closer and the princess cowered. Her cousin had never looked frightened of her before. *She should be.*

Jabbing Essy's chest, Branwen shrieked, "How *could* you?"

Tears welled in her eyes. "I—I don't know," she said, bottom lip quivering.

"You don't *know*!" Branwen yelled in her face. "Do you have any idea how much—how *many* people have sacrificed for you? For peace?"

"I'm sorry. I'm *so* sorry, Branny." Essy's fists curled around the sheet even as she began to sob, her apology tempered by defiance.

Deep within, Branwen felt the rumble of Dhusnos's laughter. She would have given her life for peace. Her mission was a failure. All because of her cousin's selfish heart. But, wasn't that Branwen's fault, too? She had always allowed her to be selfish.

Her cousin's chin trembled. "I didn't mean to fall in love."

"*Love?*" Branwen waved at the bloodied sheet. "You think one night of . . . You think *that* is love? You jeopardized peace and for *what*?"

Whether or not Branwen agreed with the laws, King Marc would expect a virgin on his wedding night. A bride whose heirs he could be certain were his. Branwen had already killed to protect her cousin's reputation.

"You did it for nothing!" Branwen shouted.

Through her tears, Essy's eyes hardened. "I *chose*, Branwen. I am more than my body and I made a choice. I only regret hurting you. I didn't intend . . . I did it for love."

Two minutes ago, Branwen had made the same choice and it had felt so right. But a queen didn't have that luxury.

"The only person you've ever loved is yourself, Essy."

"Don't blame Eseult." Tristan's voice came from behind Branwen. Taut. Low.

Eseult. He had called the princess by the name she would be known by as Queen of Kernyv. She was Essy no longer. She was Branwen's Essy no more. Not after today.

Branwen craned her neck at Tristan, searching his face for the man with whom she'd fallen in love. The man who was honorable and right and true. He pushed to his feet and, as their gazes intertwined, the hazel flecks of his eyes dimmed. He shifted his focus to Eseult and Branwen recognized the look on his face: desire, hunger, craving. The smoldering look he gave Emer before he kissed her on the beach—as if nothing else mattered.

Blood and bone, forged by fire, we beseech you for the truest of desires.

Dread froze Branwen from within. There was only one way Tristan would betray his king. His family. His people.

Magic.

Branwen clutched at her chest as if she'd been struck by a club. She expected—hoped—to feel the familiar curve of the dainty vial.

Nothing.

She patted her chest more frantically. "Branwen?" said Tristan.

No. Just *no*. This couldn't be. Dhusnos's laughter intensified. Branwen hadn't let the Loving Cup out of her sight since Essy had discovered it. She circled her gaze around the cabin like the burning torch in a lighthouse. *There.* Gold winked at her. On the floor beside the bed. She dropped to her knees, snatching it from the warped wood, heedless of splinters. Branwen weighed it.

Empty.

Rushing toward the princess, she waved the vial in jagged motions.

"You stole it, didn't you?"

The widening of her eyes was all the confirmation Branwen needed. "Why?" she cried. "Tell me *why*? When you knew it was mine to keep safe?"

Confusion creased her cousin's forehead. "I found it in the bed. I couldn't sleep. I thought it would calm my nerves—after my ordeal."

Her ordeal? "What does it matter?"

In the shadowed recesses of Branwen's mind, Keane gloated. To the princess, the wedding toast was nothing but another of Treva's fortified spirits. How could she have known that one petty act of rebellion could destroy two kingdoms? But then, she had never cared for consequences.

Branwen pressed her hands over her ears but she couldn't drown out Dhusnos's cackling. He had known what would happen. Of course he had. He was a *god.* Branwen had spent her whole life trying to protect her younger cousin from the world. Perhaps it was the world that needed protecting from her cousin.

"*Branwen.*" Firm, warm hands seized her elbows. Hands whose touch she had wanted to know—everywhere. Hands that knew the feel of her cousin instead.

She shook Tristan off. "Did you drink the wedding toast, too?" Branwen charged, and part of her wanted it to be true, wanted to believe only magic would make Tristan stray from her. "The toast Princess Eseult was supposed to share with your uncle—your *king*? You've committed *treason*!"

Shame deluged his features.

Branwen couldn't look at the lovers a minute more. And she couldn't tell them they were under a spell. Directing her fury at her cousin, she said, "You've broken my heart," and tore from the room, knuckles white around the vial.

"Branwen!" Eseult called wretchedly.

Tears ate at her face as she raced down the passageway and up the stairs. The sun was suddenly too bright. Branwen had risked everything for her cousin's happiness. She hadn't been willing to sacrifice Essy's heart for the rest of the Iverni. She'd wanted peace and love. She'd wanted it all. She'd been just as selfish as her cousin and now she would be left with nothing.

But not only her. So many lives hung in the balance.

Dashing toward the stern of the ship, Branwen's stomach somersaulted over and over. If the Kernyveu discovered their future queen had committed treason against the crown—if they punished her with death, Iveriu would have no choice but to invade.

The vision she'd had of Eseult being marched toward a pyre crackled behind her eyes. The night she retrieved the traitor's finger, Branwen thought the Old Ones had been testing her resolve.

They were warning me.

Leaning over the hull, Branwen stared at the waves, and hurled the Loving Cup into their depths with all her strength. Should she dive in as well? Let Dhusnos have her?

Her fingers skimmed the writing on the underside of her brooch.

The right fight. What did that mean now? Branwen had endangered two kingdoms, and she didn't dare believe she'd be spared retribution—she didn't *want* to be spared.

A firm hand pulled her back up. Branwen recoiled.

Tristan stood before her, half dressed. The love-knots she'd sewn over his heart taunted her. Consumed by rage, her open palm connected with his cheek. He didn't move a muscle.

Shuddering, Branwen held up her hand. "Is this why? Do I *scare* you?"

"No, Branwen. *No.*" The compassion in his voice was unbearable.

"But you could never love a murderer, is that it? Never be handfasted to—whatever I *am*?"

Darkness rinsed his face. "I love you. If Keane numbers among the Shades, then he deserved whatever you did to him." He reached for Branwen's right hand as if he truly was unafraid. "That's how you were injured the night before we left."

She didn't want his sympathy, his understanding. Not now.

"You *love* me?" she spat instead. "You love me so much you deflowered my cousin!"

Tristan pulled Branwen against his naked chest. "Forgive me. I don't know what happened," he said in a harsh whisper. "Passion overtook me. I couldn't control it."

The truest of desires: That was the spell that Branwen and the queen had cast. Her aunt wanted the princess to produce heirs for Iveriu and Kernyv. Bitter laughter flung from Branwen's mouth. She cursed herself for not asking Queen Eseult the precise nature of the spell. She'd eagerly agreed to anything not to watch her cousin waste away in a loveless marriage. But was the Loving Cup truly worthy of its name?

Who could say where the line was drawn between love and desire?

"Eseult came to my quarters. I should have sent her away, but she was so shaken," Tristan confessed in a torrent of words. "She didn't want to disturb you, so she asked me to share a drink with her. I didn't see the harm . . . I didn't—"

"I don't want to hear—"

"*Please*," he cut her off. "Branwen, please." Tristan was begging now. "I returned to the land of my enemies to find you—*you*. Something possessed me last night that was beyond reason."

Branwen struggled in Tristan's arms like she was suffocating.

"Keane threatened the peace—and I killed him," she informed him, fury simmering beneath her skin. "Should I kill you, too?" She could never tell Tristan that she knew exactly what had happened. And yet, a part of Branwen still hated him for his weakness—because his love hadn't been stronger than her magic.

"I will accept any punishment you deem fit." Tristan rested his chin on her head, forcing her to still. "What happened between me and Eseult—it was a moment of madness." Branwen sucked her teeth. It would be easier to stop loving him if he revolted her. "One night doesn't change everything else between *us*, Branwen."

There was real grit in Tristan's voice, but he had called the princess Eseult. The princess was something more to him now. She would always be something more than his queen or his uncle's wife.

One night *did* change everything.

Branwen beat his chest and Tristan tilted her head toward him, crushing her with a kiss. It was fueled by shame and regret. This wasn't the way kisses were supposed to taste. Her hate bubbled and

Branwen thrust him away so vehemently that he couldn't resist. She hated herself most of all.

"We can still be Tantris and Emer," he pleaded.

She wished she didn't love the small scar above his eye, or his messy curls, or all of the details about him. She burned with the desire not to want him. She loved him, but she wouldn't share him.

Branwen kissed him deeply. One last time. "You were never Tantris," she said against his mouth. "And I was never Emer."

Branwen pushed Tristan away, holding up her hand. It was full of flames.

She tore the tricolor bracelet from her other wrist. "This is what I think of your promises."

Holding his gaze, she fed the bracelet to the fire—*her* fire. It frayed and turned to ash.

Tristan lurched backward as if she'd dealt him a body blow.

"I won't forget the dream we dreamed together, Branwen," he protested through clenched teeth. "It was your will, not mine, that has brought us peace. I won't give up on it. I will die for it."

Branwen turned a cruelly rational gaze upon him.

"You will do no such thing, Prince Tristan. You will leave the princess to me—*I* am her Champion now. Her *only* Champion," she instructed, cool and clear. Like the fox, she was a messenger, and a protector. She would preserve the illusion of the princess's honor as fiercely from this day forward as when they'd departed Iveriu.

"You're not as strong as I believed you to be, Tristan," said Branwen. "You are not the *man* I believed you to be."

He hung his head, expression bleak. "And you could never love this man?" There was just the smallest shred of hope in his voice.

Tristan's name was stitched into her heart as surely as Branwen had embroidered the love-knots above his. But, for the sake of her own sanity, she had to kill that hope.

"No, my prince."

Branwen couldn't love Tristan and the Land at the same time. She chose the Land.

"You're wrong, Branwen. You're *wrong*." His fists shook at his sides. "I will win back your love if it's the last thing I do."

The world fell away as they stared at each other: enemies turned lovers turned adversaries. An hour ago, Branwen would have given her honor to know all of Tristan. She could no longer afford surrender. She was committed to leaving the world better than how she'd found it. For Cadan. For Gráinne. For her parents.

"Peace above all," she whispered.

Time moved like honey as Branwen walked away from the first man she had ever loved. She focused her eyes on the rocky cliffs of Kernyv. She had been hollowed out, reforged by fire. Only one path through the waves stretched before her.

Branwen would prevent the chaos of the Loving Cup from being unleashed—the chaos *she* had created. No matter the cost. She would lie, cheat, and connive to carry out her mission for Iveriu. And, from now on, that included putting the needs of the Ivernic people above their princess.

Eseult would be the queen Iveriu and Kernyv needed—whether she liked it or not.

The lovers who had burned in Branwen's mind for so many, many years weren't people, she realized. They were the spirits of both kingdoms. And her destiny lay between them. The two lovers for whom she would trade her heart.

The right fight. She wiped away a solitary tear.

The pale late-autumn sun hit the water just right and the waves turned black. She rubbed her palm and closed her eyes. No one would sing songs of Branwen's lost love.

Odai eti ama. She would sing them for herself.

I hate and I love.

ACKNOWLEDGMENTS

First and foremost, I'd like to thank you, the reader, for embarking on Branwen's journey with me. Putting this book in your hands has been quite the adventure, with heartbreak and magic along the way, and I am forever indebted to two extraordinary women for having made it thus far: Rhoda Belleza, my incredibly insightful editor who believed in Branwen from the start, and challenged me to paint her story on an even broader canvas; and Sara Crowe, my formidable agent, who has stuck by me through thick and thin—I couldn't ask for a better champion.

I also consider myself hugely fortunate to have found a home at Imprint. Thank you to Erin Stein for taking a chance on me, and to Nicole Otto for your keen second pair of eyes and thoughtful suggestions. Kerry Johnson, thanks for being my grammar maven. Ilana Worrell, for your production prowess. Ellen Duda, for the marvelous cover. Brittany Pearlman, Johanna Kirby, and Kristin Dulaney, for your tireless efforts to get SBW out into the world. Also huge thanks to the team at BookSparks.

Professor Sarah Kay, thank you for sharing your expertise with me once again and for being such a generous mentor all of these years.

Dr. Geraldine Parsons, thank you for answering my calls for help with Old Irish since 1998 and for being one of my dearest friends. ASNaCs forever!

A shout-out to my sister-in-law and Flesh-Stripping Expert, Magdalen Wind-Mozley. It's good to have a forensic scientist in the family when your characters need to dig up corpses!

My first readers for all of my projects are always my oldest friends: Georgina Cullman, Brooke Edwards-Plant, Ame Igharo, Rhoda Manook, and Deborah McCandless. I wouldn't have made it through my teens without you, and I'm very lucky our friendship has endured across the miles and years. I am also grateful to Kathleen Ortiz and the MediaBistro workshop where I began Branwen's story way back in 2012. Thank you to my first CPs: Amy Carol Reeves, Rhiann Wynn-Nolet, Susan Francino, and Teresa Yea.

One of the best parts of being a debut author is becoming friends with other wonderful, talented, and supportive authors. Kamilla Benko, I didn't know I could have a bookish soulmate until I met you. Vic James, my fellow lapsed academic and lover of G&Ts who gives me sage counsel. Rebecca Barrow, Ali Standish, Katie Webber, Carlie Sorosiak, Alice Broadway, Natalie C. Anderson, Akemi Dawn Bowman, Lisa Lueddecke, Ruth Lauren, and Rebecca Denton—it's always a party on this side of the Pond. Thank you to Dhonielle Clayton, Heidi Heilig, Stacey Lee, Annie Stone, Karen M. McManus, Linsey Miller, Somaiya Daud, Zoraida Córdova, Misa Sugiura, Elsie Chapman, Sona Charaipotra, Caroline Richmond, Kaitlyn Sage Patterson, Melanie Conklin, Samantha Shannon, and Rachel Lynn Solomon for your wit and wisdom. I am obliged to everyone in the Class of 2K18, the Electric 18s, Kidlit AOC, and the 2017 Debuts for being so welcoming. There are many other writers who have let me vent and/or made me smile at my computer—thank you, you know who you are (#FightMeClub).

Many thanks to my parents for not blinking when I told them

I wanted to be a medievalist, then a journalist, and, finally, a novelist.

Last but not least, my deepest gratitude goes to my husband, Jack Mozley. More than a decade ago we had *Ne vus sanz mei, ne mei sanz vus* inscribed on our wedding rings. Not you without me, not me without you—it still holds true and this book wouldn't be here without your unflagging love and support. *Je t'aime.*

GLOSSARY

A NOTE ON LANGUAGES AND NAMES

The languages used in *Sweet Black Waves* are based, fairly loosely, on ancient and medieval languages. As I have adapted the Tristan legends for my retelling, Ireland has become Iveriu, Cornwall has become Kernyv, and the Roman Empire has become the Aquilan Empire. I have taken liberties with history and linguistic accuracy while trying to postulate how the political realities of my world might influence the development of its languages.

Today, nearly half the world's population speaks what are known as Indo-European languages. This group includes English, most of the European languages, but also Sanskrit and Persian. One branch is the Celtic languages, which are now spoken primarily in northwestern Europe: Ireland, Cornwall, Scotland, Wales, Brittany, and the Isle of Man (as well as small diaspora communities), but during the first millennium BCE these languages were spoken as far afield as the Iberian Peninsula, the Black Sea, and Asia Minor. The Celtic languages are further divided into two groups: the Goidelic (Irish, Manx, and Scottish Gaelic) and the Brittonic (Cornish, Welsh, and Breton).

Since the nineteenth century, scholars have been working to re-create the Proto-Indo-European language—the hypothesized common ancestor to all Indo-European languages. Celtic linguists have also made significant headway in the reconstruction of Proto-Celtic, the language from which all Celtic languages derive.

Therefore, my fabricated Ivernic language is based on Old Irish and Proto-Celtic, whereas my Kernyvak language is based on Proto-Celtic and the Brittonic languages. For the Aquilan language words I have looked to Proto-Italic—the forbearer of Latin—for inspiration. Given that the Aquilan Empire occupied the island of Albion for hundreds of years before Branwen's story begins, I have also allowed for there to be some linguistic influence of the Aquilan language on Kernyvak. Since the Aquilan Empire never invaded Iveriu, their languages would have remained quite separate. Although, of course, Branwen and the rest of the Ivernic nobility speak Aquilan as a second language.

In creating the place-names for Branwen's world, I have tried to incorporate relevant aspects of the Celtic tradition. For example, *rigani* is the reconstructed Proto-Celtic word for "queen," and since the Land is a female goddess in Iveriu, it made sense for me to name the seat of power Castle Rigani. Likewise, *bodwā* is the Proto-Celtic word for "fight," which is fitting as the name of Branwen's family castle given that their motto is *The Right Fight*.

The ancient language of trees that Branwen calls the first Ivernic writing is a reference to the Irish Ogham alphabet. It was devised between the first and fourth centuries CE to transfer the Irish language to written form and is possibly based on the Latin alphabet. Ogham is found in approximately four hundred surviving stone inscriptions and is read from the bottom up. In addition to representing a sound, the letters of the Ogham alphabet have the names of trees and shrubs. The Ogham letter *coll* translates as "hazel" and represents the /k/ sound as in *kitten*. The Ogham letter *uillenn* translates as "honeysuckle" and represents the /ll/ sound as in *shell*. Hence, when Branwen and Essy trace their private symbol, they are only writing two letters rather than a whole word.

The legend of Tristan and Isolt has been retold so many times in so many languages that simply choosing which form of the character names to use also poses somewhat of a challenge. Two possible origins for Tristan's name include Drustanus, son of Cunomorus, who is mentioned on a sixth-century stone inscription found in Cornwall, or a man named Drust, son of King Talorc of the Picts, who ruled in late eighth-century Scotland.

In the early Welsh versions of the legend, Drust becomes Tristan or Drystan. Tristan was the name propagated by the French poets, who employed its similar sound to the French word *tristesse* ("sadness") for dramatic effect. Another consistent feature of the legends is Tristan's disguising his identity by calling himself Tantris—an anagram of his name—and I therefore decided to do the same.

While the name Isolt is probably the most easily recognized, it is in fact derived from the Welsh name Essyllt. The French poets translated her name as Yso(lt) or Yseu(l)t(e). I have therefore synthesized the two for my Eseult.

In the Continental versions of the story, Isolt's lady's maid is usually called Brangien or Brangain. However, this is a borrowing from the Old Welsh name Branwen (brân "raven" + (g)wen "fair"). This choice was also inspired by another Branwen from the Middle Welsh *Mabinogion*, the earliest prose stories in British literature. The Second Branch of the Mabinogi is called *Branwen uerch Lyr* ("Branwen, daughter of Llŷr"), the meaning of the patronym *ap Llŷr* being "Son of the Sea," and the connection that the Branwen of *Sweet Black Waves* feels for the sea was inspired by this forerunner.

The Branwen of the *Mabinogion* is a member of a Welsh royal family who is given in marriage to the King of Ireland to prevent a war after one of her brothers has offended him. When Branwen arrives at the Irish court, the vassals of the King of Ireland turn him against his new queen and she is forced to submit to many humiliations. Her brothers then declare war on Ireland, and Branwen is the cause of the war her marriage was meant to prevent.

Several prominent Celtic scholars have made the case that the Welsh Branwen can trace her roots to Irish Sovereignty Goddesses or that both the Welsh and Irish material derive from the same, earlier source. Particular evidence of this is that Branwen's dowry to the King of Ireland included the Cauldron of Regeneration, which could bring slain men back to life, and which served as the inspiration for Kerwindos's Cauldron in my own work.

While there is no evidence of a direct connection between the Branwen of the *Mabinogion* and the Branwen of the Tristan legends, I find the possibility tantalizing and so I have merged the two into my Branwen as a forceful female protagonist with magical abilities and a strong connection to the Land.

IVERNIC FESTIVALS

Imbolgos—early spring festival of the Goddess Bríga
Belotnia—the Festival of Lovers, held toward the end of spring
Laelugus—the Festival of Peace, held in late summer
Samonios—New Year Festival, held in mid-autumn

IVERNIC LANGUAGE VOCABULARY

derew—a pain-relieving herb

fidkwelsa—a strategy board game

Iverman/Iverwoman—a person from Iveriu

Iverni—the people of Iveriu

Ivernic—something of or relating to Iveriu

kelyos—a traditional Ivernic musical band

kladiwos—an Ivernic type of sword

krotto—an Ivernic type of harp

lesana—ring-forts belonging to the Old Ones

ráithana—hills belonging to the Old Ones

sílomleie—an Ivernic type of cudgel made from blackthorn wood

skeakh—a whitethorn bush or tree

KERNYVAK LANGUAGE VOCABULARY

Kernyvak—something of or relating to Kernyv

Kernyveu—the people of Kernyv

Kernyvman/Kernyvwoman—a person from Kernyv

kretarv—carnivorous seabird

mormerkti—"thank you"

sekrev—"you're welcome"

AQUILAN LANGUAGE VOCABULARY

ama—"I love"

amar—"love"

amare—"bitter"

Aquilan—something of or relating to the Aquilan Empire

de—"of"

est—"is"

eti—"and"

fálkr—a broad, curved sword

la—"the"

mar—"sea"

misrokord—a thin dagger; literally means "mercy"

odai—"I hate"

SOURCES, LITERARY TRANSMISSION, AND WORLD-BUILDING

The legend of Tristan and Isolt is one of the best-known myths in Western culture, and arguably the most popular throughout the Middle Ages. The star-crossed lovers have become synonymous with passion and romance itself.

When I first decided to write Branwen's story, I put on my scholarly hat and reacquainted myself with the most influential versions of the Tristan tales, then followed their motifs and principle episodes backward in time before arranging them into a frame, a loom onto which Branwen's story could come to life. Despite the numerous retellings of Tristan and Isolt throughout the medieval period, the structure remains remarkably consistent.

The names of the main characters can be traced to post-Roman Britain (sixth or seventh century CE). There was no real Tristan or King Arthur, but there are tantalizing stone inscriptions in the British Isles that suggest local folk heroes whose names became attached to a much older body of tales, some mythological in genesis. And while there is evidence that some motifs may have been borrowed from Hellenic, Persian, or Arabic sources, the vast majority are Celtic. Rather than viewing these Celtic stories as direct sources for the Tristan and Isolt narratives, however, most scholars agree the medieval Irish and Welsh material should be viewed as analogues that presumably stem from the same, now lost, pan-Celtic source.

These oral tales were probably preserved by the druids and our earliest surviving versions were written down by Christian clerics in Ireland between the seventh and ninth centuries, and in twelfth-century Wales. Because Ireland was never conquered by the Roman Empire, it didn't experience the same "Dark Age" as elsewhere in Europe. Women in early medieval Ireland also had many more rights and protections under the law, enshrined in *Cáin Adomnáin* (Law of Adomán), *ca.* 679–704 CE, than their Continental counterparts—which is echoed in the strong female protagonists of its literature.

There are three Old Irish tale-types that feed into the Tristan legend: 1. *aitheda* (elopement tales), in which a young woman runs away from her older husband with a younger man; 2. *tochmarca* (courtship tales), in which a woman takes an active part in negotiating a relationship with a man of her choosing that results in marriage; and 3. *immrama* (voyage tales), in which the hero takes a sea voyage to the Otherworld.

The Old Irish tales that share the most in common with Tristan and Isolt's doomed affair are *Tochmarc Emire* ("The Wooing of Emer"), a tenth-century *aithed*; and *Tóraigheacht Dhiarmada agus Ghráinne* ("The Pursuit of Diarmuid and Gráinne"), an *aithed* whose earliest text dates to the Early Modern Irish period but whose plot and characters can be traced to the tenth century. In these stories, the female characters wield tremendous power and are closer to their mythological roots as goddesses. Other tales that are reminiscent of Branwen's complicated relationship with Isolt include the ninth- or tenth-century *Tochmarc Becfhola* ("The Wooing of Becfhola") and the twelfth-century *Fingal Rónáin* ("Rónán's act of kinslaying").

When the Romans withdrew from Britain in the fifth century,

many residents from the south of the island immigrated to northern France. For the next five centuries, trade and communication was maintained between Cornwall, Wales, and Brittany. The Bretons spoke a language similar to Welsh and Cornish, which facilitated the sharing of the Arthurian legends, to which they added their own folktales. By the twelfth century, the professional Breton *conteurs* (storytellers) had become the most popular court entertainers in Europe and it was these wandering minstrels who brought the Tristan legends to the royal French and Anglo-Norman courts—including that of Henry II of England and Eleanor of Aquitane, famed for her patronage of the troubadours in the South of France.

The Breton songs of Tristan's exploits were soon recorded as verse romances by the Anglo-Norman poets Béroul, Thomas d'Angleterre, and Marie de France (notably, the only woman), as well as the German Eilhart von Oberge. Béroul's and Eilhart's retellings belong to what is often called the *version commune* (primitive version), meaning they are closer to their folkloric heritage. Thomas's Tristan forms part of the *version courtoise* (courtly version), which is influenced by the courtly love ideal.

The twelfth century is often credited with the birth of romance, and Tristan is at least partially responsible. Which is not to say that people didn't fall in love before then, of course(!), but rather that for the first time, the sexual love between a man and a woman, usually forbidden, became a central concern of literature. The first consumers of this new genre in which a knight pledges fealty to a distant, unobtainable (often married) lady were royal and aristocratic women and, like romance readers today, their appetite was voracious. While the audience was female, the poets and authors were male, often clerics in the service of noblewomen. The poetry produced at the behest of female aristocratic patrons might therefore be considered the first fan fiction.

However, while the courtly lady may have appeared to have the power over her besotted knight, in reality noblewomen were rapidly losing property and inheritance rights as the aristocracy became a closed class ruled by strict patrilinear descent. Legends like that of Tristan and Isolt provided a means of escape for noblewomen who were undoubtedly in less than physically and emotionally satisfying marriages of their own, while also reinforcing women's increasingly objectified status. The portrayal of women in the Tristan legends therefore exemplifies the conflict between the forceful protagonists of its Celtic origins and the new idealized but dehumanized courtly lady.

It is this conflict that particularly interests me as a storyteller and which I explore through my own female characters. Because the legend as I have inherited it is a mix of concerns from different historical epochs, I decided to set my retelling in a more fantastical context that allowed me to pick and choose the aspects of the tradition that best suited Branwen's story. In this way, I also followed in the footsteps of the medieval authors who, while they might make references to real places or kings, weren't particularly concerned with accuracy. The stories they produced weren't so much historical fiction as we think of it today but more akin to fantasy.

During the nineteenth century, the German composer Richard Wagner drew on his countryman Gottfried von Strassburg's celebrated thirteenth-century verse romance of Tristan as inspiration for his now ubiquitous opera. Gottfried had, in turn, used the Anglo-Norman version of Thomas d'Angleterre as his source material, demonstrating the unending cycle of inspiration and adaption. The

Tristan legends started as distinct traditions that were grafted onto the Arthurian corpus (possibly in Wales, possibly on the Continent) and became forever intertwined with the thirteenth-century prose romances.

Concurrently with Gottfried, there was a complete Old Norse adaption by Brother Róbert, a Norwegian cleric, and the Tristan legends gained popularity not only throughout Scandinavia but on the Iberian Peninsula and in Italy. There were also early Czech and Belarusian versions, and it was later translated into Polish and Russian. Dante also references the ill-fated lovers in his fourteenth-century *Inferno*, and Sir Thomas Malory devoted an entire book to Tristan in his fifteenth-century *Le Morte d'Arthur*, one of the most famous works in the English language.

The popularity of Tristan and Isolt fell off abruptly during the Renaissance but was revived by the Romantic poets of the late eighteenth and early nineteenth centuries, who sought an antidote to the changes enacted by the Industrial Revolution—although they viewed their medieval past through very rose-tinted glasses. Nevertheless, the preoccupation with Tristan and Isolt, as well as their supporting characters, has persisted for more than a millennium and it would be surprising if it did not persist for another.